JAMES J ACCRINGTON 40

LYTHAM ST. ANNES BOROUGH LIBRARIES.

To renew give the last date below and this Number:

M181553

Renewal may be made by personal application, in writing, or
by telephone (weekdays)—St. Annes 24711; Lytham 6745. The
Librarian has the right to refuse renewal.

30 MAY 1974
10 JUN 1974
6 JUL 1974
23 AUG 1974
28 SEP 1974
8 OCT 1974
23 OCT 1974
14 NOV 1974
5 DEC 1974
20 JAN 1975

27 DEC 1974
20 JAN 1975
30 JAN 1975
17 MAR 1975
10 APR 1975
ET MAY 1975
5 MAY 1975
13 MAY 1975
30 JUN 1975
22 AUG 1975

14 NOV 1975
27 NOV 1975
16 DEC 1975
29 DEC 1975
5 JAN 1976
20 APR 1975
JUN 1976

FROM HA
TO BB
DUE BACK 14.9.79
17 SEP 2009
8 OCT 2009

PLEASE TAKE CARE OF THIS BOOK

Damage will be charged to
the borrower.
Change of address must be
reported.
Borrowers' Tickets may be
used at any Library.

If this
on or
above
and
notic

The Lending Library opens 10
closes 6 p.m. Monday, T
7 p.m. Friday and 5 p.m. Saturd
Closed all day Thursday.

D1420379

Also by John James

VOTAN
NOT FOR ALL THE GOLD IN IRELAND
MEN WENT TO CATTRAETH
SEVENTEEN OF LEYDEN

The Lords of Loone

JOHN JAMES

CASSELL · LONDON

01397318

CASSELL & COMPANY LTD
35 RED LION SQUARE, LONDON WC1R 4SJ
Sydney, Auckland
Toronto, Johannesburg

© John James 1972

First published 1972

I.S.B.N. 0 304 29080 7

To HELEN and CLARE
who asked for a book they could read

Printed in Great Britain by
The Anchor Press Ltd, and bound by
William Brendon & Son Ltd, both of Tiptree, Essex
F.472

1

Robert Folland came into Wrackham on a misty afternoon in February. He was riding on a black horse that was not his own, and he was driving two men in front of him, in their shirts, without boots or breeches. For they had stood out of the thicket, on the heath beyond the River Loone, and had offered to shoot him.

He had come into the heath huddled in his old red coat, the same he had worn at Malplaquet, and in the pursuit after it, with the facings torn off and the collar pinned back a little. He had in his pockets three shillings in English silver, three French pennies and a Dutch stiver or two. His long sword, with its English hilt on a German blade, was his own. The holster on his saddle and the horse-pistol also belonged to him; he had for it seven charges of powder, three flints, and four balls. In one tail pocket he had a prayer-book and a pack of cards. In the other he carried a spare shirt rolled small. His campaign wig might have fetched three-ha'pence. Under his saddle-cloth tops, well hidden, he still had six golden guineas and three half-guineas, mostly with the Vigo mark, and a handful of letters. And that was all he had in the world : for that, two men had offered to shoot him.

It was not very late when he pushed his way between the trees. It was still a mile from the town, not a good place to be, and he half expected what came. He searched the mists between the trunks, and when he thought he saw a movement he loosed the sword in its scabbard. He did not slack the horse's pace; instead he shook the reins, and came from the walk into the semblance of a trot. He had been riding that horse for three days now; he had reached with it a very complete understanding. He had better horses in Spain, but that was a long time ago : he had not had a better horse in Flanders.

He could see that it was a mounted man in the shadows, trying to hide himself behind the branches. Robert wondered if there were others. If he were to do a thing like this himself—and he might well come to it, cast off from the army and never a trade—

I

then he would prefer not to be alone. Too many things can happen to a lonely man.

The event was clear to see, coming like a cannon-ball, but more deliberate. Folland's only question now was, what weapon? Then he heard the grating of the hammer that came to full cock. The horse came forward, broke cover, blocked the path, the arm came up. Not far away—Robert Folland waited for the shout,

'Stop! Put your hands in the air!'

Oh, no, not for an old Dragoon, Robert thought. His sword came out. His heels kicked into the horse's sides. Not too fast in the charge—we always learned that in Corporal John's Army, would God I were in it still. Folland stretched out his blade, rigid, in a straight line from his shoulder, like a man trying to sight a pistol. The man from the shadows shouted again, but his words were drowned in Folland's loud and angry cry, 'Ha-la-la-la-la-la-la! Ha-la-la-la-laaaaa!'

The man from the shadows tried to hold his horse still, but it bucked and curvetted, not used to an attack. He fired in sheer terror at this animate thunderbolt that came at him, flashing and deadly; with his own shaking and the movement of his mount the ball went into the leaves somewhere. Folland saw the flash and heard the bang, and a moment later he heard another ball come nearer to him.

The man from the shadows was trying to twist his horse round, tugging at the bridle. But Folland was on him. In the last moment, the Dragoon altered the line of the sword, as if he were trying for a cut instead of a thrust. The other man raised his hand to shield his head, and Folland slammed the guard of the hilt into his face. The fellow reeled back, and then toppled from the saddle.

Folland slapped the man's horse across the rump, and laughed as it galloped away. Then he turned back to see where that second shot had come from. To his satisfaction, this man was not mounted. And, stupidly, he had not moved, but was trying to reload his pistol. He was so intent on pouring the powder into the barrel that he did not look up till Folland was near enough to knock the pistol flying with the flat of his blade. The man cowered against the trunk of a tree.

'That way,' said Folland. 'Back to your friend!'

The man, rat-faced, greying, looking vacantly at Folland. He shouted in a despairing voice, 'Help! Help me! Help!'

2

Folland laughed. This was an old trick, pretending there were more than two of them. You couldn't catch an old Dragoon like that. He prodded the rat-faced man with the point of his sword.

'Back! Back, I said.'

The failed highwayman trudged in front of the horse. The other man was sitting up, younger, fatter of face as far as Folland could see under the bruising and the mud. He was rubbing his hurts. Folland laughed.

'Right! Off with them.'

'Off?'

'Aye. Your boots. Take them off. Smart about it! Throw them into the bushes. Far! Right, now your breeches! Quick before I cut them off, and what's in 'em, too.'

The younger man stood there, still half dazed, holding his breeches in his hands. The other, still entangled round the ankles, grunted with effort.

'Now, hang them up in that tree. No, a higher branch than that. Throw them up! You'll never have to climb for them. You'll be higher than that after next assizes.'

'Oh, no, please no, don't do that.' It was the younger man.

'Who told you to speak? Hold your tongue, and throw your breeches up. Hurry, or I'll have your shirt off too! Now, empty your pockets!'

Ratface had managed to settle his breeches on a high branch. He stepped back. Then, from the mists behind Folland's back, there was the bang of another pistol. A hole appeared in one leg of the breeches. Folland swung round, saw a faint shape a hundred feet away, a horseman. The younger highwayman shouted, 'Save us! He'll have us hanged. Save us!'

This time, Folland saw the flash, though the white smoke was lost in the mist. The hole was in the other leg of the breeches. The horseman laughed. Folland heard him gallop off. He could have killed me if he wanted, thought the Dragoon. He put his shots where he wanted them, and we all three here know it. And more, we know he has abandoned his comrades. But *I* haven't.

'Empty your pockets! Both of you. Whatever you've got there, throw it away. Yes, money as well. No, not drop it. *Throw* it away, into the bushes. As far as you can! And now, forward. . . . *March!*'

The two highwaymen walked in front, the younger man leaning on his comrade. They soon began to limp and whimper, their

3

feet torn by the stones of the road. They tried to walk on the grass of the verge, but brambles tore at their feet, and in the grass they could not see the flints. So they returned to the rutted gravel, frozen hard. They said nothing, and neither did Folland. He mused to himself that he had been many things in the last ten years, since he had gone off with the Regiment at sixteen, but never a shepherd before.

As they came out of the thicket and down off the heath, the mist thinned. Surprisingly it was clearer by the river. There were a few houses and a red stone church with a ruined tower by the road on this side of the bridge into Wrackham. Men and women came out to look at the little procession. Folland was relieved to hear laughter, not sounds of sympathy.

'Lost yer breeches then, Joe?' he heard someone shout; and another sang, 'Old Charley Nobbler, couldn't pay the Cobbler!'

The tollgate was on this side of the bridge. The keeper came out of his booth, laughing.

'Got yer, then, 'as 'e, Charley? All right, Squire, it's a ha'penny for you and a penny for the yoss. A farthing a leg and a farthing a wheel, that's the rule here.'

'And these gallants?'

'A ha'penny each for them.'

'Well, I'm not paying for them. They haven't got any money.'

'They can't cross then, can they?'

'Not on the bridge. Where else?'

'Oh, they could walk down to Bratton, that's on the sea, and perhaps they could steal a boat there and come across. Or . . . it be ten mile to the next bridge.'

'That's a long walk. They could swim.'

The tollkeeper grinned from ear to ear.

'Oh, yes, they could swim.'

Folland swung his horse at the two failed highwaymen.

'Now then, down the bank with you. Down you go!'

They retreated before him. He lunged the horse at them, and waved his sword. They went backwards, gingerly. Joe squealed when his feet felt the cold water, and stopped a moment, till Folland poked the sword at his face; then he rushed in, as far as his waist. Charley Nobbler, jerking away from the horse, slipped on the mud and went down, covering his front with the greasy clay. He found the hooves almost on him, and crawled crabwise down the bank. Folland looked down at the two of them, standing miserably up to their waists in water, not able to hold their footing, clinging to each other to stay upright.

Folland asked the tollkeeper, 'Do you know a Mr Kettlestang in Wrackham?'

'Oh, everybody do know Master Kettlestang.'

'Do you know where he lives?'

'Aye, everybody know where 'e lives. 'E be the Portreeve, 'e be.'

'The what?'

'The Portreeve. There's some places 'ave a Mayor, and some 'ave a Provost, and Wrackham 'ave a Portreeve. I knows you was goin' to Master Kettlestang.'

'How do you know?'

'That's 'is 'oss you're a-riding. Proud of that 'oss, 'e be. Left it in London, 'e did. Came back on a ship, three week agone.'

'Colonel Cutler hired me to bring the horse up for him. I have letters for Mr Kettlestang, too.'

'I knowed, else they'd never 'ave let you 'ave 'im : the yoss, I mean.'

'But where does he live?'

'Everybody know that in Wrackham.'

'I don't.'

'Oh, but you're not a Wrackham man. That do make a difference. Look, you goes across this bridge, like, over there, as far as the Town Wall, and you goes in through that gate there. And inside the walls, you see a wide street. That be Foregate, that be. And you go along that till you come to the Cross. And then you turns . . . this way——'

'Right, you mean?'

'Eh? Oh, aye, right. And you goes along there a good bit past the side of the Abbey, that be a big church, you see, down Watergate Row, because the Water Gate is at the end of it, through the wall. And down the end of that, against the wall, there be Master Kettlestang's house on this side, and Master Place the wine merchant his house is the other side of the street.'

'I shall find it.' Folland looked down the bank into the river. The two rascals were edging up the bank. 'Back in!' Folland shouted. 'Back as far as you were.'

They started at his voice, and the Nobbler made such an effort to obey that he fell. Trying to get up, he clung to his companion and brought him down. There was now a crowd of men and boys at the water's edge, laughing at the show, and these began to throw dead cats and cabbage stalks. I may as well leave it to them, thought Folland. He rode across the bridge, past the shattered chapel on the middle pier, through the gate arch in the walls, mouldering red ramparts of weather-rotten stone. The tollkeeper stared after him. 'Wot,' he asked himself aloud, 'is *e* a-doin' of 'ere?'

Folland did not ask himself that question. He knew that other people were asking it, because as he went up Foregate and down Watergate, people looked out from their shops and houses and stared at him. But all he was concerned with was delivering the horse, and then perhaps he could find somewhere to sit down and rest his leg. It was a big house that Kettlestang had, then, timber framed and white plastered. Folland hammered at the door. After a long time it opened. Folland looked down at the grey woman who stood there.

'Is Mr Kettlestang at home?'

'He is not.'

Folland considered her, from his saddle. He asked, as a gambit, 'Mistress Kettlestang, are you?'

She laughed shrilly.

'Me? Mistress Kettlestang? Oh, that's a good one. I wouldn't be Mistress Kettlestang for a thousand pound, nor he wouldn't like that either. There's no Mistress Kettlestang. I does the house for him.'

'Oh. Well, Mistress . . .'

'Hartsop. I be Nance Hartsop.'

'Mistress Hartsop, I have to deliver this horse to Master Kettlestang, and I have a letter for him.'

'Well, you'll no more see him tonight than the Lord of Loone, nohow. It be Council day.'

'Council day?'

'Aye. It be the day in the month that all the Aldermen meet for dinner in the Crown, and there they do all the business of the town. So he won't be here before midnight, and in no state to read letters then.'

'Well, what am I to do?'

'Well, it'd be better if you come back in the morning with your letter. Don't leave it wi' me, nohow.'

'Where do I leave this horse? Out in the street?'

'No. He do know his stall, do our Tiger.'

She patted the horse and disappeared into the house. Folland heard the bolts drawn on the gate beside the house. He rode into the stable yard. He guided his horse over to a mounting-block. He eased himself out of the saddle, and sat down on the block.

'That's a fine way for a brave dragoon to get off his horse,' sneered Nance.

'That's why I'm not a brave dragoon any more,' Folland answered. He rubbed his thigh. 'That was a Frenchman, that was. Now, is there an ostler in the household?'

'Old Josh? He went off an hour agone, when the Master was safe at the Council Feast. You won't see him afore the morning, not sober, nohow.'

'Oh, God!' Folland felt unutterably weary. He cursed all horses. He got off the block, and let the horse lead him to an open door. He unsaddled, and put the tackle where it seemed to belong. He found brushes and curry comb. He cleaned the mud off the horse's legs. When Tiger was clean, Folland went up into the loft, brought down straw and feed. Last of all he worked the pump in the yard, got water for the horse and to wash his own hands and face.

Nance came out of the house again.

'When do I see Master Kettlestang?'

'Oh, come you back in the morning. He'll be up before seven, but he don't like to see anybody before the Abbey strike eight.'

Folland hung there a moment. Then he asked, 'D'ye know anywhere I can have supper? And sleep?'

Surely to God, he thought, she can't turn me away with not so much as a sup of ale. But she did.

'Down the street, there's the Falcon. That might suit you.'

She saw him out of the yard and shut the gate behind him, barring it. He stood in the street a moment. His leg only hurt him now when he was tired or cold, and he was both. He pulled his coat collar up. He began to walk slowly down the street—he only limped now if he hurried.

He remembered passing the Falcon. It was a small place, not grand enough to call an inn, yet something above an alehouse. He heard a door slam. He turned, and saw Nance coming out of the Kettlestang house. She crossed the street and slipped down an alley. There was no one else out of doors. But at the house opposite Kettlestang's, an upper window showed a flicker of white.

2

'I slept at the Falcon,' Folland told Master Kettlestang.

He had come into the inn out of the dank cold of February, and he had been struck by the heat of the place, by the blast from the logs in the grate, from the glowing firebricks. Otherwise, it was an ordinary tap-room, with rough tables, settles all round the walls, stools, a counter. But it had that wonderful fire. Folland sat down, teetering on a stool. He fumbled with the buttons of his spatterdashes, and stripped them off, laid them on the fender to dry. The landlord stood over him, a spare man, as if his own fire had dried out his fat and rendered him down to nothing.

'And what'll ye be wanting?'

'Something to eat, and to drink.'

'A pint of yale, then?'

'Aye, ale. And what is there to eat?'

The landlord brought the ale.

'There's bread and cheese.'

'Nothing hot?'

'Nowt yet. Perhaps when the Abbey strikes six, there may be stew.'

'I'll have bread and cheese, then. And I'll toast it.'

'As you like.'

The bread and cheese came on a tin plate. The bread was fresh and hot, the cheese was Somerset, tart tasting, pale in colour and crumbly. It toasted well, and the landlord brought an onion too. Folland told him, 'Better cheese than we had in Flanders—that was the red stuff, all flabby. But this ale—you don't brew your own, do you?'

'No. Nobody does, not in town. Out in the marsh, maybe. . . . I gets it from Shillmoor the brewer, down Heath End Street.'

'Watery stuff he sells, don't he?'

'I thinks I got some stronger—next time.'

Folland stretched out his legs, drained the pot.

'Next time is now.'

He stuffed his mouth with the hot bread and cheese. He felt

the life come back. The landlord was before him with a fresh pint. Folland tasted it.

'That's a bit better. What's your name?'

'Dowgill. Amos Dowgill. I been in the Falcon this last twelve year. A Wrackham man I be out of the Vintners' Guild, born here and my fathers before me for hundreds of years.'

'What d'ye know of Master Kettlestang?'

'I do know this, that I'm a Burgess of Wrackham, and Master Kettlestang be an Alderman, and Portreeve for this turn, and like to be for next turn, and a turn last five year. And that makes him Licensing Justice.'

'You know which side your bread's buttered?'

'Aye, and where my cheese do come from. But the bread I know most of all.'

'How come?'

'Well, perhaps you don't know. The Aldermen be the heads of the Town Guilds, and Master Kettlestang be the Alderman of the Millers' Guild.'

'A miller?'

'Well, grain-merchant more like. How don't ye know, if ye've brought his horse?'

'That's all I was hired to do, bring the horse.' Folland tired of conversation. He finished the cheese. He asked, 'You got anywhere I can sleep?'

'You can have the garret.'

'With the rats?'

'There be no rats. They're all gone with the Lords of Loone.'

'Can I go up now?'

Dowgill grunted. He led the way to a low space between rafters and ceiling. There was a bed, a straw-filled mattress, a bundle of threadbare blankets.

'I've slept in worse,' Folland said. He did not add, as he was tempted, *but not much worse*. 'Let me know when the stew is ripe.'

Alone, he peeled off his coat. He sat on the bed, and unlaced his shoes with their high tongues. He stuffed his guineas and the packet of letters inside his shirt. He put his hat carefully down, and then his wig. He found a nightcap in his pocket and pulled it on to his cropped head. The blankets did not seem damp, nor more flea-ridden than he expected. He slept almost at once.

Folland was wakened by a banging on the floor, the ceiling, below him. He sat up. There was an inch of candle burning by the bed. By its light he saw that someone had brought him a bowl of warm water and a scrap of towelling. And he had slept through that? Oh, the wars were long ago, and the alarms, the prowling French. He washed, and felt his own man again, clean now. He pulled on his shoes and his coat, left his wig and went down in his nightcap.

The tap-room was full, but a girl in a dirty gown at the foot of the stairs took the candle from him and led the way to a table.

'You found the water? Ready for your stew, then?'

'Aye.' The sleep had done him a world of good. He felt like taking on a dozen French, or her, or grooming a whole squadron's horses. He touched her hand. 'And a pint of that strong ale like I had the second time today. What's your name?'

But she was gone, slipping from him with no effort.

'Liz Alley,' said a voice beside him. 'Liz Alley, that was.' It was a little man, pink-faced, toothless, very old, not easy to understand.

'Gipsy, isn't she?' Folland asked. 'She looks like one, anyway, dark like that and black hair and eyes——'

'Now, don't you go calling an Alley a Gipsy,' the old man warned. 'That's the way fights start, and fight an Alley, you fight the lot, and the Sarsens and the Blackmers. They be old out-of-Wrackham families, that came in with Lord Wrackham. But not gipsies.'

Liz Alley came back, planking a plate of stew in front of the Dragoon, and a slab of bread and the pint of ale. The little old man asked, 'You, was it, that brought Tiger back?'

'Aye. Are you Master Kettlestang's groom, then?' The man looked ostler all over, he smelt of a life with the horses.

'I am. And his head wagoner I was afore.'

'Not much, to be groom after that.'

'And if he hadn't kept me on, where else would I be? D'ye know how old I am? Guess!'

'Oh, I don't know. Ninety?' Better to guess high, thought Folland, these seventy-year-olds all want you to guess high. And then they lie to you.

'Near enough. Ninety-three.'

'Do you remember being born, then?'

'No, I swear to ye. Look, I remember when the old wars

started, I were growed then, I went off with the train. Gloucester I were at, and Newbury, and Basing House, and Chester. Sometimes it were the King's guns we was pulling, and sometimes Oliver's, depending on who would pay us, and once I mind it were the Scotchy men. I were at all them battles, and bad they was as anything you been in.'

It was possible, Folland thought. Perhaps not ninety-three, but eighty-three more like, and still leave time for it, if he'd gone off to the wars at sixteen like Folland had. Good enough for a pint, and he called for ale for them both. It was probably all the old man had to live on, tales of the wars, and, truth, what more had Robert Folland?

'Thank ye kindly, and here's to your honour's health.' And the change of tone, the unearned title, went through Folland like a sword. That so little should change him into a lackey. But the ostler caught at Dowgill as he went by.

'Hey, Amos, where d'ye get this yale? This be good stuff, this yale be.'

'Why, 'tis nobbut my usual.'

'That it be not. This be a *good* brew, this be. There be malt in this.'

'Shut him up, for God's sake,' Amos Dowgill told Liz Alley. 'What you want to give him that barrel for? That's my own barrel.'

'It's what the sodger called for. What I gave him, like you said.'

'Well, *keep* it for him then. Know who he is? He's an informer for Shillmoor, he is.'

'Then serve you right. Once you start playing with the beer, it's bound to turn out bad.'

'They all does it.'

'But it's *your* hide Shillmoor'll have at the next Assize of ale.'

'Too late to change now. Keep your wits. Don't serve any but the soldier out of *my* barrel.'

'Aye, there's no good ale left now, I was thinking,' the old man was maundering on, 'I thought it was all gone with the Lords of Loone.'

'And where are they gone?'

'Oh, you wouldn't know, being a stranger like me. I came here the year the King came back from his travels, and still I'm a stranger here. So I'll tell ye. Once there was great Lords here that were earls of all the Loone valley, and the Marsh and the Down and all the way to the sea. Endellion their name was, aye, Endellion. And all gone, now.'

'All gone? But how gone? Here, Liz, a pint of the same again —the same, for both of us, I'll taste both pots.'

'Oh, aye, gone. All gone. And the last Endellion that was here, he were a cousin, not one of the main branch, he ended up a Steward, he did. Steward to Lord Wrackham that bought all the Loone lands when the last lord did ruin himself for the King. All except that bit of land Hodman Blackmer did buy. There's justice in it, isn't there now, that Lord Wrackham went over the water and died there. The Lord Wrackham that is now nobody has ever seen to know. And that last Endellion, dead too, and his kin all gone. Gone with the Lords of Loone, that's what Wrackham men do say. And they laugh when they say it, for the Endellions were never friends to Wrackham men.'

'Are you a Wrackham man?'

'No, that I be not.' The old man was indignant. 'From Essex, I were, but I go where the hosses call me, and with the hosses I will be till the end. Tiger be a good hoss. Quiet, and not fast——'

'But a stayer.'

'Arr, you're right there. Go all day and night with ye, you must know. Master Kettlestang do usually ride him to Lunnon and back in the week. This time he came back on ship, for summat strange reason. Ah, the rich have whims and the poor have whims, but 'tis the rich can enjoy them.'

'You knew I was bringing Tiger back?'

'Aye, I knew——'

'And you made sure everybody in town knew, Josh Caddon,' Dowgill put in over the ancient's shoulder. There was a chorus of laughter all down the table. Behind in the kitchen Christopher Gunver heard it, and Joseph Carines, Andrew Pontigarde and Frederick Arkengarth. They sat there, drinking and listening, and none of them looked into the Tap, for that was not their way.

'Joe Grinton and the Nobbler tried arter ye, then, did they?' someone asked.

'Caught a Tartar, they did,' another voice out of the crowd.

'Walking in the river without their breeches.'

'And dripping up the street.'

The room was full of laughter. Folland found his pot filled, and filled again. Men clapped him on the back. It seemed that anyone who tipped Grinton and the Nobbler in the river deserved to eat at the public table. And yet, there seemed a brittleness in the air. Nothing was quite sincere. There was a phrase that caught his ear.

'Watered their wine for them proper, you did.'

More than one of them said that, or something like it. There was no point in asking what it meant. These were all Wrackham men, and he was a stranger. Popularity like this was easy bought, easy lost. Nothing but to sit and take it while it came, and thank God for the ale.

Who were these men, he asked himself. Not the poor of Wrackham, because they had money to spend on ale, or credit that Dowgill would accept. They were ostlers and wagoners, sawyers and coopers, journeymen working by the day but with work to go to, every day, with a place, even though a low one, in society. Men with a skill of some kind. But not the rich or even the middling people, not men with little shops or a site for a stall at the Butter Cross. Men, thought Folland, fit for a sergeant to drink with. Or an ex-sergeant. And men here too who seemed to be known, but not well known, come to see—what? The man who had frightened two highwaymen? The man who had been trusted with Master Kettlestang's horse and had delivered it, a horse well known in the town? Or what? Or whom?

And suddenly, the hubbub died. Not to silence, but to a mere murmur of private chats, of clinking glasses and belches and confidential murmurs. And the men fell back from Folland, sitting by the counter. They stood in a circle, men in their own hair grown long, or greasy nightcaps or worn bobwigs not fitting, men in frocks unbuttoned or in sleeved waistcoats without coats, or in aprons and their shirts. But in the midst of them now was another man, in a full-bottomed wig all white and powdered, with a cocked hat set delicately on it. The coat was new, and of a tender, unpractical pink, that must shrink from a dirty thumb : the buttons alone, of gold wire, would have paid for that whole week's drinking in the Falcon. Young, thought Folland, perhaps a year younger than I am : but he's not been through what I have; I swear I look five years older. But money there, whoever he is, money and a lot of it, not stolen but respectable. Money like that doesn't come drinking in a Falcon. He isn't here without some reason.

The young man rapped on the bar.

'Brandy,' he said.

Liz Alley brought it, hovered by him, eyes on his. The smart young man leaned his elbow on the counter, choosing a clean spot with exaggerated care. He looked down at Folland, sitting not five feet from him. Folland stared back. Fair hair showed at the corners of the wig, against the brown stubble under Folland's nightcap. But green eyes burned into green. Folland nerved himself to sit still. What if this man owned the town, and Folland had not a penny in the world? This was a public house, he'd not be stared out or put down. And he'd not stand up, nor call any man 'sir' again without good reason. Those days were over. And, thought Folland, brandy for the boys to show how big they are drinking it: strong ale in pints for men.

As if in answer the young man in the pink coat raised his glass, sipped his brandy, savoured it, then tossed it down, all of it. Folland picked up his full pint pot. He put it to his lips. Slowly, not taking the vessel from his mouth, he drained it. He thumped the pewter tankard down: it echoed in the room. The young man turned, walked to the door, went out into the night without a further glance.

He went, but the spirit of the evening had changed. Men finished their beer, without undue haste, and then left; they did not order more. In half an hour barely a third of the clientele was left. And they, from the way Dowgill addressed them, were regulars, the men he would see in every night, or most nights, the men with accounts on the slates, the men who paid for his bread. It was Folland, and the men who came to see him, who would send him this week's butter. And the cheese?

In another half-hour by the Abbey clock there was nobody left in the tap-room of the Falcon but Josh Caddon. Folland felt at liberty to ask him, 'Who was that?'

'Who was who?'

'The man in the pink coat.'

'Oh, him. He bain't no strawberry roan. He bain't but a nothing.'

'Now, Dad, he weren't a nothing, whatever else he were.'

'Well, he may be summat to all them there, but not to old soldiers. That's George Place, old Jemmy Place's son, him that is Alderman of the Vintners' Guild.'

'That has a house opposite Master Kettlestang?'

'No sooner do Master Kettlestang move into the town into what were Franky Endellion the Steward's house once, than the Places do build that there great place with the yellow brick they carted over special from Bedford. And out from over the shop Jemmy Place do move, right opposite Master Kettlestang that can't abide him, nor him neither though they talk polite enough in public. Well, thank ye kindly. I'll be back now to bed Tiger.'

Thus Folland slept in the Falcon.

Towards the end of the morning, nearer nine than eight, Folland at last stood face to face with Kettlestang.

'At the Falcon?'

' 'Twas where your housekeeper sent me. And 'twas what I could afford.'

'I have no criticism.' Kettlestang opened the packet of letters that Folland had brought out from his breast, beneath his shirt. He looked through them, drafts, receipts, they could wait. He opened the letter that Colonel Cutler had written. Folland watched him as he read. He was a prim and dapper man, thin-fleshed over the bones of his face, his dark green coat spotless, his wig curled down three aside and four behind. He fitted the room, with its square of carpet laid an exact foot from the wall all round, the oval table, the chair with its new-shape back, all in the latest of fashion, scoured with sand and clean, clean and neat. Nothing of disorder there. Kettlestang looked up suddenly at Folland standing there.

'What did Colonel Cutler tell you?'

'Only that I was to bring this horse to you, that he said he had borrowed of you. And that you would pay me for my trouble when I got here.'

'And you wait for your pay?'

'It is due to me.'

'True. And I suppose you need it. You are no longer in the Army? You are sure that you will not be having to go back?'

'No. I cannot return. I have been cast off since this wound.'

'Does it inconvenience you?'

'It is almost well. Only the cold grips it sometimes, or when I am tired I feel the pain still and I limp a little. But less and less every day.'

'You were a long time in the Army?'

'Ten years. I started as a bugling boy and I ended as a sergeant.'

'A sergeant? Can you read and write?'

'Aye. And cast up figures. Count charges for fodder or billeting, change guineas into guilders or livres, tell hay from chaff or cheese from millstones, flour from chalk and gilded lead from gold. I can stand with the order book on my knee and take down what is said as fast as it is spoken. I was a galloper for Colonel Cutler. Now he thinks of selling out. I am cast off and stand here.'

'Take a glass of ale, Sergeant. Did Colonel Cutler tell you nothing? Or give you no help? Have you nothing to do now?'

'I suppose I must look for employment. I have no trade. I have seen men already who are begging.'

'Or worse. You still carry your sword.'

'Or worse.'

'When the war ends, as they say it will this year——'

'And so they say every year.'

'True. There will be many more looking for work, and finding none. What I wrote to Colonel Cutler two years ago, and have repeated since, is that I would be glad of a man to work for me. Colonel Cutler says in this letter that he thinks that you are a suitable man.'

'Wrackham is full of men.'

'I asked Colonel Cutler to find me a . . . a confidential man. I cannot ask a Wrackham man to keep my secrets. They concern too many Wrackham people.'

'Do you think I could keep your secrets?'

'Colonel Cutler thought you could be trusted with another man's horse, worth a hundred guineas. And so you could. I do not want just another clerk. I can find frightened clerks enough in Wrackham. I want a man who cannot be frightened.'

'I was not frightened at Malplaquet.'

'You were not frightened, I hear, in the woods yesterday. And you keep your trust. I saw you this morning, mucking out my yard. That you were not asked to do.'

'I could not leave Josh to look to Tiger.'

'I want a man, Sergeant, who will move silent as my shadow, where I need, when I need. Discreet, dumb. A man who will take my messages, to wherever I send them, and carry money and guard it. And a man who will look into my books after my clerks, and into my granaries after my storemen.'

'A man with no kinsmen, here in Wrackham?'

'So I said.'

Folland considered. What else had he been in Cutler's Dragoons but the Colonel's confidential man, his doer of business. And for that, in the Army, he had half a guinea a week in pay, and seven shillings to buy forage, and his food was rated at eight shillings a week, but Cutler and the Commissary and every clerk in the Treasury pared and scraped that away till he was lucky if he saw a guinea in a quarter, in hard money. He asked,

'And what would you be paying for such devotion?'

'For a man who would offer it . . . let us say, fifty guineas in the year. And another twenty at the year's end for the man who had given it.' Kettlestang waited a moment. 'And your dinner every day you work . . . and two suits of clothes in the year.'

Folland turned his back and looked out of the window at the harsh new brick of the Place house. Was that a face at the upper window? Something white was there. He sipped his ale, deliberately, made himself count to a hundred, then to a hundred again. Then he turned to the dapper man at the table, sitting keen-faced, the skin drawn tight from chalk-white brow to scraped chin.

'What d'ye want me to do for ye today, Master Kettlestang?'

'Clap hands on it, then.' Their palms slapped across the table. 'For a year at the start. Now, list ye here. I'll have no man say that Jacob Kettlestang would not walk the streets of Wrackham without a soldier at his back. You can keep your sabre, but not that red coat. First, go to Master Carines, the tailor, and bid him let you have a frock at my charge.'

'In your livery, Master Kettlestang?'

'Livery? Am I the Lord of Loone? What d'ye take me for? Find a frock in what colours you wish, but fit to walk the street in. Here is a note for Carines. Later, perhaps, you will need a coat besides the frock, but for today the frock will be enough. And another thing—where will you live? I'll have no one live in this house but my own flesh and blood, and I have only one nephew, that is in London at the Inns of Court.'

'I am well enough at the Falcon.'

'Not well enough for me. Find some respectable house, and lodge there. Forget your army ways of billeting in alehouses. Ask

Master Carines, for he lives nearer the come-and-go of the town. Now . . . what is it you are waiting for?'

'I was promised three guineas for bringing Tiger back from London.'

'Are you so hard a man then for money, Folland?'

'The Queen's service has made me so, Master Kettlestang, because I found that if I were not hard I would never get a penny of my own.'

'Three guineas . . . three. Be sure that you are as hard always. For my money as well as for your own.'

Carines was ready for custom, not questioning Folland's order, even without seeing the note from Kettlestang. The sight of Folland on that horse, he said, had been enough to mark him as a man of trust. And now . . . 'Frocks, frocks . . . there ought to be one here to fit you, big as you are. A red one would not be to your mind?'

'I have had enough of red coats. If I cannot be a soldier, I will not pose as one.'

'What will you do with the one you are wearing? It is still good——'

'I will keep it for old times' sake. 'Twill do for stables in the cold morning.'

'As you wish. Here, this will fit. Dark brown. Or this, in green?'

'No, the brown.' If Kettlestang wore green on a working day, then Folland would not. This brown frock, with flat collar and pocket flaps in grey, was inconspicuous. He would not stand out in a crowd. At the upper level of servants, below men of a little real money or the minimum of influence—he was used to it, a sergeant's place. And where would a sergeant live? Kettlestang was right : not in an alehouse. He consulted Carines.

'A place to lodge?' Carines took stock of him. 'Eh, you are not a riotous man, Master Folland?' The ex-dragoon had already moved his belongings from the red coat to the brown. The prayer-book had been conspicuous : the cards were rolled in the nightshirt, back in the Falcon. The purse of guineas clinked heavy.

'I have tried to be so, and there was plenty of encouragement in our regiment, and not a little instruction by past masters. But, i' faith, sir, I had not the talent for it, and I failed to learn the trick.'

The tailor laughed. It was a laugh of good humour, of real

amusement, with no touch of mockery : it was not the laughter Robert Folland had heard the night before, on the river bank or in the tap-room. He realized that for the first time in Wrackham he had said something light-hearted, subtle.

'Perhaps you have convinced opinions in religion or in politics that might disqualify you?'

'From what?'

'There is here a Non-juring clergyman, a Mr Arkengarth. He was Vicar of the Abbey till he refused to take the oath of allegiance to King William on the irresponsible and frivolous grounds that he had already taken an oath to King James. So he was ejected, and it's the third time-serving Whig Vicar in the place since then.'

'And he still lives in the town?'

'Where else? Soon after the ejection, the master of the Town School, who was a Lincoln man, was caught in disgraceful conduct, or misconduct, that it was proved by many truthful witnesses he had been continuing in flagrantly and openly in the sight of all for many years. Though quite what that misconduct had been none exactly knew. So he was dismissed, and Mr Arkengarth, who was a Wrackham man born, and his great-grandfathers before him, has been master of the Town School ever since. He taught me, though what, I cannot remember.'

'And yet ... ?'

'He has a large family, and the School House is big. He would be glad to take you in. Perhaps he might then be able to pay me —after he has settled his other debts : I will not push myself before the other merchants of the town.'

'Where is the School House?'

'Next to the Abbey Gate—the School is in the gate.'

Carines bowed Folland out of the shop. He watched him walk away. Not far. Folland stopped at the next shop. Not only a new frock, thought Carines, but a new wig, too, or at least a second-hand one. Any would be an improvement on the one he was wearing. Malplaquet? It had probably gone on the long march to Blenheim and been ridden over there. Would Gunver offer him anything on it? Carines thought not, on the whole. What would he choose now to go with that decent frock? No, not a full bottom, he had too much sense for that : a plain tie wig.

Folland was at the School House door. He had, he thought, no objection to Non-jurors as such. There were not many left now

19

who held so firmly to their old oaths : most of them thought that the death of James, the accession of Anne, had wiped the slate clean. Bishop Ken was the type of the remainder, ascetic, scholarly, pious, virtuous, sacerdotal—yes, that was the word, sacerdotal, all High Church, almost Roman. Folland had seen Roman Churches in Spain, and priests and monks, too. All sorts, good and bad, like the clergy here. It was school time, but the tailor had said something about a family. A wife, perhaps, to be at home now at midday. It was a girl who opened the door, in a dull brown bodice, a russet-skirted petticoat, a yellow scarf. For a moment, Folland thought, *'tis only the skivvy*. But then he heard her voice as she asked clear, in a tone of authority,

'And what, sir, would you be wanting here? Pray you knock less loud, or you will disturb my mother.'

'Well, miss, 'tis perhaps your mother I should be talking to.'

'Then you must tell me how important it is, and it must be of the greatest urgency before I let you talk with her, because it was only yesterday that she was brought to bed of my new brother.'

And this one, Folland thought, cannot be less than seventeen. He countered, 'Then it might be your father I ought to speak to.'

'It should be plain that he is in the School. What is it you would say to either of them? For I will have to hear it at last, seeing that I do all the work of the house.'

'I am new come into the town, miss, and I am to work for Mr Kettlestang——'

'And we all know that since you rode his horse all round the town last afternoon.'

'And I am looking for lodging. Master Carines the Tailor thought that you might——'

'Did he, indeed? And like him for interfering and wanting to know other people's business better than his own.'

Folland did his best to look firm, though he found it difficult to look down on the brown curls, lighter than his own, and the grey eyes looking up at him, without laughing at their defiance.

'Now, my girl, you are trying to be disagreeable with me. You find it hard, because plain, it is not your nature. But perhaps you were taught to be suspicious of men who come to the door, in case they should sell you something you would be sorry to have. I assure you that I am none of those, though you have only my word for it. I know nobody in the town to answer for me, except perhaps Master Kettlestang, and for all I know he would not let his word go far, seeing I met this morning for the first time in my life.'

'I am sorry, sir. I have no time to bargain, because I have all to do in the house, and you will see how much it is, with my mother ill. And I am only afraid you might not like the place once you were in it, and then it were better you had not come. But we have a room, and we would be glad of someone quiet to take it, because we could do with the money.'

Oho, thought Folland, doesn't the School pay? She thought, Doesn't he know whose house he is at, and who it is he may meet here? But he looked clean and respectable, for all the long sword tucked under his arm, and it was not a good thing to seem disobliging to Master Carines, or to Master Kettlestang either. She led him inside, talking all the while in what she thought the proper way for a woman trying to let a room.

'And it is quiet here, only for a little noise of the children, because Mother has seven of us, not counting the baby, and also we keep here eleven boys of the School who come from outside the town and are not free scholars. This is where they are'—and she pushed open a door on the first landing to show a long room crammed with empty white beds. 'But we have a good little room above, if you do not mind stairs, just along here, where you have a nice lookout over the Abbey Churchyard and no trouble from the noises of the street and the market and the fairs they have down there.'

She stood there, twisting her hands under her apron and thinking, Oh, please let him take it, please God let him take it. If he takes it, perhaps he'll be quiet about—oh, let him take it.

Folland took it.

'I have little to bring. A soldier from the wars returning. . . . I'll leave this here to mark my place.'

He took the prayer-book from his pocket and laid it on the little table. There was that in the room, and a chair, a chest, a few hooks on the wall, the bed. No room for anything more. No room, hardly, for Folland, she thought, six feet and more of him. The prayer-book was old, the leather binding scratched and scuffed and the corners bent. He saw her look at it.

'My—I was brought up in a parsonage,' he told her, half shamefaced, as if it were not to be expected that a sergeant of dragoons should carry such a thing about with him. She only answered, 'You will need it tomorrow, to go to church with Master Kettlestang.'

Nevertheless, when Folland had gone she went back into the room, and picked up the book. At the top of the fly leaf she read the name *Margaret*. . . . The surname was scratched out, in a different, fresher ink. And there were other words, scratched out at the same time, below. Only the one at the foot of the page had suffered less than the rest. After some trouble she could make out a *W* and a *k* and an *h*, and at the end of it was clearly an *m*. The name came first to her mind : *Wrackham* . . . ?

3

Edward Quernhow stood within the vestry door in the Abbey Church. Above in the West tower, the great bell Timothy tolled the half-minutes to eleven o'clock, the sacred hour. Quernhow always called it Matins, having a romantic and High Church imagination. All the town knew that he was a High Church man, wearing a surplice to read the service each Sunday, not merely when he administered the Sacrament, three times a year before a host of witnesses, to such as wished to hold office under the Corporation or the Crown. On those days he saw many who on other Sundays worshipped in the Baptist Conventicle, or the Congregation of the Independents that had come down in the world since Oliver's time, or the Assembly of the Misguided Brethren. Even these last he tolerated more than Catholics, if there were any in the town : for Antinomianism was mere vacancy, but positive error was another thing.

No matter, three times a year these people came, and showed themselves, whatever their opinions, true members of the Church of England, and supporters of the Crown, and therefore qualified to be excisemen and tollgate-keepers, town-bailiffs and market wardens. This was how the Kingdom worked.

In the choir, the town band waited, at ease. The fiddles were across their laps, the trumpets idle in their hands. In front of them, the singing boys from the Town School were about as quiet as one can expect boys to be. They were whispering among themselves, and giggling; two of them were playing chess with a board ruled on a sheet of paper, and men of little scraps with letters, *K, Q, P*, written on them. But they kept a weather eye on Frederick Arkengarth. He looked to the Vicar for the sign.

It embarrassed Quernhow to see his predecessor stand there, who had been Vicar in his place. But that was that. The parish paid him as Master of the Music as well as Master of the School, so his livelihood was safe, and with the boarders and private pupils, he would be better off than the Vicar. And Arkengarth himself made little of their counter-position. He could hold no cure of souls, nor even, Quernhow supposed, celebrate the Sacraments in the Abbey. At least he had never asked to do so, although certainly he communicated more than the legal minimum of times each year. Quernhow was not sure what the legal position was. He sometimes thought he might ask the Archdeacon. Whether the Archdeacon could or would answer was another matter : the Archdeacon had no ghost to sit in his pews.

Most of the congregation were there already, those who always came to Church. These were the little people of the parish, market women and labouring men who hoped by constant attendance to make their claims to one of the seventy-three separate charities which the Vicar, under the Corporation, had the bestowal of. But today was different. There had been a Council Meeting in the week. Therefore, today, the Council would come to Church. Not formally in procession, in chains and furred robes as they did on the Sacrament Days or at Portreeve Calling Day. It was merely the tradition that on the Sunday after a Council meeting, the Fourteen Aldermen of the Guilds of Wrackham, and one of them the Portreeve, would come to Morning Prayer, and the Vicar would preach appropriate to the time. Quernhow's text was ready, his sermon composed. But the Council was not yet come, because how should they be expected to jostle with the commonalty of the town in the church porch?

When the chimes were over, and only Timothy tolled the half-minutes, the Council walked one by one up Abbey Path and into the church, out of the green graveyard into the red stone door. They were the notables of the town, and between them they held the advowson of the living. They might appoint it to anyone whom they wished—once it were vacant. But the Vicar, once appointed, once instituted, held the living for his life. No man could dispossess him of that, unless they proved him treasonable to Church and Queen, as Arkengarth had been. Therefore the Vicar could say to them, plain and loud, what he wished. And that Quernhow had done in the past, not always to the Council's liking : though today he had nothing particular to reproach them with, he would reproach them in general to show his good will.

First came the most junior member of the Council, and the only one who, though himself born in Wrackham, was not a Wrackham man by his own father's birth. Gaston Grangier was Alderman of the Silk Weavers' Guild, that had swallowed up the Clothiers. He was the richest of the French that lived, mostly, around Duck Street. His father had come from Lille, a Huguenot. Grangier wore a silk coat and a silk cravat, and his wife a silk gown, but his seven sons were all in cloth coats. His father-in-law, Raphael Fencote, the Cooper, through whom he held his townsmanship in Wrackham, would come later in his turn, and take his own pew.

Ezekiel Enskiddy followed him, the Shipbuilder, with his family. Then Jonah Perrott, the Glovemaker, and his one son, being a widower, but he was the first to have grandsons, some with him and another in the choir. Ahab Starbutton was the Waterman, and David Nosterfield the Stonemason, Elisha Keld the Cordwainer and Abel Gannel the Tallow Chandler. All these Aldermen came not alone, but with their families behind them. And besides their own kin, they brought apprentices and bully boys with swords and clubs. The Aldermen sat each in his own pew : their hangers-on spilled over into the empty aisles.

Solomon Hunderthwaite was the Locksmith, and Reuben Blackhope was the Glassblower. Gideon Conrig was the Carpenter, and Abram Kilnsey the Furrier, and each brought his train of sons and journeymen and apprentices to fill the church. And after them came Andrew Pontigarde, but although his precedence was so high, he was not an Alderman : he was an attorney and Clerk to the Corporation, a Wrackham man born and related to almost all the Aldermen. He kept the Council records, and held their money, and did their business for them. Therefore his power in Wrackham was as great as any three Aldermen put together, though they hardly knew it.

Almost all were there. But not all. Quernhow motioned to Micah Widdybank to toll Timothy ten times more. Now, when all were settled, the Places entered. All the Aldermen were rich and powerful in their own right, each the head of his Guild, chosen by his own tradesmen. But there was no one in the church now so rich and as powerful as James Place the Vintner. His wife entered first in her plum-coloured gown, and then his daughter, Sophia. And Alderman Place himself, in a fine coat of scarlet silk, and orange breeches, a green cravat about his neck. In his left hand he held his long slender stick with its silver mountings, and his right hand was laid on his son's shoulder. He went up the aisle till his son stopped him before his pew. He touched the tall Churchwarden's staff that stood at the gate before he entered; they went in, and shut the door, and sat.

The men that came with the Places arranged themselves where they could. They were out-of-Wrackham men, Marsh Pards that lived where the fens were not drained. They worked for Place, lightermen and wagoners; there were other things they were said to do as well, so that Quernhow wondered often how Keffle and Buick, Key and Glass, for such were Marsh Pard names, had the face to come to church. But one day they might repent, though it never looked very likely. They looked around in savage pride, as if they were men who had owned the town before there was a town, and waited only for the Wrackham men to go away again.

Now, thought Quernhow, there is only one left to come. And he must sit in the Portreeve's stall, with the other Churchwarden's staff, and the hatchment of the last Lord Wrackham. The black lozenge framed the ancient arms, azure, across a lunette argent, two roses of Lancaster, gules. Quernhow would not, for pride of office, for pride as a man, look towards the North Door. He contented himself, forced himself, with the counting of the petals on the roses, slowly, one . . . and . . . two . . . and . . .

It was always like this. At the last stroke the Portreeve would enter, alone, always alone. He had neither wife nor son to come with him; after he had entered the Abbey Church for the last time, borne by his own wagoners, where would all that wealth go? Who would control this great house? There was talk of a nephew in London, but no one had ever seen him, nor, mostly, believed in him, for nephew was a vague term, and the relationship hard to account for.

The Portreeve entered. And Quernhow, and all the people, against their will, turned to look, knowing by some inner sense that this was not a Sunday like all other Sundays. The band struck up their march at Arkengarth's gesture. No one listened to them, even though they made a discord : the band, like everyone else in the church, was looking at the door. Out of the February cold of the air into the chill of the church came the yellow Sunday coat of Portreeve Kettlestang, and his staff, too, rattled on the flags of the nave. But he was not alone. For the first time in memory, Kettlestang came to church in company, a man at his back that towered a head above him, a man in a decent tie wig against his master's full bottom, a brown frock behind the Portreeve's golden coat. But at his waist, under his frock, to echo his patron's staff Folland wore his great horseman's sword. The brass of the hilt showed through the slit by his left hand, the chape of the scabbard shone, polished, under the hem of the frock. So, thought Quernhow, so . . . the Portreeve has his bully boy at last.

The music came to its end. Parson Quernhow settled his wig on his head, and walked into the choir. He stepped up into his place in the new three-decker pulpit, the latest fashion, lately paid for by the Council and built by Master Conrig's men from drawings Master Kettlestang had got, somehow, in London. He looked over the people in the nave. He was not interested in Robert Folland any more. His eyes roamed over the congregation to see who was not there. An Alley and a Sarsen in the school choir : but no one else of those families, even though they might live in the town. No Gunver, no Carines, no Bridgward.

Folland followed the Portreeve up the nave. He did not feel embarrassment, let alone shame, at being seen to obey a master, or in appearing to display this other man's power. It had been his place for so many years, first as a trooper, and at the last as a sergeant. But as he came to the door of the pew, and bent to open it for the Portreeve, he felt eyes upon him as if he were on guard in a public place, booted and spurred, in scarlet and polished brass. He straightened from the latch, he stood aside for Kettlestang, looked across the aisle, into the Place pew, the other Churchwarden's stall, next an Endellion tomb. Yes, there he was, the young man of the Falcon tap, in his pink coat, his covered buttons and his well-ironed wig, his eyes, his insolent green eyes, that burned into Folland as if they would strip the brown frock from him, and leave him naked in his shirt to the cold air of the church.

It was Folland whose eyes dropped first. What of it? he

thought, it is his affair. I have nothing to do with such childishness. I know who he is, I have that advantage of him. What do any of them know of me? What do they know of why I chose to come to Wrackham, why I seized the chance when Colonel Cutler threw it in my way. He offered it in that diffident manner of his, as if it were something I might well refuse. Refuse? What else was I to do? And what have I to do with any of these—yet?

He looked along the pew, to where she sat—not the mother but the daughter. What was it that drew his eye there? He had seen women enough in his time already. This was no nut-brown maiden like the school-house girl, but yellow haired and green eyed like her own brother beside her. Something made him look, some vague surge of sentiment. For till he had to turn to follow the Portreeve into the pew, look away he could not. But then he could, must, look away. Look anywhere, he sensed, but there. It meant danger.

Schoolmaster Arkengarth watched the look. Well, there's a thing now, he thought. There's Portreeve Kettlestang, that has no more child nor kinsman in the place than Adam, that has always been so proud of himself, that he would always walk alone, comes now into church with his fighting man behind him. What does it mean? At last, does he feel himself to be old? Can he no longer collect his debts? And that's the man my Prisca let the top attic to. I wouldn't have had it if I'd been there. Not now I see who it must be. Me, the schoolmaster of a great town, to be letting out rooms. But she says she can't manage on the money, and with my Nellie so bad, what am I to do? But it's a woman's place to manage.

He turned to his choir. It was a fine great church, and where was there a better choir of singing boys? The church itself was fit to be a cathedral, as good as Chester any road. Why should it not have as fine music as any cathedral? For seven years it had been his, young as he was then. All gone, now, beyond recall, and yet he could never tear himself quite away.

He raised his hand. They began the *Venite*. It went fine enough with his band, fiddles and trumpets and flutes. But if the Corporation would buy an organ . . . There was fine music written for the organ and he could play it for them. If he had an organ instead of this unruly band, he would be able to play music as written, not as they misread it. And only if he had the one instrument under his hand, could he then hear the sounds

27

he wanted to hear, the tunes he wanted to make, and find whether what he had written was what he imagined. Arkengarth had once been back to Cambridge, and there on Father Smith's organ in Trinity College he had heard three of his anthems played—but not sung.

Sophia Place looked sideways at the man in the opposite pew. She flickered her lids over her pale eyes. He was at least a new man in the town, someone perhaps to steal a glance at when he could see it, to motion with her eyes, to tempt, to tease—perhaps, even sometimes to talk to if no one was looking. Someone new in this boring town, where everything was always the same since the beginning of time. Where he had come from she had not heard, any more than anyone else in the town, and yet she was certain she knew; she could not believe herself mistaken.

She knew when he had come. George had come in in a bad temper that afternoon and refused to tell her why. Except he said that Nobbler had done it. What it was the Nobbler had done she did not know. But a little later, she had sat, as every afternoon she sat, in the gallery window at her embroidery, and she had seen this man ride up on Tiger. There weren't many men like that in Wrackham, walking with that swagger that showed through his limp, that showed through that ragged red coat. He walked the streets like a lord, although he tried to hide it. But *she* knew.

Oh, so she's got her eye on him, thought Arkengarth. I've not seen her look like that at any man before. And my Prisca knows what she wants in the house, or she'd not have let him have that room at first asking. And no recommendation, either, has he, except that he is going to work for Kettlestang. But why so straight to our house? Why should he come out of nowhere and at once seek a room in the house of a Non-juring parson? And if I ask that of myself, who else will not ask it? 'Up, now, boys, and let us give forth our tongues in praise. *Te Deum*, sing it loud and clear, that all the Hosts of Heaven may hear.'

Prisca Arkengarth sat in the back row of the nave, where she could look up the long aisle to her father in the choir, and slip out unnoticed when the sermon started, to make her father's dinner ready, and see to her mother. This was the furthest she ever went from the School House now. These few shillings for the music, it was all useful, or would be if she or her mother ever saw it. But it went, as often as not, into other pockets. She

28

grudged that loss more than any. Was there ever going to be any more in life for her than washing and cleaning and mending and saving and skimping for an ever pregnant mother and eight brothers—two of them half-brothers, and the more work for that because they were grown men. But, she supposed, after that, she could manage an extra man in the house well enough. Hardly an extra man, indeed, only a replacement because the Nobbler would hardly show his face again after what had happened in the woods.

'Stretch forth the right hand of Thy majesty,' prayed Parson Quernhow. The words were automatic, the thought too. Whose majesty? How long now would it be Anne? She could not live for ever. If only she could. What ought he to pray—Oh Queen, live for ever? If it be George, then all would be well. But if not—perhaps James again? And if James, there might be civil war raging over the country, perhaps before the year were out. And if James won, who would read the Service at this desk? Himself? Almost certainly not. Little chance then for an Arminian like Quernhow. Perhaps Arkengarth, as a reward for old loyalties . . . for a time. But not for long. There would soon enough be a Papist here to say his Latin Mass. Quernhow shuddered. He recited '. . . that we, trusting in Thy defence, may not fear the power of any adversaries. . . .' Is this man an adversary? Is he come to bring one stranger King or other from over the seas? Has he come to prepare my downfall?

Is he come to prepare my downfall? wondered George Place. We might have had him in the thicket, if the Nobbler had not been a coward. So I left him and Grinton to face it. He wouldn't have given me away, they wouldn't have had a word out of old Nobbler. And if he had talked, would they have believed him? People would have thought it a prank, what we would do to any stranger, and no harm done, nor thought. But it was so tempting, that rumour. A thousand pound they said that man was worth to Kettlestang, a thousand pound in gold. It'd have been worth the having even at the risk of murder. Indeed, murder would have been the safer—we'd have buried him six feet deep, and with a few leaves on top, who would have ever found him? And for murder, the Nobbler could be risked. Everybody knows what kind of man he is, a finger in every stinking pie, and yet never to the hanging limit. The Nobbler must go too far, must be hanged some day. He could be risked.

But he was not risked, did not himself take the risk. So here comes that proud horseman, now, and still as proud, for all he plays the lackey's part.

James Place, standing between his wife and his daughter, also thought more of the stranger he could not see than of the service. Who has brought him here? He has come to spy us out and betray us. He is not here for nothing. But surely even Kettlestang would not bring him in here for that. So Kettlestang must have been deceived, to have left it to that fool Cutler to find a man at a venture to bring the horse back from London. Space enough there for anyone to insinuate himself into Kettlestang's confidence. And deep into it already, to be walking behind him into the church. What was it the boys were singing now, in that complex anthem Arkengarth had written for them, and taught them with as much weeping as true notes?

'Why art thou so heavy, oh my soul? And why art thou so disquieted within me?'

Reason enough for disquiet, with a stranger so thick already with the Portreeve, and that poor man accepting all he was told at its face value. Oh, Kettlestang was no more than a fool, be he never so rich. Someone would rue this day. But who? The Places would take care.

The anthem ended in a tangle of eleven different voices, and only boys to sing them. Oh, thought Arkengarth, for a dozen good men, basses and tenors, to sing like the boys. Oh, what blessed harmonies, would we not hear the voices of Angels.

In the conventicle of the Misguided Brethren, Carines writhed under the burden of the living Christ, under the weight of the sins that He carried, and all Carines's besides. The spirit came on him, and he cried out, spoke with tongues, shouted aloud in the congregation. 'Unigenhedledig fabduwgenhedledigdimgweuthuredig orunhanfonartad drwyrhwnyrgwnaethpwydpopbeth.' Around him the poor, market men and Marsh Pards, turned and danced in the ecstasy of worship, in surrender of themselves to God. And they knew it was through the mouth of the wealthy, the proud among them, that the humility of God was made known.

Arkengarth sat far back in his stall, pressing to the oak where he could not be seen from the nave. He prepared to sleep through the sermon. One of the boys would wake him at the end. But sleep was hard to find today, with that stranger here. He heard the text.

30

'For it is a shame to name those things, which are done of them in secret : but all things when they are brought forth by light are made manifest.'

It was from the epistle for the day. The congregation settled back in their pews to hear the rounded periods, the scholarly clarifications of difficult texts they were used to. And more. What else had they come to church for, but to hear the sins of others denounced, or at least described. Better by far than it had been twenty years ago when I was a boy, reflected Andrew Pontigarde : then I heard Arkengarth flay his hearers, by name, man by man, sin by sin, and 'twas the sins of the heart that he exposed and scorched the worse, not sins of the deed. That had been the trouble with Arkengarth. A mere matter of an oath could have been hushed up, but it was what he had said otherwise. He had been confident that whatever he said he could be dispossessed by no man; it had been his undoing. It had brought Arkengarth down, that accident of a glorious revolution, and that boast in liquor that he had taken one oath and now no power on earth would make him go to the bother of taking another. But now—who would be brought down? What was this man here for, sitting in the Portreeve's pew, at Kettlestang's side? Would he show forth secrets, more than Kettlestang ever knew?

Up the street, in the cellar of the Falcon, Christopher Gunver knelt before the altar of God, even the God of his joy and gladness. Two sailors from a Liverpool boat were with him, old Josh Caddon, an Irish quarryman, three women and a child. Amos Dowgill served the Mass. The priest was a man they had never seen before, might never see again, passed from place to place in one disguise or another. Gunver made his prayers, for the coming of the King and the true faith again in the land. To be a Catholic was no longer dangerous in England : but in Wrackham it was still unwise. Gunver's special intention was in respect of the stranger, that he be not in danger, nor lead anyone else into it.

'And there be some that do dispute the interpretation of this text, whether those things that are hidden are by the light brought forth to be made manifest, or whether being otherwise brought forth, are in the light made to manifest themselves. But are not both interpretations together to be held? For God is not simple as we mortals are, nor is his forthshowing of our hearts to be thought of as one single act.'

At the Falcon, Liz Alley sat firm on the trap that led to the cellar. Sometimes, four or five times a year, Dowgill would ask her to do this. She did not ask what they did down there. An orgy, a vile feast of sodomy and vice, a coven of witches, it might be anything. It was none of her business. All her business was that Dowgill was kind to her, and few others were or ever had been. Folland had been, not actively kind, perhaps, but he had treated her as if she were someone, not a utensil.

'Every time we deceive others, each time we deceive ourselves, we face a new judgement day. For nothing can for ever be hid, though to the end of time it pass from view. For at the end of time must every mystery be made clear in the face of all creation. For then, my brethren, will we not have to face the contradiction of our own lying?'

They must all end in time, these deceits, thought Pontigarde. Someday Lord Wrackham must come home. Born in France, after his father fled with the old King, he had not yet come into his inheritance. It was Pontigarde who hired the bailiff and the steward, looked to the accounts, saw to the sale of wool and wheat, and found ways, in war and peace, to send the rents to France. Lord Wrackham, now, would be about this dragoon's age, and, if he took after his father, about this dragoon's height. Nobody in the town had ever seen him, except Pontigarde, when the lad was twelve, before this war had started. I will keep my counsel, thought the attorney, and hold my own faith, and when all secrets are revealed . . . even in the cold of February, in the great draughty church, he could not keep awake against the drone of Quernhow's voice.

'Who knows when a judgement may not come upon us?' the Preacher asked. 'Not from one day to another, are we safe. Not from one night to the next are we sure that some awful event will not cause us all to choose, to speak or not to speak, to join or not to join.

'And next, my brethren, let us consider what the most learned authorities do so earnestly debate, whether in that day . . .'

Oh, true, thought Arkengarth, it all hangs on that one woman's life. When the Queen goes, what then? For then they will all have to choose. When the Queen dies, who will take the throne? Will the Stuarts come back, and Lord Wrackham with them, to take up again his father's quarrel with the town and this time with the King and judges in partial on *his* side. Or will Marlborough bring in the Elector in his baggage, to turn us all into Germans and give this living, next turn, to a Lutheran? Or and most likely, will Marlborough come in himself, to be King, or Lord Protector? And will he then govern the land through Major-Generals, men like Cutler, and at their backs, Dragoons, Dragoons. . . . How many of these men sitting here have already given their word to one side or another? How many are committed on two or three sides at once? Now, there was a question for Quernhow to ask : but he could not ask it directly.

'Choose now, my brethren, that ye may be found on that awful day of Judgement to hold the true secret in your hearts. Choose now in faith and righteousness, and hold steadfast in your souls.'

4

Folland walked with Kettlestang through the dark mists of the February morning, out of the postern gate in the Town Wall at the end of the Watergate. Out on to the river bank, along the towpath to the Watermill. And beyond the mill, two barns and a cottage, and between them a yard lined with stables, and filled with wagons. The far side of the yard ran along the river, as a quay, and there were two ships alongside, and men loading grain. Beyond that, again furthest downstream from the bridge, was the old Miller's House, where Kettlestang had been born, and his father had been the miller, before all this sending of grain out of Wrackham.

'D'ye see that?' Kettlestang pointed to the ships. 'D'ye know where that's all going?'

'No. How should I?'

'Why, what did you eat in Flanders? Or in Spain?'

'What we could find. If we could pick up a hen or a bit of bacon, or perhaps oranges off the trees, or a turnip or two and some carrots in a garden—we shared it between us. But that was only luck. Mostly we had the cheese the quartermaster issued, and bread, or biscuit. That we could depend on unless we were in the most headlong retreat. Sometimes it was biscuit ready cooked, and awful hard it was, or sometimes we got the meal to bake our own. Mostly the biscuit, though, new baked in the town ovens, and we could depend on it.'

'And where did the meal come from then? Did you never ask, boy?'

'I never thought to ask. That was not my affair, so as only we did not starve. The French starved, often, and them so much nearer their homes, but not the English; we fed the Dutch out of what we had left over, too. But—you mean this meal is for the Army in Flanders?'

'Yes. I send two ships a week all the winter through and when the campaigning season starts we double it. Easy.'

'So your living—I suppose the living of all the farmers around here—depends on the army. What will you do if the war comes to an end?'

Kettlestang shrugged. 'If it had stopped a dozen years ago I would have been in a sad way. But myself—if it stops tomorrow, I shall hardly notice it, however the farmers take it.'

'How is that, Master Kettlestang?'

'Oh, when I was young, and stupid like my father, I made money out of grain. But now, I make money out of money. I leave the farmers to make their ha'pence out of wheat. I make my guineas—do you know double entry book keeping?'

'I do not.'

'Then Bridgward will show you, young Robert.'

They came into the great room, where five generations of millers had eaten and drunk, with their workers and their families. It was set out as a counting house. Along the walls were set high sloping desks. Bridgward came forward, leaving his under-clerks sitting still on their tall stools.

'I have told you about young Robert Folland. You are to show the lad everything in the books with which you deal. You are to make him familiar with the workings of the house. He need not become as expert as you are in casting accounts, but he must know how it is done. His main work will be outside; he will do some of the travelling for me. You will always remain here supreme.'

Bridgward bowed. He had a sleek face, a stately air, that of a great ceremonial officer of state. His little narrow eyes, set deep in the fat, raked Folland like a deck of guns.

'Master Kilnsey is here to see you, your Worship.'

'Then let me see the statement you have made. Thank you. You see, young Folland, Bridgward has made arrangements and preparations without consulting me. That is how you are to act. Now come up with me into the parlour, and stand by the door. You are not to speak. Stand, only, and listen, and learn. Learn.'

Folland followed Kettlestang into an upper room.

It was like a parlour : there was a large table, chairs, a cupboard, a carpet. Kilnsey was a big man, comfortably rather than fashionably or even smartly dressed. Folland stood by the door, listened, watched. Might he be called on to do this some day? Kettlestang greeted his visitor, opened the cupboard, poured two glasses of Spanish wine. The preliminaries were long, formal, a chaffering about the price of corn, a drizzle of platitudes about the weather. It was a dance of men avoiding the point, sparring about it, hinting at something. So that bluntness, when it came, bringing reality into the room, seemed itself an intruder.

'It's my rent, Master Kettlestang. How do I stand? It's not long off Lady Day.'

'I have your accounts here. Let me see . . . yes, you are well in credit. Shall I let you have the money now, in gold, to take out to Master Shillmoor, or shall I look after the transactions myself?'

'Oh, you do 'un, you do 'un, Portreeve. Save me troubling, it will, and carrying all that coin about. Oh, yes, I mind me, I be a mite short of seed corn, too, this spring.'

'That will be supplied. I shall send a wagon out to you . . . are your roads mired?'

There were more details, then another flurry of chat. When Kilnsey left, Folland estimated that he had been with the Portreeve over an hour. He escorted the farmer to the yard gate, held his horse while he mounted, and returned to find Kettlestang now in the counting house again.

'Come here, Folland. You noticed how embarrassed Kilnsey was, how long he took before he mentioned money? That was because he was not sure if I owed him or he owed me. Now, look at the accounts Bridgward brought me. See in this column what I paid him for corn last October—or at least the sum agreed on, because he left it with me. Now, this is what I have paid for him, on his orders. This to a tailor, though you would never think it to look at his coat, here to a grocer for comfits and fruit, so much here to Master Place for wine . . . all by orders on paper, and

35

never a coin passed. So now we enter his rent in this column . . .
for seed corn, say . . . now young Robin, cast that up, if you
please. And we take that from the price of his corn . . . see . . .
how much do you reckon that to leave? Over the half year, so
far . . . near two hundred and fifty pound; unless he do something quite unlike him, next harvest he will still be showing two
hundred pound profit over the year. And I don't think he would
know within a hundred pound either way if you asked him.'

'He is worth all that in money? And you hold it here?'

'Oh, more. There have been years before. Look here, carried
over . . . he owns—that is, I have on credit for him—near on a
thousand, for he had some bad years a while ago. And though
that is his credit here, he probably does not credit that in his
mind either.'

'But—if he came and asked for it? Sure you do not keep the
money here or in your house? Is it safe?'

'That money is not in my house. Very little of it is in Wrackham either. It has gone to the Indies.'

'The gold? Gone to the Indies?'

'Almost exactly that. See here, I have a thousand pound of
cargo in a ship that went last month to Muscat. Muskets,
powder, wool cloth . . . it will sell there for three or four times
that in gold. Then my agent in Muscat will buy goods for me,
and they will sell here for three times that again. But there will
be no return for three years, because that is how long it will take
to do all the business to India and back, and there is a thousand
pound locked up all that time. Not more than three or four
hundred per cent profit in the year.'

'Per cent?' Folland seized at a familiar sound, not that he
knew what it meant, but it had an usurious ring in his memory.
'You will pay Farmer Kilnsey interest for the use of his money?'

'Oh, yes, one per cent a year—the usual rate. Nearly enough
to cover the charge I make for carrying his rent to Master Shillmoor, and carting out the grain, and settling all his other debts.
I said, I trade in money, not in grain, and what I am about is
making profits. Look, here, another farmer. Hodman Blackmer,
he owns a little farm between the Marsh and the sea. Clay land,
hard to work. I owe him nothing. But he owes me two hundred
pound on the security of the land. When I want that farm, I can
have it. But I don't want to be a farmer. I shall let him struggle
on with it till I think I can sell the place at a profit.'

'You do not want the land?'

'What would I do with land? I have his goodwill. In my next cargo from the Indies there will be a parcel of raw silk, promised to Master Grangier. I shall ask him for six hundred pounds—barely double what my agent will have paid in Muscat out of the profits on thirty guineas' worth of brass pots. But if he go to any other merchant, he will have to pay seven hundred and fifty at least. Even that six hundred he cannot pay me till the silk is woven and sold, when if he ever had a hundred guineas in ready cash to venture . . . well, if a man is a spendthrift fool, then a spendthrift fool he must be. Learn from me, friend Folland. I take the risk. If last month's ship go astray, then the whole thousand pound is lost.'

'And if it be lost?'

'It is not the only ship in which I have bought hold-space and taken a share in the bottom. I have never ventured so much before in one ship; need I tell you why I must split up my trading, and never take a ship all to myself?'

'I was in a transport that nearly foundered once, between Spain and England. Nothing is safe at sea. But the grain still goes.'

'In Dutch bottoms. I charter them for the voyage out only. What they do on the journey here is no concern of mine.'

'And what would you have me do now, Master Kettlestang?'

'I told you. Stay here for the day with Bridgward; he will teach you how to cast up accounts in *our* way.'

Folland's eyes ached from the books. First in the good light of the day, under the window. Later under the one tallow candle, flickering over the pothooks. Money owing, money owed . . . names, names, Dowgill, Sarsen, Grangier, Pontigarde, Penmeller and Staffield, Azerley and Keld, all the harsh Wrackham names, every name in town—except Place. Not a word of these books of Place, except as someone to whom money was paid on another man's account. Folland thought of asking Bridgward; then he decided it would be better not. There was a part he was expected to play, it came through Kettlestang's manner as clear as through the Colonel's lips. He was a sergeant, nothing more. He asked nothing, said nothing, looked and listened and absorbed and waited.

In the School House, he pulled himself up the creaking stairs by the rope knotted from staples along the wall in place of a banister. The noise had been loud on the first landing, it was intolerable in his own room. He stamped down the stairs, threw open the door to the boys' room.

'Quiet! Quiet, all of you! Is a man to have no peace to sleep?'

There was quiet for a moment, a terrified stillness of a dozen lads standing frozen, from running, jumping, fighting. Then one of them, Benny Alley, said hesitantly,

'We're sorry, sir, please sir, we're sorry sir.'

'What are you all up to? You ought to be in bed. Get into bed all of you. And GO TO SLEEP!'

'Oh, please sir, it's too cold to sleep, sir, it's cold in bed, sir.' But they scampered about the room, picked up blankets from the floor, rolled again into little shivering balls, trying to be cosy.

'Well? You'll soon be warm. Why don't you all go to sleep?'

'We're not tired, sir.'

'It's too early.'

'We can't sleep.'

'It's too cold.'

'Nonsense,' Folland told them. 'Lie down all of you and be quiet, and you'll all be asleep in a winkie.'

There was quiet for a moment. Then a small voice from the end of the room,

'Please sir, were you a soldier, sir?'

'Were you at Malplaquet, please sir?'

'Or they say you were at Almanza, sir.'

'Tell us about it, please sir.'

Folland looked at the long row in the moonlight, the beds set close side by side, the eyes that sparkled at him, far from sleep. He laughed.

'I was your age once, and never been to the wars.'

'What, sir?'

'Oh, never mind. Was it Almanza you wanted to hear about? I thought it would only be victories.' It was easy, the tale he had told in a dozen alehouses in London and got a pint for it, or sometimes even a plate of beef, when he was just limping out from Chelsea, and glad for anything to keep his ribs from his backbone. The boys lay and listened, silent, from the beginning, that three-day march across the dust of Spain, through the opening charge, the way the French centre fell back, and the horror as the enemy wings came in from either side to encircle the English foot, and the Spaniards ran away.

'So there weren't more than three hundred of us came out of it alive in our Regiment of eight hundred that went in to the fight, and they didn't even trouble to reform us there, but shipped us back to England and filled up our ranks and went out to Flanders under the Duke.'

'And after that, sir?'

'Oh away to sleep with you, I can't go on telling the tale all night.' He laughed, and left the chamber, a chorus of 'good-nights' following him. He stood irresolute on the stairs. His tallow dip was burnt nearly to the end. He would need another one to dress in the morning. He knocked on the kitchen door. There was a reply. He entered.

Prisca Arkengarth looked up as he entered, from her sewing.

'Always sewing,' she remarked. 'With all these boys in the house, and the mending paid for in their fees along with their food—always sewing to do.'

'And you have to look to all.'

'And to my mother, while she is still so ill. She is asleep now, so I have a little time to sew.'

'My light is out.'

'It has died of the cold, by the look of it. Sit here by the fire for a while. You are always welcome in these cold evenings. It's freezing across the other side of this room—see the milk in that jug?'

'You are very kind.'

He was clumsy, she thought. Probably he had not spoken to a young woman for heaven knew how long. She said as much.

'It's true. I went to the army when I was sixteen, and that's been ten years, and all that time and I haven't been in a private house—not of right, if you see what I mean.'

'Not even in Spain? Or in Holland? Sure, and are they not our allies? I know all about this war. I have read some pamphlets.'

'I have been billeted in both countries in houses. The people have no choice but to take us. You can guess how welcome we are then. We pay, or the quartermaster pays, or he will pay if he ever has the time or finds the way. But they have no choice, and the money is not much.'

'So they would not sit with you in the kitchen?'

'Not unless they were paid.' He did not think it decent to men-tion what women could be paid to do, and not only in the kitchen, decent respectable women too by the look of it, if you waved money in front of their eyes. He did not want to spoil this. It *was* the first time, ever, since he had been a man, that he had sat to talk with a girl in his own language. It was enough to sit still in the light of the one candle, watching the shining needle, the white thread, the dark patch. He laughed at that.

'It makes no difference,' she told him. 'Whatever thread I use, the boys have it black in a day. Besides, I have only white by me till the pedlar come again, and that will be the end of this week.' They both laughed. She flicked the shirt on to the pile. She looked about her, could find no more.

'Have you had supper, Master Folland?'

'I had dinner down at the mill, with Obadiah Bridgward and the clerks.'

'That was long ago. I had dinner with the boys. We shall have some supper, now.'

She went to the cupboard, brought out a loaf, cheese, two pewter mugs. She sliced the cheese into thin slices on two tin plates, put them on a trivet in front of the fire. She found bottles in the bottom of the dresser, small beer for herself, strong ale for him.

'Better than Shillmoor's,' she told him. 'I brewed this.'

She cut bread. The room filled with the smell of toasting cheese. It was warm and quiet. Folland felt at ease, at peace for the first time he could ever remember. He drank his beer, and ate the hot runny cheese, the good wheaten bread. Prisca belatedly set another plate by the fire, took the first dish up to her mother.

'Aye, that's good,' Folland told her when she came down again. 'Now, one of these times, I'll show you what we did in Flanders. We'd take a couple of rounds of bread, thick as your hand, mind, no good any thinner. We'd toast one side of each. Then on one we'd put a slice of cheese on the raw side, and toast that, and for the other we'd find a nice thick slice of ham. And then clap the two sides together and eat them in our hands. A clout, that's what Dan Miller called it, that came from Stafford, a clout. That'll put the fat on you, that will.'

'It didn't put much fat on you. Was that what you ate all the time?'

'No. Sometimes. When times were good and living was high.'

The once only, he remembered, the week before Malplaquet,

they had found a place to shelter in that Flemish farm, and the people there too frightened to argue as their good ham and their round red cheeses went down with the new-made bread in that awful waste. And Dan Miller, who had called out to start, *let's have a clout of ham and cheese*, was dead three days later. Not in battle, he never had the satisfaction of seeing that, but from the kick of a horse, as he might have died anywhere in England that day, if that was the day fated for him. Folland shook his head.

'No, we didn't grow fat. There's some as grew fat on it in England, but we stayed lean in the Low Countries.'

'And in Spain? Were there oranges growing on the trees like apples here? And grapes where we have blackcurrants?'

'Oh, aye, well enough. And every third man a priest, and every other house a nunnery, and no sitting at ease in them. Oh, 'tis a strange land, a strange land.'

But this was stranger, after what he had seen done even in a nunnery, that he should sit here alone in a room with a young girl, this small slim girl with the deep calm voice, and do nothing but talk to her, though there was no one to be their duenna. Oh, now he was sure he was back in England, a country he hardly knew—it was an innocent country, where no harm was thought of a harmless act. He drank his ale and asked,

'Is your father at his studies?'

Prisca laughed.

'He is studying the art of . . . hawking.'

'Hawking?'

'He is in the Falcon almost every night.'

'I did not see him there the first night I was in town.'

'You sat in the Big Room, in the Tap. You can always find him there, but in the Kitchen. He drinks with Master Pontigarde, or anyone else who will come there, and pay his round. They'll let you in there in those clothes, if you ask : they would not have had you in that old red coat. You may go there if you wish, or come to sit here in the evenings. The Kitchen of the Falcon, or the Kitchen of the School House, whichever you please.'

He was going to answer, 'it pleases me here', when there was a noise outside.

'Your father?' he asked.

Before she could answer, the back door opened, and a man slid in, quietly, from the washhouse. He was shabby in worn boots and a stained riding coat, a stout blackthorn stick in his hand. He shut the door behind him, stood with his back to it. He blinked in the candlelight, not seeing Folland clearly in the shadow. The Dragoon rose to his feet, his stool in his hands. He would be sorry to break the furniture, but he had no other weapon. It would serve. He would take what advantage he could.

'Oh-ho, and have you come for your breeks?' he asked. The newcomer started, recognized him, and cowered back against the door as if he wished he could fade into vapour and slide out of the cracks. Folland swung the stool with both hands. He tried to look savage, as if he would use it. It was stouter than the stick, heavier; it would do a great deal of damage.

Prisca went quickly between them.

'This is my brother. Charley.'

Folland remembered.

'Old Charley Nobbler?'

Nobbler did not like the situation. He tried to be placatory, hoped that his sister would shield him. He said, nervously,

'But 'tis all over now.'

Folland decided that he could risk sitting on his stool again. He asked,

'What do you want?'

'A bit o' bread and cheese, like you just had, if you an't ate the lot.'

Nobbler sat down, leaning his stick against the wall. He took off his coat and huddled over the fire.

'What were you after? Were you trying to steal the horse?'

'No, 'twere the thousand pounds we thought we could get easy.'

'What thousand pound?'

'Why, 'twere common knowledge that old Kettlestang had a clerk coming up from London with a thousand pound in gold, and that's why he had the old man's best horse to come on. Seemed so easy like, and what would you ha' done?'

'I didn't carry money.'

'No? 'Twere common talk. A thousand pound, they said, in Vigo guineas.'

'I carried nothing but letters of recommendation for this post.'

Nobbler considered this while he took a bite of cheese. Prisca stood and watched. So there wasn't a fight, she thought in relief, perhaps there wouldn't be any trouble after all, perhaps he wouldn't lay an information against Charley, she had better be nice to him for that alone, who wouldn't be nice to this man once knowing him? Nobbler went on :

'The thousand pound were common knowledge, and so is that you will be riding to London next Monday.'

Folland was shaken. 'How do you know that?' Kettlestang had only told him at the end of the afternoon.

'Why, it stands to reason. 'Twill be the first Monday in't month, and old Kettlestang, he's always been used to riding to London that first Monday. And he's not a one to keep a dog and bark hisself, not if he paid for the dog.'

Indeed, it was a reasonable deduction. Nobbler sank some of his ale, wiped his lips.

'Wouldn't be surprised if there was other people didn't want errands gone to London for them, either. Nothing too heavy. There's a carrier for that, but that do take three weeks, there and back with waiting time, and some things won't be waited for when it do cost as much for an ounce as a pound and no faster. There'll be letters to carry—you'll be safer than the post, and more direct and private. And there'll be apothecaries' stuff to come. And principles for silk dyes. Nought heavy, but good, if you see my meaning.'

'You mean that people will trust me with things? Me not a Wrackham man, and so lately come?'

'If Kettlestang trust you with a thousand pound and his horse as well, then everybody else in the town will trust you. There's not much carrying and stowing that's safe enough for Kettlestang, not without double sending and splitting of parcels.'

'Will I be safe?' Folland felt a little more relaxed. Yet, there had been that shot on the heath.

'You'll be safe enough. A clerk, the tale was. They've seen you now. How d'ye stand? Nineteen hands?'

'Nearly that.'

'And a hundredweight and a half. And that big sword. Enough to frighten anyone, that might be that way inclined. The word's gone from Watford to Worcester, among all the Gentlemen. You'll be safe.' Nobbler stood up.

'But—' Folland asked, 'what about Master Kettlestang? Will he let me take these errands? Or did he not use to do them?'

'That's all right. He'll not say yes nor no, so long as you do his bidding. But them as wants the things fetched and carried, they'll pay. I'll let the word go round. You'll take the messages to London.' He kissed his sister on the cheek, slipped out through the door, snatching up the heel of the loaf as he went.

'His breakfast,' Prisca explained. 'Father will not have him in the house. He often comes in for supper like this, when no one knows.'

Folland blinked.

'Where does he live?'

'Oh, somewhere. I don't think he sleeps in the same place twice together.'

'But how does he make a living?'

'As you see—in short, he doesn't. He works odd days, by the day, for the Places, on the barges, or loading wine casks, driving horses when they're short of a man. And sometimes he works for builders. He has been all over working for builders, Lynn and Norwich and Cambridge. He is a good builder. Have you seen, he built our privy himself, out of waste bricks Master Place had piled in his yard and doing nothing that were left over from his house. It's a fine privy, isn't it?'

'Aye, a fine one. I like the columns at the door.'

'He would like to be a builder. I'll show you his drawings some day—he keeps them in my bedroom. Great houses he draws and churches, all to be built in brick. But that's all he's built so far himself, a privy. Or he grooms horses. Or he rides horses in steeplechases, or prepares them for races, and if they win he gets a share of the plate money.'

'And sometimes worse things than that?'

'Aye. Sometimes worse things.' He did not ask, she did not tell, what worse things. He only asked,

'Why? A parson's son, a schoolmaster's son come to this?' And he knew that it was what they would have said about him back there in Gloucestershire, Parson Bowbank's boy gone for a soldier.

'It was a great quarrel he had with my father. He had—my father had it all arranged. He could have had a sizarship at St John's College in Cambridge, and been at the University and had his Master of Arts and become a parson and had a curacy and, who knows, perhaps a snug living after all, and been safe for life, like my brother Martin that is at Cambridge now and a scholar of St Tibb's Hall. My father still has friends, that remember what he has done. But Charley said he would not sink to wait on tables that was a Wrackham man born and no one's servant, and he would not leave his own town neither for 'twas here he belonged. And they had it all out here, and no one could make anything of him, and like this it has been ever since.'

Folland nodded.

'I was sixteen when my mother died. I quarrelled, and I ran away from home and joined the Regiment.'

She understood. He was just another boy. There had always been a houseful of boys here, big half-brothers and little whole-brothers, and boys in the school. She watched him as he sat, his head in his hands, bowed over the table. He thought on, of how he had flung out the day of the funeral, when he had learnt that . . . *he* was not his father. And his very name now, Folland, he had taken from the landlord of the Inn where Sergeant Doggett had pressed the shilling into his eager hand. And he had buried Doggett, himself, in Spain, and wept as much over him as over his mother. It was Doggett had taught him to be a soldier; he had taught himself to be a man. Sudden he said, aloud but still softly,

'But who am I? That I don't know—who *am* I?'

And as she looked at him, puzzled, there came a voice from the entry, echoing his, loud and clear as music in a great nave, as Timothy in the Abbey Tower,

'Who art thou?'

Folland and the girl stood up. The door opened and Frederick Arkengarth stood there, leaning on the door jamb.

'Who art thou? Art thou he that should come?'

It's the drink, Robert Folland thought, that brings truth and hidden things, as good as a light to men lost like me. And the Schoolmaster called again, before he finally sank into a stupor on the scrubbed flags of the floor,

'Art thou he that should come, or do we look for another?'

5

'But I know who he is,' said Sophia Place.

'How should you know that?' asked her brother. 'There's many have guessed, and there's no showing that any guess is wrong.' They looked down into the street from the window of the Place House. It was eight in the morning. Folland was at Kettlestang's door, in his brown frock, the brass sword hilt showing through the slit. He had already been down along the Quay, past the ships where the wharfingers were readying their tackle in the morning gloom, to check the great doors of the mill, greet Bridgward. Now he reported to Kettlestang. This they knew, he did it every morning. When he rode to London, Kettlestang did it in his stead as he had done in the time before Robert Folland came.

'I know because I see him walk here every day,' Sophia insisted. 'He would not walk like that if he were a nobody. He must be somebody really important, walking in disguise.'

'You think you know who he is just from watching him walk along this street? You've never even spoken to him. Have you?'

'No. Not in the whole two months. But I have seen him here and there. Going to church, sitting in the Portreeve's stall, not deigning to look sideways at us, doesn't that show he's somebody of importance? And when I walk in the afternoons along the Wall, I can look down on the Quay; sometimes he is there giving orders to the stevedores and the ship men. I can see he is *somebody*. The men know it—you ought to see them jump when he gives them orders.'

'So they would jump for anyone in his place. They jump for Kettlestang who put him there.'

'Nobody jumps like that for you. I want to talk to him—I never have. I want to meet him.'

'And how often have I heard that before? The last time it was Captain Gavelkind, that rode in so brave and fine and ready to spend, and 'twas you that yammered on how handsome and brave he was and what a catch for somebody till the very day, nearly, we went up Staddle Gibbet and watched them string him up for not quite robbing old Shillmoor.'

'But am I to sit and watch the street for ever? I never meet anyone. I want to see the world, to go to London. I want to be married. How am I ever to get married?'

'Oh-ho!' George Place laughed. 'Married? And you think even of someone like that? A man without a coat on his back except what Kettlestang puts there? A man who walks behind his master, and rides to London on errands for him, and isn't too proud to take half a crown to carry a letter?'

'I told you. I know who he is. He can't be anybody else. He's come out of nowhere, but he must have come from somewhere. No one ever comes to Wrackham unless they've something to come for. So he's come for something.'

'What?'

'His inheritance.'

George regarded his sister with some suspicion mixed with his amusement. 'What inheritance? Who do you think he is?'

'He's Lord Wrackham.'

George Place laughed aloud, then stopped sudden.

'It might be.'

'I'm certain sure,' Sophia insisted. 'He's about the right age. And nobody knows what he looks like. The Harnes have had money enough out of the place since they've been Barons Wrackham—even after they went to France—Pontigarde sees that safe. But now his father's dead, he has the title. He's come back to see that the property is safe, how Pontigarde has kept it for him. If all is well, he'll come here openly, and drop King James. And if he does come home—he'll have to be grateful to people who helped him when he was in disguise? Won't he? Won't he? And stranger things have happened.'

George Place looked at his sister with new respect.

'You'd have to be careful. You'd have to be sure. Let nothing go till you are sure.'

'I am almost sure. You've seen the pictures in Wrackham Hall —all brown-skinned men like him, brown haired, not like the Alleys but still brown haired. It must be, George, it must be.'

George laughed, but it was only at her enthusiasm. Not at her idea. It was true, nobody in the town knew what Lord Wrackham looked like. Whether the new Lord had really taken an oath to the Pretender, no one knew. There were rumours. But the Harnes had never been dispossessed of the land : they were not friendless parsons.

In any case we may see the Baron back in Wrackham Hall there, across the river, and then? What then? A peer that can buy us all up, Kettlestangs and Places and Pontigardes, out of his breeches pocket and never notice it? But, they say that Eli Harne, that was the first of the Harnes to take Wrackham Hall, had begun as a locksmith : and the old Baron, that had been a Colonel in Ireland under Oliver, and then been made a peer by Charles II because he played such a good hand at cards, always losing to the King and winning with the King, why, he had married a brewer's daughter, Shillmoor's cousin. So what was there against it for the Places?

'Surely you can make friends with him?' Sophia insisted, nagging on like a wife, only worse. 'Can you not meet him in the Falcon? You're in an alehouse most of every night, can't you go to that one? Key tells me he spends most evenings there.'

'Or at home with Prisca Arkengarth,' George put in, cruelly.

'There's no danger there,' Sophia brushed this aside, it was not worth thinking of. 'You can go and make friends with him.'

'It would be much too marked, if I were to go into the kitchen at the Falcon.' It was typical, he thought, of this man, who had come to spy out the town for . . . somebody, that he did not come to the Dragon, where the aldermen and their sons were wont to sit in comfort in the parlour, nor to the Two Roses, where the gay gentlemen that plied the road could be found drinking with the Pards, but to the kitchen of the Falcon. There he would sit with the attorney and the schoolmaster, with sober shopkeepers, men of little account, though of some worth. And even there drinking only a little as if he mistrusted the good ale. 'I might see him if I went to a cockfight, though—I might find how to chance to meet him.'

'Do that. I must meet him, know him. Then perhaps when he comes back all plain and known to claim his lands . . . perhaps then. . . .' She was daydreaming again, thought George, dreaming of a marriage to bring her not merely fine clothes and good living, because she had that already. But it was the gay life she wanted, London and the routs and balls and theatres. And a place that no one could take from her. George watched Kettlestang and Folland come out of the house opposite and walk down towards the Postern. The grain merchant asked his man,

'D'ye like the town? D'ye like living here?'

'I like it well enough.'

'You should settle down. Do you not wish to be settled and have a house? A house, now, that means a wife. You ought to marry a Wrackham girl, my boy, and be a Wrackham man yourself. Be a burgess and share in the rents of the town lands, and the candidates' largesse at Parliament Picking time. A guinea a vote Shillmoor paid. Wouldn't you like that?'

Folland did not answer. He thought, it's not a good thing to be teased, a landless, moneyless man. I have to earn all I have. I have to walk behind him, keep my place, ride his errands, repeat messages learnt by heart because they are too secret to be written down. They were in the upper room of the Mill before Kettlestang spoke again.

'There was a letter came in on that London ship last night. It was from a merchant in London called Newall. You may have seen his name in our books. You ought to read it.'

Letters came to Kettlestang in all manner of ways, by land and sea, by private messengers and public post, and even sometimes thrust under his door at night. There were many letters, Folland knew, which he did not see, knew nothing about. Nothing surprised him. That was what he was paid for, not to be surprised. He took it, observed,

'As I read it, with a great deal of flowery writing, the man asks for help. A great deal of help, four hundred guineas. Will he really be in Caroon Row if he cannot pay?' He meant the debtors' prison.

'He will indeed. All his bills are due on the last day of this month. If he can pay a little, or look as if he can pay, they will let him ride on another month. He must have ready money to show. Not much, but enough to jingle.'

'Will you help him?'

'I may. On my conditions. If I do, you will have to ride with the draft, and leave in the morning. But I will not help him for nothing. He wants the money against an option on the cargo, but I will demand to buy the cargo. Look, he is in trouble because he has laid out too much money in stock, not keeping enough liquid by him. He has put shares in eight or nine ships, and the whole share in this one ship, the *Norman Pride*. She should have been home a month ago, and he counted on that to pay off his creditors. Because it is delayed, or perhaps lost, if he shows one sign of weakness, then his creditors will tear him to shreds and he will lose the ships that are to come, worth ten times four hundred guineas at the least. If he has four hundred to pay off the dogs that snap at his heels, he may live till one of his part cargoes comes in. But he must be in the last straits or he would not call on me, so far from Town; no one else there will cover him.'

'But you will?'

'Oh, I will send him the money. But look here, young Sergeant, would you not like to earn some money? I shall spread this venture around among men I have to keep sweet. I shall let Master Pontigarde pay a hundred guineas of it, and Keld shall be in for thirty. You see, when that ship comes in, it will sell for at least three thousand. Now if you had twenty guineas . . . I could let you in on this.'

'Why should you? Why not take that profit yourself?'

'If it all comes to wreck, is that not twenty guineas of loss I've saved and passed to you?'

Folland, standing, looked down at the grain merchant.

'I have known your ways for two months. That is long enough to persuade me that you would not risk two hundred and fifty guineas unless you thought it would come back.'

'True. I have been in this business long enough to see a chance.'

'But why give me this chance?'

'Well it is not fitting that you should be walking about doing my business, and not have all the things a young man needs like fine clothes, that you would have had by now had you not come, naked as it were, out of the Army. And a good place to live. And a fire of your own to drink your wine by.'

'I live well enough. We are commanded not to be covetous.'

Kettlestang turned to the window, looked out at the ships. Then, 'I will be frank. You have travelled to London for me twice. Tomorrow you go again. I trusted you at first because you did not know what you were carrying. But now—you know enough about the business to think how much you might earn if you were bribed. I want a messenger who cannot be bribed because he sees his way to make for himself by honesty more than anyone would offer. Bridgward has a share in everything that goes forward, and I know that he is safe. I would have you safe. I offer you a way to make money.'

More than that, thought Folland, he is offering me a way to

make money through him, and only through him. So I am tied to him. He asked,

'What makes you think I have twenty guineas?'

'Oh, that? I can advance it out of the pay due to you. It will be only a movement on paper. You have seen how we do it.'

I *have* seen it, thought Folland. And tied to him in debt for half a year, and perhaps longer, if it does not succeed. And after that? How many more chances? How many more half years? He thought a little more, then said firmly,

'I have twenty guineas. It is safe away. I can bring it in tomorrow morning before I start.'

Kettlestang's eyes did not move, but Folland saw the fingers shift on the arm of the chair. So that was a surprise to him, was it? Folland heard himself, against his will, blurting out a shame-faced explanation,

'There have been errands, little messages and packets, to and from London. And an evening in the cockpit behind the Falcon....'

'You were gambling? Waging money on the chances of the birds? This will be a surer chance.'

'I would not have called it gambling. I lost half a guinea on the first bout. But the last bird belonged to Baker Sarsen. Liz Alley told me. I reckoned that if anyone knew, she would.'

Kettlestang laughed.

'No, that was not gambling. We shall make a banker of you yet.'

'But this is gambling.'

'In its way. All banking is a gamble. You shall see.' Kettlestang went down to the outer office, where Bridgward stood at his ledger.

'Write the Sergeant down twenty guineas in the matter of Master Newall's ship. He will pay in cash. In the morning.'

Folland felt still a need to explain. 'It was what I was always taught at home. "Owe no man money" and "Always take your pay in arrears".' But he did not add what Parson Bowbank said so often: *'If a man persuade me earnestly to a thing, I ask whether it be not to his advantage rather than to my own.'*

Three days later he was in London, at Newall's door. The man looked at the draft in Folland's hand incredulously, as if a last desperate shot had hit a vanishing target, and then he wept real tears. Folland had never seen a man weep over mere money.

Men might weep when they were wounded, or before they were turned off the gallows, or like that night in Spain, when they had been three days with nothing to eat, and Jim Mann had stolen two eggs between four of them, and dropped both and smashed them on the ground. Jim Mann had wept in sheer desperation and shame at wasting what the section had been waiting for. So, this man wept. It was true, he told Folland, there would have been nothing to look for at the end of the month but the debtor's prison. As it was, he might now be able to borrow something, his credit being good again, and then—but Robert Folland could not follow the complicated scheme which was on foot.

'But all hinged on that ship. If it had come home I would have made five times my money. As it is, I am glad to get half my money back.'

'But if it does come home?'

'Oh, it will never come home now. If I thought it would, I would never agree to this from old Kettlestang. Sell my share in a ship like this if I thought it would ever come to port? I would be mad. Kettlestang's lost this money. Mind you, he's had to borrow from me before. We must run these risks; it was a close thing this time. I was nearly in gaol again. I've been there once before, and I do not want to have it happen again—it interferes so much with business. But if only that ship . . .'

'What was the cargo?' Folland asked, thinking, I'm a part owner, little he knows it. He seems sure enough it's lost. I might as well know.

'It went out in brass chamber pots and old clothes to the Guinea Coast, and from there in Negroes to the Indies. And back in a mixed lot of tobacco and cane sugar to Bristol. There's a mermaid smoking that baccy now, for sure. If I weren't so positive I'd never let it go.'

Folland left, concealing his own gloom. Twenty guineas of his own, hard earned by long riding, by trudging round the streets of London as he was doing now to pick up a paper of patterns for Grangier, all gone. He was as badly off now as when he first came to Wrackham. But if he had not yielded, had not put his little money in, would he still have been allowed to work for Kettlestang? Or work at all in Wrackham, or anywhere where men would say, *that's him that Kettlestang turned off, and no reason given*, and no character neither.

Carines watched his long face as he came riding back over the bridge. He told Gunver,

'It's not been a good errand for him, whatever it was.'

'Have you had any business out of him?'

'Since that brown frock and the blue coat that Kettlestang paid for, nothing. And there's little else he's bought in the town.'

Robert Folland turned along the river bank, past another Dutch ship tied up at the wine warehouse, two loading flour for London by the Mill Wharf. He went into the Mill House. It was barely seven in the evening. Kettlestang was still at his desk—where else would he be at this time?

'The ship is yours.'

'Oh, but the ship has been mine for a long time. It was the cargo you went to buy.'

'I am sorry. These distinctions——'

'Are the most important part of our business. Still, you have everything there. Yes, this is all unambiguous.'

'I worked through it all with him before I left. There was a clause . . . here . . . which was not clear, so I had him qualify it . . . here . . .'

'You are learning exactitude, my young Sergeant.'

'I am learning to lose money in exactitude. And so, I suppose, is the Attorney.'

Kettlestang laughed.

'Why should we lose any money?'

'The ship. Newall said that there was no chance of its coming home.'

'Why should it not come home? It has only to come across from Dublin, where it lies in the Liffey.'

'Dublin? But—when did you hear that? While I was in London? This is luck beyond dreaming, Master Kettlestang.'

'There is no such thing as luck. Luck is for Gipsies and fortune tellers. Never trust to luck, young Sergeant, unless you can arrange it yourself.'

'When did you learn the ship was safe?' Folland stood with his back to the window, looking down on his employer.

'Oh, the day before Newall's letter came.'

'You knew the ship was safe already, and yet you took the man's fortune from him?'

'Of course I knew. What else do you expect? Did I not say

I own the ship? I was not speaking in parables. The hulk is mine.'

'The ship is yours?' The plan came clear in Folland's mind. 'You ordered the Captain not to go to Bristol? You sent him to Dublin instead, without Newall's knowing?'

'He will stay there till he hears from me. So you have a profit, young Robin. Bridgward will credit you with a hundred pound in the books, in advance. It is likely that there will be more to come.'

'I cannot take it. Not when you . . . we have cheated a man like that.'

'Cheating is a strong word, young Bob. I will show you in the books how this man, four years ago, laid a trap for me that would have cost me I do not know how many thousand. As it was, he cheated me of more than three times what he has lost here. And *you* had no hand in the deceit. You need this money, now, don't you, Folland? More than I do, or the Attorney. Take it, and feel you have something solid behind you. Not only the money, young man. You have started in trade, and you are learning how money is handled. It is a fine sport, and you will find the thrill of a clever gain like this a fair exchange for the thrill of battle.'

Folland hesitated. He remembered Newall's tears. But he remembered also, the man said he would not move to pay off any debtors till the end of the month. He had in view some transaction in shares that would bring him a profit, and let him double the four hundred guineas in a week, so he only had it in ready gold to put down, and yet the reputation of having it was by itself sufficient to stave off his creditors. Oh, they are all as bad as each other. Besides, if anyone makes a profit out of it, 'twill be Kettlestang, and since he pays me so little for carrying his bloodmoney, I may as well take it.

He did not tell Prisca about it all. He let her know that he had had a piece of luck, as they sat by the kitchen fire, eating their clouts, for he had at last remembered to bring in a piece of bacon for them. He did tell her about London, where she had never been. Robert had sat in three coffee houses, more or less fashionable, to meet one man and then another on Kettlestang's behalf. Not Newall—he had had no credit that week even for a coffee house. And in one of them someone had pointed out to him the learned Doctor Swift, drinking tay but with someone else to pay, that had written all those pamphlets against the Ministry.

54

'I have one of them here, since I thought you would like something new to read.'

'Is what he says true? About the Whigs keeping on the war for their own profit?'

'Sure, any war is for someone's profit. See how fortunate we are, to know whose profit we fight for.'

'But then the poor soldiers get killed for someone else's gain—were you stuck in the thigh only to bring money into the Duke's pockets?'

'O, 'twould be the same for us whoever commanded. If there had been no war, and no army raised, half of us would have starved to death in England that grew fat in Flanders on Master Kettlestang's biscuit.'

He laughed. He had not thought of his thigh now for weeks, except to note the scar, pink where it had used to be an angry red. Able he was now to ride six days with only one day's rest, and that spent walking round London. He didn't want to talk about the war, he did that with the boys. He was sorry he had brought that pamphlet, it reminded him of the bad times, the things he could not tell the boys : it made the whole thing real again, not a bad dream he was putting behind him. He told her, 'I have bought something else for you beside, in London. Something you did not expect.'

'Something for me? Besides the pamphlet?'

'Oh, the pamphlet was nothing. Besides, I wanted to read it, so I would have bought it anyway, just so as to say I saw the man who wrote it. No, I had an errand to do for Pontigarde, that was worth a guinea to him, and another for Grangier, and so this was within my purse.'

He fished into the deep pockets of his coat, and laid a bundle on the table. He reflected that probably no one had ever bought her a present before. It was no more than even payment for the warm evenings before the fire, for the beer, the bread and cheese, and he had thought that when he bought it, and really it was not beyond his purse.

'It's something in fur—what can it be? Oh! It's a muff. But—it's so small. Not half the bulk of the one Sophia Place wears to church.'

'Then you shall wear this on Sunday and make her writhe with envy all through the Lessons. These small muffs are just come in, this winter. No one of quality wears big muffs now . . .'

'But it must have cost a great deal. I cannot accept it, Mister Folland.'

'Come, Miss Arkengarth. You know it could not have cost a great deal, because you know I have not got much. In short, Miss Arkengarth, it's Master Pontigarde who has paid for it, and he would not know what to do with it if I gave it to him.'

She giggled and took it. The next Sunday, she wore it to church. She walked behind the boys from the school, holding her four-year-old brother within her joined furry hands. The child liked it, and he was so good in church. Nevertheless, she took him out, before the sermon, to see to the dinners, and did not hear Parson Quernhow preach three turns of the glass on 'The hired servant fleeth, because he is an hireling and careth not for the sheep'. And Arkengarth listened.

6

Folland rode the long road from Wrackham to Bratton. He went up over the top of Staddle Down, and looked back to where the town lay in the crook of the River Loone, the walls shining red around it in a shower of rain, the ships tied up along the quay. From there, the river wound in a great half circle round the base of Staddle Down. It was a long day to the sea on a ship, drifting down on the stream or carried up on the tide. It was only two hours by this road, on a horse. But you could not bring a wagon over the top. The flat road along the river bank was fit for that traffic, but it took as long in time as a ship.

Nevertheless, there were ships now that were too deep in the water to come up to Wrackham. There was trade in offloading them, as they lay inside the bar at Bratton, into lighters that went up the river. Some small parcels might come up on wagons : but for bulk goods, grain or wool cloth or wine, lighters were cheaper, and even slower, dragged by a couple of horses and poled by an odd group of men, a race apart. Pards they were mostly, from the Marsh.

The Marsh you could see from the top of the Down, inland again from Wrackham, a waste of land and water mixed. People there were proud of being marsh men born, and Pards they called themselves, fierce and lone as big cats. Endellion had been their Lord in the old times, they knew no other, living in a great castle on an island in the Marsh, ruined now. When that house had lost much of the Marsh to the Harnes, back in the fifties after the War against the King, Rupert Harne that had become Lord Wrackham had brought in Dutchmen to drain the land. Then he had let it out in farms, and even given it, or sold it, to his own men. The ullage, land not fit to work, he had sold to desperate outsiders like Hod Blackmer. You could see the drained land from the Staddle, a velvety surface in front of the sage green of the Marsh.

Going over the Down, Folland stirred up the sheep to run. There was a ship in the river mouth to catch before she sailed. He had letters for the Captain to deliver by hand. Letters for someone in Gothenburg, too important to have gone down in the lighter, with the bolts of woollen cloth. What it was all about, Folland did not ask. He only carried the letters, and a full bag.

This was a part of his life, now, riding alone on country roads. It had been odd at first; he had been used to finding himself looking for another knee close to his. You were never alone in the Regiment. This was the first time in his life that he had been alone so long, a man on his own, with no comrades. It was the first time in his life he had had a room of his own to sleep in, to keep his things in, to sit in. It was the first time in his life that he had had space to think. He was getting so used to it, he was irked sometimes now by company and clamour. There were evenings now he could not bring himself to go to the Falcon, where he had his own corner in the kitchen. They were all older than he was, richer and more settled, with a chance to plan what they would be doing next week, or even next year. But they accepted him. There were times he had no wish to go even into that grave and silent company where nobody asked after another man's business. He just wanted to be alone, in his little room under the roof and wonder. Wonder, who he was.

He stopped this morning at the turn of the road, where he could look back to Wrackham and then forward to the sea. He hated the sea, the very smell of it as it came to him. He had been four times in a ship. The first three times, it had meant storms and looking to terrified beasts in the hold, himself sick as the horses were, listening to them scream in terror and die under his hand; each death would terrify the others even more, and the final hoisting out of the hold, whether a dead horse or a live one, was something he did not want to do again. And that last voyage, short but worse weather than any other, himself not able to stand, and his thigh feeling as if it would burst, the pain enough to make him sick even if the world stood still. No, Folland did not want to see the sea again from a ship's deck.

Far in front of him there was another horseman. A slight man, on a slight horse, a grey, and in a cloak of russet, standing out on the green grass as much as his mount did. Yes, thought Folland, that was George Place. He was in the Falcon again three nights ago, and had had the temerity to come into the Kitchen. It was Liz Alley's fault. She had been too nervous to say no to him, swaggering in his strawberry coat and absurd little sword, and Dowgill had been down in the cellar at that moment. George Place had come into the Kitchen and called for brandy : but all those solemn men sat saying nothing and drinking their ale. Nobody made room for him, no one spoke. He could—or at least his father could—buy any one of them three times over. But they had kept silence and given him no room and after a while he had gone away.

Now, he was here again, a mile or so in front of Folland. There was no mystery here. It must be something to do with the wine ship that was inside the river mouth; it was come in yesterday and was like to prove too deep to come up the river. News like that went like wildfire through Wrackham. It was what the grave silent men in the Kitchen talked about. He'd be wanting to settle the matter of the lighters.

'You are going to Bratton yourself?' James Place had asked his son. George looked back into those filmy blue eyes.

'I shall have to.'

'The lighters—that's nothing. Let John Mellin go or Cock—even Key could manage it, a mere matter of counting.'

'But Alexander is gone. There's a new man there.'

'Go carefully.'

'In any case, it will be expensive.'

'It cannot be more expensive than Alexander,' put in Sophia. 'I cannot abide Scotch men.'

'Your abiding has nothing to do with the matter,' her father told her. 'But go easy all the same, George.'

George, riding down the hill, had seen Folland behind him. He had not seen the Dragoon on this road before. There must be something to it. He was twisting Kettlestang round his little finger. He must be. Had he been dipping in the till? See him last Sunday, a new coat, five guineas' worth at least, and a new wig—why hadn't he gone the whole hog while he was about it and got himself a full-bottom? Sophia had marked it all, and told him.

'I am sure he is *someone* in disguise. He speaks so well. He must be Lord Wrackham, he must be.'

'How did you hear him speak?'

'Why, did you not see me drop my prayer book so he had to pick it up? Not that *you'd* have picked it up for me if you had seen.'

'What did you say?'

'I thanked him, and asked whether he thought it would be a good year for roses.'

'Oh, you asked that, did you? And what did he reply?'

'That he had been out of England so long that he could hardly remember whether roses bloomed in June or November.'

Oh, but that was a sly answer, George thought. It was June for the Pretender, the tenth was his birthday. But William had come in November, on Bonfire day. There was still no knowing. Sooner or later, someone would have to know.

There were in Bratton several alehouses, fit for seamen, but only one Inn. Folland put up the horse there, a hired one. Tiger was saved for the long journeys. Four ships in the river. There was no way of getting out to them or even finding which ship was his without a boat. It cost a shilling, after he had found a waterman, to be taken out to the *Gustavus* and be waited for. This was an expense the Swedish Captain objected that Folland could have been spared, since he had twenty lazy fat men and boats. But Folland thought he might have to come to Bratton again and come out to other ships : he would need a connection.

In the cabin, he ate rye bread and salt herrings, and drank aqua vitae; it was like the army again, and being in a ship made it no better. Every time it swung to the anchor chain he felt queasy. But talking a mixture of English and High and Low Dutch and a few words of Spanish, he made bawdy conversation

59

with the Swedes. Here again, Folland thought he *had* made a connection, well worth the bag he had brought out with a cheese and three fresh loaves and a few green cabbages.

The letters were handed over, the instructions for delivery memorized; yes, the Swedish Captain knew the man well, and there would be no difficulty. And laughing they helped Folland into the wherry, and so he came ashore between two beached lighters.

He got out on to the sand and was glad to be on dry land. He was some way from the Inn, and he set to walk along the water's edge. He stepped on the bladderwrack and laughed to hear it burst under his feet. He picked up the butcher-board of the dog fish and wondered what it was. He had grown up inland, and this was the first time he had been alone to play on a beach, on a fine day. He was a little light headed with the aqua vitae, and he looked to the wind to clear it from his system.

He crunched over the pebbles towards the crust of houses above the high water mark. The first in the row was an alehouse. As he came to the door a voice suddenly cried out,

'Ahoy there, sodger!'

Folland stopped. A man sat there, outside the alehouse. A short man, well fleshed, but not fat, older than Folland, a brown face, scoured by salt winds. He smiled at Folland.

'I thought I knew you, sodger. I can't place it but I do know you, I do.'

Folland reached back into the stores of memory. There was something familiar here.

'Aye, and I think I do know you, but I can't for the life of me . . .'

And there was no reason that Perkins should not look familiar, because he had been two or three times in the Falcon, but in the Tap, where Folland might notice him in the crowd without noting him specially. And there had been a little asking round, so that then Perkins could burst out convincingly,

'The *Valentia*, that was it. In the old *Valentia*.'

'Were you on her, then? When we came back across the bay?'

'Aye. Don't you mind me? I was the Bo'sun.'

'Maybe I do.' Folland was not sure he could remember him, but one sailor was very like another, and he had been too worked then to notice anybody.

'You were a corporal, and the only man that could stay on his feet. I didn't tell ye then, but it were one o' the worst blows I were ever in.' There was nothing here Perkins had not heard said in the Falcon. 'What you a-doing of now, then?'

'I'm out of the army. I got hurt and out that way. I work for the corn-factor.'

'Oh, aye, old Kettlestang. That's why you just been out to the *Gustavus*?'

'You saw me there?'

'Oh, it's my business to see who goes out to what ship.'

'Why's it your business?'

'Sit down and have a pint and I'll tell you. Not bad beer for a place like this. Here's to your good health, sodger.'

He was right, it was good beer. Better than Shillmoor's, anyway.

'Remember my name, now? Perkins. Matthew Perkins, I am. Now, let's see, what was yours? Falkirk . . . Fodder . . .'

'Folland.'

'Aye, that's it, Folland, I had it on the tip of my tongue.' Perkins seemed a lonely man, eager to talk to anyone who would listen. 'Unsociable lot they are here, and you can't trust them, neither.'

'Do you live here?'

'Oh, I does for the time being. And the longer the worse. And it's my being here that they don't like. D'ye see, I swallowed the anchor a year agone, and I has a bit of influence, some interest as you might say from the great ones I did meet at sea, helping them to ease theirselves over the sides. So I puts in for, and I gets it, a Tidewatcher's berth.'

'A tidewatcher? Do you watch the tides to see whether they come in late, and complain to the Almighty—direct is it, or through the parson?'

'Ah, that's what I mind about you, always one for a joke. Oh, 'tis an Officer of her Majesty's Customs I am now, that's brought many a parcel of contraband in, in my time. Set a thief, they say . . . and it's always a stranger a Customs man must be, so it's good to have an old comrade to talk to.'

'So then you watched me go out to the Swede?'

'And I knows who you are now, and what business you have, and it don't concern me at all, that ship leaving as she is on the top of the tide. But there's one I'm watching, that flute there, the Dutchie.'

'Why, are you watching her? Here, have some more yale. There's no customs on that, is there?'

'Thank-ye, I saw it brewed, I did. I gets nothing out of the ale. That's a Bergen boat, that is.'

'How do you mean, a Bergen boat?'

'Well, she come in here three days agone, and I goes on board like I always does. And she's full of brandy, French brandy, all in little kegs, when the law says you mustn't bring spirits in anything but big casks, too big for a man to lift into a small boat or hide in the bilges, d'ye see. So I says, "I'll be having you, I will, let's see your bills of lading," I says. And the Master, smirking all over his fat face, he do bring out all the bills and the papers, and he tells me a long tale about being short of water, and coming in here to fill his casks. So I says to him, I says, "Why don't ye drink brandy, then?", but he do laugh and say that it's all sold already in Bergen as he can show, and he don't broach his cargo unless he's in exterminis. And he laughs in my face, he does, 'cause he knows, and I knows, and he knows I knows that that brandy will be ashore somewhere between here and Newcastle before the month's out.'

'But you can't touch him?'

'No, you can't do nothing to him, nothing at all, because it's all legal so far, d'ye see. We got to catch him running it ashore, or you can have all the lawyers you like for the persecution and there's not a magistrate but will throw it out. "Where's your proof?" they'll say. "Where's your proof that he had cheated the Queen or was going to try to cheat her?" And o' course, you ain't got no proof, save only if you can get one of the sailors to blow on him. No, you got to take them in the act, bringing the stuff ashore, and even then have fifteen bishops to swear they saw it, or there's no justice you'll get in a smuggling town. And for why? Because they're all waiting for their cheap drink, Magistrate—aye, and Bishop too, and they won't find against a villain unless you shame them into it.'

Perkins spat into the dust and called for more beer, and pipes and tobacco. Folland could see which way they were going, and he did not trust the beer to lie well on the aqua vitae. Nevertheless, he could not see how he could break off this conversation : he felt dimly that to have a friend in the Customs might be an advantage. He asked,

'You're just waiting and watching her on principle?'

'Well, I wants to see what's going on, because if she's caught further on the coast, then there's them as is above me will want to know what I saw of it, and how she lay so snug under my nose, and me going aboard her and all, as I have done in my report. So I wants to see who goes aboard her—or into that other ship, too.'

'That one moored just this side of her? With the lighters alongside?'

'Aye. That's a wine ship out of Lisbon, all clear and paid up on. I'll pass that one. It's for a Master Place, up river. You'll know of him?'

'I do.'

'Then you know who came down the hill in front of you, and had a boat out to the wine ship?'

'Oh, yes. that was young George, old Place's son, and like to have the business after the old man is gone. Very respectable, that family.'

'There's none too respectable to cheat the revenue, sodger. But he went in the wine ship. Now, it's what goes between the Bergen boat and the wine ship I can't always keep track of, one lying so near to the other. So I watches him go out there to her, and I watches him come back from her like he's a-doing now.'

George Place was leaping from the dinghy on to the sand. It had been a long and tedious wrangle, with the Dutchman out of the Bergen boat demanding more, and yet more, than he had already agreed to take. It was not only carriage money he wanted, but danger money, and no way of refusing it. Too much trouble already for one day. He stood a moment on the beach and looked round. There was the Customs officer as always sitting on the bench with his spy glass in his hand. Didn't he ever do anything but sit and drink and watch all kinds of people who had no more to do with him than the man in the moon. It would be hard to prove anything—George stood stock still. The hairs bristled on his neck.

'I saw it,' he told his father that evening, trembling. 'I saw them there. Folland talking with the Tidewatcher, and drinking with him, and I'll be bound the Customs man was paying.'

'Why, there may be nothing in it at all,' his father objected. 'Are you sure it was Folland?'

'Sure? Why, I saw them with my own eyes. *Saw*, SAW them together, if you know what that means—*saw, saw, SAW-SAW-*

63

SAW!! Thick as two thieves together. It's a plot and a conspiracy against us.'

'Have you told the Bergen boat?'

'I sent John Mellin out with a message to them, as soon as I was sure who it was drinking. They'll move nothing tonight.'

'And the *Flora*? She cannot remain in the river when she is light, or it will look suspicious indeed.'

'It will that. She'll have to come up to the wharf tomorrow when she can take the shoals, because that is what the arrangement was and everyone knows it. But the *Gouda* must clear.'

'If we hold the *Gouda* for three days more, it will cost us——'

'If we have the *Gouda* for three days less and lose her to the Customs, and have all known, what will that not cost us? We cannot trans-ship. We will have to run her.'

'Can't you try to sell further up? There's always them as will take brandy in Lincolnshire, as if it were the thirstiest county in England. Or drop down to Dorset, where they're near as bad.'

'There's no time even for that. We must have the cargo out of the *Gouda* before the Customs think to have a sloop to watch her at sea, and catch her landing. She must clear this coast and be well out by the day after tomorrow.'

'Where will you do it?'

'I can have enough men and horses tomorrow at Farm creek. Then it's only three miles across the land to the river, and if we have a lighter with empty hogsheads to pour the brandy into, there'll be no trace but that it's what we've been lighting out of the *Flora* to work her up the river. As we planned.'

'And the empty casks? What will you do with them? If we left them in the *Gouda*, we could have filled them with water to hide the loss of weight, but now ... ?'

'Knock the heads out and sink them in the river.'

'They'll float, even full of water,' Sophia put in. George made a face, she could always find a way of making the work worse.

'All right, we'll put a handful of stones in each one. But we'll have to have it all out of the *Gouda* before the Tidewatcher thinks to call the Soldiers.'

'I' faith,' observed Sophia, 'is this not a better way than the old? It were always a waste of money bribing Alexander not to be there the night we moved the cargo out of the Bergen boat into our own lighter through the wine ship.'

'It was safe. And not too many to know about it.'

64

'Only the whole of Bratton to know. And to tell the new watcher.'

'And them all in the secret and coining money out of it. Perhaps you're right. This way, there's only Pards to know, and we can pay them off with a keg apiece, and no money to change hands. We'll risk it. It's six and eightpence a gallon duty on the brandy that we'll be saving, that costs us barely sixpence to buy even from the Dutch. We'd never sell at the legal price while there was anyone else left to run it. But as it is, a clear profit of three shillings on every gallon . . .'

'So ye'll run it,' commanded James Place. 'Ye'll do that and be sure of it.'

'I wish I could be sure,' George retorted. 'A Customs informer in the town, and us with a thousand gallons of spirit at stake. Lord Wrackham, indeed. A Customs nark, and you think he's Lord Wrackham. You've no wits in your head. I'll lay he's talking with the soldiers this instant.'

In this George Place was right.

'Don't ye drink in the Falcon,' Perkins had told him, wagging a long finger in his face. 'Don't ye drink in that Falcon. There's nobbut a parcel of hoodie crows there, that sit solemn and still all, as if their dads had died a'Friday and left their goods to the Parish. Go you to the Black Bull, at the Bridge, where the cavalry are quartered. There's two dozen good Dragoons there I can call on. The Sergeant's named Freeman, you tell him I sent you, and he'll look after you. Have some more ale.'

'No, no, I can't. I have to ride back to Wrackham and tell Master Kettlestang that I took his message.'

Folland stood up, suddenly, with an exaggerated movement, and held at the corner of the table. 'I hope I can get back. How the devil came I to drink so much?'

'You've been mixing it, lad. I knows them Swedes, and demons they are for it, too. Never mind, the horse will look after you.'

'I wish I could be sure of that.'

'A good horse?' Perkins asked, as they trudged along the shingle to the Inn.

'All right, if a horse is all you want. Not the best in town, though—that one belongs to Kettlestang, and I ride him on long journeys. They calls him Tiger.'

'Funny name for a horse. Biter, is he?'

'No, gentle as a lamb. If I fell off, he'd pick me up in his teeth

and put me back in the saddle, I'm sure. Not fast, but steady—
a glutton for the going, as they say. Not like this walking hound's
dinner. What did you say that Sergeant's name was?'

'Freeman,' Perkins called after him, 'Sergeant Freeman, of
Harley's Regiment. At the Black Bull.'

Folland felt better when he had the wind in his face. By the
time he had reached the town, he was fresh enough to take the
horse back to the livery stables and then report to Kettlestang.
It was now too dark to work on the books. Instead of going
straight through the Postern, Folland turned along the quay to
the Black Bull.

Inside the Inn, he felt himself back a year. An Inn with
soldiers quartered in it, he'd lived in places like that all his time
in the army. Sergeant Freeman had been two years in Flanders,
long ago, and though he had never been engaged, he felt himself
a hardened campaigner, brother to Folland. None of his men
had ever been out of the country—indeed, they had only come
from the next county, but still they felt foreigners among the
Wrackham men.

'Joined to pull the French King down, as the saying goes,' he
told Folland, 'and here we sit waiting for the Tidewatcher to call
us out. Not a real military career, you'll be agreeing.'

'But better than Flanders.' Folland had the right to contra-
dict, he had paid for ale for all. 'And Spain was a first time in
Hell for us, what with the heat and dust and no water. And let
no man tell you different, at Almanza we ran, and we didn't
stop for three days and nights. Always look after your horses,
lads, and when you have to run, you'll live. Like I did.'

They didn't believe him. They thought they'd never run.
Poor lads, he thought, none of them more than seventeen, except
the Sergeant, and don't know how lucky they are at home, not
in Flanders. He only stayed for one drink, and that he bought.
At least, now, they knew him if ever he tired of the Falcon. He
came back late to the School House, where Prisca sat in the
kitchen at her eternal mending.

'I've bought you this. It cost me nothing.' He put a big whelk
shell on the table.

'Only the remembering. Was that not worth something?' She
smiled up at him. 'Where did you get it?'

'I picked it up, on the beach. There were any number.'

'What? By the sea side?'

'Aye. Show it's true, listen into it and you'll hear the sea loud.'

She listened, and laughed at the waves in her ear.

'Is that what the sea sounds like?'

'Have you never heard it?'

'I've never even been as far as the top of Staddle Down, and they say you can see the sea from there. I've always wanted to see the sea. I wonder if I ever will.'

'One of these Sundays, I will take you to the sea.'

'Oh, but on Sundays I have to take the boys to church, and see to the dinner, and—oh, lots of things. It's my busiest day. And I have to see to my mother.'

'Some Sunday we can find you a deputy.'

And they talked about the sea, and listened to the shell again, but most of all she listened to him. Further down the street, Sophia Place listened to her brother.

'It's true, I have the proof of it. John Mellin heard them talk, loud to wake the dead, about him going to see Sergeant Freeman at the Black Bull.'

'That's nothing,' Sophia Place told him.

'But it's not. Mellin came here as fast as he could—he passed Folland on the hill, your Lord Wrackham indeed, he was so fuddled he could hardly hold on to his horse's neck. I watched him when he came from the Mill, and where was he in two shakes of a lamb's tail? In the Bull, drinking with the troopers, buying them ale, as thick with them as he could be. What more do you want? He's an informer out to ruin us.'

'It may be innocent,' said Sophia. But to herself, she thought, if he's not Lord Wrackham, come to reclaim his own again, then he's no common soldier. He's a captain or a colonel or whatever they have, come to seek out smugglers—why cannot he be that, and Lord Wrackham too? But he'll not catch our George—our George is clever. A Wrackham man born is too clever for anyone.

7

George may have been too clever, in his own estimation, for Robert Folland. He was not too clever for Matthew Perkins. Perkins sat on the shore all that day. In the evening, his junior came to relieve him. By dawn, Perkins was watching again. This time, he had as visitor not Folland, but Freeman, in a plain hat and an old grey cloak over his scarlet.

'How would you do it, then?' Perkins asked. The soldier pondered.

'I come down by the river road,' he volunteered at last. 'There's a lighter there, close in under the bank, about three mile up. Nobody watching after it. I think they'll take the casks out of the ship and row them up to the lighter in the night.'

'Maybe. That'd be a long job, and they wouldn't do it with me watching here. So they'll go to sea and run it ashore. Now, which side would you go?'

The soldier looked puzzled for a moment.

'Go?'

'Aye, go. I want you there, in the night, watching the place. If they land it up the coast, they'll have to bring it over Staddle Down to get to the lighter or troop it through Bratton, and they'll never do that with me here. But if they go down south about . . . Yes, I think I know the beach. There's a shoal where they can run her aground just before the turn of the tide, unload her onto the sands, and be off again in an hour. Them as takes it will have to come across the fields . . . I know for certain the path they'll take.'

'Where?'

'I'll tell you. I want you out there.'

'Tonight, you mean?'

'May be. I'll wait till she sets sail, and then I'll send for you. I'll meet you on the marsh, about a mile and a bit from the creek, where there's a ruined sheep fold they use for a lambing shelter. There's a hedge runs along behind it. You line the hedge—on the land side. I'll come to meet you from where I can row across

68

the river. I'll be on foot so bring a spare horse for me. Wait for me. Don't do anything yourself.'

'And what do you want me to do now?'

'Go back to Wrackham.' Perkins tried hard to be patient. 'Make sure your men and horses are rested. Have them saddled at nightfall, and ready to move if the lad comes to you. Go over the bridge, and take the creek road, as far as the Dane's Cross, and go down the left fork there past Hod Blackmer's farm, the brick house, and along the hedge beside the ruin. And wait.'

He hoped the Sergeant would understand what he was after. If he could take the ship with the brandy half in and half out, and the men too, that would be worth something. Alexander had been a fool, to think he could take bribes and have no one notice it and no one be jealous either. But now—they wouldn't be able to switch their cargoes in the river again. Another thing—he told Freeman,

'Mind that Folland.'

'Mind him?'

'Don't tell him what you're up to, old soldier or no old soldier.'

'You think he's in with them, then?'

'I don't think that, not for certain. Keep him dark.'

In Wrackham, Folland stood at the counting house desk and checked through bills of lading and a long account of trading in wool and hides and tallow and beeswax and Stockholm tar and timber, that left money owing to Kettlestang from Gothenburg. And out of the fat credit with a Swedish timberyard, two hundred guineas paid on a bearer draft to someone . . . no name given. Perhaps it could be made clear from another ledger, but where? Folland shrugged. None of his business, only curiosity, only a lesson in this business he was beginning to learn. The Portreeve had said that he did not deal in grain only, but in money itself, as something to be bought and sold and rented. And why, Folland asked himself, should I not do the same?

In the warmth of a fine May afternoon, Gunver and Carines stood outside their shops and gossiped.

'He was drinking with the soldiers yesterday afternoon. And with the Tidewatcher before that.'

'It means nothing.' Gunver was sceptical.

'It may mean nothing. But the Tidewatcher goes in secret to report to Shillmoor.'

'He must report to some Magistrate, or he will never be able to have warrants sworn out.'

'Watch, my friend, and pray.'

'And fast, too, I fear.'

'Are you going to run it tonight, then?' Sophia Place asked her brother.

'We will have to. We cannot leave the cargo in the ship any longer. We will have half at least.'

'But is it safe?'

'Only if no one has warned the Customs that the lighter is hidden by the bank. We have it well under the trees.'

'Will you beach the ship? The tide is right?'

'The tide is right, but we won't beach. We will hoist half the cargo out tonight into boats, and the rest in a week's time, if I cannot have it sold higher up in Lincolnshire. We must have the ship where she can put to sea at once.'

'Will you take your pistols?'

'Not on this affair. A Scotchman drowned in the river, and there a week, that's nothing to worry the justices about. But a Customs man shot in the Marsh, and many there to see it and to know the reason why, that no one can ignore.'

'Is there anything more to do?'

'Nothing. Mellin is going on the ship to show them where to come ashore, and the Nobbler has been collecting Pards from high up the Marsh. When it's dark, Key will run an empty lighter down the river to take the place of the one we pole up.'

George rode along the quay in the twilight. There were few people about, only urchins playing and a man walking along. George thought he knew him by the stride, the swagger. As the hoofs clattered on the cobbles, the man turned his head to see who it was. George swore under his breath—it *was* Folland. *And* he was going into the Black Bull. But the lighter was gone from its place, Folland must have seen it moving. And who knew what the Nobbler might have said, or let his sister know that she might have passed on to Folland. Still—everything was launched, and not even a man to spare to pin the old Dragoon down.

Folland turned in to the Black Bull. It was a pleasant place, and he felt in need of a wet before he went home. He stopped as he entered the tap-room. The whole detachment were there, sitting round in marching order, swords at sides, and pistols on their knees ready to slip into the holsters on the saddles. In the backyard, the horses were all saddled. Freeman leapt up to greet him.

'Have you the message?'

'What message?'

Freeman looked abashed. He could never quite understand all the hints that Perkins dropped him, but he could have sworn that Folland had come into it somewhere.

'Oh, nothing, nothing. All right, stand easy again, all of you.' Because all the troopers had got to their feet. 'Keep them muzzles pointing up there, loaded or not, else we'll have a man killed some day if you don't learn the habit now.' He turned back to Folland. 'God knows how I'll ever make soldiers of them, I don't. Give them a chance and they'll fire off good powder as if it cost no more than sand and we could pick it off the beaches as easy.'

'Oh, we must have been as bad in our time,' Folland comforted him. 'You'll be going out this evening, then?'

'No, there's nothing toward, just having a bit of exercise. Stay and have a dram with us.' It seemed to him essential, that he should keep Folland with him for some time, so that he should not tell anyone else that the soldiers were ready to move. He poured a tot of gin. 'There's good Hollands for you, best in town, and if you make it worth my while I'll tell you where I gets it, because it's not in this tavern.'

'Not much worth smuggling gin, is it?' Perkins was still fresh in Folland's mind. Freeman looked sideways at him.

'Made in this very town, excise paid, and you should know.'

'Oh, yes, I know. At least, Kettlestang sold the grain to distil it. But he doesn't own the distillery.' Not yet, he thought, but in a few months if the distiller doesn't stop drinking his profits. . . . And Folland followed Freeman's eyes. There was a young man behind him making frantic conspiratorial signs. Freeman shouted, and the troopers scrambled from the tap-room into the yard.

'Stay here till we come back,' Freeman yelled at Folland. For a moment he wondered if he ought not to leave a trooper to keep Folland company and make sure he did not leave the Bull. But he thought that if he were going to tackle smugglers he wanted all the men he could take. Perhaps Folland would wait some time. The gin bottle would keep him : sure he would not leave before he had finished it, all open for him. Freeman himself would not have left it if he had the chance. He would finish the

dram, anyway. Freeman heaved into his saddle and led his little
force over the bridge, the way George Place had gone an hour
earlier.

He was half right. Robert Folland finished the one drink,
slowly. He wondered idly where Freeman had gone, then
shrugged his shoulders and dismissed it from his mind. He had
been, he supposed, too long a sergeant to act as a principal, as
an independent man. These things were the concern of his
betters. The Magistrate would know all about it. In fact, no
Magistrate did. Perkins was not risking any leakage.

Folland walked home to the School House. It was the second
evening in succession he did not feel like going into the Falcon.
He still had a bad head from the day before, and the gin had
done nothing to settle it. He sat close on the settle by the kitchen
fire, while Prisca held the pamphlet he had brought her from
London close under the lighted dip and read aloud.

' "It will, no doubt, be a mighty comfort to our Grandchildren,
when they see a few rags hung up in *Westminster Hall*, which
cost an hundred millions, whereof they are paying the Arrears
and boasting, as Beggars do, that their Grandfathers were Rich
and Great. What use is it to us that Bouchain is taken, about
which the Warlike Politicians of the Coffee-House make such a
Clutter? What Advantage have We, but that of spending three
or four Millions more to get another Town for the Dutch, which
may open them a new Country for *Contributions*, and increase
the Perquisites of the General?" Why, d'you think this is all true,
Master Folland?'

'What if it be true? What odds to me?'

'Did it not matter to you when you were in Flanders? Did you
never ask why you should attack this town or that? Did you
there think it was all to the Queen's advantage, or would you
have fought as well for the Dutch?'

'It would have been all one for me. Look here, Miss, we fought
for money, and for the means to keep body and soul together. I
tell you, we fought as other men might plough a field or carry
sacks of grain. It was employment. And easy to get, too, and no
questions asked, and it was something that would take us far
from our homes that we wanted to leave. As to why we fought,
why the Queen fought, well, it was nothing to us.'

'But what if, as this pamphlet says, it was all to fill the Duke's
pocket?'

'There was no way I could fill mine. I tell you this, Corporal John may be a miser and a lecher and all the rest, but he is a good general. For in Spain we fought a battle whenever it offered. But in Flanders the Duke would only have us fight when there was no other course open, and the rest of the time we marched hither and yon, and the French would not stand before us when the Duke had us in a good position. How do you think we took those towns for the Dutch? By fighting three battles in ten years? No, but by always being where the Frenchman would not have us be, and where he ran rather than have to try to shift us. If there was to be a war, then he was a good general to be under, and safer than a hundred Peterboroughs.'

'But do you not think of the cause of the war? Do you not ask why you fought at all?'

'No. Why should I? I was never more than a Sergeant. It was none of my business.'

'That is a turn of speech I have heard from you too often, Master Folland. Is nothing any of your business? Is even your own business your own business?'

'I work for Master Kettlestang. I do *his* business, not mine. Is that not business enough?'

'But you work without curiosity. You do what you're told, you say. But what are you trying to do? I suppose you don't want to admit that you know this, but all the town is asking who you are and why you are here.'

'I came here for peace. I have had ten years at the wars, and I want somewhere quiet to live. There was employment here offered me without my asking for it. Would you rather have me walk the streets begging my bread? And remember, I have for all that time been a man under authority, not in authority. All right, Miss, so I have been a Sergeant, and had men obey me. But I had my orders from my betters that were officers and had bought their places when I had to work for mine. And as to why we should march here or here, or dig this trench or climb that glacis or shoot those Frenchmen, that was not my business, my business was to see it done in a smart and soldierlike manner. And I am in the same position here.'

'Surely you do not want to be an underling all your life? Doing what other people tell you?'

He wanted to retort, what business was that of hers? He wanted to ask her why she should want him to make any motion

73

of his own. But he thought it simpler to ask,

'Is this not a night when your brother is likely to come here?'

'I will get some supper, if that is what you are asking for.'

We are wrangling, he thought, like some old married couple. Sure, there are married couples who talk less than we do, much less, and that only on subjects of the house, who find no pleasure even in wrangling any more. He pressed the point, if only to keep the talk away from himself.

'But where is your brother tonight?'

'Charley is out working for Master Place tonight.'

'Tonight? In the dark?'

'It sometimes happens. Sometimes he is out the whole night. He is a man under authority, like yourself. We poor have to obey to live—you have been telling me that.'

'Your father did not obey.'

'And so we are poor. Are we not paying now for his disobedience before we were born? If he were still in the Vicarage, with eight hundred pound a year clear, and myself living like a lady on it——'

'Yet, with the School you should be comfortable enough.'

'As many as we are? And him—he drinks it all. Haven't you helped him? Drinking the money that ought to pay for our bread.'

'Is there nothing we can talk about tonight without quarrelling?'

'Nothing,' she snapped.

'Then I will go to bed.'

'And sleep for two nights, because tomorrow we will have the fair in the street, and that will not be over till morning.'

He came to the first landing. The door to the long room was open, and a little voice bleated, 'Sir! Please, sir!'

'Oh, what is it now? There'll be no stories tonight, it's far too late. You ought to be asleep, Moses Alley. Why aren't you all asleep?'

But it was lost, he was inside the room already.

'Oh, sir, please sir, we were arguing, sir—you never told us how you were wounded, sir. Was it in a battle, sir?'

'No, few men die in battle. Most die of kicks of a horse, or of the plague, and for every man that dies, there are four ruined for life.'

'But your wound, sir? It was a wound, wasn't it?'

'If you must know, I had it stealing horses. There were a score of us, with an Officer, went to raid the French horse lines. They caught us. The Officer was killed. A Frenchie stuck me with a pitchfork. That's all it was. Think, lad, if I'd done it at home, they'd have hanged me. But do it in Flanders, there's a hero I am, and have free licence to beg in the streets as my reward. Look, I've got you a bag of apples. Fair shares, mind! Now, to bed, all of you.'

He heard a scuffle of small bare feet. They must have all been close to him in the dark, he thought. But he let himself go to them, said things he dared not even say to Prisca. Ten years in the field, and nothing to show for it at the end. While the Duke . . . but a soldier had to be loyal, and never think if loyalty was deserved. He was ashamed of thinking it now—he could not get used to being able to think things like that. He stripped to his shirt and slid under his rough blankets. Through the window, the moon shone full.

Perkins was running under that moon. He was breathless and sweating. He had sent the lad off as soon as he saw, for sure, that the Bergen boat had upped her anchor and was standing under topsails for the open sea. He did not dare move before it was dusk, in case anyone should notice. He used the time for a meal. But it was a long walk in a hurry past the village, by the high-tide mark on the slippery sand, to the river bank. And then the row across the river—he told himself, he ought not to have done it on a full stomach. He had been banking on the rising tide to carry him upstream, but it had not lessened his rowing. He felt dizzy. The moon was getting up, and he was glad of a little light. He was afraid of losing the tide and having the stream catch him and sweep him heaven knows where, and him never knowing about it if he could not even see the opposite bank.

But he did come ashore, a quarter mile below where he ought to be. He beached the boat, reasoning that he could make better speed on land. He soon began to regret it. He found the greasy clay led him slithering down into a succession of drainage ditches, running into the river. He was wet to the knees. Water squelched from his boot tops—he considered slashing them open at the toes to let out the water, but decided that he would never get their value back from the Crown however eloquently he claimed for them. At last he found the beginning of the path. He stopped there, took off his boots, poured out the water. His feet

75

now felt cold as ice. He began to run to warm them up, and was alarmed at the noise he was making. He tried running on the grass at the edge of the path, but caught his foot in a rabbit hole and came down on his face. He returned to the pathway, walked as quietly as he could, and as fast. Even this he was not able to keep up for long, but slowed down to his usual pace. By now his breath was coming from deep in his chest, with a conscious effort, and hurting.

The moon was well up. He came to Blackmer's brick farm house. He stopped and watched it in case there was anyone moving. Inside, Hod Blackmer heard him and drew the blankets over his head. Then he went into the field opposite, to walk quiet on the grass under the hedge, not to be seen and, more important, not to wake the dog. He got past in quiet, but that was more a feat of self-control than of foot work, because he came down on both knees in a cow pat.

A half mile further, and he knew where he was. He found a half-taken haystack, and climbed on it to get a view to the beach over the flat land. For the first time in that horrid night he felt a flash of pleasure. He had been right. He could see the ship under the moon. It was the *Gouda*. Perkins had been twenty years at sea, even if he had never been in the *Valentia*, and the shape of a ship was as good as a face to him, to know and remember and recognize. No two ships anywhere were alike. This was the one, and if bound for Bergen, she would have been ten leagues to the north by now. But there she was, under topsails only still, close in to the shore. Perkins prayed to God, sincerely and devoutly and convinced that his prayer would be answered because he was in a just cause, that the sinners would not be too quick in starting to unload.

Now he had to go warily. There were two dangers. He might come on smugglers; if he were caught, there would be a vacancy for a Tidewatcher again at Bratton. He would not be the first taken like that and, if not killed, then beaten till he was not fit for any service again. He had met a man that had happened to, and all he could do was sit in a chair and mumble and shake. Perkins was willing to take the risk, but he prudently wanted to be sure the risk was a faint one.

The other danger was more ludicrous. He had little trust in Freeman's sense or his control over his troopers. He had seen Dragoons before, and that was why he was so sure that Folland was something more than an old soldier. He did not behave or talk like a Freeman, and Freeman was a good Sergeant. Perkins had no particular wish to be killed by Dragoons rather than by smugglers. So he kept low, trying to see the soldiers' heads against the sky. He found them, all pressed together, peering over the hedge at the beach. They had not so much as a man on look out behind them, let alone flankers. Perkins was able to walk up to the sergeant and tap him on the elbow.

Freeman started; his horse shifted nervously, and voided itself over Perkins' boots. The sergeant got down.

'What's happening?' Perkins asked him.

'She's anchored. There's a boat coming ashore.'

'Then watch it.' Perkins asked, 'Have you seen anybody on the shore?'

'There was a man showed a light over there, a while ago.'

'That's the way to the farm. That may mean nothing. Nobody come down to the beach?'

'We've seen nobody.'

'That boat's moving slowly.'

'Perhaps she's got a load in her.'

Perkins snorted. That was the obvious conclusion, and there was no need to waste breath in drawing it. He was, however, too happy to make any comment. This was what any Customs man dreamt of in the long lonely watches by the shore. There was actually brandy coming ashore, and men waiting for it, and himself with a troop of soldiers in ambush. Nothing to do but to wait, till he was sure that they were going to beach the ship. The thing was to catch the shore men and their beasts loading up. And enough sailors, at least, for someone to blab and give sufficient evidence to have the ship herself seized at sea. Then he heard a loud voice, a country voice, one of the troopers.

'Look, there they be, there they be, look at 'un. Don't ye just see 'un, Joe? Look at 'un!'

'Shut up, there,' Perkins hissed as loud as he dared. He could see men leading horses down the shingle.

'But it must be smugglers, sir,' bawled another trooper from the end of the line. 'Don't ye see them there, sir?'

Have they heard us? Perkins asked himself. Or have they stopped there because that's as far as they can take horses laden over the wet sand? If only we can stay hid a few minutes longer, till they are all busy. But then, CLAP! He heard the hiss of the ball going away from him across the beach, in the general direction of the horses, which were far out of range.

'Stop that!' shouted Freeman. 'What man fired? Stop that! Keep hidden.'

'Too late,' Perkins shouted back at him. 'You'd better rush them. They've all heard it.'

Freeman hoisted himself up again to stand in his stirrups. 'All right, boys, after them! Catch any you can!' Perkins jumped aside as the horsemen crowded to pass one by one through the only gap in the hedge. The troopers came out into the field, and Freeman got them into a line before he had them charge headlong across the marshy ground, shouting and yelling like boys let out of school. They did not keep a line long. Each caught a glimpse of some shadow, some grass moving in the sea breeze, and went off on his own, a different direction for each of the dozen men. Only Freeman held straight for the boat, and Perkins ran after him.

Perkins stumbled over clusters of reeds, squelched into holes full of foul water. He heard the bang of a pistol from his right, where the horses had been, then a regular fusillade. Something might be happening there. But he held to his line for the boat. Where was Freeman? He stopped to catch his breath and look ahead. Freeman was trying to get up on to his frisky horse. He's been thrown, thought Perkins. I've seen two of his men come off, and there'll be more. I wouldn't like to gallop over marshy ground in the dark like they did. He came down into the sand. The sailors were pushing out the boat, in water up to their waists. It was heavy : full of brandy, Perkins thought. They had stood there, and calmly restowed their kegs before shoving off. There were three still lying on the sand, but the surface cut up and indented around the mark of the keel showed there had been several more.

Perkins shouted at the boat to stop, to come back, in the Queen's name. He thought he heard laughter. He took out his pistols, stowed in their holsters close to his body under his frock. The charges and priming were dry. He aimed carefully, and fired. One bullet and then another went over the boat, as the oars splashed free in the water. Freeman came up with him, hauling a reluctant horse. He passed the bridle to Perkins, took out his pistol and fired. They thought they heard wood splinter. Then the boat was out of reach and the pistols empty.

78

Perkins wandered over to the kegs, and sat down, drained, exhausted. Freeman came over, took the bridle, hobbled the horse.

'What can we do now?' he asked.

'Can you rally your men?'

'I don't know where they've all gone to. I suppose they'll come back here. Or go to the Black Bull.'

'Didn't you give them a rallying point?'

'I never thought they'd get scattered like this.'

They sat glumly on the shore and waited. The Bergen boat stood north. The sails glinted under the moon. After about an hour, a trooper came along the beach, leading a limping horse. Then another rode back. Then two more, and they had a prize, a prisoner walking between them.

'Look, Sarge, we got one of 'em, we got a smuggler,' they shouted from a hundred yards away. Perkins remained seated on the keg till they brought the man up to him. He was small and wiry, dark haired and, Perkins thought, sallow faced though it was hard to tell in the moonlight.

'And what's your name, my man?'

'Baker Sarsen . . . me lud.'

'And what are you doing here at this time of night? Come on, man, answer!'

'We'll have him answer, soon enough,' said Freeman. He whirled a strap round his head, made it whistle in the air. 'We'll have a bloody back and all the answers you want out of him.'

'I'll have none of that,' snapped Perkins. 'Now, Baker, what were you at?'

'That's my business.'

'It's my business. D'ye know who I am?'

'No, sir.'

'I'm Her Majesty's representative. Now what are you doing here at this time?'

'Oh, I come out for a bit of fresh air.'

'Where do you live?'

'This side of Wrackham Bridge.'

'Far this side?'

'No. Just this side.'

'And you walked all this way for a bit of fresh air? A likely story. Who employs you?'

'Eh?'

79

'Who do you work for?'

'I works mostly for Master Kettlestang. I'm a carter in season.'

'But tonight, you've been a carter for smugglers.'

'Smugglers?' The man was visibly frightened. 'Oh, no, not me, not for the smugglers, sir. Them's all Pards that do do that, sir, and us and the Pards don't agree. They come down here and spoil all that us decent folk be trying to do with their noise and rushing about.'

Light began to dawn on Freeman. For Perkins, his suspicions were confirmed.

'You've been poaching, haven't you?'

'Aye.'

'And it's a hanging matter. It's Lord Wrackham's land beyond the hedge. Rabbiting, isn't it?'

Grudgingly, again, 'Aye.'

'I'm not concerned with poaching, not here. I'm partial to a nice rabbit, or a bird, myself, occasionally. Hard to get, aren't they? Master Pontigarde looks after his master's interests well, don't he?'

'He do that.'

'Did ye see the smugglers?'

'Saw sommon here wi' pack horses back there on the lane.'

'Who?'

'I don't know. Pards they was mostly, from up-Marsh. Not down-Marsh Pards. Couldn't put a name to any of them, I couldn't that.'

'But not all Pards?'

'Some didn't talk like Pards. More like townies they did talk, like.'

'Would you know them again?'

'Not in the dark, I wouldn't.'

'How're you taking the rabbits?'

'Slipknots.'

'Can you show me.'

'I left three along here.'

Perkins followed the poacher along the sand. He noted on the beach the deep indented footprints of John Mellin, put ashore with the brandy. He did not know whose they were, only noted that they were too big, too heavy-booted, to be Baker's.

'You could be hanged for this.'

'Too true, I could.'

'And so could I, come to that.' Perkins stowed a rabbit into an inner pocket of his frock. 'Now, off with you.'

'I can go?'

'I said, poaching's not my business. Smuggling is. If you want me, the soldiers will know where I am.'

Perkins returned to Freeman.

'You've let him go?'

'Of course.'

'We could have had a guinea from old Pontigarde for taking him back. And 'twould have been something out of this night.'

'He'll be more use to me alive than hanged. Have you got all your men?'

'Near enough. Two still to come.'

'Then let's be off. Where's my horse?'

'Your horse?'

'I told you to bring a horse for me.'

'Oh—I clean forgot.'

'Well, I'm not walking. Where's the man who called out, the man who saw them first?'

'Oh, that was me, sir, Trooper Bragg, sir, I saw 'em first, I told you, sir. And I was first to shoot at 'em, sir, you'll remember that when you write it down won't you, sir?'

'May all the Gods who watch over the Customs forgive me if ever I forget your name, Trooper Bragg. Get down off that horse. Quick! I'll have that to ride back.'

'What? Do I have to walk, sir?'

'You're not walking tonight. You'll sit here in the dark and the cold till I send someone out to you.'

'What, here, sir? But, sir——'

'And you'll guard these kegs with your life or whatever else you find handy. And mind, if I find one of them stove in when I come back in the light, then I'll bash your brains out with my own bare feet and I'll have you hanged for smuggling. Three kegs I'm leaving, and three kegs, full, I'll have when I come back.'

'All by myself, sir? All night, sir?'

'You've got your pistol. And you've reloaded—you haven't? Then reload it, you fool. And when the other two come down to the beach, make them stay here with you. Keep awake. Right, Sergeant, we'll be off. I hope you give me a good breakfast at the Black Bull. Bragg's breakfast.'

Somewhere in the darkness, Perkins knew, the smuggling party was scattered, lost in the labyrinth of lanes and dykes, green water and grey mud. There was no use looking for any of them there. But to sit in the front parlour of the Black Bull, and eat bacon and eggs and watch the town end of the bridge might not give him proof, but it could tell him who came home late, on a blown horse covered with the unmistakable greasy muck of the flats.

Charley Arkengarth came through in the grey light of the dawn. Perkins saw him and noted him. He had no idea who this man might be, thin and shabby looking of no importance. But he would know him again. Anywhere.

Charley Nobbler had nowhere else to go. So he went round to the School House.

8

Folland had gone into the School House kitchen to drink his morning dish of tea, standing. Charley Nobbler was there, haggard and muddy. He looked dog tired. Folland took no notice of him. It was not his business. He felt ashamed of his bad temper of the night before. Prisca was bustling about, finding something for Nobbler to eat, looking out a clean shirt for one of the schoolboys, heating gruel for her three youngest brothers. Folland tried, for some time in vain, to catch her. Time was passing. If he did not get his word in, he would have to move off to make his check along the Quay, before he reported to Master Kettlestang. At last, he slipped in front of her.

'Now, Miss Arkengarth——' he began.

'Sir, you are in my way,' she retorted. He took no notice of that : where else was he trying to be?

'We did talk of going to see the sea some day. There is something we can do before that.'

'Indeed? And what, I pray?'

'Today is Saturday. We have almost a half holiday at the counting house. I can leave at four of the clock.'

'And I am to have you under my feet before you go off to that Falcon, I suppose?'

'No, not *under* your feet, Miss.'

She looked at him suspiciously.

'Then that will be a change.'

'Come out tonight and let me buy you a fairing.'

Prisca turned abruptly away from him. Folland did not realize it, but at that moment Prisca grew up, and she knew it. She thought, he has asked me to go to the fair. And he has asked *me*, to my face, direct, not gone to my father over my head as if I were a baby, as Grinton did last year. And I would not go with him, just to make a fourth with Charley and . . . who was it Charley was after? One of the Alley girls?

'If you are ready when I return . . . then perhaps . . . if you will consent . . .' He was still not sure that she would consent. But she turned and told him,

'I will be ready when you come in. I will find someone who will look after the boys and my mother, for the night.'

'How is your mother today?'

'Very poorly, very poorly.'

'She will not grudge you——'

'There will be no question about that.'

Folland stood all day before his desk in the counting house. Perkins stood before Shillmoor. He had ridden over the slope of the down to Dunnet House, that had been the Dower House for the Harne family, in the three short generations that the Wrackham Barons had held the Hall and the land which went with it. But Dunnet House and five hundred acres had had to be sold to pay the last Lord's gaming debts, not to speak of bribes here and there to make sure that there was no impeachment, no scandal even though he had held to the wrong King. It was a long low house, timber framed, clunch filled, like most of the houses in Wrackham or on the Down. Shillmoor had it now, and Shillmoor the brewer, the gin distiller, was a Justice of the Peace and sat in the Parliament. He was at home, and received Perkins in the gun room.

'It was a night wasted, sir,' Perkins ended his tale. 'All that work, and the troops out as well, and nobody caught, and nothing but to beg a cart from you to bring in the brandy we caught.'

'You are not employed to *catch* smugglers,' Shillmoor told him.

'No, sir?'

'No.' Shillmoor ran his hand over the stubble of his head. 'You are here to prevent the evasion of duty that ought to be paid. You did that last night, most effectively. I shall make a most favourable report to your superiors. Now, that ship had to put North. Let the Lincoln men look for the brandy.'

'But there was nobody caught.'

'Do you *want* to catch men? Do you want to have people round here fined to ruination or thrown into the County Gaol or be hanged up on the Down perhaps, when you have to pass their brothers in the street every day after it?'

Perkins said nothing. He cursed in himself, railed at heaven at these local magistrates. That was why a Customs man was always a stranger, so that he could not be made a prey to local loyalties. But magistrates came out of the very soil where the smugglers grew. And this one owed his seat at Westminster to the Burgesses. What would *he* do to offend anyone over a few bottles of spirits? All he cared was that if people could not find cheap brandy, they would have to drink his gin.

Folland checked the books the clerks had made out, found some errors, missed others that Bridgward found and pointed out to him with scorn and mild ridicule, friendly, but patronizing. He sat at table, at Kettlestang's left, in the counting house, with Bridgward opposite him and the lesser clerks below him. He ate the rabbit stew with onions and carrots, and good wheat bread, and ale—well, Shillmoor's ale, but better than anything he had had in the army. Kettlestang talked about the fair.

'Aye, we always had a fair on Saint Ragnfrith's day, outside the Abbey. I mind going with my father, holding his hand, the year that—what d'ye think? There was hardly anybody there at all. Nobody to buy, and precious few stalls to sell. That's the first Ragnfrith fair I remember. D'ye know why, then, there was nobody to buy?'

The clerks shook their heads. They could think of no reason why anyone should miss the fair.

'Because it was the Plague year, that's why, and nobody would come to the Fair for fear of the Plague, and because they thought the stall-men would bring it. But my father, he was Portreeve then before me, said he would go. And he went, and took me with him by the hand, to show there was no danger from the Plague. That was the first year I remember, only one little row

84

of stalls—I can see it now in my mind's eye. And there was a-many that shunned the fair that died of the Plague, but we didn't, nor did any of the stall-men that came.'

Kettlestang laughed at the memory, and all the table dutifully laughed with him. Folland mopped up the last of his stew with a crust and laughed too. Kettlestang had come through the Plague unharmed, as Folland had come away from Almanza, neither by his own will. Both had lived. Why, he supposed, God knew. Everybody was born for some purpose. Why was he born? Folland had often asked himself that. He did not know, but surely there was some reason in it, that he had come through ten years of war, and at the end the only man in the Regiment that had joined it in England at its first raising. That's the way I came to be a Sergeant, he used to say, forgetting that he had been a Sergeant before Malplaquet, and that was where most of them had been killed. Killed like Baker Alley killed our rabbits.

The long day, no, the short day was over, and he walked back with Kettlestang to his house, and then along to the School House. He went, unusually, to the kitchen, and popped his head in to Prisca.

'Why, miss, when will you be ready to come a-fairing?'

She leapt up, scattering her mending.

'Why, sir, I did not think you meant it.'

'I say nothing I do not mean.'

'That is a common boast, sir, and not easily justified.'

'Still, miss, will you answer my question, or should I ask the cat?'

'When you ask me as nicely as the cat, sir.'

'Then please, Miss Arkengarth, will you come with me to the fair?'

'I will come in half an hour, sir, because I must take my face out of the paint closet.'

'But who will mind your mother? And the boys?'

'The boys are gone to the fair before us. And Mistress Carines will come in and sit with my mother.'

Folland went to his room, and washed, and changed for the evening. He looked at his big sword. At last he decided not to wear it. His sword smelled too much of his daily work : or of being a gentleman, which he was not. He tied his cravat with care, buttoned his waistcoat, buttoned his coat, considered again,

85

then unbuttoned it to show his new waistcoat. He picked up his hat and returned to the kitchen.

Prisca joined him. He bowed to her, deep, sweeping his hat-brim in the sand of the floor. She curtsied deep, too, and they both laughed. She said primly,

'My Lord, your Lordship's most humble servant.'

'Madam, you spoke too late, for I was your Ladyship's before.'

He stood back to look at her. She was in a white satin petticoat and a deep red gown over it, open fronted, and a lacy handkerchief for a modesty piece. It made a brave front indeed, but sure it was easy to see that it was not made for her, but was probably her mother's, and the hoops under it too. Folland thought, I will get her a better dress soon; he did not dare venture to say so, seeing she felt so fine and smart. But she sensed what he suppressed, and laughed to cover her embarrassment, saying,

'But you must know, sir, whom you serve. I had my eyebrows of a mouse, my face from the flour bin, my patch from a Dutchman's breeches, and my shoes from a farrier's. And pray, sir, where got you that weskit? I am sure I never saw it on you before. Have you found a mine of new clothes?'

'Aye, and I labour in it mightily, under London Bridge. For I bought it there, and I have kept it against today.'

'I think that light green goes mighty well with your brown coat, like new wheat on plough land.'

'New wheat with roses growing in it?'

She looked closer. 'Roses? I have seen babies embroider more like. Though perhaps not more artistical and fanciful.' She felt like saying she would embroider him a better waistcoat, but she was too shy. Folland offered her his arm, and they went out into Butter Street, to walk around the Fair.

The stalls were in long rows along the cobbles. It was a cloth fair, some called it a flannel fair, where spinners and weavers had once been eager to get rid of the last of the year's work. A New Year's fair, indeed, for the Clothiers. But now, not half the stalls were of the old kind, with two or three families joining together to sell their cloth. Most of the weavers now sold to the clothiers, and some of them were as fast in debt to the factors as Hod Blackmer was to Kettlestang.

Nowadays, even some of the cloth stalls in the fair were selling silk, heavy corded stuff woven in the town by the French. They helped the day to be known, still, as Rag Fair. Some stalls sold lace from Nottingham, and ribbons, but the people who sold them would set up their counters at twenty fairs that year. They were professionals at selling, not at making. And all the stall-holders who were not burgesses paid high for a place in the fair : burgesses put up stalls and paid nobody for it.

Robert Folland walked between the rows of stalls with Prisca on his arm, and looked at things, and tried to buy her a fairing. He offered her a bracelet of coral that she saw on a jumbled stall of bits and pieces, and she said no, it was too much. Then there was ribbon, or a piece of silk, and again, she said no, he must not throw his money away if he had any, he worked hard for it. So they strolled on, and looked at a man who was playing a game with three cups and a pebble, and she wanted to put a shilling on her certainty where the pebble was, it looked so easy. But Folland guessed that the shilling was almost all she had, and said it was all rigged, it would be a certain waste. And she stood for a bit and realized that Robert was right, and no wonder, for he had been all over the world, more or less, and seen things like this before.

The crowd was thick, as always, Marsh people and shepherds from the Downs, mixed together with yokels from the clay farms beyond the river. You could look at a man in his smock and tell where he came from within a mile, by the embroidery on it. It wasn't a hiring fair, so you didn't see men standing about in sad groups, holding their crooks or straw bridles or whatever they had to show their trades. They were come empty handed today, and full of pocket as far as they ever had full pockets. The sailors had come from the ships along the Quay, and they had money to spend, and sometimes something to sell : you might find a sailor with a handkerchief spread on the cobbles, and on it a set of whalebone stays, carved at the top with hearts, and engraved on the front of the busks with scenes of ships and fish. Or another would have a coiled rope mat or a wooden spoon with a carved handle, anything to sell for drinking money. The sailors kept an eye open for the Market Warden, Lazarus Uckerby, because they did not bother with any formality of Market Dues. But Prisca would not buy from them either.

There was one stall with a little awning over it, and a bit of fun there. A man stood on a platform and offered to fight any-one who would come, bare chested and bare fisted, for five shillings a side, winner to take all, and the loser to be the first who failed to come up after a knock down, or the first to own himself bested. Robert wanted to stay and watch, and Prisca was at first ashamed; she puzzled why it drew her so to see two men, young country lads, bigger than the challenger, get up one after another, and both knocked down, and almost senseless, with the second or third blow. Because, as Robert pointed out to her, the youngsters spent some time after they were up waving their fists about for their friends to see and pondering how to go about it. While the man in the stall who did this for a living was only interested in how much he could earn in an hour. And he was used to it, knew where and how to strike, and how to knock a man sick and silly. Prisca was impressed at such wisdom, and thought that Robert, if he stood up to fight this man, would surely guard himself properly and win his five shillings, the fighting man being small and wiry and grizzled, not even young. But of course, it was not dignified for a man of importance like him to fight in public.

And the same went for the next stall, where there was a crowd watching a man who would fight anyone with single sticks. Here Robert was eager to try it, but Prisca was not willing he should risk blooding his fine coat, cutting heads being the object of the sport. Folland remembered what he had been used to do with a sabre, sheathed, in the bivouacs, and knew he could settle this man by the sheer strength of his arm bearing down. Still, he let Prisca persuade him from an easy crown. There was no dignity in brawling in public, however much money you could make. So next they found a stall where they could have a dish of strawberries and cream, the first of the season, and therefore well worth threepence each, even though a trifle sour, because they could wish on it, but not tell their wishes. And Robert Folland wished for peace, and at the same time wished to know who he was, though he knew the two wishes were opposed : but Prisca wished for Robert Folland.

And after the strawberries, they came on little Benny Alley and the other boys from the School gazing sadly at a stall which sold marzipan. Robert spent another threepence on them, and they cheered him, which made people laugh. And next, again, there was a little booth all hung with gay cloths, and an old woman brown-faced and black-haired like a gipsy—though she was not a gipsy—sitting inside it calling out that she would tell fortunes.

'Only sixpence,' she was calling, 'only sixpence and I will tell you true.'

'Come along,' Robert urged Prisca, 'and have it all told and hear what marvels will happen.'

'Not at such a price,' she objected, ''tis too great a sum of money for a puff of breath.' And then she was afraid that she had offended the woman, but she in her turn had heard such things often enough, and knew that if the man had suggested it he would pay whatever the girl said. So she grinned toothless out of her brown face as Folland held out his sixpence. But he said to Prisca,

'It's like a silver bullet. If you want to have certainty, you must pay for it.' The old woman laughed aloud in agreement; Folland went on, 'If you can tell the future, surely you can tell the past. It must be easier.'

The old woman looked at him, eyes narrowing.

'You want that, Maister? You want me to call your past out aloud in front of all these people? There's few as wants that, Maister, few indeed so brave. The future, people think there's no harm in that, Maister, but the past—it hurts terrible, though it be dead as the Lords of Loone. And it shames, too.'

Folland stopped smiling. Still he had come so far, and there were people pressing close around him to hear. So he pressed the old woman in his turn.

'What was I doing a year ago today? Now, tell me that.'

'A year ago today? A year ago today? Give me your hand, Maister, give me your hand, that's how we tells. Let me feel the blood and the bones, that's how we knows, we feels the blood and the bones. Oh . . . yes . . . last year . . . there was pain in these bones, Maister, there was pain in them, and yourself lying on a pallet in a big place, a big house next a river. And there was a man on a pallet by you, an Irishman, and he died that day. All that day he cried for his mother, and only you to look after him. You couldn't walk, Maister, and when he died you couldn't call nobody else, and so you laid by his dead side all night long, didn't you, Maister, didn't you? Tell me Maister, don't I tell true?'

Folland shuddered, all the people around saw him.

'Aye, that's true. I'd forgotten it was today last year. I clean forgot. Lawrence MacBride from Derry. D'ye know what he died of?'

'Oh, aye, I knows that. A musket ball in his side was the start, but 'twas not from that he died. It was from ague and coughing, and consumption of his flesh utterly that he died, and a long dying he had after all, when his ribs were long healed and the scar fleshed over. It was a long dying, you know it well, that he had.' She watched Folland's face, determined to follow home her advantage, try him further. 'Come now, gallant Maister, shall I tell you where you were the year before? Or what you did three years ago, in the Orange Groves? Shall I tell it in front of all these who listen?'

Folland, again, shuddered. He remembered the Orange Grove and the dead men by the wall, and the way the woman screamed when they—when he—it was too much to remember. He shook his head and rubbed his hands on his coat. It was time to change to something harmless before he was harmed.

'You are telling the truth about the past. What can you tell about the future?'

'That will need more silver, and a handsome man like yourself is generous.' Folland shrugged. He took out a shilling, but he said,

'Not one fortune only for this. Tell the lady's as well.'

'I shall, not for the money, but because I likes the look of you.' And she thought, because by saying I speak true you have made me for the day, and there'll be a hundred sixpences to follow after that wild guess. She looked now at the hardened horseman's hand, and wrinkled her brows impressively, dredging deep for ambiguous sayings and possibilities. She built quickly on what she had already heard of this sodger. The first guess had been lucky, even though she knew from Liz Alley, her niece, that he had been in Chelsea Hospital the summer before, where men died like flies of consumption, and that he had been once in Spain, where everyone knew there were Orange Groves. She bent low over the hand and crooned strange songs, like she thought real Romany would use, gibberish her mother had taught her, and her grandmother that had been one of the first Sarsens to come to Wrackham when Elias Harne brought them from . . . somewhere. And at last, she began to speak in a tranced voice which she had practised long.

'O ullukbarullukbar allullulla, oh, 'tis a searching man, for there are some that are losing men, and some that are finding men, but 'tis you that are a searching man. There will be trouble for you very soon, yet it will not lead to sorrow. But trust in cold iron, and you will see the end of your trouble. And after that, in the end of things you will find your beginning and if that's what ye were searching then 'twill all be well, but if there is anything else you search for, then that same night ye will find it. And lift up your heart for the best of your time is to come.'

Folland shrugged. 'No more? No clearer?'

'Oh, yourself said it was easier to see into the past than to see into the future. And with so little time to peer into the mists, what more should I see? But if you were to pay for the smoke now, and the blade bone of the sheep, and the secret cards and the tray of sand . . .'

Folland laughed. He told her,

'No, but you must read the lady's palm now.'

Prisca hung back, but Folland urged her forward, taking her hand in his, the first time he had touched it and this only to place it in the old woman's. After his firm fingers, the bony hand felt chill cold. She understood now why he had shuddered, twice. The old woman looked at her plump young palm, close, so that she felt the breath and said :

'Oh, what can I see here, what can I see here? First there is sorrow, my lady, great sorrow, sorrow that is great without equal, yet not with trouble and worry, but sorrow of a kind we must all suffer. And after that, there will be worry and anxiousness, and concern for others . . . but in the end, and before there is another rag fair, I can see a fine marriage, my lady, because a fine strong line is here, marriage to a man who is kind and handsome and brave. And there will be some wealth, my lady, and happiness in the end. So lift up your heart, the best of your time is to come.'

Prisca laughed at the conventional ending. There was nothing more in the rest. She was sure she could make as good a hand-reading as the old woman, and she said as much to Robert as they walked away. Then, suddenly serious, she asked him,

'Are you a searching man, Master Folland?'

'I think I am that.'

'And what is it you are searching for?'

'What I think I have found. Peace and a place to be.'

'A place to be?'

'Yes. In the Army I was a wandering man, indeed, and a losing and finding man when there was anything to find and lose again. But there was no place I was welcome to return.'

'You think you have found it?'

'Oh, I am sure I have. Here I am in Wrackham, and see how welcome I am here. I am as settled as if I were born in the town. I have my place in the tavern when I need men's company, and my own room when I need solitude.'

And our kitchen when you need a girl's company, she thought, since he was too cautious to say so. But she warned him,

'Do not take anything at its face value. People here are deceptive. You are not a Burgess.'

'What difference does that make? I don't want to choose Aldermen, and I don't want to keep a stall in the market. That is all I would have by being a Burgess.'

'Indeed, and there is more in it than that. There are two ways of becoming a Burgess in Wrackham; one of them is being the son of a Burgess and the other is by marrying the daughter of a Burgess. But there is no difference, because there is not one Burgess daughter in a thousand marries except a Burgess son, so that all the Burgess families are related and all Wrackham are my cousins. If you are not a Burgess, then you are no man's care, here.'

They had strayed to the edge of the market place, where more sailors had spread their goods. Robert chaffered with them in his few words of Dutch and German. They had some English; they all knew him by name. He asked one of them,

'Hey, Johnny? How much the shawl?'

It was flaming red, and shimmered as the Swede let it flow over his hands.

'Oh, that a good scarf, Skipper, that a good one. I buy him from an Indian man. Look, real Indian silk.'

'How much, then, Johnny? Two shillings? Here, see half a crown?'

'Oh, it real silk, Skipper. Ten shilling for this.'

'A crown, then?'

Prisca realized that Robert was in earnest.

'Oh, no, Master Folland, don't!'

'But it matches your gown exactly. It's very hard to find reds that go together. Hey, Johnny, look! A crown in your pocket, and a net of cabbage before you sail.'

'And eggs, skipper.'

'All right, two dozen eggs, the same day.'

They clapped hands on it. Robert draped the scarf over

Prisca's shoulders. She coloured—he thought he would never see her blush, women with that golden-sallow skin rarely did, but now she was almost the colour of the scarf. She knew it so close a match that she thought it fated. She let him pay and promise, and went forward on his arm. He picked up the conversation where they had left off.

'You are very old fashioned.' They had gone into the tent where the man showed wild beasts for a ha'penny. He had there a shabby wolf, three monkeys which huddled together in a corner, a parrot, gay feathered, that cursed foully and snapped its beak at Folland when he tried to stroke it. Prisca retorted, 'I am not old fashioned. A Wrackham man and you have no more in common than ... that wolf and a monkey.'

He laughed. He had laughed a great deal that day, more than he had for months. It was easy to laugh with her on his arm.

'Pray, Miss, which am I—a wolf, or a monkey?'

She turned on him, her face serious.

'Sir, you are most of all like the parrot to laugh at.'

9

In his own house, George Place ramped up and down like a caged wolf. He had come home, across the Marsh, at midday, in a foul temper. He had taken some of that out on the men at the warehouse. There was plenty left to let out on his sister, but that was a mistake. She came back on him, direct.

'It was sheer folly to go out last night. Once the Tidewatcher had seen the *Gouda* in the river, he must have guessed. He took the chance that it would be unloaded there, and not go on into Lincolnshire. And up there it's gone, isn't it?'

'Aye, and half the profits lost. But he knew where we were going to land it. He must have had a whole squadron of horse out there, charging about chivvying us into the bushes. And he knew when to come. They had us, they nearly had us; it's only the will of God that we got away. We'd have been all up before

Shillmoor in the morning, and once that'd happened, he'd have had to send us to the Assizes. And he'd not have wanted that, however eager he is to stop us coming ashore. Every drop of brandy we bring in, one way or the other, is a drop less of his gin to sell. Someone must have told the Tidewatcher where we were coming, and when.'

'He could have guessed that. Where else is there to go on this part of the coast? And would you have kept the boat if you had not run last night?'

'There must be a dozen places within an evening's sail.'

'My dear brother, did you not spend the whole of last summer, in your patient placid way, wearing your breeches' bottom out going looking for a better place? And did you find one?'

'But he must have known. That beach is four mile long, and he had to be waiting for us at exactly the right place. Why could he not have been two mile the one way or the other? He would never have reached us in time to interfere.'

'It was the nearest spot of the beach to the road, and the easiest place to come to the lighter—what if it were two mile from the river mouth?'

George snorted. This was not the argument he relished. He had never been able to talk his sister down. The more unreasonable she seemed, the more certain he could be that she was right; she would not stop pointing that out to him. The more she pointed it out, the more certain he felt that he ought, in justice, to be right. He ended stubbornly,

'Say what you like, someone told the Tidewatcher, and I know who it was. He was a go-between for the Dragoons; I would not be surprised if he were not out there with them. Did I not hear old Kettlestang in the Dragon the night before last, tell Father how eager the man had been to go to Bratton, that very day? That night, he was in the Black Bull. Last night, I saw him myself go in there, and not half an hour later all the soldiers rode out ready for a fight. It was us they nearly fought. I tell you, it's not very pleasant to hear a pistol and know it's fired at you. I don't care if you think he is Lord Wrackham, I don't even care if Father thinks he may be Lord Wrackham. I don't believe it. All the better if he is. I shall have it out with him. There's a score of good Pards would have been hanged if he'd got us caught.'

George flung out of the house. He was dressed for the fair, in a new coat of his favourite sky blue, with his court sword set with brilliants and a silver mounted cane. But he did not go straight to the Market Square. His sister waited till she was called for, and then she did go straight to the fair. Folland saw her go by, and he bowed to her. He asked Prisca,

'Who is that who has her on his arm?'

'That? Oh, 'tis Paul Shillmoor, the brewer's son. And a fair catch for him, too, if he wants vinegar in his porridge.'

'Why, Miss, are you not a little tart yourself?'

'And with reason, sir. You have never had her spite to contend with.'

Folland shrugged. Quarrels and jealousies between a rich girl and a poor girl were something he could imagine. He could not tell Prisca, and he still wondered if Sophia Place knew, how Shillmoor had been overstretched when he had bought that house and land. Folland felt that that knowledge gave him a kind of power as he walked among the stalls, and bowed here and there to the tradesmen of Wrackham. Newall's ship had come into Bristol, Kettlestang told him, and been sold. So now he had a hundred and forty pounds in the stocks, that Kettlestang held for him, and another thirty ventured to Sweden, and still thirty guineas to his name in Kettlestang's books. And he wished he had the courage to spend twenty-five pound on his own judgement, not on Kettlestang's, because last time he had been in London he had talked with one of Mister Cardonnel's clerks at the Horse Guards, and if only . . . he saw no reason to tell Master Kettlestang all he knew. He dreamed his way through the fair, till his nose twitched his head round of itself, and the old soldier in him woke to the smell of food.

'Why,' he said in awe to Prisca, 'there's someone roasting an ox whole.'

He stopped to look at the spit, the carcase revolving above the charcoal flames, the shovels and pokers leaning against the tripod.

'Master Crankley is a butcher,' Prisca introduced Folland. 'He roasts a beast at every fair. You may have a plate full for three-pence.'

Folland called for two platters, and Master Crankley cut them, smiling, and made them bigger than most people would hope for for sixpence, for Parson Arkengarth's sake, his boys going to the School though he himself was a Baptist, and so he told

Folland all in one stream without drawing breath while he sliced the meat. Folland stood there with Prisca, and they ate the juicy rare beef with their fingers, and mopped up the gravy with their bread, and were happy with it.

And the marsh men came around, the Pards, by ones and twos, till they were in a circle about the roasting ox. Crankley saw them out of the corner of his eye and began to worry, wondering what they were at. In 'ninety-two, he remembered, there had been a fight at the fair between the Pards and the Burgesses, and there had been a great riot in 'seventy-eight that some people like Josh Caddon still talked about between Pards and the Dutchmen that the Harnes had brought in to drain the Marsh. Even three Pards could mean trouble before the night was out, a man beaten to the ground, or a tavern gutted with barrels stove in and pewter dumped in the river. For the Pards from the Marsh would drink beer when it was offered free, or when it was all they could afford : but when they had the money, and on a Fair Day, somehow, they all had the money, Pards drank brandy.

Folland, cleaning his plate, saw Crankley's eye, followed it, saw the Pards around. The talk died away, the decent Burgesses held back. Folland stood with Prisca in a circle of rough men, dressed like sailors in coarse shirts and knee breeches, with heavy boots to the knee. He had never seen so many Pards together before. And then he looked over their heads, and Charley Nobbler was pushing through them. And the Pards, knowing him, let him pass.

Folland felt something was hanging over him. He smiled to welcome Charley, put out his hand. But Charley did not smile, did not even look at Folland. He spoke at once direct to Prisca, urgently.

'Come home, love, come home.'

'What is it?'

'It's your mother, love. Come home with me, now.'

'My mother? What——' And she looked beyond the Pards and she saw Mrs Carines, with her handkerchief to her face, and she knew. She buried her head at once in Charley's chest, and he hurried her away. Folland felt a wave of concern, anger almost, that at this moment she had not turned to him, and he made to follow. But the Pards blocked his way.

And it was at this moment that George Place came through the line, with the Pard that had gone swift to bring him. He had already been into the Falcon and found no sign of his quarry, though it was seven o'clock. But the Pards had searched out the prey, Keffles and Keys, Dees and Buicks, Adairs and Peascods, running through the fair like their own dogs in the Marsh.

'So I've had to look for you?' George stood face to face with him. 'So I've had to quarter the town for you, eh? And now there'll be no running.'

'Pray, what business have you with me?' Folland asked seriously, genuinely.

'You have no business with me, and that's what I'll have to teach you,' George snarled, more the hound himself now than the huntsman. 'Keep your nose out of what's not your business. I warn you—you're a traitor, you'd have us all hanged.'

Folland looked at him. He could not remember having spoken with George Place before. His attitude of surprise, his blank questing eyes, infuriated George, who screamed,

'You know what I mean. I saw you, everybody saw you, hob-nobbing with the soldiers and the Customs bastard. You've betrayed us all. There's a couple of hundred of pounds of good brandy you've lost us already, besides——'

George stopped. He was conscious of eyes on him, he knew that he had said things better not said in public, certainly not at a fair, things he might have to answer for to Pards even, though every man in town knew how they got their brandy cheap. It was the brandy speaking now. Brought up short in his speech, George looked for a gesture. He groped about a moment, then found on Crankley's counter a pewter bowl in which the butcher had been setting dripping over water. It was not yet solid, not all liquid. He flung it, bowl and all, into Folland's face.

Folland just stood there, still and quiet, grease trickling over his wig and coat and fine new waistcoat, soaking into the expensive silk. But he did not move. He could feel an overpowering anger come over him, at this wanton spoiling of his clothes. The fat had been hot enough to sting. Now, he told himself, as long as you do not move, then it can all be smoothed over, it can all come to a peaceable end. He remembered wild nights in camp. Let nothing be done that cannot be hidden after, as if it had not happened.

What it all meant he had no idea. He only knew that *something* had happened in the night, from the way the Dragoons had ridden out, from the weary Charley sitting in the School

97

House kitchen that morning, mud-covered and depressed, from a little undercurrent of whispering between lightermen and sailors and clerks. What, he had no idea, and he did not ask. It was none of his business.

'You betrayed us,' he heard George screech at him again, driven beyond all containing by this man standing like a log, this man who never did take the slightest offence, never did anything of his own initiative. 'And now I'll kill you for it, by God I'll kill you. Get up and fight or I'll kill you where you stand!'

George drew his sword, a long slender whip of steel, shining in the last sun of an early summer evening. It might have an ornate hilt, but the blade was real enough. He swished it through the air, men waited to hear it crack like a lash. 'Fight, damn you, fight! Have out that big sword from under your coat, that sword you're so proud to hide behind, and fight, or I'll kill you here like the coward you are.'

Only Folland in all that crowd knew that he wore no sword under his coat. Half the town was there behind the Pards, watching George stab within an inch of Folland's naked throat. Robert Folland said quietly, but plain, so that most men around heard, Carines and Gunver and Pontigarde heard.

'If I fight you, my lad, then I'll kill you for sure.'

'Then be killed yourself for sure, if you'll not fight, you coward,' George Place screamed. Josh Caddon, pressing his head between the Pard's elbows, saw him stab at Folland's chest, touch it, with a flick of the wrist tear open the cloth from breast to waist, and dance the blade away again. Folland also backed away. He groped behind him, and felt cold iron. His arm came up. He was holding, not a sword, but the big poker the butcher had used on his fire, a bar of black iron, three feet long, thumb thick.

George saw the flash of metal without knowing what it was. He stepped back, saw Folland advance his left foot, thought, I have him now. He lunged. Folland parried, crossing poker and sword below the hilt, pressing against the guard to force the sword away. He pushed it out and down, locking the poker against the curve of the guard. George pushed back against him, not thinking, feeling only his stubborn fury. It seemed to him all-important that he should overcome this strength that forced his wrist, his forearm, out and away. It took all his attention, drew his thought, he did not step back to disengage. But against the strength of Robert Folland's arm he could do nothing. The Dragoon pushed the sword away as if he were playing with a baby. And then, when the arm was forced back against the joint, the poker slammed horizontally backhanded to thud, squashily, into George's shoulder. The arm dropped like the limb of a doll, pivoting as on a pin. The sword rattled on the cobbles. George screamed in fury and in pain. He fell to his knee, clutched his left hand to his shoulder. Robert Folland only said,

'Quiet, you fool. 'Twas cold.'

Ned Grinton came forward and helped George to his feet, sliding his arm round the sound shoulder. Grinton helped George Place away into the crowd.

For a moment, Folland felt that the pressure was off him. He had done nothing he had not been forced to do. There was no one killed, nor even badly hurt : he had not heard bone splinter. It had been an act of providence that stopped him wearing his sword. 'If I had been properly armed, I would have him dead by now,' he murmured, aloud, wondered who had heard, looked around him.

No one could have heard. There was no one near him. Folland stood with his back to the trays of burning charcoal, the spit where the carcase still turned. But all about him, in a semi-circle, the nearest perhaps five yards away, stood the Pards, silent, grim. Small men they were mostly, thin and wiry, their hair curly and light brown like Folland's own, and their eyes blue. They were marsh men used to punts and light boats, living by cutting reeds for thatch and willows for baskets, by catching pike and otter, and by working lighters for anyone, except for Kettlestang. And they closed round Kettlestang's man, that had hurt their employer, the source of their brandy, all in those heavy boots, nailed.

Robert Folland held his poker. He looked round at the Pards. There were no swords against him. It was worse. They carried their own tools, sickles and reed hooks, short single-edged blades that would shear through willow branches. Or through flesh. With these they had faced the Dutch and even the Irish soldiers King James had sent to put down the rioting. Brandy eager, the Pards were, and it was the Places who brought them brandy, and found them a hundred ways of making a living. While there had been Lords of Loone, the Pards had followed the Endellions, blindly. Now they followed anyone who would pay them. The

Pards stood around Folland, and well back. One came forward, swinging his reed hook.

'All right,' Lew Key said, quietly, 'we'll have you now, we will. There be no Endellion to be Lord of Loone. So Place we follow, and Place you'll pay for.'

Folland looked round them, beyond them. He was frightened. It was like Malplaquet, when Cutler had trotted them up close to the French gun-line and they had waited for the blast. His blood ran chill again. Over the heads of the Pards he saw faces he knew. He called,

'Master Carines, help me! Master Gunver! Master Pontigarde, Bridgward, Dowgill, help me!' They did not move. 'What is the matter? I work with you. I drink with you, I throw dice with you. Come and help me! For the love of God, why do you not help me?'

And then he knew. It was none of their business. They were watching this as they would look at a man who dropped an egg in the street or stubbed his toe. They might laugh, or perhaps shake their heads in sympathy. But it was none of their business. He was not a Wrackham man. There was no help from them. This was a quarrel between outsiders. It was by accident that it was happening in Wrackham. It was none of their business.

Folland knew it, in a sick moment of despair. He swung the poker. It had the weight of a sabre, but not the balance. It had served against that light foil. But not against short chopping tools, rough bludgeons, several at a time. These men were not obsessed with being gentlemen. They would not fight according to rules. They would come in with feet and fists as well as weapons. And those boots were weapons to frighten anybody.

Robert Folland had his back to the glowing charcoal under the ox. It might keep a man from stabbing him in the back, but it would not stop the thrown log. And it was not like a wall he could lean against. It was a thing they would try to push him into.

'All right, then,' said the Pard again. 'We'll have you, soldier.'

And then, over Folland's shoulder came the creaky voice of Josh Caddon.

'I'll keep your back, sodger. Us what've been to the wars, us'll stick together. They'll keep back here, they will.'

And Folland heard the crack of a carter's whip, harsh tough leather, that could take the cheek off a man's face. It could clear a space of twenty feet. But not for long. There was nothing Josh could do except show that he was not a Wrackham man.

There was a clatter on Folland's right. He turned his head, quickly. Not a Pard, but a big man, in a smock, one of Kettlestang's carters from up the Down, a chalk farm man. He held the iron rake from the charcoal bed; the teeth glowed red. And another carter was close to him, holding the butcher's long slicing knife. Three, then?

Folland risked a glance round. Then he knew why the Pards came so delicately on their feet. They would not hew him to pieces, like Agag. There were three soldiers from the Black Bull behind the carters, men he could not tell by sight except by their clothes, but he had bought them beer once. They were unarmed, but a fourth was pushing his way through the crowd with their swords, panting with running. And there was a Dutch sailor with a belaying pin. Two lightermen, not Pards, with boathooks. No Wrackham men, but no more Pards. Folland twirled the poker and wished it were a sword.

Over the crowd, Folland saw others coming to him. Another lighterman, a couple of Finn sailors with long knives, grinning like the Pards. And, then, coming by the Abbey Gate, a solid group, a dozen at least, slight black-haired men, sallow faced— Folland knew these by name, Baker Alley, Taffy Sarsen, Homer Blackmer, others of that close-knit group of families. And they carried better steel than pokers.

Suddenly Folland realized there was a small army at his back, or at least a company. As many as the Pards, any rate. They faced the Pards across the market square. The Wrackham men had melted away to the shelter of the houses. The market people scurried about, trying to take down their stalls, hide their goods —but there was at least one pedlar now behind Folland, with a hollywood staff, a steel spike on the end. There was quiet now, a quiet he remembered from the hour before the assault at Malplaquet. This was a silence that was like home to him. A sweeter sound than music. Now Robert Folland knew where he was. He shifted his grip on his poker, and looked round in pride at his supporters. This was a game, wasn't it? The Pards who were not Wrackham men, against all the rest of the world—and the Wrackham men standing aside. And the Wrackham market place for the fight to rage in, and the Wrackham windows to smash in, the Wrackham doors to batter down. Folland looked at his enemies and laughed. He took a step forward. The leading Pard stood still where he was, not coming forward, but not going back either. It was a grasshook he had. Folland began to think how he would deal with that sickle. With a sword it would be easy. And—suddenly he had a sword. Young Benny Alley came running with it, sheathed and almost as tall as himself, from the School House, where Liz Alley had sent him.

And now Robert Folland knew what was his business. He turned his back on the Pards, deliberately, to draw his sabre from the scabbard that Benny held for him. He left the scabbard in the boy's hands, and with precision saluted him, the sword reached out to the right, raised above his head, then the blade to his lips, down to his side again. And he turned on the Pards.

Another step forward, and still Key did not move. Folland thought, he would soon settle this trash. A third step forward and they would be in contact, the two mobs launched at each other in the empty market place. He hoped the soldiers, if no one else, would have the sense to back him close. There was no one left to interfere but the ox on its spit.

It was dead quiet. Both sides stood still. Well, if they are waiting for us, thought Robert Folland, they will not wait long. But at the edge of his attention, he could hear on the cobbles shuffling steps, dragged feet. The Pards were looking past him. Folland did not turn his head. He saw them come out of the corner of his eye, saw them walk between him and the Pards. It was James Place, his hand on Parson Quernhow's shoulder. The two men moved slowly between the two lines, ready for the riot. Place's light blue eyes, clouded, almost sightless, moved from side to side, questing, seeking. Quernhow stopped, murmured into the Alderman's ear, nodding to one side and then to another. And Place turned first to the Pards, to his own followers, and said, not loud, but firm,

'Go home. It is done. The fair is over.'

The line of Pards hovered a moment, broke, melted away towards the Northgate. As they went, Place turned again to the men from outside the walls.

'Go to your homes!'

And Folland went.

10

'It was as if a veil had been taken from my eyes,' Folland told Newall. They were in a coffee house, near the Strand. It was not chance. Robert Folland knew where Newall would be, sitting in the little stall, doing business as if he had never been on the edge of bankruptcy. 'It was as if I had been asleep for—for months, near a year, ever since that man stabbed me in the thigh. Was there a poison, d'ye think, on the prong? Or did he let all my manhood out?'

'Those months lying in Chelsea, struggling with death, would have let the manhood out of anybody.' Newall was sympathetic. ' 'Twould have been a wonder if you had come out of it a whole man or a well one.'

'But it was more than that. I was blind. I could not see what was going on. All that town, and the Burgesses so bound to each other, so centred in their little world, that outsiders are less than the dust. We can work, we can be used, but we do not matter— we do not count. While the Wrackham men—they are all related, so that there's not a marriage in the place that is not incest, nor a blow struck that is not fratricide. They take notice only of each other. And—' Folland spoke low, earnest, 'I *will* be taken notice of.'

Newall watched him with interest. This was not the inert messenger he had known. This was a man who had ideas of action. He asked, as offhand as he could manage, 'Then you will be leaving Kettlestang?'

'No, not yet. I am so complicated in my affairs already, and I do not know whether I am worth two hundred pound or whether I owe him money.'

'In his books, that is?'

'In his books. There have been dealings I cannot follow.'

'Be careful. I do not know what kind of a miller Kettlestang is but as a book keeper there is nothing I would put beyond him.'

'Nor I. But that is something I must talk of with you. Kettlestang cheated you over that ship, the *Norman Pride*. When you were so worried about whether she were lost or no, Kettlestang knew she was safe. He knew she was in Dublin. He sold the cargo and made a great profit. And he persuaded me to venture part of the money he was sending you, so that I show a profit in his books. He has cheated you, Master Newall, and I have been a party to it. I must clear my conscience.'

'Are you mad?' Newall stared at Folland as if there were no two answers to that question. 'You say that Kettlestang sold the *Norman Pride*?'

'Or at least her cargo.'

'How do you know?'

'He told me. And he has allowed me credit on my share—he paid me some of it in real money.'

'Kettlestang told you? It's just as well you found me in this tavern where the Poole Captains come to look for cargoes, and the man I want is here—not that a dozen others might not be of the same service, for the thing was notorious and we thought only how to keep it secret from Kettlestang. Here,' and Newall stood up, called a man from another stall in the coffee house. 'Captain Kitchin, come and tell this gentleman about the *Norman Pride*!'

'The *Norman Pride*? Oh, that was a bad business.' Folland was used to sea captains by now, was not overawed, did not scorn him either. 'I saw her strike. That was on the Tusker. I were outbound from Bristol, and the winds were very bad from the sou'west. And we saw the *Norman Pride*, not two mile ahead, and coming between us and the shore as she tried to beat across it, and I said to my mate, she's too near the cliffs. And just as I says it, strikes she do on the Tusker, and we watches her break up. And the people in her, they goes down into two boats, and one we picks up, with about seven men in her. But the other was overset by the sea, and they was all lost. Still, that's how I know that it was the *Norman Pride*. I carries on, and come round the Lizard and up into London, as I was bound, and I comes in here and I tells the tale, not telling nobody till then because I knows Master Newall were heavy committed in the ship. And 'twas all the gentlemen here that did counsel me urgently to keep silence, for Master Newall thought he knew of a gull to sell the cargo to, she being lost already.'

'And I sold it,' Newall said triumphantly, 'to Kettlestang, and that letter I always counted a masterpiece of writing, to be counted with Lyly or Shakespeare for wringing the tears from his heart, if Kettlestang had a heart, which we who know him so well beg leave to doubt.'

'There's a tale,' Kitchin reminded Newall, 'that in his youth, if he ever had a youth, he was sore in love with a maid against her father's will, but while he was still pondering what to do, there was one man of the town did cuckold him and have her first, and yet another did marry her in front of him. So 'tis sure he was counting the cost all the time, if it ever happened, which I doubt.'

'You see,' Newall told Folland, 'I did cheat Kettlestang roundly, selling him my rights in that ship when I knew she was lost.'

'But he told me he had cheated you.'

'Oh, he was boasting. Do you think he would have told you I had bested him?'

'And lost four hundred guineas on it? And he has paid out nine times my stake to me. And far more to Master Pontigarde,'

'You saw the payment made to Master Pontigarde?'

'No.'

'But, 'tis in the books?'

'I have not seen it.' Folland looked puzzled. 'The ship dealings are in one of the foreign trade books, and many of those Master Kettlestang keeps himself, and I do not see. I only see the books of his dealing in the town—money lending and such.'

'That is strange. But do you not see the hold he thinks he has on you? First, there is money he owes you—on paper. He does not believe you will leave him, or betray him while he holds money of yours.'

'But that he has already told me. He said he wanted me to have too much money in the firm to be capable of being bribed.'

'And he thinks that you will be too fearful of the law, or too troubled in your conscience to let this be public. Therefore you will not leave him lest he tell others that you are willing to cheat. He did not count on such a tender conscience as you have. You are too honest to make a business man, Master Folland.'

'Let me tell you, Master Newall, I am not such a slave to conscience as all that. I would not have told you if it had not been for last Saturday. If there had been any help coming from

Wrackham men, I would have been faithful to the Portreeve. But there was never one of them would help me. I saw clear what I was against.'

'And that was?'

'The Town. I felt I was there, with all the other out-of-Wrackham men, to be a show for them, to fetch and carry, and be convenient. Just as I am convenient to Master Kettlestang.'

Folland and Newall walked by the river. It was a hot day, and they sweated under their wigs. A stench rose from the water, and another stench came in the streets. And the people themselves stank, Folland noticed, as if he had never known it before, and they covered themselves in scent to hide the stink, which no one in Wrackham did : Prisca did not.

'What will you do?' Newall asked him. 'Will you work on for Kettlestang? I suppose you must go back with the errands you have done on this visit. But then, what? Will you leave him at once? Or work out the half-year's money he owes you, and then leave? Would you want to come to London? I know many would offer you employment. Think of all the bankers you have been talking with on Kettlestang's business, where you have carried messages he preferred not to have on paper. They will jump for you. You don't know your own worth.'

Folland laughed. 'My own worth? Maybe I don't know my own name, but by God, Master Newall, I know my own worth well enough. I will tell you what I am worth, and it is more than every man in Wrackham put together, for not one of them has ridden at a gun-line as I have, or lived rough as I have—not one of them has commanded men in danger of death. And let me tell you, that is a situation which teaches a man to think. And I have been thinking.'

'What have you been thinking?' Newall was curious. This, he thought, is not a man to be disregarded.

'I have been thinking and talking. There is a friend I have, a clerk at the Horse Guards. He was one of Mr Cardonnel's clerks when he was Quartermaster to the Duke in the Low Countries. And there was something he told me. . . .'

Robert Folland paused. Newall waited, had to ask,

'What?'

'It would be worth the paying for.'

'Perhaps, if it is worth . . . I *might* pay.'

Folland laughed. 'I am not a buyer and seller of secrets for ha'pence. I am a man of business. If there is no profit in it, I will get nothing. Take it unseen, Master Newall, and agree first. I am an agent. Give me . . . ten per cent of your profits, if any, and let me see your books.'

'And if there is no profit?' Newall probed him.

'Then there is ten per cent of nothing. And we will have a memorandum of this, in writing.'

They struck hands on it. Folland sat in Newall's house and wrote out the agreement himself, two copies. He sanded the ink, then he told his secret. Newall whistled.

'That is what I have always wanted. A quick turnover and a large profit.'

'How much can you put into it?'

'How much can I raise? I think I can promise this—at the end of the summer you will be a man of substance.'

'That is what I want. For, Master Newall, I want to buy a farm.'

Newall's wife served them supper. It was worth while for Newall to open first one bottle and then another of wine.

'And none of Jemmy Place's bringing in, either,' laughed Folland.

'Place? What Place?'

'No, 'tis a wine merchant, in Wrackham. I tell you, Will'—they were on short name terms now—'that there is something going on in Wrackham. There are strange things done in the night, and whispering behind my back. In the end, I tell you I shall be taken notice of. I *will* be taken notice of. But first I will take the notice. I am going to see who does what in Wrackham. It is none of my business'—and Folland laughed at the remembered words—'none of my business, and that is why I will busy myself with it.'

He drank again of the Spanish wine, and as he looked into it, he was again looking down on Wrackham from Staddle Down. The whole town lay open before him, clear and sharp. He had looked down into a pool in the stones at Bratton. Wrackham moved under his mind's eye like the crabs in that pool. And he thought, I shall have you, I shall hold you all in the hollow of my hand, because I am not one of you and I care for you not at all. And I shall bring you down.

'So you will go *home* to Wrackham?' He heard Newall's voice from very far away. He tried to bring himself back from the top of the Down, and could not quite do it. He heard his own voice far away, far away.

'I have no home in Wrackham, not now.'

He had gone back to the School House after the affair in the Market Place. He had his naked sword tucked under his arm, and the soldiers had marched with him, in case the Pards should try again. But nothing had happened. The soldiers had wanted to parade around town, looking for Pards, since they were sure there were still a few lurking, but Folland would not have it. He had bought them ale and hot pies and waited for the dark, but if there was to be a fight, it could happen some other day. The sides would be even, then.

He had come to the School House, before he realized that anything had happened. He had his hand on the knocker of the door before he saw it was wrapped round with cloth—black cloth. A muffled knocker. It came straight to him, it was ten years and more since there had been knockers muffled in any house where he had lived. There had been enough dead in his world, but not decent and civilized like this. And the last time, it had been *his* mother : for her, the blinds had been lowered all over the house in the daytime, for her they had strewn rushes in the village street to keep down the noise of the carts. So now, he knew.

'I have no home in Wrackham,' he told Newall. 'The first thing I have to do is find somewhere to live.'

He had not needed to knock on the door, Charley must have been watching for him, anxious to avoid a scene. He had stood there barring the way, not welcoming, his weak mouth quivering and the tears not far to come. He held a bundle in his arms, all Folland's belongings. Clothes were there, and boots and the empty scabbard for the long sword.

'It's all there,' Charley said, as Folland searched through, found, at last, the prayer-book, slid it into the pocket of the coat he wore. 'Prisca says . . . Prisca says . . .' he could not bring himself to say all that Prisca had said, the self-blame, the passionate accusations. Her mother had died because Prisca was not there with her. It was her fault, and if so, then it was Robert's fault.

So there was no place for Robert there, not any more. Just seeing him there would remind her how selfish she had been, going running off into the fair, not caring about her mother and leaving her to die alone. And now Prisca was alone, with all those boys to look after; to that she could see no end. And *him* to look after too, still in the Falcon, most like, not bothering to come home for such a small thing as a wife dead, why, 'twas his second and he was used to it.

But Prisca did her father an injustice. Quernhow knew where he was. Often he had seen Arkengarth there, sitting still in his place in the empty choir, his head tilted as if he were listening to some angelic voice, to some message that no one else could hear. Arkengarth did not pray—at any rate, he did not kneel, his mouth did not move, he did not cry out in his sorrow. He only sat there listening.

Arkengarth was listening. It was, then, the end of eighteen years of something like happiness, something like stability, something like a home. The best a turned-out parson could hope for, a poor schoolmaster. He had wanted to weep, he had tried, but there was nothing to come. Nothing from him : only to him. And what came to him, perhaps someday if he were clever enough, if he could only catch it, other people might hear. On the boys' voices, they might catch it, or the poor jumble of fiddles and trumpets : but what would catch it properly he did not have— the great organ of his dreams. Still, what he could, he would. If he had been a Papist he might have written a Requiem, a great Mass of Lament. He knew how he would have treated the Creed, the Sanctus. But he was not a Papist, however he had suffered for that Papist King. He was an Englishman, and this was an English church. It would take time. It would not be ready for this funeral, nor for many months. He would have it written, ready, rehearsed, for some future Great Day of Judgement. He would have it done for when—when the Queen died. For then the whole kingdom would be in a state of flux, as his soul was now.

'I shall turn them all into confusion,' Robert Folland told Newall. 'I shall bring a judgement on all these conceited men of Wrackham and leave them weeping.'

Yet even now Arkengarth did not weep. He sat quiet in his pew and listened, while the Devil spoke in his ear. And it seemed to him that the Devil came in the form of Jacob Kettlestang.

11

To casual view, there was no change. Robert Folland had changed his lodging, men learnt, as they tried to seek him out for errands. For a few nights he slept at the Falcon. But he was now too used to comfort. He toyed with the idea of going into the Black Bull, where at least he would have some company. But would being so thick with the soldiers help his plan? And he had no plan yet.

No plan without a base secured, that was a good military maxim. And to secure a base? Strange, there was soon an excuse for a handy place to live.

Three days after Robert returned from London, he walked from the Falcon down to Kettlestang's house, and then behind his master to the Quay. He had already made his first visit to the Watermill. What the carters had told him had made him return to the Inn for his sword. It might do no good now, but at least it might add a reassuring touch. As they walked down to the Watergate, Robert told Kettlestang what he had found.

'There had been some effort made to force the yard gate,' he told the grain merchant. 'They had been at it with a crowbar, by the marks. They had not taken an axe to the wood——'

'They would have raised half the town,' Kettlestang cut in to explain. 'You have only to knock hard on the gate at midnight when the wind is in the south and you will wake me, let alone those who live nearer.'

'There was more that should have waked you,' Robert told him. 'They failed at the door, so they came over the wall, and broke the shutter on the counting house window. But the bars on the inside beat them. Had they not wasted time on the door, they might well have got inside before it was light.'

'If anyone had been sleeping here, they would have been caught.'

'If they had known anyone was sleeping here, they would not have come.'

'Were they from inside or outside the town? If they were inside they would have tried my house rather than the Mill.'

'The wall is no protection, Master Kettlestang. You could get over it in thirty places in two jumps. But you sleep in your house.'

They walked on in silence, Robert following Kettlestang's turns as he went the length of the Quay, then back again from the bridge to downstream of the old Watermill. He murmured, 'If I could get any of my people to sleep in the Mill . . .'

'There is no room,' Robert objected. 'There is your private room upstairs, and the counting house.'

'A man could sleep in the cottage.' It was at the corner of the Millyard, and had a door opening into the yard, and one on to the Quay.

'That is too valuable as a store for hay. I don't see how we would do without it,' Robert objected.

Kettlestang let the matter go by. It was three nights before the next attempt. This time, the intruders got over the high wall, and forced open the shutter on one of the counting house windows. But the bars had resisted them. They must have been surprised by the dawn coming up, before they had been able to do more than work the bottom end of one batten loose.

'There is no doubt, one night they will be inside,' Robert warned Kettlestang. He had not been prepared for the effect this would have. The man stood stock still, gaping at the broken wood, the splinters and the marks of tools. After a little, he recovered and said,

'What did they want? I do not keep money in there.'

'Perhaps not, Master Kettlestang. But who in town is sure of that but you and myself and Bridgward? You are a rich man, Master; there are tales told of that in the town. And if men believe you are rich, they will think there is money in any house you spend much time in.'

'Oh that was an evil day I left off living here, and moved into the town.' Kettlestang stood, shaking a little. 'But they would only have to look inside to see that there was nothing.'

'Nothing?' Robert smiled, waited just long enough, then said, 'There may be nothing in the counting house, but upstairs . . .'

'Upstairs? They would not go there surely. The door is always locked when we leave.'

'It's a locked door that tempts thieves. They believe you would not lock it if there were nothing there to safeguard.'

'But what is there?'

'I have seen a man hanged for stealing worse candle sticks

than you have there. And you keep wine in the cupboard—men steal drink anywhere.'

'But not in that room.'

'There is a good carpet there, and cushions. If a man really has nothing, then anything he can steal is a profit to him. I have been in such a state.'

'You have?'

'It was after Almanza. When you lose a battle, you lose everything. You feel to have anything at all is better. So you steal. Even as you run you steal. We ... I went into a church, I remember, and took a kind of surplice, that had lace on the edge. Dan Miller stole a cope, and we carried them a few miles and threw them away, because they were too heavy. Other men came in after us and found nothing so they broke the windows and made water on the floor.'

Kettlestang made a face. 'The stable lads could take it in turn to sleep in the cart shed.'

'It might be,' Robert agreed. They moved into the parlour. Kettlestang began to look through his letter books. Robert stood and watched. There was no hurry, he would not be going to London till the morning. Kettlestang would give him instructions as the day went on. He suddenly looked up, asked,

'You will be moving back into the School House? The funeral is over, and the place is serene again.'

Robert shook his head.

'I am no longer welcome there. I will stay at the Falcon. I am quite comfortable.'

Kettlestang's next remark was not what he had expected, certainly not what he had been inviting.

'Then you will not be taking Miss Arkengarth to another fair? That is a great pity, young Bob, that is a pity. Every young man ought to have a young woman to take a-fairing.'

Robert only smiled ruefully, shrugged his shoulders, said,

'Women change their minds.'

'There are other ladies in the town. We will see. You must have been having a sad life, young Robin, to have so little choice. Now, now ... let us see. For tomorrow ...'

It was three nights to London and back, if he stayed the shortest possible time. This time, Robert Folland made sure he was delayed; he had to stay over the fourth night. He met Newall in the same coffee house.

'How goes it?'

'Slow. I think the first step is yet to come. I have begun to make my plans.'

'Have you found out why he made you, one might say, a present of all that money?'

'I cannot ask him. You ought to come up to Wrackham, and talk to Kettlestang. Chew over old times with him, boast of your mutual coups.'

Robert rode back to Wrackham in mid-afternoon, not a usual time, and yet he had no usual time. He had seen to that. He appeared, silently, in the door of the Parlour, where Kettlestang sat. The grain dealer looked up at him, his face lined with anxiety. He spoke before Robert could open his mouth.

'They have been again. They have been into the counting house, and tried at this door.'

'When?'

'The night before last.'

'Did they get in?'

'No. But I think now it can only be a matter of time. They know the Mill is not guarded. They are bound to succeed. It is plain they are determined to get into this room.'

'You will have to set a guard. Employ a watchman.'

'I have asked the carters, but that was a mistake.'

'Why?'

'It may have been one of them. Or the thieves could get a carter in league with them. Or they could bribe him.'

Robert said nothing. Oh, now we see the great man of Wrackham, the Portreeve, that knows his own workers so little that he does not think he could trust them. He does not know them even as well as I do. He waited. Kettlestang said, bitterly,

'I am not a Place, or a Lord of Loone, to have a pack of Marsh Pards to follow at his heels like dogs. I am an honest man. I do not know where to turn.'

Robert Folland only asked,

'Do you not want to hear the news from London?'

'No, no, that can wait. We must make this place safe somehow.'

'Then you could move back to live here, as you used to.'

'No, that's out of the question.'

'Or we could move the books and papers up to your house

113

every night. And empty this room, so you could entertain your ... visitors in your house.'

'No, that would mean too much moving about and carrying. The only thing is for someone to sleep in the cottage.' He looked sharply at Robert. 'You might well consider living there yourself.'

'When I came,' Folland reminded him, 'you said you would have no one but yourself live in your house. Had you asked me to live in then, I would have refused. I want a little space to myself.'

'But the cottage would not be the same thing at all as living in. It would be yours all to yourself, and you could come and go as you wish.'

'I live in the Falcon now with no labour of my own. I am not a great hand with a broom.'

'No, if you live here, Nance Hartsop could come in here every morning and set all straight for you.'

'But I would still be at charges for my food.' Robert caught at himself, told himself he must not press too far, it was out of character. Would he have been so demanding even a week before? Since then he had seen that first deal made. Six thousand greatcoats ordered for the army, for regiments not in the end raised, and so, by a stroke of a clerk's pen, to be sold off cheap as dirt. And Newall to buy them, on the grounds of what a man could pick up who had friends at the Horseguards, and talked to Swedish ship captains. Six thousand more greatcoats to go marching into Russia on Swedish backs. Fifty guineas to the clerk, to keep him sweet and be sure there would be other chances. More than fifty guineas to Robert Folland, ten per cent of the profit, and the money in coin lodged with a goldsmith till he thought what to do with it next. Real money at his back, not just figures in Kettlestang's books, that was something that braced him. But he must not go too far.

'You do not think I would charge you rent to guard my property?'

What else were you meaning to do, thought Robert. But aloud, he said,

'Why, would you let me have it free? That would be kindness indeed. But 'tis not in a state to live in.'

'We can have the hay out in a day.'

'And then, we can see if it can be made ready for a man to sleep in.'

114

'You will do it, then?'

'Oh, we will find *someone* to do it.'

'But who will I trust?'

'There must be someone. Besides, remember I am not always there. What of when I go to London for you?'

'You do not go often. And even now, you slip away with little warning, and no knowing ever when you are coming back. How would anyone depend that you would not be there?'

Robert laughed. 'If you offer a house rent free, there will be a hundred will want to come live in it.'

'But not a house with a door in the Millyard.'

They left the subject. The rest of the day was spent in entering up the results of the latest London affair into the books. Outside, seven men struggled with the hay. After the end of the day, Robert went, not to the Falcon, but for a change to the Black Bull. He asked Freeman for news.

'News? You've come from London, I'd have thought you would have all the news.'

'Nothing happened at all?'

'Oh, well, we had an officer here yesterday. Not in much of a humour, he wasn't. He were robbed where he left the London Road, watch and purse and two good pistols all gone.'

'Who did that?'

'How should anyone know? I don't think it was anybody around here, myself. I think it was one of the gentry going to London. Still, we had to take a section out and sweep the road. Wonder we didn't pick you up.'

'I came later.'

They sat a little, looking at the lighters moored in the river. Then Robert asked,

'How is Mr Perkins?'

'Now, there's another thing. Any time he feels like it, he do call on us to go and sit out on the marsh all night. And not enough of us to do that and sweep the road.'

'Short, are you?'

'Five men here below the establishment.'

'Recruiting?'

'Are you offering yourself?'

'You've more sense than that.'

'I suppose I have. But a man or two would come very handy. If you could find any—I'd share the bounty.'

' 'Twould be on my conscience. But not for long. They say there may be peace any minute. They'll be cutting down regiments then.'

'But not yet. We're still wanting soldiers ourselves.' Freeman puffed a while, then added, 'You've heard, Colonel Cutler's sold out.'

'What, sold the Regiment?' Robert was surprised, and yet could not think why. He admitted, aloud, 'He's had it for near on seven year. It were Barnard's when I joined it. He was my first squadron commander. What's he doing?'

'I did hear, he was a-coming back to his own place somewhere around here. Staddle House, they said, over the crest of the Down. That'd put old Shillmoor's nose out of joint.'

Robert said no more about it. Instead, he thought. The situation was complex. Cutler was a new factor. He might serve to simplify things, a celebrated cutter of knots : but with any luck, he might make them so tangled . . . Robert could see what he could do. He called for more ale, set himself to make a night of it. He would return to the Falcon late. The Constable might shut and bar the water gate at dusk, but out of the Black Bull's yard, three steps up in the holes of the wall and he was in the town—in Obadiah Bridgward's back garden, too. And that might be useful.

In the morning, Kettlestang returned to the theme.

'Would you not come to live in the cottage, Rob my lad?'

'It is not fit to live in, Master Kettlestang.'

'No, boy, come and see what it is like now the hay is out.'

Robert looked at the place with a critical eye. The roof had not leaked to spoil the hay. Now the earth floor was swept clean. There were two rooms, and a ladder to the attic. One door opened on to the street, another into the Millyard.

'I have not slept on the floor since I was in Chelsea Hospital,' Robert remarked, grudgingly. He did not think it politic to make a firmer promise. If Kettlestang would not go as far as he wanted this time, he could always leave it, and Charley would do the rest in a night or two. It would be easier, now the cottage was clear, to get into the yard.

'Oh, we can have a bed in here.'

'I do not own a bed,' Robert said coldly.

'I can let you have furniture,' offered Kettlestang. 'A bed, a chair, a table——'

'Two chairs. A man cannot sit alone,' Robert objected.

'Oh, aye, two chairs, three if you like. I have them spare,' Kettlestang insisted.

'Yet, 'tis not a very cheerful place. The plaster is peeling from the walls.'

'Oh, we will have a plasterer in. Nay, better, to keep out the wind, and make the whole somewhat nearer to your dignity, I shall have an upholsterer in, and both these rooms panelled in pine.'

Robert raised his eyebrows. This was more eagerness than he had bargained for. He might as well have a pine floor laid too.

'I will need a cupboard.'

'Naturally. And something to hang your clothes in. And a pot or two, in case you would wish to make yourself a dish of tay, or mull your ale. There is a pump in the yard.' Kettlestang's eyes sparkled. 'Oh, that I had had such a chance when I was a young man, to lie snug in a place of my own, and not to worry that my father would hear all I did. Oh, you are a lucky young Robin, indeed.'

'*If* I should come here.' Robert Folland pressed home his advantage. I see what it is, he thought, he has so entangled his mind with the picture of myself lying here, and confused it with what he wished he had been, that there is now no denying him. And he does not count the cost. Aye, I will have a floor here, and a piece of Turkey carpet over it yet.

The next day, the panellers were in, and Robert Folland was on the way to having his floor. He saw to it himself. Of course, it was not finished in one day. Folland and Bridgward together saw that the outer door was locked, so no one could come into the yard by way of the cottage, and let themselves out into the Quay.

'Come and have a wet in the Bull,' Folland urged Bridgward.

'That be Rupert Staffield's house,' observed Bridgward. 'His father's father was a great King's man in Oliver's time. Not that it brought him any good, though. And them soldiers don't make his trade any more select.'

'You wrong the company. Sit here, and taste this yale. Have you ever drank any that were kept better? He brews his own, too, and the last in the town, almost, that does that. All the rest do buy from Shillmoor.'

'Then that be why Shillmoor quarters the soldiers here, to see he pays his duty,' Bridgward pontificated. 'So you be the Gaffer of them all, then?'

'Gaffer? That's a strange sound of it, but I suppose you may say that,' Freeman agreed, sitting down with them. 'Now, that's hardly a start. Bring us another pint apiece. Now, doesn't that hearten ye? I can't understand how ye sit so long in the Falcon over that gnat's brew.'

'Oh, 'tis the company there. No offence meant,' Bridgward added hastily, ' 'tis not a matter of liking, but there's often business to be done in that kitchen. For real company, cheerful, I dare say there's none like a good crowd of soldiers, all singing away like they are now. Oh, but I often think it would have been a fine thing to have been a soldier, if I had been bred to the strength for it.'

'Oh, you have the strength for it. Come some time in the day, and we will let you try the exercise of arms.' Freeman caught Robert's eye : the other shook his head. 'Now, off you must be back to your missus.'

Bridgward rolled off into the night. That was something for Robert to remember. The Clerk might do well enough on a pint of Shillmoor's ale sipped slowly through the evening. But two quarts of home-brew, and he might be . . . irresponsible? He was well enough next morning. They had a cart up to Kettlestang's house, and put the bed on it, and the rest of the promised furniture. No carpet, but that, thought Robert, will come.

Kettlestang was beside himself, giggling like a schoolboy. He might have been furnishing for his bride, the Dragoon thought. I have met men—but he is none of those. He would have shown it earlier. He has played into my hand, not but what I helped him a good way along the road. But that he should travel it so readily, why, 'twas almost a miracle. A base the Dragoon had now for operations. The plans, half made, could proceed.

12

Or had Kettlestang plans, too? It still worried Folland. Why had he been handed those two hundred pound, for nothing? Just to hold him in his place, a bonus promised against good behaviour, perhaps never to be paid? But it was there, in the books, and Robert Folland was here, in the Cottage, next to the books. Not all of them. Some were in Kettlestang's house, and there was no getting in there. But from the cottage into the Mill House, even in the dark, was an easy step, and to someone who knew just where every ledger was, no problem about getting them back into the cottage, where there was a candle.

So there was little sleep for Robert Folland. For night after night he sat and worried over the books, traced again the intricate pattern of loans and bargains. This town was a cobweb, he thought, and a spider in the centre, attracting flies to him. All the flies? There were names that did not appear. Never a mention of Place, father or son? Were they perhaps hidden somewhere in a secret place of the web? And never a mention of Colonel Cutler—till here. A fortnight after Robert moved into the cottage, there came a solitary line in the day book, a record of a payment by a draft on a goldsmith in London : *From Coll. Cutler, in payment of debt, three thousand pounds.*

Where it came from was obvious. Cutler had sold out, and would have had money now to spare. But why was he is debt in the first place? The money had been cleared from the day book, was marked 'entered in the private book' in Kettlestang's hand. That was not unusual. Folland thought on it, smiled. Cutler had a house on Staddle Down; perhaps he had mortgaged it to buy his regiment. Common enough.

And the entry in Kettlestang's hand was genuine. Folland knew all the writing in the books, Kettlestang and Bridgward, and the clerks, Caldbergh, Azerley, Darnbrook. He could recognize them all. Kettlestang could recognize them too, could he? Let us see, thought Folland.

He sat for long nights with the quill pen. He had watched these men in the counting house. The first thing about each was the way he trimmed his quill. Kettlestang so, and Bridgward, a different cut at the tip. And Azerley was left handed and trimmed his quill with that hand, but wrote right handed and awkwardly. Folland went no further till he could change the pens in the counting house overnight, and see each man write with a pen he had not trimmed and not see any difference.

Now, if the pen were right, it was a great help that each of them had the same writing master, Arkengarth. Letters formed on the same model for each : it was simple. These books were easy. The same words, only a few, repeated again and again. And the figures.

In five weeks, Folland could do it. He could finish a man's work for him in the night, so he would not notice in the morning that there were five extra lines in the book. But before he was that good at it, he had ridden over the Down to Bratton to catch a ship. For once he had not stopped to drink with the Dutchmen, or eat with Perkins. Instead he had come back in the middle of the afternoon, and then turned out of his way to Staddle House, a long low mansion of crumbling stone, once a grange to Wrackham Abbey.

He had ridden to the front door. He nerved himself for that. told himself they were neither of them soldiers any more. He told his name to the flunkey who answered his knock.

'Tell the Colonel that Master Robert Folland is here on private business.'

It sounded fine enough. The flunkey went, returned, ordered Robert to follow him into the depths of the mansion, to somewhere near the back, where Colonel Cutler sat in a small close room, full of the smell of oil and powder, filing at the sear of a flintlock trigger, to make it the lighter on the finger for snipe shooting. He was wearing a shabby old waistcoat and his greasy campaign nightcap. He looked, Folland thought, ten years older than last year in Flanders. Perhaps it has happened to us all, Robert thought. Have I aged too? Was I too old and terrible for Prisca? Did I terrify her? But he had decided he would never think of her, so he did not. It was too late now, it hurt too much.

'Well, my sergeant? What is it I can do for you?'

'There is nothing I require, sir. I have called to pay my respects and to thank you for what you have already done.'

'What have I done, then?'

'Was it not due to you I got this position with Master Kettle-stang?'

'Have you come to reproach me with it?'

Folland looked at his Colonel with curiosity. He had never been so defensive, so apologetic before, with no excuse. Perhaps without his red coat, his gorget . . .

'The position suits me very well, sir, so far. I think I am beginning to prosper.'

'I hope it will last. Do not build too much on it, Folland, do not build too much.'

'I think I know where I am, sir. I have a part in the making up of Master Kettlestang's books, and I see what is done.'

'A part?'

'I do not see all. But most of the business. I see enough to know I am safe.' Surely that was what Kettlestang wanted him to think. But what did Cutler want him to think? Robert was sure, now, that the grain merchant did nothing by chance.

'Then be sure you remain so. Now, will you have a glass of something with me?'

'Thank you kindly, sir.'

The something was gin and water. A change from the old yale, thought Robert, but a drop of brandy would have been more to taste. More body in that, and more colour, too. But he knew better than to expect brandy here. He ventured the observation,

'There be a lot of spirits come in here, sir, with no fuss about customs, or so they say.'

Cutler snorted.

'Disloyalty! 'Tis not so much evasion of duty that I dislike, but buying from those French dogs. Not that I like Portugees much better, but they're legal, at least, and so is this stuff. Don't drink any more of it. Pour it out of the window. Marl! MARL! Bring us a bottle of port, Marl, and two glasses.'

Marl, the Colonel's butler, appearing for the first time, opened his eyes wide at Robert; then, knowing his master, brought not one bottle but four, one opened, and left a corkscrew. Robert savoured the sweet port, smooth and soothing after the raw spirits. He accepted the pipe offered him, lay back, filled his lungs with the smoke, and suddenly seemed to float outside himself and see what was happening, see it clear for the first time. And seeing it, he coughed in surprise and spluttered as if smoke and port had exchanged paths. That he, a sergeant, should be sitting at his ease with his colonel showed what peace did to a man. Or what Master Kettlestang's man rated in the Colonel's eyes.

For it *was* peace, for them, he had to tell himself. He was no longer a sergeant, but a man of business, and Colonel Cutler, for all his money that he must have made from selling out and that he was a Justice of the Peace just like Shillmoor, what was he but another farmer? A bigger one, maybe, than Hod Blackmer that was so near to losing land and house in one stroke if the barley failed; but still, a farmer was no more than a man of business, selling what he made to merchants like Kettlestang, and through him to the brewers. And the good ale sent out to the troops in Flanders, and the biscuit too, had nothing to do with Cutler or Folland.

So the two men of business gossiped about the barley and the rain and the price of corn and whether it would go up or down this harvest time. And it seemed now and again as if Cutler were about to tell Folland something, but he never did. So when that bottle was finished, and it was four glasses to the Colonel and two to Folland, the Dragoon took his leave.

Robert Folland walked behind the butler towards the door of the house.

'I've sent the boy to catch the hoss. He's in the paddock,' the butler said. Then as they stood on the porch, looking at the comic scene where the lad could not run as fast as Tiger nor think as fast either, Marl changed his tone, his voice. 'Sarge. Sarge! What be ye up to, Sarge?'

'I'm not up to nothing, Lemmy.'

'Oh, yes, you be, Sarge. Look, wasn't I his batman all the years you was his trumpeter and then a corporal and all the time after that you carried his letters? I seen your eyes like that afore, Sarge, and it were always something you were up to.'

'Not now, though, Lemmy.'

'Aye, now, Bob. I mind that time we went out at night down to the gun park, and them fusiliers didn't keep good guard. And we stole all their breeches when we was cruel short of breeches. What be ye short of now, Bob, boy?'

Folland regarded Marl, critically. Was it so obvious, then?

'How many of you are there?'

'Out of the Regiment? Oh, not more than three or four. But if you wants more . . .'

'I might.'

'I could find you . . . oh, a dozen lads, game for a lark.'

'Horses?'

'Aye. Not riding horses, mind you, but shires out of the carts.'

'And guns? A few fowling pieces? Not to use but to make the moon shine on the barrels? And feathered hats?'

'For a whole army, then? An army of dragoons? I've known you do that before. Ride 'em round and round, eh?'

'Could the Colonel . . . asleep, perhaps?'

'I knows Shillmoor's butler. I'll have him there for his dinner.'

'I may think of a better way. But there'll not be much warning. I depend on others.'

'And not saying nothing, eh, Bob?'

'You've not named a price.'

'I'll come for a bit of fun. And the rest will come because I tells 'em to.'

'Oh, there'll be a drop or two and to take away.'

Folland had no clear plan in his mind yet. But he had a tool. The plan would come. The horse had come, too. He swung himself up on to Tiger.

'Aye,' went on Marl, 'that's how I remembers ye. Best seat in the Regiment you had. You going to chase him?'

'Chase him? The boy's been doing that.'

'No, you don't understand. They do have a race every September, as soon as the barley's in, out of Wrackham, round through three villages to the pole the Marsh Pards puts up on the Down that time every year, and down again.'

'The beast's got no speed. He's a long goer, but he can't run.'

'Don't need to run. That race be over eight mile. You think about it. Colonel Cutler be going to ride, and a lot of the gentry, but that be for the excitement. Do you race that hoss, Bob Folland, and we'll make enough money out of the betting boys to drink all night.'

'I'll ask Master Kettlestang.' Robert was decided that he would do no such thing. But, looking down, he thought to ask, as a last word,

'You a Wrackham man, Lemmy? You a Burgess?'

Marl did not even shake his head. He only spat. It was answer enough.

It was a fine hot day in early summer. In Wrackham it would be intolerable. The heat would be beating off the walls. The ramparts were a walk of, perhaps, two miles from Northgate back to Northgate, and inside that tiny space five thousand people lived and defecated and died. Prisca Arkengarth went yet again to the well in the School House yard, and pumped up water for the boys. She did not feel this a labour. She had been doing it most of her life, and when she stood at the well she could look over the fence to where her mother lay. She could almost touch the grave from where she worked the pump. If her arm was as long as Robert's, she could have touched it, she thought —and then remembered she must not think about him. Although she thought about him most of the time. And sometimes, of an evening, when her father was in the Falcon, she would wrap herself in her red silk shawl and dream. She was not disturbed. Father Krantze the organ builder who had Robert's room sat with Arkengarth in the Inn and they talked of music.

Ten miles away, on the Heath, by a thicket of unripe hazel nuts, Robert Folland faced a highwayman. Charley Arkengarth made the introductions.

'The gentleman will not be alone?' Captain Taberon asked. The rank, if not the name, was assumed, but everyone on the road knew who he was, what he was capable of. Now Folland would find if the man were capable of keeping his word. Taberon measured the ex-Sergeant with his eye, the height of him, the hard lines about his jaw, the steadiness of his eyes, the way he used few words. Taberon decided that now, for once, he would be trustworthy. Especially when Folland answered, 'He will be alone, yes, as a man rides alone. But he will be watched and covered. He must not be harmed. I promise you he will not resist.'

'He will be protected? But what about me?' asked Taberon.

'You will be protected, too,' Robert assured him. 'There is nobody in this business who is without protection—except myself.'

Sitting in the gallery of the Place house, Sophia jerked her hands and sent the cards flying across the blue cloth. She had been playing a complex Patience, that required two whole packs and three jokers. In seven years it had never come out. It seemed to her that she had been playing Patience for seven years, just playing Patience and waiting for marriage, not marriage to anyone but just a marriage. There had been this marriage and that marriage mooted but the Patience had never come out, for this suitor had been too old, and that one more crooked than even Doctor Wormset could cure, and another so ugly that there would be no hope of handsome children, and one ill-tempered in drink, or so her father said, for Sophia herself had never seen a one of them. It was not her affair. She knew what would happen—she would search the orchard and find the crab. Not if she could help it.

Now, there was a fine pippin ready to fall ripe into her hands. This was a man, at last, handsome and young and strong. And clever—why, if he could bring her brother into ridicule twice, he was clever enough for her. Money—that was another matter. There would be money. She was not quite so sure now that he was Lord Wrackham : a Lord might have endured this labour for a week or two as a disguise, but not for these months. But if he were not Lord Wrackham, then there was no doubt that he was Kettlestang's heir. Perhaps not an heir by blood, but they said, in the streets, in the shops, that it was he now who did the business in the Mill House, the bargaining down to London that Kettlestang had always kept to himself. There would be money there, lots of money, and she would have it. But how?

For him to court her was difficult enough—she never doubted that he wanted to. He would have to approach her father, and what *he* would say she could not think. He would peer at her, as if she were no more than a dimly located cloud, and then screech his contempt, loud and long. And for her to court Robert, to attract his attention in some way, to speak first, or at all, to him, why it beat all her imagination as to how it was to be done.

13

Robert Folland stood dutifully, as was his wont, and waited while Kettlestang read the letters he had brought back from London. This was in the morning. His verbal report was different. He had delivered that in the night as soon as he had reached the house. He knew what knock to use. He was expected. Kettle-stang always examined him from an upper window, watched him put Tiger into the stall, before he came to the back door. And then he would be admitted, to make his confidential statements about the worth of the written things he carried, whether a man's word could be trusted, if looks supported an offer.

But on this, that Kettlestang waved at him, he answered that he had nothing more to say.

'He only came to me in the coffee house and gave it me.'

'You remember him?'

'Master Newall? Oh, yes, I remember him. You lent him—no, advanced him money that saved his fortune, or so they say.'

'You have not heard anything? What he is proposing now? What he is trading in?'

'I do not know. I have heard nothing. He is waiting for a ship to come home, and planning great impossible things.'

'It seems he is grateful for what I did for him. Look, my boy, he wishes to come here and visit me. He says he has a project I might be interested in. Have you no inkling what he is up to?'

'He did not tell me.' That was at least true, thought Folland, I told him.

'Well, it is not often that we have visitors like this coming from London. We will have to do something about it. I will have a Rout. I will give a Wine. We will have everybody in this house, and I will entertain them. I will have a reception, they shall come, all the Aldermen.'

Folland was taken aback. He had not expected this nervous activity, this sudden jumpy excitement. But Kettlestang moved about sharply as if he were playing with a ball. Indeed, he went on,

'We will have a ball indeed, a ball, there has not been a ball in the town this ten years.'

Robert Folland still looked at his employer with caution. How this would work out to his advantage he could not now see, but there would be some way.... He asked,

'In your house, Master Kettlestang?'

'In my house? There is not room for a ball in my house. We will have it here.'

'Here?'

'Aye. We will clear the floor and strew it with clean rushes, stow all the books in your cottage for the night, hang the walls with flags and curtains. I will buy candles enough to light Saint Paul's, and we will make the church band come and play for it. Do you think they know any dances? Or that they can learn any?'

Robert shook his head. 'I have no knowledge of their capabilities.' It was more and more an effort to retain the old sad self that had come to Wrackham.

'You can dance, of course?'

'Alas, I have not had the chance to learn.'

Kettlestang laughed, cackled. 'Then I will teach you, young Bob. We will have you dancing like an Easter sun. When is it he is coming? June the ninth? Then we will have our Rout the next night. And by then, I will teach you to dance.'

And that he did. Of a dinner time, when they stopped work and had finished the rabbit stew or the boiled beef and dumplings, Kettlestang would call Bridgward to bring out his flute, and stand on a chair at the end of the counting house. They would clear some of the stools and tables to one side, and while Kettlestang called out the steps, the three clerks and Robert Folland would go through one of the dances which had been, sometime or other in Kettlestang's youth, fashionable.

So, somehow, Robert Folland learned to dance, and that to Kettlestang's calling. But not again, he told himself, not again. I have other things to do, and other games to play.

But for his new games, Folland had to wait on George Place. That he was content to do. The word would come at the right time, on the night. He had his ways of telling, his ways of finding out. Some of them were simple. What Perkins did, surely Folland could do as well, or better. The first time, Folland was in London : nevertheless. he guessed what was coming, and when, by the cargoes that were moving on the river, by the way the Pards gathered ready in the lower taverns of the town, to which the Black Bull was a Palace, and the Falcon a Versailles. When Robert returned he could tell from the looks of the Pards that the Places had succeeded and run their brandy.

Perkins knew it, too, now. He stormed and swore at Freeman, at anyone handy to catch the fury. He railed, to the Sergeant, at Shillmoor and all local justices who were so mixed up with the smuggling they were supposed to put down. Freeman was sympathetic, but not really fully comprehending how a man could so wish to damage his own trade. Why should Shillmoor let the Pards bring in brandy when he could sell them gin?

He put the point to Perkins.

'Buy gin? What a thought,' the exciseman dismissed it. 'They'll never buy gin.'

'But if there be no brandy?'

'They'd never buy gin. For did you ever see a Pard with two halfpennies to rub together? They get nothing out of that Marsh but their bread, and not much of that. Game and baskets, that's all that comes out of the Marsh. And you don't know the Pards' way, either. 'Tis the Marsh women do hold all the money there, and decide what's to be bought. Them Pards are ruled by their wives, and there's not many women will spend their all for drink, as most men do, given the chance. So either they gets their brandy for their labour, or they gets none at all.'

'So you'll be looking for it?'

'And if I found a barrel of brandy in a man's cottage, how would I prove it was smuggled? And how would I catch them? It's *them* I wants, that runs it under my very nose.'

Freeman told this to Robert, as one sergeant to another, as they sat in the front room of the Black Bull, looking at the river. Robert stowed it away in his mind.

Newall rode into the town in the middle of an afternoon, a hot June afternoon, but he was hotter than the air or the sun that beat down. Going by the directions Robert had given him, he turned right from the Bridge along the Quay to the gate to the Mill House. He was not merely hot with the sun and the strain of riding : he was red faced and blistering with rage. He flung the reins at the boy who came to hold the horse's head as he got down on to the mounting block. Kettlestang came out of the counting house to meet him, his hand outstretched. Robert Folland sood behind, his face calm, unmoving. He forced himself to be placid : otherwise he would have laughed. Josh Caddon, fussing round with a blanket to throw over the horse, with fodder and water, heard Newall's opening words, a blast of invective. It was all round the town by sunset, Josh saw to that, and the bridgekeeper who had to wait for his toll till he could collect from Kettlestang.

He'd been robbed, they told everyone, that friend of the Portreeve's, he'd been robbed. The Gentleman had stopped him up there on the Heath, and pointed a pistol—no, two pistols it was, must ha' been, two pistols—at him. Thrust it—them—full in his face he had, near knocked his teeth into his throat with them, and left him in a state, shivering with fright and no wonder, it was not to be expected that a peaceful man should have to face something that made even soldiers blench. Enough to frighten a soldier, aye, even Folland had said that, old Josh had heard him, so it must be true. And robbed him of, well, it all depended who you listened to, a hundred guineas in gold, a fortune in diamonds, papers that were worth as much to the right buyer, why it was certain that this stranger was almost ruined, sure he must be by the way he was carrying on. And all his finery too that he had brung up special for Master Kettlestang's rout that all the town was talking about, if not working on, that everyone was toiling for and bringing in wine and glasses from the Places' warehouse. There was no work in the counting house that day, only a kind of general clearing up, a heaving of the desks to the side and, later on, near the end of the day, out into the yard and to store in one of the granaries.

The Counting House once cleared, it looked what it had always been under the dust, a fine large hall, a little low of ceiling perhaps, but for all that well proportioned, the walls of good stone that the monks of Wrackham Abbey had cut for a great tithe barn, and the watermill built on to it at the end as an afterthought.

On the day of the rout, the day after Newall had come, the clerks were all hard at work, and Robert Folland standing over them, cleaning out the room from end to end, carrying presses and stacking papers. The stable boys came with buckets and mops, to scrub the floor and the walls and lay the dust—Kettlestang regretted now that he had not started a day earlier, when there would have been time to whitewash the walls again. But in the candlelight they would serve. White was white. And the walls would not show all that much. He had brought in hangings, flags and sheets of bunting to make a gay colour all through the room.

There were barrels rolled in, empty, to stand at the end of the room, and planks put upon them to make a platform for the parish band. And others along the wall opposite the door, as a long table on which he meant to have the food spread, and the drink. For the Portreeve was determined that his guests would lack for neither. Aye, there would be magnificence here, Kettlestang could imagine it all, a rout such as no other Alderman of the town would ever have thought of giving. It would have him remembered in the place for generations. He became quite carried away. He forgot that the rout was to welcome Newall, to get him at a disadvantage in whatever undertaking he wanted to discuss, to impress on him how wealthy and powerful Kettlestang was, not to be disadvantaged by any little financial failing, by the loss of any one ship or a trifling fall—or rise—in the rate of the Stock.

For this was the Portreeve's first attempt to entertain on the grand scale. Shillmoor had done it, some years before, when he was first trying to be a Parliament man, and Grangier once at a son's wedding. But never Kettlestang. He had enjoyed being a guest at such fêtes : he had not realized that it was more exhilarating, almost intoxicating, to be the host, even in preparation. He could see it already. Perhaps the first time he had given a rout, but would it be the last? There were merchants in London who made a habit of it, who kept open house on known evenings in the year, in the month even, who—but they were all married, had wives to preside, to dispense their largesse. That was possible. After his plan was complete, perhaps the Portreeve would look round for a wife.

But it was not yet all over, it was hardly begun. Last night before their desks were picked up and tucked away, all his clerks had been engrossing invitations as carefully as if they had been writs for slander. Writing them by hand, and then in the dusk, carrying them around the town, Robert Folland sent to carry some out into the country on horseback. On Tiger, to look the bigger and better and make the greater impression. Newall, pleading fatigue, retired to the George Inn, and was no more seen. Kettlestang spent the evening at the White Hart, and went home late, and in liquor, to his lonely empty house, his cold and single bed.

That was the night. The invitations were hardly needed for the clerks had talked, the lists were spread well around the town. The gossip was spread even further. Dowgill, for example, knew all about it, and talked in his tap to Josh Caddon and anyone else who would listen. He jerked his head toward the Kitchen.

'Most o' them, even, he's got coming. Not just the Aldermen, oh no. He's got more coming than that.'

'Why's he want all them?' asked one of the Sarsens, another

small wiry man, with the added complication of one grey eye, one black. Dowgill laughed.

'It's a wonder he's not asked me. Look at it, now. He's been Portreeve for a whole term, five year already. That's a good place to have. Take your share of market moneys, the quay rents, the tunnage on every barrel and the pannage on every basket that comes out of the ships on the quay. And that's supposed to mend the quays and the stairs and keep the channel free. When did you ever see any quay mended before it were falling right into the river? No, them Aldermen do keep most of what's paid, and the Portreeve do get the lion's share. But there's more to pay when Parliament time come round. It may be that it's us Guildmen and Burgesses do elect the Aldermen, but the Aldermen elect the Portreeve, and with the Portreeve the Parliament men bargain for votes. Last time it were Shillmoor that did pay a guinea a head for us Burgesses : next time, they say that Cutler do want the seat, and there's a fine lot of argifying there'll be while old Kettlestang forces the price up. Thirty shilling us want next time.'

'If it's Kettlestang,' he was reminded.

'And who else would you want? For me, it's worth the Portreeve's share of the dues for him if he does what he did before. There's no harder man, nor no craftier in the whole town, and there's none of the other Aldermen can screw a harder bargain. Maybe I don't stand for much in the Vintners, but I've told Jemmy Place, and I told him to his face, that Kettlestang was the man for me.'

'But he's not asked you to his ball,' one of the wagoners sneered.

'Nay,' and Dowgill laughed. 'He's done better than that. He's paying me good money to be there, and to have the ale down in the counting house and serve it to them as is asked.'

'You'll stand for that?'

'Stand for it? I'm no flunkey, I'll have you know, I'm a tradesman, and that's my trade, and what's the odds to me if I get paid pint by pint or for all the barrels together. I'll have the ale down there by six in the morning, and it'll stand and be sweet to drink again by the evening. When did I ever get custom like that from Jemmy Place?'

'You're doing the ale then. But I suppose that the wine, that's the Places, isn't it?'

'Oh, eventual like, it is. But 'tis Zekiel Angram from the Dragon that's serving the wine. And Sam Galphay from the Greyhound, he's doing the cooked meats and the cold. That's why we all wants Kettlestang for Portreeve again, he do remember who shouts for him, and he do share around what he do get from the dues. It's trade and spending that do make us all prosperous, not hoarding it away. He bain't no miser, whatever you say.'

The clerks were going around the town. They took the invitations to this house and that, to Grangiers and to Fencotes, to Nosterfields and Starbuttons and Gannels, Perrotts and Kelds. All the Aldermen were invited, and Pontigarde, of course, that held all the secrets of the town in his deed-books and his strong boxes. And with him, of course, Parson Quernhow, who held as many secrets, but in his heart and his memory only. And a host of tradesmen below this in wealth and standing, Gunver and Carines and their like, all that had some voice in their Guilds, that influenced their customers or their debtors, or the men they prayed with or plotted with—or against.

But no invitation went to Arkengarth. He could influence no one. He was only a schoolmaster. Kettlestang could safely leave him out. Besides, it was not in Kettlestang's plan, it might even interfere with it, even though he had got Folland to move out of that house. Kettlestang now gave himself credit for the move.

Only Prisca was disappointed. Her father did not notice the slight, hardly knew that there was a rout arranged. It was nothing to him. But Prisca—she knew what would happen. She had been certain of it for two weeks now, since she had seen from the School House window the Aldermen and their families come out of the Abbey Church, stand talking on the Buttermarket in little groups, break up to go to their homes by ones and twos. It was a day when George Place was somewhere absent, she did not know or care where save that he had carried Charley off with him, and that disturbed her. Anything could happen when Charley was away. There might be disaster.

But no disaster could happen to Charley like the one that happened now to Prisca. She saw Robin Folland come out of the Church, her Robin, and stop while Kettlestang passed the time of day with James Place. And then, she noted it well, the two groups melded into one to walk down the street toward the merchants' houses, and there was Sophia Place walking with

Robert, talking with him, no, it couldn't be, but it was—her hand was on his arm. Prisca took hard hold of the dish that was in her hand to stop herself moaning, to grind her fingers against its edge to drown emotional pain with physical. And then, going beyond that, she deliberately broke the dish against the window sill, and it was a good dish that had cost threepence in the market. But threepence, she thought, threepence, it would be worth all I have in the world to break that hussy's head—and I haven't even got threepence of my own. It was at that moment, from that day, that Prisca ceased to be herself a passive watcher. She would, from now on, she ordered herself, be a worker and an agent, a doer, no more passive. Unknown to herself, it was the same vow she took as had Robert : to find myself, to settle myself, to gain my own desire, I will take this town apart. She counted her allies in a moment : Charley was a broken reed and a pawn of the Places, her father not much better, and a dozen schoolboys who missed their apples. They would have to serve.

Robert Folland knew nothing of this as he came out of the Church, offered his arm to Sophia Place, walked her down the road. He still knew nothing as he stood in the Counting House in the light of the candles, close behind Kettlestang to welcome the guests. He had thought himself there as a major-domo, to see that things worked smoothly, to watch that the great ones had their liquor and their ladies their sherbets and trifles. But that was not his place at all. Kettlestang kept him at his right hand, presented him, by name, to the Aldermen as if he were, well, not an equal but at least out of the same level of wealth. He is presenting me, thought Robert, as if I were some day to be one of them, just as George Place will be one of them, and Francis Grangier, and Augustus Kilnsey, all to be Aldermen in their fathers' places, unless they fall into poverty. And they can fall into poverty, a misjudgement of the market, a change in fashion, even a new material for hats or house-building can bring them low. They could be as poor as I—nay, poorer, for all I have is a future, while all they will have is a past.

So Robert Folland stood there as if he were almost an Alderman, and the Aldermen were not slow to notice it. What also they knew, was that the Millers' Guild had once been a large company in Wrackham, and the Millers had been some of the most important men in the town. Now there were few members of the Guild, and the most important man in the town was the only Miller in the place that had a Mill. This last Miller was Portreeve : after him, would there be another Miller to take the chair? They took the hint that Kettlestang offered them : this then was the next great Miller of Wrackham.

Only one thing was lacking in this man Folland, and Hunderthwaite knew it, and Nosterfield, and all the others. Folland could not be admitted to be Alderman, or Portreeve, or even have a Parliament voice, unless he were admitted a Burgess of Wrackham. He was not a Wrackham man born : it was a little late for apprenticeship and the seven-year wait : it would be necessary that he should marry a Wrackham man's daughter. Hard fathers and grasping mothers in that instant made their decision, and the daughters, not speaking, concurred : Martha Blackhope and Eliza Gannel were already on the block, showing their paces : even Phoebe Pontigarde, barely fifteen, was in the hunt, calling *say-say, saw-saw* in her soul. Shillmoor the Brewer cursed the town laws that said that the Burgesses need not choose one of their number, but might take anyone their fancy dictated to be their Parliament Man, so that he had never, when the opportunity had been offered, thought it worth even the nominal apprenticeship : and the opportunity was gone, and Shillmoor had four daughters.

The gesture was made, the position shown plain, as Kettlestang introduced Folland to the Aldermen and the Justices. He did not need to say in full words, *this is my heir*—he was careful not to say it—but they all understood what he wished them to understand. Even Folland, not a Wrackham man, not tuned to the nuances of this close company, could understand that. He understood it best of all from the looks of the women. He stood there, in his coat of green and his new silk waistcoat, Wrackham woven, and felt as proud as he had ever been of his scarlet in Spain. And yet, he thought, if they knew what I am about. . . . The women admired, they speculated, and then they fell into despair. For the matter was already decided.

The Places entered. Folland was presented. Martha and Phoebe and Eliza saw him make his leg as if he had been brought up at the Court of Saint James—and who knew, they agreed, it might well have been the Court of Saint Germain for all anyone in Wrackham knew. They saw his lips move, words exchanged, smiles, compliments, but the band drowned all that. And then they saw James Place smile, saw George Place scowl, impotent in obedience, and Sophia Place glisten in triumph as she had Robert Folland lead her off into the dance.

That was the end, the girls knew. There was something planned already between Vintner and Miller, whether Sophia had known it before or not, and she had sworn to them that she had no idea what was in store for her. But what she had planned, Sophia saw now within her grasp. Kettlestang's heir he might well be, but would Kettlestang have taken a pauper, a stranger to continue his house? No, she was absolutely sure now that this was Lord Wrackham, and nothing George could say would shake her. She was on the point of asking him point blank, but thought better of it. Let him have the pleasure of breaking it to her on . . . on her wedding night, she forced herself to think of that.

Folland was at a loss. The way she looked at him was puzzling. He held her hand, released it as they parted in the dance, held it again. She was a good-looking girl enough, as well built as any he had had in Spain or Flanders, but yet . . . how was it, he could not warm to her. Nevertheless, Kettlestang was eager for them to come together, he was always dropping hints that Folland ought to marry. He was looking as pleased, now, as if he had planned the whole ball for this one purpose, to bring Robert Folland and Sophia Place together. And Sophia looked as if she agreed with him.

James Place gazed vaguely into the blur, through his cataracts. The young man sounded well enough, whatever George said. So he said nothing, merely looked approvingly into the mists. He chatted with Kettlestang, about the prospect of the barley harvest this year. Good barley meant good beer, cheap barley meant ruin to the poorer farmers. Barley that was scarce and good meant dear gin, because there was a limit to the scarcity of ale, and dearer gin and scarcer meant a better market for wine, and for run brandy. Bad times meant more farmers in Kettlestang's pocket. And more tradesmen in Wrackham that would owe him money, and depend on him to stay alive, and to pay their town dues. But not the Places. Place would never be in debt to Kettlestang. To be wed to Kettlestang, either to the man or to the business was another thing. That might well be managed. It would be good business.

'Aye,' Robert told Sophia, ' 'twas warmer in Spain in summer than it is here. But there was times in winter when it was cold as ever I have known it in England.'

That, she thought, shows it. For we all know that Spain is a hot land, and he has *never* known a winter in England, that is what he means to say. It's clear enough.

'But the fashions?' she asked him. 'How did the ladies dress?'

Folland was tired of being asked about Spain. Was there no other subject of talk? He seemed to have the same conversation again and again, only the interlocutor changing.

'The women, in the fields,' he answered, 'were whom the soldiers mostly saw. They dressed sadly enough, in what they could find, or what the armies had left them.'

'But the great ladies,' she pressed him, 'how did they dress? Did they dress, for instance, as the great noblewomen do in France?'

'The ladies in the towns, the wives of the merchants, dress always in black,' began Robert lamely. And then he thought, the hell with it, I'll have her listen and believe whatever I say. Turn the town upside down, aye, and start with her. But not to hurt her. He could not harm anyone who looked at him that way. It was strange that he could feel no warmth in her touch, and yet, there was something between them. 'Oh, the fine ladies wear all manner of colours, and lace in abundance.' There was a lady he had seen lately outside the theatre in Drury Lane, being handed into her chair, and he had noted all she wore to describe to Prisca. He told Sophia, only transferring the encounter to the Cathedral of Cadiz. He felt that it was a kind of theft from Prisca, even though she would no longer accept such gifts of words. But it was strange; Prisca would have listened in all seriousness, but Sophia showed an unexpected levity, and the arrangements of patches on the lady's face, that Folland had thought privately to be funny, she laughed at while he described them with a straight face.

The other girls saw her laughter, saw his face break into a smile of genuine friendship, and they were furious. Not as furious as George Place, who swore to himself and greatly shocked Eulalia Fencote who stood close enough to him to take it as meant against her. But Kettlestang saw it and rejoiced. *His* plan, he saw, was beginning to work out. It had been worth the expense of the rout, all the trouble of clearing the Counting House and the interruption to work. Newall had been a good excuse, the gaining of support of all these groundlings would cover his costs, make him Portreeve again, but the match of

Robert Folland and Sophia Place would stand him as clear profit. And he was in business for profit, not for stability.

Besides the little men and the working Burgesses, the Aldermen of the Guilds were here, all of them. Master Shillmoor and Colonel Cutler, with all their tribes of wives and children, were also here, would have to talk to him, would have their little achievements and plans to expound and boast about. They were both Justices, but what was that? They were Justices by grace and favour, had been picked by the whim of the Sheriff : but he, Kettlestang, was a Justice and sat on the Bench because he was Portreeve, and owed that to no one man's favour but to his own substance and skill. He could look down on them even as he heard Cutler talk of how he was going to tear down his old house, three centuries old, built for Monks and no warmer or more comfortable for that, as soon as he had a new house built, and this new one of brick.

'Aye, brick is the coming thing,' he told Shillmoor across Kettlestang's front. ' 'Tis the material of the age. There are things one can do in brick no builder will attempt in timber, nor yet in stone, for bricks come for the most part in set size and shape, and yet beside that in any shape that a builder can desire or the mould encompass.'

That was sheer boasting, Kettlestang thought. There was not a builder in the Loone valley that was used to building in brick, nor yet any brick works. The brick for Jemmy Place's house, brought all the way from Bedford, had near bankrupted him, so that there was not likely to be another house like that in this end of the county as long as any man here would live. Clay there might be, like on Hodmer Blackmer's farm, but not enough wood here for burning bricks. His eyes strayed around the room, saw Robert, were satisfied.

Robert Folland was still talking with Sophia Place. To tell the truth, he did not know now how to get rid of her, and she gave him no help. They were in the end window of the Counting House, looking out over the river. In desperation, Robert called Josh Caddon with his tray, and offered her a glass of wine, fine sweet Madeira, and watched her roll it over her tongue, close her eyes, judge it, price it—she was a vintner's daughter. She faced him across a great silver bowl of flowers, the buds beginning to open, their feet in water.

'A tolerable wine, sir,' she told Robert. 'True, we sold it, and we could not sell a bad wine.' And her eyes twinkled at him. He searched for the right reply, answered,

'A wine fit for you, Miss, must be fit for a Queen.'

'And a King,' she answered, and held out her glass to clink against his.

'A King?' he asked, dully, then cursed himself for slowness of wit, and clinked his glass with hers, and so they drank across the white roses. And Joseph Carines saw them, heard the words 'The King', and the glasses touch across the bowl of flowers in water before they drank. And then his attention, and theirs, wavered across the room to where Kettlestang stood between Newall his guest and Pontigarde his attorney.

14

'They are my buttons,' insisted Newall. He was loud as well as firm. He was on sure ground here. He was not certain what Robert Folland wanted him to do, but he could not go wrong if he insisted on his rights. They had not imagined he would have to do it so soon, in public at the rout. It would look strange if he ignored it now, he could hardly hope to carry conviction later. So he said loudly,

'These are my buttons,' and for good measure, he added, 'and my shoe buckles, too.' He was not so sure about the buckles in that light, but he could see that they were very like, and he took the chance. If anyone had taken the buttons, then sure they would have the buckles as well because they matched, and he had had them made specially, when he had been paid for the greatcoats. Silver buttons, silver buckles, and none of them to be matched anywhere in the world. The plan had been to find them in Gunver's shop next day. Now they were thrust in his face.

It made Pontigarde start. He had expected anything from Kettlestang's visitor, because any out-of-Wrackham man was capable of eccentric behaviour. But he had not really expected this. He drew himself up, looked down his nose as haughty as he could manage, tried a sneer, but Newall said again, firmly,

'They are still my buttons. And pray, how did you get them?'

Yet Pontigarde was not as surprised as Kettlestang. The grain dealer had no idea what his guest was talking about, nor why he had burst into such energy at the sight of Pontigarde, since he had been conversing with Place when the Attorney entered. But Pontigarde was conscious that he was wearing a new coat, and that the buttons were very splendid—and so had been the cost. Newall's words were not the first to stagger him that day, but he was now in practice for recovery. He had gained something, a guinea or two, by bargaining earlier, he would try to bargain now. So he said, as vacantly as he could,

'Your buttons, sir? They are my buttons. I am wearing them. They are sewn on to my coat. Therefore they are my buttons.' He hoped that would, if not settle the matter, at least put this confounded man off. But Newall reached rudely out, took hold of one of the buttons and twisted it from the coat. Pontigarde pulled himself away. Newall kept hold of the button, and Pontigarde felt the strain on the cloth, as if it would tear out of the coat. So he leaned toward him and relieved the pressure.

'Look here,' said Newall to Kettlestang, ignoring Pontigarde. He pulled the button up to the grain dealer's face, making Pontigarde stand on tip toes not to hurt his new coat. 'Look here, sir. See these letters, close to the Hallmark? What do they say, then, what do they say?'

Kettlestang squinted at the tiny letters. He had a little difficulty in making them out, but not as much as Newall feared, since he was becoming a little short sighted in the left eye. He was about to speak, when Newall demanded,

'Do they not say "W.N."? How, sir, do they not?'

'They do indeed, Master Newall,' Kettlestang admitted, and if he had had so much trouble in reading them close up, he could not imagine how Newall had read them. He must have recognized these buttons from their faces. And Newall went on,

' "W.N." for Will Newall, I had the maker put that on. And you will see his own mark there, too—"T.B." for Toby Bertram. Now, can anyone here decipher the rest of the Hallmark? 'Tis a London mark, not Lynn nor Chester. Britannia and the Lion's head is it not, and a small "q"?'

Peter Hunderthwaite pushed through to them.

'Aye, 'tis the London mark for last year,' he agreed. 'And it do look like Bertram's work on the face of the button, too, never mind the mark on the back.'

'You see?' Newall demanded triumphantly. 'If these buttons had not been in my possession, how should I know the mark? And how came you by them, Master Punchinello?'

This stung Pontigarde, who was more and more conscious that bending over his books was arching his back. He sneered,

'Sure, any man may know what is on buttons bought and sold and passed around by pedlars in way of trade.'

Newall bridled. He did not like being called a pedlar, if only because he had once been one. He demanded, 'And my initials stamped on them, at my order, in case of just a night like this? My buttons, made for me, and stolen from me. Faith, sir, speak a little more and let me see if I know the voice.' The word pedlar reverberated in his mind—he would have this out now for his own sake, quite apart from Robert. He turned to Kettlestang, and asked, 'Have you, Master Portreeve, had the *pleasure*'—and he rolled the word on his tongue—'of this gentleman's acquaintance previous to tonight?'

Kettlestang was still not quite in command of the situation. He said pompously,

'Master Pontigarde is one of our most respected and worthy townsmen——'

But Newall, warming to his work, snapped,

'Then heaven help those who face the villains here.'

Kettlestang was acutely conscious that the music had died almost to a whisper, that everyone in the room was watching and listening. He swept his glance round Pontigarde and Newall, included Shillmoor and Colonel Cutler as out-of-Wrackham Justices, and said,

'We will go to another room. I will sit on this case.'

In the upper room, the tables were set for a more select supper. The two waiters from the Dragon stood agape, and then at a sign from Kettlestang they stripped one of the tables. Kettlestang sat behind it, in the middle of the long side. He waved the two Shire Justices to sit beside him, as sometimes happened when the Portreeve sat in Justiciar in the Town Hall, to give advice, but not to judge themselves. In Wrackham, only the Portreeve had power to sit and judge and assess, to fine or to send before the King's Justice at the Assizes. He sat now, and Bridgward, scurrying upstairs with his flute still in his hand, opened the chest and brought out the gold Town Chain to hang around his master's neck. All was to be done decently and in order, even if it were in the wrong place. The Aldermen, such as had heard that something was toward, had come upstairs, found chairs and benches and sat, a backdrop of fine cloth and fur in the flickering candles.

There was a moment's pause. The back of the room, about the stairs, was full of people. Robert had come up, and Sophia had clung close behind him, determined to see what went on. Her brother was somewhere there too. Kettlestang was sitting as Portreeve for a court, they could all see that, but Pontigarde was not in his usual clerk's place, behind the Magistrate. Kettlestang had beckoned Bridgward to come there, and take down what was said. Pontigarde stood at the end of the table, on the Magistrate's right.

Kettlestang poured himself a glass of sack, then rapped on the table with the heel of his hand. The noise in the room diminished a little, but the music below still shook the floor, and the dancing rattled the timbers of the walls. Only a few of the guests had noticed the absence of the host. The Portreeve said, very firmly,

'I sit here in a civil cause. Master Newall, have you then a case?'

'I have indeed. D'ye want to hear about it, then? Or am I to have no justice here in the wilds?'

'I think there is no necessity for you to be sworn,' was the Portreeve's diplomatic answer. He did not wish to give Newall the opportunity for saying in public what he had already said in private about the rights of the subject in Wrackham. 'Tell us your plain tale, pray.'

'Well, I was on my way here, and in the thought of doing business with you, Master Kettlestang, and with any other gent of this town who would wish to be making his fortune out of his neighbours, and sharing the wealth of the town around in a different way. Well, I won't be making a song or a parade of my own virtue,' and that would be as dangerous for you as it would for me, Newall added to himself as a caveat—'but 'tis true, that I was doing and meaning no harm to nobody around here at all. I came, quiet and inoffensive, riding my old grey horse that has carried me so far all these years'—seeing I bought him only last week, and next month I can make ten shilling on him at the knacker's—'and I had nothing to think of at all but the hospitality I was sure to receive at your hands. But when I was in a little thicket of hornbeam and hazel where the road was narrow and not well repaired, look, a great big brute of a man on a horrible big horse, a bay I mind it was, came out of the woods in broad daylight, and pointed a pistol in my face, and told me to stand and turn over all I had. There was another one behind him even bigger and nastier looking, and what was I to do against all those pistols, a whole row of them, as fierce as the broadside of a first rater pointing at me. So I stopped my horse as best I could, the brute having a head like a bucket and a mouth like leather, and I said to him, "Sir," I said, "what would you with me?" And though I answered him so sweet and reasonable, he did not think it proper to reply in anything but a shower of oaths, saying that he would have my guts to lace his shoes if I did not do all that he bade me, and I feared for my own bodily virtue, for though he was very big and very fierce, there was something mincing and effeminate about him that I could not like. I therefore agreed that I would do his will, but I kept my seat firmly in the saddle.

'Now behind my saddle I had my valise and all my clothes in it. But the few coins I needed for the journey were in my boot-toes, and in my hat lining I had the letters of credit and the notes of hand which I was to present to your Worship, and which I have presented as you well know, otherwise I would be penniless now. I could do nothing——'

'Other men here have defied highwaymen,' put in Sophia, rather spoiling Newall's narrative. He recovered himself, seeing that no one else took any notice of her, and carried on :

'The villain commanded me to drop my valise on the ground, which I did. He then cut my horse across the rump with a switch, and of course he bolted and carried me into the very town gates without a stop. And in that valise, Portreeve, was my best new suit that I had made especially for this ball of which you warned me, and on the coat were my own buttons, and the buckles were on the shoes. I can see my buttons on the coat of this—this confederate of yours, and on his feet, not merely the buckles, but the shoes themselves !'

'So you say that Master Pontigarde, who is a respected burgess of this town and known to us all as a man of substance, has stolen your buttons?'

Newall felt a sudden chill : he must be careful. Luckily, he had covered himself.

'I have made no such accusation. I only said that yesterday afternoon my buttons and my buckles were stolen from me, and this evening he is wearing them. I am sure that he can produce some story about how he came by them.'

Pontigarde was used to standing in courts, but not like this. He usually acted as clerk to the Justices of Wrackham, and had on occasion been to the assize town to brief a barrister. But his real home was in an office with his conveyances. He was not used to arguing without a written draft, not even with his wife, and now he was sadly unprepared. He cursed the nagging that had led him to go at such short notice to buy a new coat for this evening, and the powers of persuasion that had saddled him with new shoes too. He thought for a moment of trying to brazen it out. His nerve for that failed him. With never a twinge of conscience he prepared to abandon his friends. How to do it with the least damage to himself . . . he havered a little.

'I must submit, Master Portreeve, that your worship is not bound to listen to nor to take cognizance of any statements made nor speeches rehearsed here not made on oath, since a man not on oath may say what he likes and be in no fear of the everlasting fire, which torments more than doth the rope.' He remembered that, he had written this as a speech for the barrister at the last assizes prosecuting a Pard, but the jury had brought the man in not guilty of bigamy for no other reason than that they thought that marriage, being better than burning, was therefore equivalent to hanging. 'Nevertheless, I being a man of honour will not demand that this stranger repeat his evidence on oath, but I will accept that what he has said is in substance true, namely that he was robbed yesterday of buttons and buckles——'

'And shoes, and much else,' growled Newall.

'——and shoes, then, to which those I now wear do bear, and offer, a patent and superficial resemblance sufficient to allow him to state his honest belief, though it may yet be a mistaken one, that they are the same.'

'They are mine,' said Newall, in a cold tone, 'and I will have them back.'

'There is no better way to examine this gentleman's claim to be the true and rightful owner of these articles which bear so close a similarity to his descriptions, than for me to declare briefly and simply and directly how I came by them. It being late on last night ere I received your Worship's most gracious invitation, it was only then that my dear wife who is so well known to you and all here being Master Hunderthwaite's sister and cousin to so many Nosterfields and Kelds, and having already made her own gown of Master Grangier's silk, taking out my best ball coat from the press did observe that the moth had corrupted it and that the buttons being of steel were now rusty. Therefore in the morning, I did take myself early to the shop of Master Joseph Carines, who is well known also to you all. And he did take out from *his* press this coat which he had already made there, of a size to fit me. But this coat had no buttons at all, and he did go into his inner room and brought out a variety of buttons, of silver and pewter and brass, for me to choose from : the which I did. And the buttons I chose, your Worship, were the most expensive that he had in his shop and he did sew them on to my coat there and then, and I went home to my wife rejoicing. And so I came in my new coat to the ball, not having asked Master Carines whence he had the buttons, or any other of his buttons, no more than I would ask him whence came the cloth or the thread or the needles he used, or than I would ask Master Place whence came his wine or yourself, your Worship, where you had the grain you sell.' At that, Pontigarde was pleased, feeling that he had now involved everyone in the room either by the call of kinship or by veiled threats of revelation.

'What about my shoes?' grumbled Newall, but Kettlestang ignored him. He called, loudly,

'Is Master Carines here, that can tell us whether all this be true and whence he had those buttons?'

Master Carines was indeed there, pressed in the crowd at the top of the stairs, many of them there merely because they had heard of this upper room of Kettlestang's but never seen it and were grasping at the chance, no one having turned them back. Master Carines wished heartily that he were somewhere else. But there he was fixed; now he was pressed close against Folland, who was twice his size as he well knew having measured him, and waiting to do the Portreeve's bidding. So in terror of being seized by those huge hands, and pulled forward, he pushed himself to the front and said humbly,

'Oh, your Worship, your Worship, and here I am and I hope

that you will not be listening to any awful slander that is said against me.'

'Listen I must,' said Kettlestang, wishing that he had been bred to the law like his nephew so that he could sit, as surely as Nat would in the end, in wig and scarlet gown on an Assize bench. 'But whether I believe what is said is another matter, and you must convince me of the reasonableness of whatever you have to say. You have heard Master Pontigarde's evidence, have you not?'

'Oh, yes, your Worship,' and Carines was thinking fast. This was worse than selling a worn-out coat to a suspicious Pard, but not different. It was the same kind of persuasion. Pontigarde had let him down, blamed him, had he? And not told the whole truth, or even the whole lie? Then Carines would jettison Pontigarde, and anyone else who stood between him and the gallows; nay, if he were flung into gaol, he would sure die before the Assizes of bad food and rank water and lack of air.

'Oh, yes, your Worship, I admit that I did sell Master Pontigarde these buttons, but it was at his most urgent entreaty. They were not for sale, your Worship, since I had the gravest suspicions myself whether they had come into town honestly, being of such good quality seeing the price I was asked for them. I therefore had not yet paid for them myself and had them separate in my strong box while I bethought myself what to do with them. But Master Pontigarde was so finicky and choosy about his buttons, and would not have these that were too small, and those that were too plainly brass, and above all none that were not gaudy and showy to let all see their value and the expense he had been to. Therefore, on his urgently praying me to see whether I had any that were larger and brighter than those I had shown him, I was persuaded to take these from my strong box and let him have them, on his promising to pay me at the week's end, which day of reckoning has not come, and now not likely to come, I suppose, a greater judgement having intervened.'

Pontigarde quickly interposed, 'I am, of course, willing to restore these buttons and buckles to their proper owners whoever they may be or to pay for them on the appointed day.'

'But from whom did you have these buttons, Master Carines?' asked Kettlestang. He added, unnecessarily, 'Remember that you are not yet upon oath, since theft of such a great amount as these buttons must represent will be a hanging matter and beyond the jurisdiction of our court in Wrackham.'

Carines trembled. For a moment he was so terrified that he left the body. He stood before the living God and worshipped, and spoke, in desperation, with tongues, 'Ichhateinenkamerade einbesserfindstdunicht.' The clouds passed before his eyes, and he knew what he had to do. He said, loud and clear,

'I bought them from Master Gunver. He sold them to me.' Let Gunver suffer that had let him in for this. And Carines thought in terror of the coat from which the buttons had been cut, still in the press in his shop and harder to defend than buttons. 'Master Gunver knows where they came from. I would no more think of asking him whence they came than Master Pontigarde would think of asking me.'

Kettlestang shook his head. 'There are deep matters here, Master Pontigarde, cloudy waters in which to dredge for buttons——'

'And my shoes are drowned therein too,' said Newall in a resigned voice. He caught Kettlestang's eye. The Portreeve shuddered. There were two of the Justices of the Shire sitting here to watch him, and he would have to press the case further. He ordered,

'Find Master Gunver.'

'Master Gunver!' they cried down the stairs, across the counting house. The dancing had stopped, guests and band were engaged in a struggle for the food and drink that was now being carried in. Gunver had managed to seize a ham and a loaf, and his wife had got hold of a bottle of sack. They were sitting on the floor near the stairs, sharing the booty, when of a sudden he found himself seized by a dozen pairs of hands as big as the ham. He was haled to the stairs, half pulled, half pushed up them, without an explanation, and sudden, found himself before a court. It was a court, he saw at once, with the Portreeve sitting in his gown and chain, and his clerk as well, and it was all his worst dreams beating at him through the fog of sack.

'You are Christopher Gunver?' Kettlestang asked him.

'Oh, yes indeed, your Worship, you know me, your Worship, and you knew my father before me.'

'What is your business?'

'I am a shopkeeper, your honour.'

'Ah, but what kind of a shop, Master Gunver?'

'Oh, your Worship, your highness, what kind of a shop? Why, you know what kind of a shop.'

'But how would you describe it, Master Gunver? What is it you buy and sell, and when and how?'

'Your Worship, you know how it is. Now my father was a goldsmith, and his father before him, but being much hindered by unfortunate matters into which it is only painful for me to go here, not unconnected with the politics of the late reign, I have taken to buying and selling whatever occasion offers, besides gold and silver, such as wigs and clothes and anything that a man wishes to get rid of. And I will also take pledges in pawn, and keep them safe, having lent money on them at a very moderate rate of interest, being no more than twenty per cent per month——'

'Indeed, that we all know, Master Gunver, But tell me, was there anything you bought or sold yesterday, later than the afternoon, or perhaps in the early hours of this morning?'

Gunver's head was beginning to clear. He could make out fairly well in the light of the candles the faces nearest to the table. The Portreeve's guest was there, and Carines, and Pontigarde, with his buttons shining—his buttons! The pawnbroker summed up the situation in a flash. Abandoning his friends had caused Pontigarde a long moment's calculation, had occupied Carines' conscience for a split second in physical time, though an eternity of mystical experience. It took not a tenth of that interval for Gunver: jettison was automatic. The plan was made in an instant, the pose of the honest trader, unfamiliar as it was, was assumed.

'Indeed, your Worship, I had a caller last night, who had objects to pawn. This is not an uncommon thing in my trade, your Worship, since there are many who come to pledge their goods who do not wish it to be known, and indeed there are some here tonight who would not be able to show their faces in company were it not for the money they owe me. Even if I cannot lend it on farms, yet there are many choice items which I have in safety.' Gunver looked defiantly round the room. Let them attack me who dare, he thought. Only my power to destroy credit has kept the True Faith alive here all these years. He fixed Pontigarde, in particular, with a malevolent eye. He went on. 'It was late last night that there came one man to the back door, but he wanted not to pledge but to sell, though I would not buy.

I therefore lent him money on a set of silver buttons, and on a pair of shoes with fine buckles, on promise of repayment at the month's end, but I have heard that before from the likes of him. So though I lent him money out of pure charity, I must look on it as money gone from me, and I know that I will have soon to sell those buttons and buckles to cover the expense I am put to in keeping them safe, for the wear and tear on locks and chests is stupendous.'

'So you took them as pledge?' asked Kettlestang. 'You did not actually buy them? You do not think of the ownership as passing from him to you?'

Gunver caught at the tone. He agreed.

'I did not buy them. I may have to consider them as forced on me.'

'But then?'

'Why, then I showed them, in the morning, to Master Carines, and he was so taken with them, that he prevailed on me to lend them to him since he thought he might wish to wear them himself tonight, and such is often done, for jewellery of this kind if not worn but left fallow in a press do lose its lustre.'

'What say you to that, Master Carines? Did you consider them yours to sell to Master Pontigarde?'

Carines in his turn grasped at the straw. 'Indeed, your Worship, I did not, but I merely put them on Master Pontigarde's coat for this one evening.'

'What about my shoes?' asked Newall, in a voice of thunder that made Gunver jump, being only three feet from him.

'Shoes? Shoes?' Gunver had not realized those cursed shoes were also in the case. 'Oh, yes, there was also a pair of shoes that this man did pledge with me, and Master Pontigarde going by on his way to the Ball, I saw him so down at heel and the wet of the horse-stale coming in at the sole, that I did offer in pity for his poverty to lend him any pair of old shoes out of my stock that would fit him, and these were of a size for him, more or less, though that did not matter his necessity being so plain and pitiful. And I suppose he wears them now, he did an hour ago.'

Pontigarde saw thus his reputation for wealth destroyed, in front of Kettlestang and, worse, Kettlestang's heir. But there was no help for it, he had to agree. He nodded. The Portreeve continued to question.

'And who was it that came to your back door then, Master Gunver? Who is it will come again for his pledge?'

Gunver hesitated.

'Ah, well, I can't be saying. I give out them pledges to whoever has the piece of paper, and I don't try to keep in mind all them faces that come to the door.'

'But all the people of Wrackham come, you say, sooner or later, to your door,' Kettlestang objected.

'To your door or to mine, high or low, your Worship,' agreed Gunver.

'Then it is true that you know everybody in Wrackham, Master Gunver? You are not yet on oath. Be careful. I will have you sworn, if you do not answer, and when we find out all the truth—why, men may still hang for perjury.'

The room was still, although the hubbub came from below where the guests rioted and fought over the casks of wine and the ruins of the food. In the upper room nobody stirred, and they all watched Gunver. James Place, only, gazed into the milky space before his eyes, not turning to the voices. Pontigarde watched, his own soul a turmoil, full of hatred for Gunver that had exposed his meanness. And George Place watched in perturbation of mind, wondering what Gunver would say, what now would be revealed: Leyshon Keffle, at his elbow, sensing his leader's mood, fumbled in the waistband of his drawers for his reed-knife.

Gunver was silent a long time. At last he began to speak, babbling a little, not able to form a sentence, as if even in the act of speaking he had not made any decision, as if his words were dictated by something outside himself.

'It were, well . . . it were dark, you know . . . there was little chance to see . . . he were all muffled up . . . it were a greatcoat, a riding coat . . . he did have the inside collar buttoned up and the outside one turned up . . . it must have been powerful hot . . . it were a lightish drab colour . . .'

That coat is enough of a description, thought George Place, it was the one I was wearing three years agone, and I gave it away, and they all know who I gave it to and what we have done together before.

'But who was in the coat, Master Gunver?' Kettlestang's voice was grim. He felt the eyes of Shillmoor and Cutler on his back. He must go on.

'It were . . .' Gunver looked in terror at George Place's hard eyes, at Keffle's clenched fist inside his waistband. He swallowed hard. 'I couldn't swear . . . no man could swear . . . it looked uncommon like Charley Arkengarth.'

There was silence again. Then Kettlestang, quietly,

'Fetch Charles Arkengarth. Does anyone know where to find him?'

'I think,' and it was Robert Folland who spoke, 'he will be in the Two Roses, for I saw him this afternoon, and he seemed very full in funds.'

'Then fetch him, someone.' It was Bridgward running down the stairs, thrusting through the confusion, to find Charley, sitting quiet in the Two Roses Tap, with a crowd of Pards, as if he were expecting to be called. Meanwhile, George Place stood telling himself, oh Charley won't talk, he's a good fellow is Charley, he'll never let us down. Only his sister knew the rage that was in him, saw the fist clenched tight around Keffle's arm above the elbow.

At last Charley came up the stairs, followed by Bridgward. The Schoolmaster's son blinked in surprise at the candle light, at the crowd of notables, at the Justices. He stood there, alone, in the middle of the room, in his drab-coloured riding coat worn in spite of the heat because he had no other, nor waistcoat either underneath. He was conscious of his shabby shoes, his greasy wig. He heard Kettlestang,

'Charles Arkengarth, we are here in the matter of fifteen silver buttons, each of the bigness of half a crown, and of two silver buckles and the shoes with them that were the property of Master Newall.'

'Nothing is yet proved,' murmured Pontigarde in token protest, but no one heeded him.

'Master Gunver here says that it was you who sold them to him, coming to his back door last night, in the hours of darkness and with intent to hide your face.'

'A moment,' said Newall, but Kettlestang went on,

'What have you to say, Arkengarth?'

'Indeed, sir, I . . . I . . .' Charley looked round in desperation. He had not expected the crows would come home to roost so soon or so publicly. He stuttered in echo almost of Gunver, looked round, opened his mouth again. Then, Newall said,

'A moment. I must speak.'

'What is it, Master Newall?'

'Is this indeed Master Arkengarth?'

'It is.'

'The same Master Arkengarth that Gunver alludes to as having sold him *my* buckles?'

'There is only one Charley Arkengarth in the town, and it would be a good thing if there were none.' Kettlestang was in a hurry to have this over. It had spoiled his rout already, and it was a pity that it had to come to something so unpleasant for a Wrackham man, but there. . . .

'I am acquainted with Master Arkengarth. At what time is he said to have come to Master Gunver's door?'

Kettlestang looked at Gunver. The pawnbroker writhed, looked about, caught Keffle's eye, then answered miserably,

'It was about ten o'clock by the Abbey Clock.'

'I am acquainted, I said, with Master Arkengarth.' Newall's voice was firm and smooth. 'He came to me last night in the George Inn, quietly. We heard the clock strike nine together, and ten, and eleven. We were talking business. We were together all that time.'

'You were together?' Kettlestang was surprised. 'What business could you possibly have with . . . with this man?'

'My business is my business, Master Kettlestang. Would you have me discuss it with every chance comer? These may be Wrackham ways, but not London.' Newall was careful what he said. He had been twenty feet away, in the shadows, listening to the murmur of Charley bargaining with Gunver. And Robert Folland had had his hand then on Newall's arm. But there was no reason to tell that. It had not been asked.

Charley gasped with obvious relief. But Gunver was still on the hook. Kettlestang glared at him. There was a way out, then.

'Do you still swear it was Charles Arkengarth who sold you those buckles?'

'No, your Worship. Not swear, I never said I could swear. But 'twas terrible like.'

'More like him than it was like anyone else in Wrackham?'

'Aye, terrible like.'

'Perhaps, then, not a Wrackham man at all?'

'If not him, then not a Wrackham man at all. Nobody else in the town if it were not him.'

151

'Yet, it might have been someone from out-of-Wrackham? Might it not have been one of the gentry? Say, might it not have been Captain Taberon?'

'Oh, no, it weren't Captain Taberon.' Gunver was in terror. He was not to know that Kettlestang had called up the name at random, merely as the latest in a long line of disturbers of the peace. If Taberon thought that I've told on him, he'll kill me, thought Gunver, but Kettlestang pressed on him with relish. To equate his own business, his lending on mortgage, his credits and interest, with mere pledging and pawning—he'd make the little runt wriggle.

'You are acquainted with Captain Taberon, then? You are so sure that it was not him? Hey?'

Gunver sweated. George Place sweated with him. He had been a fool to go in with Taberon, pay him good money for the tip. And when there was no money in the bag, he had been a fool, again, to throw it so contemptuously to Taberon and Charley to share between them. But Charley would not talk, good old Charley. And he knew what he had been about with Newall. There was a matter of nobbling on Newmarket Heath, that Charley could arrange. There was no one like Charley for fixing a horse to run—or not to run. Yet, what would Gunver say? Or Taberon, if he were caught? Gunver was in a lather. He lashed out, like a cornered badger biting at the terriers' necks.

'No, no, I don't know him. 'Tis only what we all hears. But, if 'twere not *him*'—and he motioned at Charley—'that come to my back door, then it were him that did the deed. I do hear things, and I knows it.'

'That is a serious accusation,' warned Kettlestang, but Newall was talking again.

'I know the man who robbed me. I saw his eyes over his kerchief. And I heard his voice.' He looked round the room, slowly, his glance pausing here and there. George felt himself shrinking, against his will, closer against the wall. 'And when I find him, I will not put you to the trouble of a court here or of transport to the Assizes. I will do the hangman's job myself.' The last words came out with a malevolence even Newall had not thought himself capable of. He looked straight at George Place. In the silence Kettlestang spoke.

'The buttons, then, are the property of Master Newall, and the shoes also.'

'That has not been proved,' complained Pontigarde, but he was ignored.

'And they must be returned to him. Master Gunver bought them—or received them in pledge, in all good faith, from some out-of-Wrackham man. There was no man of this town involved in this iniquity. It is a matter for the Shire.' Shillmoor looked bleak, Cutler puzzled.

That, thought Folland, is how it was bound to end. The Wrackham men have stood together—more or less. None of them is blamed. They would not help me. Now, in spite of what Kettle-stang has said, they are shown not ready to help each other. The solid front can crack. They are united only in their indifference to the world outside. Their end begins. Now I shall discover . . . what? Newall was speaking again.

'And now, I will have my buttons. And my buckles.'

He reached out to catch Pontigarde, but the attorney stepped away. He stepped into Keffle's arms. The Pard held him, tight, though he wriggled, grinning from ear to ear as if he were doing this only for fun.

'Now, now, my little man,' he grunted, 'stand still and let the gentry have their goods back.'

Newall advanced, took a knife from his pocket. He caught the front of Pontigarde's coat, and carefully, expertly cut the threads from each of the buttons, on the front and on the cuffs, and slipped them one by one into his pocket. He winked at Keffle. The Pard, not a tall man, but powerful, hoisted the kicking lawyer off his feet, and Newall, watching his chance, seized first one shoe and then the other.

Pontigarde stood there in his hose, showing a hole in one toe and in the other heel. His coat hung open. He was purple in the face, and he looked round, in anger, at the Wrackham men, his townsmen, for help, for sympathy. And they laughed. And that, more than anything else, thought Folland, will settle them.

15

'What,' asked Folland, conscious that he was greatly daring in asking such a question of the Portreeve, 'was the business Master Newall wanted with you? I believe that you refused him.'

Kettlestang laughed. 'I told him to peddle his dirty wares elsewhere.' He had become more communicative in the fortnight since the ball, in spite of the confusion in which it had ended. He did not see it as a failure. He saw himself sitting as a righteous judge, settling others' affairs even in the middle of the festival, sacrificing his enjoyment to the common good. He had seen justice done, had delivered Newall's property—well, some of Newall's property—to him, and had made sure that no Wrackham man was blamed. Let Shillmoor ravage the county, looking for Newall's bag and Newall's better clothes, not to mention Newall's razor—it was nothing to do with Wrackham, and he had shown it.

'But what were his wares? I must know, in case he tries to persuade me.' Folland wanted to know what Kettlestang would say to him, not what he had said to Newall.

'It was a matter of . . . to make it brief, he has bought, or rather someone has sold him, probably when he was drunk, an interest in a sea-coal mine at Newcastle, and in a brig which carries the stuff to London. He was trying to persuade me that I should buy his coal and put it to market here in Wrackham.'

'That sounds very reasonable.'

'Who would buy? In winter, there is always plenty of wood from the Marsh, and the Pards bring in peat, too. And besides, if people began to burn coal, what would the Pards do?'

'If you do not deal in sea-coal, others will. But perhaps you intend to lend someone money to bring in the first cargoes?'

'Nobody will sell coal on Wrackham Quay. I have put a new bylaw to the Council, and because I am Portreeve, they will pass it. No man will henceforth be allowed to land coal at the Quays at Wrackham, either from a ship or from a lighter. We'll have no dirt to mar our clean river, and no soot to spoil the roofs of our town. Have you not seen the condition of London, where almost every house now burns sea-coal all the winter through? Would you have that happen to Wrackham?'

Robert did not care what happened to the roofs of Wrackham. He had plans for the walls, and they could not mature till the early autumn. Still, he was very content with the Portreeve's ruling on coal. He had his own affairs to attend to. The Portreeve had a plan of some kind, that was clear, into which Robert knew he fitted. And so did Sophia Place. He could date this relaxation in Kettlestang's manner, the way in which he would now confide about his business coups, the admission that he ruled the Council, from the moment that Robert had taken Sophia into the dance at the ball. One might almost think he had arranged the whole entertainment to bring about this one social meeting, to fling them together. Was this part of Kettlestang's plan?

Kettlestang's plan, thought Robert, is something which I can only begin now dimly to divine. He has laid it, and once he has begun, nothing can alter its progress. It will all be made plain in his time. But my plan . . . rudimentary as it is, it must wait first on other men's movements. I must seize at chance and circumstances. I can prepare, I can plot, but I must wait for execution. It was the middle of July before the opportunity came.

The news came three days in advance, and not only to Folland. Sergeant Freeman was summoned to Bratton. He found Perkins, agitated, sitting on the shore in his usual place, and buying beer for Baker Sarsen, which Freeman could not think to be his usual custom. The Sergeant sat down to windward of the old man, which was in itself a gross insult, and asked what was up.

'Tell 'un.' Perkins said.

'They be a-goin' to run it agen,' said Baker Sarsen in a confidential tone.

'Not that,' objected Perkins. 'I could tell that myself, by the state of the tides and that Bergen boat laying there.'

'Ah, but ye don't know where, and that's what I be a-goin' to tell ye.'

'There's only one place to run it here,' objected Freeman, 'across the river on the beach where we near got 'em the last time.'

'And whose fault was it we didn't?' asked Perkins petulantly. He did not believe in letting up on Freeman. It might happen again. They were both happily unaware that a cargo had been run in May on this same beach. Baker Sarsen cackled, as well a man may who is being paid not twice but thrice for variants of the same service, and promised a bonus in addition from the favourite in the field. He went on, ignoring Freeman's defence.

'Ah, there's a place this side of the river, don't ye know?'

'There's not.'

'Ah, but there is. Five mile north from here, where the Dean and Chapter do stick out of the sea——'

'Nobody will risk a ship there,' objected Freeman.

'Ah, but that's what you're meant to think,' Baker told him in triumph. 'You ask any of the fishermen. Just t'other side of them rocks, at the right run of the tide, you can lay at anchor as sweet as you like. And there's a beach there you can put a boat on neat and tidy. You try 'un.'

'Likely enough,' grunted Perkins. 'If it be true.'

'It be true,' Baker told them. 'I do pick up the dirty pots in the Roses, and all the world do know that that's where the Pards do always drink. If you knows where to go, you can find out anything in this town.'

'Well?' Perkins looked at Freeman. The Sergeant shrugged.

'It's worth a trial. When's it to be?'

'Night arter the night arter this.'

'Can you be here—no, there, in time?'

'High tide's at half past one. If we saddle up at last light, and ride hard, aye, I think we can do it.'

Sergeant and Exciseman chattered on, laying their own plans, ignoring Baker Sarsen. It did not matter much. Once the night was decided on, there was little choice as to what the troop would do. After a while, when he saw there would be no more ale, he crept off. He walked back over the Down to Wrackham, and told all to Robert Folland.

Folland thanked his Maker again that this time he was not in London. He was sure of his plan, now. With the soldiers out of the way, it would be easy. He wrote a letter, a long one, and pressed it back into Baker Sarsen's hand.

'Now, that's for Marl, you know, Colonel Cutler's butler. Not for the Colonel, mind you. Go to the back door and ask for Marl. Tell him it's from me. He'll give you a supper for it, and a mug of ale besides. There'll be better than yale in your throat in three nights' time.'

Baker went obediently. A small spare man, wiry, like all the

Sarsens and Alleys and Blackmers, he seemed able to walk, or run, day and night without a rest. Anything, Robert reflected, to beat the Pards. He felt, sometimes, as though his brain might burst. He had all to think of. There was mischief he knew he must accomplish if he were to enter into Wrackham as he wished. And his plan to make himself somebody, as important as any of the Aldermen—that, he was working on, too. And to make sure that he could do that, he had all his schemes and money that in London, with Newall, seemed to grow like magic. And his smaller sums in Kettlestang's books. But not always in the books where Kettlestang thought they were. And on top of that, he could not stop thinking of Sophia. Everything he did, he imagined her as if she were taking part. And yet, when he spoke to her, he saw, floating like a veil, Prisca's thin face. Can a man, he wondered, love two women at once? If intensity was anything to go by, he certainly can. And yet . . . he could see Sophia in all he did, and yet he could not bring himself to see her in his arms, or in his bed. There was something wrong, some way she had of moving, or speaking, that he could not quite accept. There was something awry in it.

By the night of the run, it did not matter. George Place had assembled the Pards, the horses were found, the carts were brought down to the woods above the beach, the lighters moved up the river and down till Perkins could certainly not have kept count. The run was to go on where it had always gone on, south of the river. That was where the Places ran their brandy, always had, always would. It had cost George Place five shillings to get old Baker Sarsen to spread that story about going north. As soon as the Dragoons had left the Black Bull, a young Pard had gone south, across the river, on the fastest horse in the Place stables. Folland had been drinking in the Black Bull. He knew early where the soldiers were going.

When he reached the edge of the big wood above the beach, he found George Place watching the Bergen boat. He raised the lantern, saw the reply from the mizzen sheets, and laughed.

The long cavalcade of light carts and floats straggled down on to the sand. The boats were coming in. It might be more conspicuous to load up all the carts and then move off together, but it was safe. Charley could keep an eye on all the carts, and the casks, as long as they stayed together. Three times the boats came and went.

At the gap in the hedge, Robert Folland watched. He waited till the Pards were walking round to the horses' heads. He motioned Marl, led the way out on to the sand, halted there. Half his mounted men were old soldiers, back from the wars in Spain and the Low Countries, or even from older wars, in Ireland, before he ever was born. The others copied their movements. The horses might be from the plough, but the riders were used to them, not talking except to whisper little sounds of comfort to beasts nervous at the smell of the salt sea.

There were half a dozen fowling pieces among them, and a couple of swords; not much cop, Folland thought, but enough to shine in the moon. He began to worry. Had they not been seen yet? It was a good thing that young Abe Sarsen, that blew the trumpet in Bratton Church Band, had thought to bring his instrument. If the Pards did not wake up soon, he might have to blow it.

George Place felt his blood run cold and slow. There they were, under the moon, and not the Dragoons from Wrackham, he was sure of that. He could make out the plumed hats and the glint of the moon on the musket barrels. He knocked up the pistol Dave Key raised, shouted,

'Run! All of you!'

'It's our horses,' complained Leyshon Glass.

'It's our necks, you fool,' George answered him. He lingered to see that all his men were coming. That was Charley furthest away, mounted, turning and caracolling his horse, threatening the Dragoons with the pistol he carried to impress his will on the Pards.

Robert could not hold his own line back too long. He could see George at the end of the beach, counting his men past him into the wood. If I were in his place, Robert thought, I wouldn't stay so far behind my Pards. But Charley was nearer still. The two horses bumped, the men to all appearances grappled.

'Get on, you fool,' Folland hissed, 'or we'll have to take you and how could we explain that?'

'He'll guess anyway,' Charley grunted. 'I'll have to——'

He raised the pistol so that it shone. Robert thanked God for someone in the town who could think fast, leaned gently away and let the shining steel barrel come down the edge of his arm. It would look good enough from the edge of the wood. In turn

158

he slapped Charley's horse across the rump with the flat of his sword, felt the hooves fling sand into his eyes.

And that was that, Robert thought. He turned again to his little crew.

'All right, let's get 'em away.' There was a horseman at each cart, leading the beasts back across the sand, heaving as the wheels sank in. Robert and Marl left them to it, and sat sentry like, watching the edge of the Big Wood. Maybe they can see us, thought Folland, but there's little likelihood they'll try to get it back. What the Pards would do in the morning, he did not care. They were bound to find out the brandy was not in any bonded store. But they would not know where it was gone.

The carts came on to the track across the saltings. They were slow, but carried more than pack horses or men's backs. It was about half a mile from here to the river where the Pards had brought the empty lighter. Robert spurred the horse on to pass the carts, scrambling between track and ditch, past them to the river bank.

Josh Caddon rose, ghostlike, out of the reeds. Robert pulled the horse up, leaned down to him. 'Have we got the lighter?'

'Oh, aye, don't fear about that, we got the lighter. You be calm now.'

Robert Folland came to the waterside, and looked down into the ungainly square-ended craft. A mumbling in Swedish came up from it.

'They be good lads for furriners,' Josh mumbled. 'Better than the Scotchy men, any road.'

'Was there any trouble?'

'Oh, aye, there was three Pards here.'

'What did you do?'

'Oh, them Swedeses did hit 'em on the head. They're behind the hedge.'

Robert looked over. There were three figures lying there, laced round in an intricate pattern of ropes, rags over their mouths.

'You've not killed any of them?' Robert asked. For answer, Josh walked along the line, and kicked each of them hard, choosing the spot with care. Each of the Pards jerked, made vague noises through the rags. Josh cackled through his toothless gums.

'All right, back to the carts,' Robert ordered. There were more men waiting. Everything was easy, he thought, if only you had enough men. There was a line between the leading cart and the lighter, just as he had told them. You could do what you liked if you had a sprinkling of old soldiers. If he could do this the first time he tried . . . it was tempting. But other things were just as tempting. He bent, clawed a lump of the greasy clay from the ditch side, and smiled. There were things more profitable than this, because more steady.

As the carts were emptied, they were turned aside into the field, the horses unharnessed and left to roam away along the river bank. There'd be no charges of horse-stealing here, but the pounder would be chasing Pards for stray-fines till kingdom come. The troop horses were already being got rid of. Five of them belonged to Hod Blackmer : the others came from farms here and there within a mile or two. There had been enough of Pards riding through this land at dead of night, beating anyone who looked at them. It had been easy to find horses, and hiding places. From now on, it might be a little more difficult.

The casks were all in the lighter. Now, the men were aboard, and they poled it off, across the sluggish river to the Hard on the other side. There were carts waiting here, traps and floats. There were seven Swedish sailors. They went first, with a keg of brandy each, sculling in silence back to their ship. That was worth a load of cauliflowers, Robert reflected, and another load every week for a year if they ask for it. Pards would be able only to blame it on foreigners, perhaps on the sailors out of the Bergen boat.

But there were no Pards here, on the Staddle Down side. They were all Alleys and Sarsens hereabouts. The Pards did not roister here, or make poor people stay indoors at night. They only came once a year, when they set up their big pole on the top of the Down, near the Giant's Table. The people who lived around here were not indoors. They were driving their little carts away as soon as they were filled. The kegs would be hidden everywhere but in the Place cellars. None of this brandy would go down Place throats. There was enough for everybody, a keg or two for every adult, a sip for the children, and plenty to spare for what Robert Folland wanted.

But now it was nearly over. Robert Folland called Josh to him. They had two horses waiting, out of the Kettlestang stables. Not Tiger. It would have been hard to bring him from under the Portreeve's nose, and he would have been known. Laughing and singing quietly, Robert and the old, old man cantered back, across the smooth turf of the Down, and down into Wrackham.

Kettlestang slept through all this. In the house opposite, Sophia Place sat up and played her Patience. It cost her candles to do it, but she could not sleep while her brother was out on a run, and she could not sit and do nothing. So she played Patience, and made up in her mind soft fantasies. Lady Wrackham walked in the Queen's presence, bowed and curtsied. She saw the new King, James III—or was it George?—stand Godfather to the infant Lordlings as she herself was Godmother to a Prince. She sat in her chair, and was carried through the golden streets of London, as fine and glistening as Jerusalem.

Further up the street, Prisca sat in her kitchen. She could not sleep either. There had been a time when she had not worried about her brother being out with George Place. Then there had been a period when she could go to bed, but not sleep till she heard his whistle outside. Now, this night, she could not even bring herself to undress. She sat close to the fire, her scarlet shawl about her shoulders, to read by the light of the burning log a book she knew almost by heart, because it was the only book that had been bought express for her.

'And as a War should be undertaken upon a just and prudent Motive, so it is still more obvious, that a Prince ought maturely to consider the Condition he is in when he enters on it : Whether his Coffers be full, his Revenues clear of Debts. For, if the Contrary of all this happens to be his Case, he will hardly be persuaded to disturb the World's Quiet and his own, while there is any other way left of preserving the latter with Honour and Safety.'

Then let Honour be curst, she thought, if so be only safety is assured. There was never a clear moment she had this night, with Charley out there doing Merciful God knows what. It would not be so bad, but there were things he had said, and words he had let drop. This was not what they had done before. Robert was mixed in it somehow—Charley had said just that, we'll come off well tonight if yon Folland keeps his head out of trouble. What that meant she did not know, but it chilled her. Robert was in it, was in danger, and Charley too. . . .

Charley was lying close under the side of a haystack. The position was more exposed than he would have liked, and he would have preferred to get into a hole at the back, but George Place had got there first. They had turned the horses loose in a field, and thrown the harness up on top of the stack, but it would still be very awkward if the Dragoons came on them, seeing they were who they were. They had been there silent for an hour now, and no sounds of pursuit, only the racket of Pards lost and floundering in the unfamiliar fields, seeking a way back into their accustomed marsh. Just let them get into the reeds, and nobody will ever catch them. But out there, quiet as it might be, who knew? There would be Dragoons moving around, faces hard under their stiff hats, eager to catch any poor brandy-runner and punish him now with boot and pistol butt before ever magistrate or judge or hangman had his chance.

The hard-faced Dragoons lay out on the cliffs seven miles away. They could not smile because they were stiff with cold, even on a summer's night. They were all drenched with the dew, for Freeman had not let them bring their blankets; they none of them had a drop of anything warming in their flasks, only water—they were stiff-faced with misery. They remembered well enough what had happened last time. They were determined, every man of them, that they would not give tongue tonight if they saw a thousand bands of smugglers moving whole distilleries ashore, not if all the sea were brandy and the little stream that ran beneath them were pure gin. And they wanted their breakfast.

They were bad tempered. Freeman was bad tempered, hating Perkins. And Perkins blamed the troopers for this new stroke of bad luck. To be warned exactly where and when the run was to be, and then to find nothing. Someone must have talked. He looked balefully over the soldiers. All young lads—whoever thought you could hunt smugglers with little boys?

It was getting lighter. It would soon be sunrise. Perkins, seting himself low behind a bush, scanned the beach again. It was too late now for a run, surely. He looked out to sea. And he swore.

It was the *Gouda*, he knew that by the cut of the sails. She was moving due east. Away from the land. And she had cleared Bratton at noon the day before. He knew it all, in an instant. He had been cozened, swindled, gulled, he went through all the words for it in his mind, but there was not one which sounded any better than the others.

He walked over to Freeman, dismal by his horse.

'That's all. We're going back.'

'So they didn't come.' It was all one to Freeman, he had done what he was supposed to do. He was only a sergeant, and he had to obey orders. He had brought his men, there had been no run, now he could take them home again. He could not understand why Perkins was so angry. 'I'll be getting 'em home, then.'

'*You* won't.' Perkins hoped he sounded as brutal as he felt. Why should he take the brunt of it? 'You can *send* your men back to Wrackham.'

'And not me?'

'No. You're coming with me.'

Four miles away, in Dunnet House, Shillmoor faced Cutler over the table, the ruins of supper, the remains of a midnight snack, all interfering with breakfast. There were six empty port bottles, a decanter with not much brandy in it. Two packs of cards and some dice were mixed horribly with the cold meats. And the two Justices were heavy eyed, flatulent, drowsy. No smugglers had been brought to them, as Perkins had promised. They had been awake—at least they could swear, or would swear at any rate that they had stayed awake all night. Well, most of the night, anyway. And nothing had happened. Soon, they told each other across the table, they would know why.

16

It was a long night. When it ended, the mists rose off the Loone, thick and milky. Aged peasants looked from their doors, wagged their heads, and said, 'Aye, 'twill be a scorcher.' And then vanished inside again, and huddled under the blankets, if they had any, to arm themselves for the battle of the day. The Pards did that, and the chalk men, the shepherds and the valley farmers who grew wheat. But not the Alleys and the Sarsens and the Blackmers. They revelled in the sun, unnatural like, and there were them as put it down to foreign blood, said it were a curse that was on 'em all.

That morning, though, the Alleys and the Sarsens and the

Blackmers stayed fast indoors, sleeping the sleep of the just-in-intent. They had worked hard in the name of God the All-merciful, the Protector of the Fatherless; they had smitten the Pards. The Pards, though, many of them, were out early. The mist was nothing to them, they lived in it. But it burned off the fields and the dry chalk fast, the sun blazed at them as they straggled back towards their huts in the Marsh. They were furious. They raged at the soldiers who had come down on them, and they raged at the traitor—there must have been a traitor—who had led the soldiers there. For the Dragoons from the Black Bull had set off the other way. They must have come back across the river.

The carts were abandoned where they stood, by the river. But the Pards walked miles under the sun to catch their horses, one by one, strayed here and there along the bank.

They raged at the heavens. They were madder far for lack of drink than they ever were in liquor. Had they had a leader, they would not have needed much urging to sweep into Wrackham and raid the Black Bull, aye and the Town House too, or wherever the brandy had been hidden. The Pards always sought a leader, and they had none. The Lords of Loone had led them for generations till the last of the King's Pards had died in a shattered mess of pikes before the great guns at Marston Moor, and six Endellions with them, the cousin and nephews of that last Earl of Loone but one. And since there were no Endellions left, and the Lords of Loone gone, why they might as well follow a Place, seeing that he paid them.

The leaders were miles away. They had waited till it seemed almost light, and there was no sound anywhere of the Dragoons, unless they sang like the blasted birds that always destroyed a man's best sleep. George and Charley crawled out from their haystack, and silently brushed each other down, scraping the green clay from their coats and sieving straw from their scant hair. They put on their wigs, and caught their horses with great difficulty, since both animals thought they had had enough of the sea shore for that year, and were not anxious to face it again. But at last it was done. Still in silence, they mounted and rode inland. There were empty ways by which they could cast south, and come out on the London Road near the thicket. There might just possibly be a rider at the thicket, and something to pick up at pistol point, out of sheer spite and frustration.

In Wrackham, Josh Caddon scurried about the Millyard. He had already groomed Tiger, and mucked out into the street; he had an arrangement with a man who grew lettuces and such small greens for the market. And some bran here, and a few oats there, they all made a difference to a poor man.

Robert Folland stood at the ledgers in the counting house. He blinked at the swimming figures. He had been up all night before, and he knew how it took him. He was jaded, and if Kettlestang thought again of dancing lessons, he'd kill him, that he would, because the one thing that Robert meant to do in his dinner time was to sit tight in his chair and steal a few minutes' sleep. But one night wasn't bad. It was only after three nights that he began to feel it.

Marl was polishing silver in Colonel Cutler's pantry. He felt gay. His stomach glowed. The Colonel was away, likely to be away for the rest of the day. It had taken tact, to deliver an invitation that Shillmoor never knew he had sent, and to convey an acceptance that would not mention the invitation. But since the Colonel was notoriously shy of writing, and sent such messages by word of mouth, as all the county knew, it had been managed, especially as Shillmoor's butler, Ullock, had been, well, if not in the Regiment, at least a Fusilier himself in his time. Without Ullock they would never have been able to do it : he'd kept two gentlemen sitting up all night. Sitting up was the word for it, though every time Marl or Ullock had peered through the crack of the door, the two had been snoring over the table. Now, belikes they were shouting for breakfast, or another breakfast, and with sad heads after the night, and Marl wished Ullock luck with the pair of them, and went off in the day as craftily as he had come in the dawn.

The two Justices were now eating their second breakfast, a civilized habit which Cutler had brought back from Germany. At the Elector's Court, he assured Shillmoor, everyone always ate a *zweite freistuck,* and so, in time, would all loyal subjects of the King, when England had a King again. Shillmoor agreed heartily. It was not very often that he could talk with someone of whose political loyalty he had no doubts. He could even broach the delicate subject of vigilance.

'There's them in Wrackham that would have the Pretender in,' he assured Cutler. 'They're only waiting for the message.'

Cutler laughed at that. There was the Army would have something to say about that. The Duke would see they did the right thing.

'And what is the right thing in his mind? What he'll be paid?' Cutler bridled.

'The Duke's a loyal man. He's loyal to the Queen first, and the country. And after that, he's loyal to the Elector.'

'All the same,' Shillmoor insisted—after all it wasn't always he could have the chance to suggest it. 'Couldn't we do the same ourselves? Be ready against the Pretender?'

Cutler laughed.

'You're not a Wrackham man, are you, Shillmoor?' He could not feel he really liked the man, but he was someone to talk to. He could be warned. 'I'm a Wrackham man. We've had that land for a hundred years, but my great-grandfather came out of the town then. Still, I am a Burgess of Wrackham by birth, and so will be all my sons after me, and I know those people. They won't move except for their own ends. Not for King George or King James, when the time will come. Only for Wrackham town. If you want to keep down the town, then ask your Dragoons and your Exciseman. Look, here they come now. Ask them. I don't see that they've a long tail of prisoners to bring us.'

Perkins reached the front door. He hung there till Freeman caught him up. The Sergeant was reluctant to come any further, Cutler could tell that by the man's gestures and his eyes, that sad dejected look like a dog expecting to be beaten, for what he is not sure, only understanding from the tone of voice that he is in trouble. Surely, thought Cutler, Shillmoor does not have this placeman come in through the front door? He was reassured. When Freeman had come up Perkins led the way round to the kitchen. Shillmoor showed that he was just as appreciative of the proper way to do things as was Cutler.

'Come round here,' he told the Colonel. 'I'll not have them in the dining room. We'll go to the Butler's pantry. They'll be more at home there.'

The pantry was a barren place—a table, a bench, bottles stacked ready for the needs of the day, some of the common-use silver ready to be polished, an ale cask in the corner. Exciseman and Sergeant came in, heavy footed and weary, their eyes hardly open, white chalk staining their coats. Shillmoor sat on the bench behind the table. Cutler did not wish to stoop to share it with him; he looked outside, found a three-legged stool, and

brought it back to sit on. The two newcomers were left to stand
—they weren't gentry or even respectable. Neither Justice saw
any reason to treat them with consideration.

Perkins unfolded his tale in detail. While he talked, Shillmoor
absent-mindedly took a bottle of port from the rack, twisted out
the cork, filled a silver tankard and drank, meditatively. He had
heard somewhere that it was a sovereign cure for headache, to
drink the same again. It was a cure he always used; it was a pity
it never worked. After a little he realized that Cutler was looking
at him disapprovingly. He passed the Colonel the bottle, and
another tankard. The Colonel's face cleared : he had heard of
the same cure. It never worked with him, either.

'So, acting on this information received from an informant
whose identity it would not be politic to reveal,' Perkins droned
on, hoping that by sheer weight of words and complexity of con-
struction he could hide the completeness and enormity of his
failure from Shillmoor, 'I took a Sergeant and twenty-three
Dragoons of Harley's Regiment, quartered in the town of Wrackham for the purpose of aid to the Civil Power in the apprehen-
sion of those who wish to evade Her Majesty's Customs. Acting
therefore under the warrant given me by yourself, Master Shillmoor, to seize and apprehend the persons of any man or men,
acting sole or in concert, in contravention of the laws of the land
and of all Her Majesty's Decrees and Orders in Council regard-
ing the rates of Duty and the methods of payment . . .' Perkins
felt proud of his achievement. He had managed to keep this
going now for five minutes without having to come to the point.
He could keep it up for at least as long again. Not like Freeman,
who was looking decidedly ill-at-ease, casting sideways glances
towards the bottles in the rack, and licking his lips every time
their Worships poured more port. It irritated Perkins. It irritated
Shillmoor also. Finally, he said sharply,

'Here, Sergeant, get yourself something to drink. And something for the Tidewatcher too. No !' for Freeman had reached an
optimistic hand toward the bottle rack. 'There's ale in the cask,
and there's mugs behind you.'

Freeman's spirits sank a little. Even Shillmoor's ale was better
than nothing, though not much. Water was better. But if there
was only ale, and that offered free, then ale it was. He filled two
mugs, noting that there was no head to it. Nasty flat muck, he
thought, trust Shillmoor to have the worst of his own ale in his

167

own house. The stuff that he can't sell he keeps for his callers, for poor men what can't answer back. He passed one mug to Perkins, who let it lie on the table in front of him : drinking, thought Perkins, would break his chain of thought. He droned on. He numbered the Dragoons name by name, described where they had been placed on the cliff top, identified the horseholders. . . . Freeman for the first time raised the tankard and took a long draught. He pulled the top back on his mind, struggled with himself, strangled the desire to laugh, to scream aloud. He stood as stiff as if he were on sentry outside a General's tent. In a little while, the first cannonade in his head subsided. Cautiously he sipped again.

In the School House, Prisca sat in the kitchen shelling peas. She was sitting on a small keg. What was in it she did not know. All she did know was that there was a knocking on the door in the dawn. She had opened it to find Baker Sarsen there, grinning from ear to ear.

' 'Tis for the Schoolie,' he hissed. 'Not much, but 'tis for the Schoolie. 'Tis for looking after our Benny.' He lifted the keg and twirled it across the floor to where it was now, by the table. Prisca asked no questions. In a twinkling, he was through the door again, out across the yard and over the wall into the Abbey Walks.

Prisca looked at the keg. It was full, she sounded it to establish that, and very heavy. There was no need to move it, it did very well where it was till her father came home. After she had fed a breakfast of sorts to the boys, she found it made a very good seat, and her skirts hid it. There was no asking her father about it till after the morning canings were over. He always came back for his breakfast while the boys were learning their ration of Virgil for the day. They would be quiet enough—the work would be tested, and any time wasted now, even in breathing too often, would be paid in blows. It was a good school, everybody in Wrackham knew it, and Arkengarth was as good a Schoolmaster as they could have hoped for, seeing that he was a Wrackham man born.

In the stable, Josh Caddon, wide awake, moved cautiously behind Tiger. There'd be nobody looking in that manger. Aye, there it was, the little beauty, the keg he'd started. There was another tucked away in the loft, too. He worked hard to pour off a moderate amount into an earthen bottle. Too moderate. He doubled it. Well, it might be a long while before he saw as much brandy as that all at one time together, and all his own and not a penny to pay, so he'd better not waste it. Might as well drink it while he'd time. If he had the chance, why waste it? He settled down with his bottle on the hay, discreet, sheltered, and dreamed of the girls he had known, long ago, when he had gone with the guns to Marston Moor.

Perkins was babbling on. Shillmoor had spent a little energy in trying to find a pen, and ink, and paper, and sand, to take it all down in detail, word for word, but he could see none of those in the pantry so he gave up, saying he would have Perkins tell it all again to some discreet amanuensis later in the day, or the month, or the year. Perkins was thankful, since he would have hated to be made to swear to all he was saying now. It was the thoroughness with which he had had the beach searched which had taken his imagination now.

'The Dragoons, at my instructions, did look behind every rock, and into every nook and cranny of those dreadful cliffs. There was no one whatever on the beach, though in truth, your Worships, we searched in every place that a man could hide, or a child either, the smugglers not being too nice in their discretion . . .' He trailed off, nudged Freeman. The Sergeant was making little singing noises, happily. He went on, 'And there was nobody there at all. I think we can say that we have prevented any brandy being run on that coast last night.'

Josh Caddon was sound asleep now, in the hay, smiling like a little child and clutching his bottle of brandy to his breast like a doll. His snoring annoyed Tiger, who shifted about and whinnied to show he didn't like the smell of spirits.

Parson Arkengarth, too, smiled. He had investigated the cask with care, made sure that it did not contain gunpowder, or clay, for the latter awful trick had been played on him before now. It was certainly full of liquid. He moved it into the pantry and hid it behind a sack of onions. He was afraid of Father Krantze's six apprentices, who slept in the attic of the Falcon, but came to Prisca's kitchen for their dinner. He would broach the keg that night : it would take a little time to break it down into a host of separate bottles for concealment here and there in House and School. Still, he blessed the hands that had brought it. It would see him into the winter, easy.

Prisca, knowing who had brought it, was worried. When

169

Charley had been fortunate, it was often a Pard who would come to the back door and leave a something in a bottle. But there had never been as much as this left, and it was not a Pard who had left it. Charley had certainly been about a run. Therefore, somehow or other, he and the Pards had lost the brandy. In an hour of thinking by the kitchen fire, in a stroll around the market, in greetings with neighbours and market women, in seeing who looked sleepy and who was wide awake, Prisca made herself a reasonable outline of what had happened. She returned to her fire, sweated in the hot June noon over boiling beef for the boys and laughed to herself. It was the out-of-Wrackham men who had done it. And there was one person who might have been able to hold together the out-of-Wrackham men, and that was . . . Oh, but he could not be courting Sophia if he was robbing her brother at the same time. He would not dare to do it. George would kill him if George were lucky.

Out by the thicket, George felt near to killing somebody. He had not been lucky. He and Charley had spent some time sitting in the bushes, where they could see about a mile along the road for anyone coming out of Wrackham. It was, soon, a hot day. First Charley dozed, then George felt himself nodding. The grasshoppers and the birds sang their conflicting lullabies. He was almost off when he felt, pressed against his neck, where the bone bulges out behind the ear, a cold ring.

It was there just long enough for him to recognise it, and then was withdrawn. He sat still, frightened to move. Then he heard the voice,

'Up! Over there by the oak. And wake Charley.'

George obeyed. The two of them stood sadly against the trunk, and faced Captain Taberon.

'Just this,' said Taberon, 'and I'm off. You made a fine comedy of that last job, after I brought you the news of it.'

'I paid you,' objected George. 'And besides, he hadn't any money on him.'

'All the same,' Taberon pointed out, in the patient tone of a Master with a lazy stupid apprentice, 'it was the most stupid thing to go into Wrackham with the only things of value and sell them to the pawnbroker there.'

'He made me do it,' Charley objected. George snapped,

'You should have had the sense to get more than the pledge price.'

Taberon laughed.

'If you show no more wit between you, you'll never get far in this trade. Turn out!'

Gingerly, wary eyes on the pistol, the two turned out their pockets on the ground. Taberon waved them further off while he inspected his gains. Charley had fourpence ha'penny in small coppers, and George had nearly four pound in gold and silver. Taberon picked it all up.

'Nothing else to take except what I'd have to sell,' he explained, 'and that means somebody like Master Gunver to run my neck into a noose again. So it's only money that's worth taking; and some stock in trade as you might say.'

He took their powder flasks and spare flints. Charley's balls would fit his pistol, he said, so he picked up those. The pistols he left, being very scornful of George's because it was of musket bore and therefore too heavy for any great use. Charley's he condemned as cheap.

'I'll leave you here, then,' he ended, somewhat unnecessarily, since there was nowhere else he could leave them. 'I wish you joy of a poverty-stricken road. I'll have no more of it.'

And he rode off again, to Cambridge, for he was in private life a Pensioner of Saint Tibb's College, and depended on what he could scrape up in this way in vacation to feed him through the terms till he could take Holy Orders. And he kept in the Gate Tower, across the staircase from Master Arkengarth.

In Shillmoor's pantry, the argument was continuing. The Exciseman was trying to defend himself. He found it difficult. Now, the man tells me that I am there to drive smugglers away, and not to catch them, and again he tells me I am to catch them and this morning he is furious because I have no prisoners. Perkins had no patience left, and he was now much put out by the happiness of Freeman, laughing and humming to himself. The words of the songs were now more distinct, and more filthy, but the Sergeant seemed unaware of Shillmoor's raised eyebrows, of Cutler's mounting fury. At last, Perkins could stand it no longer, and rapped Freeman on the shoulder. The Dragoon laughed aloud at this, and then, taking it as a cue for speech, said,

' 'Tis good ale, Master Shillmoor, good ale. Better than you sell in your inns, any road.'

Shillmoor bridled. He did not want to lose his temper in front of Cutler. He said, shortly,

'The contents of that cask are precisely what my Innkeepers sell.'

'Oh, cheap stuff, is it?' and Freeman squinted into his empty pot. 'Then I'll be having 'nother pint, just 'nother pint.' He spun through eight hundred and ten degrees clockwise, took two steps across to the cask, stood a moment aiming his mug uncertainly at the spigot, and then sat down heavily on his bottom. He giggled again.

'Oh, dearie, upsy-daisy, upsy-daisy-doo.'

Perkins looked down at him in disgust. He looked to his own pint still standing untasted on the table. He picked it up, and took a first delicate, exploratory sip.

'This is your ale, Master Shillmoor?'

'Oh, yes, of course, it is my ale.'

'This is what you drink every day? Or perhaps the servants?'

'I drink it every day myself,' Shillmoor insisted. 'It is my own special brew. I will admit between friends it is a better brew than you will buy in Wrackham, but what is the use of owning a brewhouse if you cannot have ale as you want it.'

'This is as you want it, then, Master Shillmoor?'

'Oh, pretty well.'

'So you do know what is in it?'

'Only what is usually in it,' answered the brewer, trying to make out through the fumes of all the night's carouse what the Exciseman was at.

'Taste this, sir.' Perkins pushed his pot across the table to Cutler. The Colonel picked up the silver mug, put it to his lips, took a good gulp, an ale-sized taste, a mouthful. There was an immediate effect. He kept his lips clamped close together, as if he did not dare to swallow; but he did not splutter, being brought up to believe all waste was sinful. His face went red, purple almost. His throat moved, and at last he opened his mouth to breathe out, a fragrant alcoholic breeze. He was sweating, his eyes were staring. He whispered,

'Good God! But he drank a pint!' He pointed to Freeman kneeling on the floor by the cask, trying to fit his lips around the tap. 'He drank a whole pint, and he's still moving!'

'What is it?' demanded Shillmoor.

'Why, 'tis your ale, sir, as you told us, what you keep here for your own use.' The Colonel sounded indignant, but he drank again, as deeply but more slowly. Freeman, on the floor, suddenly sang out very loudly,

'With a tow-row-row-row-row!'

He then lay flat on his back and ceased to take any active part in the debate. Shillmoor at last took hold of the pot, sipped, and said,

'Brandy! Good God! Brandy!'

'Aye, sir,' said the Exciseman, 'and drawn from the cask which you say is your own ale, and we all saw it drawn.' He exulted in himself. Now I'll have my own back, he thought, for all those nights on the coast, for all that trailing about chasing poor beggars who wanted nothing more than a drink. 'How, Master Shillmoor, will you be accounting for that?'

There was never any accounting. Only the strange appearance of the brandy, only Ullock's assurance, in front of Cutler and the Exciseman, that it was indeed the same barrel as he had set up there the night before, and if there were anything wrong with it then sure 'twere the Master's fault for starting it before it were well settled. No other explanation.

The argument went on till well into the afternoon. When the sun began to look yellowish, Perkins heaved a giddy Freeman on to his horse, and set off to see him back to Wrackham. Across the bridge, two other travellers came slowly towards the town. George's horse had cast a shoe. He had got down to walk, and Charley, deserting him, had ridden gaily ahead. But after a little time, George had caught him up. His horse had picked up a stone, and was already lame. They sat a little while and bewailed their ill luck. That did them no good, so they agreed at length to do what they had already agreed on, to enter Wrackham from altogether the wrong direction to be accused of any part in running the night before. This took them some time.

At about seven o'clock, they came in sight of Saint Lawrence-across-the-River, with its ruined spire, fallen in the civil wars, shot down, said some, by Oliver's cannon; no, no, said others, rocked to pieces by the mere sound of them. On the red stone stump, the parishioners had built a wooden gallows in which they had rehung the bells, and to George's surprise, the bells were ringing again. Charley stopped to ask in the little clutch of houses by the church,

'Why ring the bells? Why not?'

'Old Charley Nobbler,
Couldn't pay the Cobbler,'

chanted the children. Men reeled about, happy and in full song.
They danced about George Place, laughed at him, offered to buy
his horse for tuppence, asked if he had slept well. They waltzed
near enough to him for him to know their breath smelt of brandy.
And they laughed in his face.

All through the streets of Wrackham, the out-of-Wrackham
men made merry. They filled the alleys, singing and dancing,
shouting rude slogans about the impotence of the Aldermen. All
the town was *en fête*. Good Burgesses stayed indoors, Hunderthwaite and Gunver, Dowgill and Nosterfield, Pontigarde and
Kettlestang, all the Wrackham names kept close behind their
shutters. Sober and sad they were.

At the Black Bull, when Perkins finally delivered Freeman to
his Dragoons, the same disorder ornamented the tap room. Each
trooper had had the same ration, his water-bottle emptied and
refilled with the pale spirit. All about the quays they roistered,
Dragoons and Alleys, Sarsens and shepherds from the chalk,
Dutch sailors and Blackmers. And above all, they swept the
streets and sought out Pards. They beat in the door of the Two
Roses, pillaged the Kitchen, demolished the Tap. They caught
the Marshmen, and drove them out of their hiding places, forced
them down towards the river, flung them, when they could catch
them, into the water, beating them first. And always the
triumphant cry was the same.

'Go with the Lords of Loone! Be gone with the Lords of
Loone!'

17

'And all this achieves . . . what?' Newall asked Folland. They
were beside the Thames.

'It has achieved a great deal.'

'I do not see how.'

'Can you not?' Folland laughed. 'When I came into Wrackham, I thought these men were as other men, living together, trading, and dealing, marrying and giving in marriage. And then after, I thought that they were not as other men. They seemed to me, as I watched them, a solid family, all living in agreement against the world outside. Wrackham men trust only Wrackham men, I thought, and they do trust each other.'

'And do they not?'

'You saw what happened in the Upper Room. We made the lesson clear in their eyes, as well as learning it ourselves. If we had to do what we had planned, and find the buttons ourselves in Gunver's shop in a day or two, with a warrant to search the place, it might not have sunk home so hard.'

'That Gunver receives stolen goods?'

'There's not a man in town does not know that. He is a laughing stock.'

'No one moves against him?'

'Not till now. But you saw what happened. As long as they were in no danger, they were ready to deal with him; as soon as their own skins were in danger they were ready to desert each other. There were three who did that—Pontigarde and Gunver and Carines. And in the end they were willing to sacrifice another Wrackham man, Arkengarth. True, Kettlestang papered over the cracks, but they know now, they cannot trust each other.'

'How does this further our business?'

'The Portreeve has decreed that they will not land coal at Wrackham, nor sell it from the Quays.'

'So what do we do?'

'There is a Hard further down the river, on Hod Blackmer's land. We can lighten ships in the river mouth, and land coal at the Hard. That avoids Port Dues at Wrackham, and an immense amount of cartage. If they refuse to handle it in the town, they cannot complain that it is landed elsewhere. And yet, they cannot trust each other any more. They are ready to deal as individuals, not as a town.'

'And what is it you are doing?'

'I know what I am doing. At first, I only groped blindly. I was like a man out of a wrecked ship. I laid hold on fragments of wood as they came by. Little by little, I got together enough wood for a raft, and now, you helping, I have built myself a whole ship. And I know where I am going.'

'You are going into the port of Wrackham? But why? I cannot understand you. Why do you not cut your losses and find somewhere else to live? I will put you in the way of business here in London. We get on well enough together.'

'I am going into the port of Wrackham only because they wish to keep me out. Look, that is why soldiers fight to enter a Fortress. Not because they're paid to do it or because they hate the French, but simply because they will not bear to be told they cannot be let to do it. I tell you, I will enter that town of right, and I will pull it apart and before I die I will rebuild it all.'

Newall laughed.

'You'll wear yourself out while you do it, and stifle from loneliness. And how goes your courting? You were making great progress that evening.'

'Oh, that.' Robert tried to brush it aside. 'What am I to do? Her brother hates me, her father cannot see me, but is civil enough after Church, and she walks with me when she sees me. I have done nothing.'

'Marry the girl, be a Wrackham man, and live wrapped in silk and wine to the end of your days.'

Newall could laugh at it. He was envious of someone who was offered the chance to marry money, when he could see what could be done with money. If only he had had the sense to marry a bit of capital, instead—but Molly did him very well, did not ask too much of him, comforted him when bad times came, enjoyed good times to the depths. Robert shrugged. He could tell Newall some of the reasons, but not all. He could not tell him about Prisca.

'I cannot marry,' he told Newall, 'till I know who I am. And when I know who I am, I will know why Kettlestang has done all this. When I know his plan, I can complete mine and do it.'

'You think that Kettlestang knows who you really are?'

'I cannot imagine he would do what he has done if I were only what I thought I was—a poor parson's son from Warwickshire, that went for a soldier when he quarrelled with his father, after his mother died.' He hesitated. There was no one to whom he had told the story of that last quarrel. Could he now, to Newall? He swallowed, decided.

'It was . . . I do not know if he was my father. In that last quarrel, he called me a . . . he said I was . . . she was scarce dead . . .'

Newall shook his head.

'Don't say anything more. I understand.' He was concerned. He had seen Folland depressed when the Stocks went down, or when a ship was overdue. He had seen him elated at success, even slightly drunk once or twice. But he had, Newall would have said, a gamester's temperament: emotions had never stirred him from the road he wanted to go. This was the first emotion he had shown that seemed like to break him. Newall found another topic. But he had learnt enough to ask Cutler, met by chance in the Strand a week later,

'What does "Bowbank" mean to you?'

'Bowbank? It sounds a Wrackham name.'

'Were there Bowbanks, oh, twenty-five or -six years ago in Wrackham?'

'I don't know. I will ask about it.' Cutler too knew Newall too well to doubt that there was some real reason for asking.

'Make no great noise about it.'

Robert Folland was making no great noise either. Of the Wrackham men he had counted his friends, who had abandoned him to the Pards, there were still two who had not been humiliated. One was Carines. That, he thought, was easy.

Carines had been an easy target for a long time, ever since he had seen Robert and Sophia clink their glasses over a bowl of white roses in water, ever since he had heard their voices whisper, 'the King'. Robert found the tailor too often at his heels, near him in inn or market place, hovering over him, and catching his eye as if expecting him to speak, yet never coming to the point. It was not too difficult for Robert to guess what the intention was, nor what Carines must now take him for. It was August before he let himself whisper into Carines' ear, as he passed him in the street, 'The time is almost come.'

Three days later, Carines found a letter in his pocket. He could not recognize the writing. It was neither signed nor dated. It said only,

'Do what you are bid.'

It was noted that evening, in the Falcon, that Carines was light hearted, almost gay. He drank a pint more than usual, Gunver looked at him curiously. They were on speaking terms again. But they were no longer each other's confidants. The betrayal in the upper parlour had left a scar.

The next note came a week later. It was in the same hand. How it had come into the roll of cloth, tucked into the topmost fold where he was bound to find it, Carines could not tell. It said,

'Walk thrice above the Watergate at ten of night, wearing a blue coat and scarlet breeches.'

That night, Carines did walk on the wall above the Watergate. But, economically, he wore his usual drab grey coat and black small clothes. It was a week before he found yet another letter, slid under his shop door at night. It told him sharply,

'Obey my orders. Dress as the King desires.'

As the time went by, Carines had much fault found with his clothes. He made himself more. He walked in his new clothes on the walls above the Watergate, above the Westgate, on the Quays, on the banks above the river. The coat facings were wrong : he had, in his innocence made them in scarlet to match his breeches. He was rebuked,

'Is such a way for the King's Civil Officers to dress?'

He replaced the scarlet with binding of the same colour as his coat. He was told peremptorily,

'Are you a sea officer?'

At last, when desperate he came out a second time in the dark blue facings, he received some help :

'The King's Magistrates wear light blue facings.'

He tried a sky blue this time. Folland had not the energy to think of any more criticisms of the coat. He turned on the shoes. The plain tongues were condemned, and scallops were to be worn; the tongues were to be lined in violet.

By now, Carines was bursting in himself. He had been loyal all these years, and his father before him. No one spoke of such things, but his devotion to the House of Stuart was well known in the town, and respected. It was understood everywhere that someone in the town must sit the other side of the fence. The role was made for Carines. He had accepted it all these years. Now, he was to be rewarded.

His altered clothes were noted by his friends. He gave no explanation, not even to his wife. He lay beside her at night and thought how pleased she would be when the King was brought in and she found herself a Magistrate's lady. Carines did love his Eliza dearly.

178

The change was noted most in the congregation of the Misguided Brethren. There ostentation was frowned upon. Therefore, the first two Sundays after the letters began to come, Carines changed into his old drab for the Assembly. He stood in the Conventicles and spoke with tongues and the other Brethren waited respectfully for him to receive revelation before it came to them, as befitted the economic order. But he was rebuked for this, too. Were the King's clothes not good enough for the Conventicle? Was he then so ashamed of his devotion? Did he wish to continue in favour? Therefore, Carines wore his fine new clothes at last to the Conventicle. And the Brethren wondered.

They sat in their Conventicle, in little groups of four, on four-legged stools, each group a square, to represent the foursquare walls of the New Jerusalem. They sat in silence, broke out spontaneously into shouts of praise, Hallelujah and Hosanna, spoke words, sentences, whole paragraphs of truth and virtue. Thus they always did. That was the common lot of every man, to say what was true in a plain tongue that all understood. Or they sang together, lifting their voices in strange dirges, with neither metre nor tune, because these ornaments were inventions of the devil. Other Christians, they knew, sang the Psalms of David, but they did not. For it would be a denial of the spirit to repeat formal words.

That first Sunday that Carines wore his scarlet breeches in the Assembly of the Misguided Brethren, he felt ill at ease. He knew all eyes were on him as he entered, as he took a seat at considered random, opposite Mistress Carnigill, whose husband was a carter. Yet she was a comely woman, young and luscious, filling her skin like a peach, bursting from her drab gown. It was obviously at random that Carines so often sat opposite Mistress Carnigill, for there were times that the fury and frenzy of devotion and the power of the spirit set all the Brethren, and the Sisters, spinning about the room and joining each to each in carnal fury. And on such days, Master Carines found it agreeable to be by pure chance opposite Mistress Carnigill, for all that he loved his wife.

But on this Sunday, though he sat opposite Mistress Carnigill, Carines waited in vain for the spirit to come on him. He waited for words of power to come into his mouth, for strange language to fill his mind and lips. He waited, and all the other Brethren waited. They waited and waited, and the 'Praise-the-Lords' and the 'Thanks-to-Hims' were repeated. But power did not come on him, and the comforting speaking grew slacker and less frequent, the pauses more marked and longer, while they waited for him to begin. He writhed under their expectations, he tried to empty his mind, but the Lord did not come to him. He tried consciously, he opened his mouth, he tried to remember what the sounds were, what came from his mouth, from others' mouths, when the spirit was among them.

'Ba . . .' he brought out doubtfully. 'Ba-ma-ba-ga-bo . . .' He could not go on. He dared not look into Mistress Carnigill's eyes. Across the Conventicle, a voice rose loud and clear. Azerley, Kettlestang's clerk, sang out,

'Ochieemilieeprekrasnie kaklioobliooyavas kakboioosyavas.'

The following Sunday Carines entered the Parish Church. Fine in his blue and scarlet, he took his place in the old Clothier's chapel. He was unused to the service : he stood when he should have knelt, he said, 'Oh *God* make haste to help us,' but it was done. Master Carines had returned to the Church of England.

Bridgward thought it a great joke. He himself was a Baptist, although he came to take the Sacrament once a year to qualify for his other post under the Corporation, Collector of Port Dues. This was by no means a heavy task, since he employed his nephew as Under-Collector. He paid his nephew a set weekly wage : he himself drew a percentage on all tolls, and though no one was supposed to know, but everybody did, he paid a tithe of that to Kettlestang who had appointed him. He wondered what hope of gain or office had caused Carines to become so respectable, and was troubled for his Collectorship.

Josh Caddon wondered, too, what had happened to Carines. The tailor had received an instruction which made him doubt his sanity. Never before had he been compelled to give something away for nothing—even the winter bonnet to Mistress Carnigill had been payment for definite favours. The note he found tucked into the hollow handle of his great smoothing iron. It said,

'When you are a Magistrate, your Bailiff must be dressed to walk behind you. Josh Caddon shall have a new suit.'

Caddon thought Carines was mad, indeed, when the tailor called him into the shop.

'Now, what would you say to a new coat, Josh.'

'Nay, Master Carines, this one will see me out.'

'It will not see this winter through. You must have a new one for *you-know-what.*'

Josh stared at him, then laughed.

'I bain't got no money for new coats, I bain't.'

'Oh, money doesn't matter, does it, if it's for *you-know-what.*'

Josh didn't know what. But he knew better than to hint that the coat had been a free gift. The men in the tap of the Falcon noticed it, laughed at it, asked Josh if he were going courting, took exaggerated care of it, pretended to spill ale over it but didn't—for they knew good workmanship when they saw it, and they would not for the world's sake do wanton damage. They were not Pards : they were men who worked with their hands. It was a fine brown coat and fitted him well, too—they had not seen Carines taking the groom's measure, or heard his wailing over the peculiar shape of body he had to mould a coat to. The breeches were easier, because the coat would hide where he had botched them.

Josh showed how pleased he was with the new clothes, and didn't care who knew it. He still wore his old ones for stables, and in the day, but this new coat was for the Falcon and for Sunday Mass, when a priest came. But they put ideas into his head. Courting, they said? Why not? There was Nance Hartsop, she were a widow, and younger than he was by a good bit. She had a house around there in Gut Run, by the shambles, and if he could get in there for the last few years. . . . Last few years? He'd outlive her yet, and have a house of his own to bring somebody fresher and prettier to.

Robert Folland watched this with amusement. If the old goat thought he could bring off another match at his age, there was no reason why he should not be helped. But even if that were not possible, he could be given a little more comfort. A Bailiff, a Magistrate's Bailiff, must be looked after. To Josh's further amazement, he found that Carines bade him eat with his apprentices. At the beginning it was a Sunday treat only, but later he was invited for Wednesdays, and the Fridays and so on till Josh was getting a hot dinner nearly every day. It gave him a new lease of life, all said how kind Master Carines had become now he had left off that low Conventicle which had made him so much of a miser. The only cross Carines had to carry was that his wife remained still obstinate in her following of the Brethren, and refused him any kindness while he backslid thus. And he could not tell her the reason, or the great honour and dignity in store for her, because the letters forbade it, so he burned.

They told him many things. Once a week he perambulated the walls of the town, from Watergate to Watergate. He took with him paper and a piece of blacklead, and he drew in detail, as best he could, the damage the years had done to the ramparts. In one or two places, the holes done by the Parliament guns seventy years ago had not been filled in, though the wide breach by the East Gate had been rebuilt in the same year. For his first task, when the King was come again, and he was Portreeve, not by the vote of the people but by command of the King, would be to renew the defences of his town.

Slowly, as the letters flowed in on him, a picture began to build up in Carines' mind. He was sworn to secrecy, that was understood. There were many of his persuasion in the town, scores perhaps, and none of them known to each other : or if they knew each other, they never mentioned their common link. Men of the White Rose did not gossip together or drink stupid oaths as did the Elector's party, or the Marlborough men. Sometimes, of course, they pretended to be members of these conspiracies against the best interests of the nation and of the Stuart cause. This was a secret group, loyal and silent.

The most surprising people were members. Perkins, the Tidewatcher, Carines read, was one of them. He would arrange the landing. Oh, yes, it was easy to read between the lines. As soon as the Queen was dead, it was here at Bratton that the true King would land, and Carines must be ready to hurry down to the sea to meet him on the beach, kneel before him, perhaps even lie down on the sand that the Royal feet might keep themselves dry on his back. And then to walk backwards before the King into Wrackham and hand to His Majesty the keys of the town, which Bridgward would have filched from Kettlestang's cupboards. Kettlestang would be safe in the town gaol by then, haled there by Alderman Keld's three sons.

Carines was almost hysterical with his secret. He must, if ever he had the chance, declare himself. He was himself, putting two and two together. For there was one family never mentioned in the letters. You could guess by the Christian names the head of the house had chosen for his children. There would never be a true Jacobite who would christen his children George and Sophia.

Folland was on the whole very satisfied with what he had done. He debated within himself whether he could not get Charley a new suit also. Regretfully, he decided that it would be too risky. It would mean bringing him into the town again. A few people marked that Charley was absent from Wrackham. None regretted it. Nor did they know where he was. Folland did.

Charley slept in an attic in Colonel Cutler's old stone house, under the eaves. He was up early. With two Dutchmen who had jumped ship, he hauled stone and mixed mortar. He sorted and stacked the blocks from what had once been a barn. In a little shed that he had built first, he had papers and pens, plans and drafts and calculations. Under his hands, for the first time, something real was rising. They were building a new stable for Colonel Cutler.

18

Perkins suggested it. Cutler thought about it, and talked to Robert Folland. Marl was very anxious it should happen. But Folland did nothing till Kettlestang came out with it.

'There is a horse race, at the beginning of September.'

'A horse race?' Folland did not think it politic to appear to know anything Kettlestang wanted to explain to him.

'They call it the Wrackham Run. It is a long race. On the first of September, the Pards all go up to the top of Staddle Down, and they raise a pole in a hole at the top.'

'Why?'

'Why does it rain? Because that is what they have done since time immemorial. And they hold a kind of fair of their own there on top of the Down. Now, the Friday following there is always a half-holiday in the town, and the weavers stop work at noon. An hour after noon all the gentry and yeomen from the farms around race from the Northgate up to the top of Staddle Down, and back by a long way, to the Watergate. They go over hedge and ditch, young Bob, in and out of water, through thorn thicket and bog.'

'It sounds a hard course.'

'And so it is, for horses, young Robin. But once, it was a race for men. The Pards used to make the run, on foot, and they used to do it as soon as the pole was raised. I have heard tell, it was run the other way, from the Down to the town and back again, to touch the pole. That was before Oliver's time. The Parliament men quite put it down, Robin, quite put it down. After the troubles, the gentry started it again, as a horse race this time, and the other way about. And once Old Rowley came to watch it, and bet on it. Think of that, Robbie, the King himself coming to see our little race.'

Folland made appreciative noises. They were eating dinner in the Counting House, and his mouth was luckily full of boiled beef of quite a distressing temperature.

'Now, I have been thinking, Robin. Do you know what I have been thinking?'

Robert shook his head. He had somehow taken a whole boiled onion in his mouth, and it was distended. He was hoping that he would not have to answer. He would only guess ahead too accurately.

'Now, at the end of this month, Robin, there is Portreeve Making day. That is the day of Saint Matthew, who is the patron of this town, being a tax collector and a sinner. The Portreeve is made then, but he is picked on the Sunday after the Run, so that there is time for all the preparations to be made.'

'Who is to be the next Portreeve?' Robert asked. 'I know that the Portreeve is elected every fifth year, and you have been Portreeve——'

'There is no guarantee, but I tell you this, young Bob, I tell you this in confidence'—there were Bridgward and three clerks within ten feet and Kettlestang was talking at the top of his voice—'I have some reason to suspect that I may be elected again. I may be the first Portreeve since the days of the Abbey to serve a second time, to carry the Oar as we say.' Kettlestang sounded unusually pompous. It was obvious to Folland that he was playing a part, asking himself how a Portreeve ought to behave and doing it.

'Then I should felicitate you.' Robert had long given up

expressions of respect : Kettlestang seemed not to demand them, he conveyed that by his manner.

'Now would it not be a great thing, hey?' The Portreeve giggled, nudged Folland in the ribs.

'Would not what be a great thing?'

'Why, have you not been listening to what I have been telling you?' Kettlestang was not rebuking, he was laughing at Folland. 'The Run, lad, the Run! I wish I were young enough to do it myself. But if you don't do such things in your youth, they will never be possible. Would it not be a great thing if when the Portreeve rides the bounds of the Town and Port of Wrackham as he must as soon as he is made, he were to do it on his own horse that had won the Wrackham Run?'

'The Portreeve's horse?'

'Why do you think I prize Tiger so much? I bought him on purpose for this, young Bob. I have reared him for this. His sire and his dam were stayers, that would go all day, and so is he. And this is a long race.'

'So you mean to ride him in the Run?' Robert steeled himself to appear stupid.

'No, lad, I want you to ride him.'

'I am no man to ride in a race. I weigh fourteen stone. Tiger can carry me at a jog all day, but he cannot run far with me.'

'Nonsense. You have never made him gallop.'

'Only the once, when I was being shot at.'

'Then you must take him out and try him. It is a very curious way the Run goes, that the Pards laid out long ago. Now tomorrow, try him.'

'Tomorrow is a working day. There are books to be kept.'

'And is this not work? I looked round long enough, my boy, for a rider who could do it. Colonel Cutler assured me that if there were anyone who could ride a course like that, it would be a Dragoon.'

'It is not my ability I worry over. It is the horse.'

'Here, try him. Tomorrow afternoon, I will get a horse and we will ride round the course. Walk round it first, then if you think it can be done, you can take it faster. Look, I have watched this race every year of my life. I can tell you about every fence, every ditch. And I know that it is not the fastest horse that wins, but the horse that has most heart for it. And Tiger has heart.'

'He has that. But will it be a fair advantage, to ride round the course first and practise?'

'Why, everyone else will.' Kettlestang laughed. 'There will be scarcely room at some places for men riding it to learn the course.'

They went round it together, Robert Folland on Tiger, and Kettlestang on a quiet old bay. They did not take the jumps, but only looked at the hedges, sought for good places to get over, and then sought the gates. It was a good eight miles, up the wide open down dotted with sheep. They paused at the top, and looked over Wrackham to where the Castle of Loone, still proud in its ruins, stood on its hillock.

'Ah, you see that place?' Kettlestang asked Folland. 'When they built that, it was on an island in the Marsh. They had to wait for the last Lord of Loone to die before they could drain the Marsh there. He'd not have an easy way to his house, even though he had not two pennies to rub together and nothing to live on but the pike the Pards brought him. Now, look the other way, to the sea. That's where the modern life is, and wealth, and power, in trading with—what's that ship, there? See it?'

'The Swede? That's the *Upsala* out of——'

'No, that one. The brig.'

'Oh, I couldn't tell you.' Robert was punctilious for the truth.

'No matter. If you find out, tell me.'

They turned down the hill again.

'That's a fair old ride,' Robert remarked, when they were back at Kettlestang's house. Josh Caddon unsaddled Tiger and rubbed him down and saw him safe in his stall, before he thought of taking the sweating bay back to the livery stable.

'Ah, yes, it is. You'd better be taking Tiger round a time or two before the day, to learn the way. But there'll be no going to London on him. He's too precious to be risked.'

'No gallop round there, at full speed?'

Kettlestang understood.

'We don't want him lamed. You'll treat him carefully from now on.'

'I'll have some of my own money on him.'

The banker laughed.

'There'll be more wanting to bet on George Place. He was the first round the last two years running. And you won't let anyone get at Tiger, either, will you?'

'Get at him?'

'They were saying last year, that George Place only won because Charley Nobbler was a friend of his, and made sure he would have no competition. How shall we keep the horse safe from that, eh?'

'Charley Nobbler is out of Wrackham. He is building a stable for Colonel Cutler.'

'Then if he doesn't nobble Tiger for George Place he will do it for Cutler. We must keep the horse safe. He is not safe here— anyone might get over the wall while I am out. There is only one thing for it. We will have to move him down into the stables in the Millyard, with the draught horses.'

'How will that be safer?'

'No one will dare to try to get at the stables when you are in the cottage.'

Folland opened his mouth to speak, then closed it again. There was no use in objecting with everything coming to the boil. It was Kettlestang's way. He would go out at night, to the Dragon or the White Hart, where he pleased. But if Robert were to guard Tiger, he could not go out. That was Kettlestang's way. He was the Portreeve, the banker, the Magistrate, the great merchant. What he wanted, what he ordered, other people would do. He never asked. He was quite satisfied that his plan would work. Even now, thought Folland, he is decided that he will win that race, merely by entering for it. And if it means I have to stand guard over that blasted horse every night . . . oh, there will be some way out of that, my reputation will keep it safe, and I can get Azerley to spend a few evenings there, with a light behind the curtains. And in the early hours, nobody will believe I am not there asleep.

I will have to think of something to say about the Brig. It was unlucky he saw it. I can always say that it was watering, but I must bring it up. If I leave it till he asks me, he will think I am hiding it. And yet I *am* hiding it. There is very little time left to hide.

There is little time left to hide. That was the message that went now to Carines. Be ready, you do not know the day nor the hour, he read in the tight-rolled billet that came into his pocket he knew not how. He was to stand ready to take his place as Chief Magistrate of Wrackham. The Aldermen were to be abolished, there was to be no governing except what came from the King.

And the King had been pleased to appoint him, Joseph Carines, the only faithful follower of the Stuart cause, to be ruler of the Town and Port. Not long to wait now for that proud day. He made himself another coat of the French blue, he made the facings of gold lace and thin gold wire. It cost a great deal, all his profits for a fortnight, but it was worth it. What else would he wear, then, on the great proclamation day, when he would be known to all as the holder of the King's own Dormant Commission? The effect of the news was noticeable, even though he kept it a secret. He became distant in the Falcon kitchen, more dignified in the shop, disdaining to serve anyone who came after the second-hand cast-offs which formed the greater part of his stock. He left that to his apprentices. When he went to Church now he strode up the aisle proud as an Alderman, and the three shop lads trailed after him. The Aldermen did not like it, but there was nothing overt they could do. They too waited for the right time.

It was three days before Tiger was moved down into the Mill-yard. Kettlestang made as much fuss as he had over the furnishing of the cottage. The stable selected, the nearest to the cottage, had to be cleaned out, even scrubbed. The walls were white-washed. And to Robert's surprise, when the work was almost done, Kettlestang said to him,

'Go up, now, lad, and ask Miss Place if she will do us the honour of leading Tiger into his new stall.'

Robert looked at Kettlestang as if he were mad. The banker laughed.

'True, I promised her that it should be so. You will find her ready and waiting.'

Robert left Kettlestang, the carters, and Tiger, in the Mill-yard, and walked to the Place house. He rapped on the door. A little servant maid opened it, curtsied to him, and asked him inside. He stood, awkwardly, in the hall. This house was unlike any other in Wrackham that he had been in. He had not been asked into above half a dozen. There was a separate apartment to come in to, which was not a room with a function of its own. It might have been one of the fine new London houses. He seemed to have heard that they had brought a builder from London to make it, since no one in Wrackham was used to working in brick. Well, he thought, those days were over, or soon would be.

Already, in Staddle House, Charley faced Colonel Cutler across the table, all strewn with drawings.

'Robert Folland recommended you.'

'Yes, sir. I hope he——'

'I have been looking at these drawings. The house looks good enough. Can you build it?'

'Oh, I can build it. I worked for Henry Bell in Lynn for two years, on and off—I was a foreman for him——'

'I know. I sent to ask. Why did you not stay? He was sorry to see you leave.'

'I couldn't live anywhere but Wrackham. I thought perhaps I could build here.'

'But you *can* build here. I have your stable.'

'Aye. 'Tis only a question of . . . of . . .'

'A question of what?'

'Men. Not skilled men—I can find carpenters. Anyone can learn to lay bricks in a day—I did. But there will be foundations to be dug, and thousands of bricks to be burnt. We need men to dig clay. We will find them, I think. I have someone who will find them.'

The maid sent Robert through a door into what seemed to be a parlour, for he thought it looked like the best room in the Vicarage that his mother called her parlour. He looked round. There was new furniture, carved and ornamented of Indian woods. There was fruit in a silver dish, brocade hangings at the window. And he could smell money. There were only wax candles used here : he missed the stench of tallow. In every other house he knew, clothes, curtains, cushions, everything was soaked and reeking of the smell of frying, of burning fat. Not here. That was the surest sign of wealth.

Wealth was the word. Not merely comfort, such as Kettlestang lived in. Kettlestang might be more wealthy, but he did not show it. Kettlestang was not interested in money for living with : he was interested in power, and whether he had power as Banker or Portreeve did not matter to him. That much Robert had learned. But here wealth was, not so much on display, for the Burgesses of Wrackham did not entertain each other—Kettlestang's ball had been almost unprecedented, and even that was not held in his house—but in use.

It took him aback. The last time I saw a house as rich as this, he thought, we looted it. Little good it did us. But to live like this, and have servants to do all, to light fires in the cold of a morning, to place food on the table, to bring ale, or wine . . . And as Sophia Place turned to him, held out her hand, he realized that he could live like this, could have all this.

It took him, oh, two minutes, perhaps less, to realize that this was not merely an idle dream. Sophia was standing with her back to the window. She had planned it so. The light irradiated her golden hair, made it spread like a halo on all sides of her. But there was a pier glass above the mantel on her right that reflected the sunshine into her face. The modelling was soft, but clear. The rounded shapes of lips and cheek-bones, the fine line of her nose set out an angel's face, a saint's within the halo. The virtue was what she intended to be seen, not the actuality. Her jacket's round neck showed the parting of her bosom. It shaped close to her slender waist, in a sheath of pale yellow, laced in a green cord. The sleeves came midway between wrist and elbow, leaving visible the fine boned wrist, the fair skin with a hazing of golden down. The cuffs were overlaid with lace. From the waist, the jacket flared out over her wide skirt of green, flowered in yellow. And all was silk. Sophia had decided long ago that these were her colours, green and gold, and she wore them with her own air.

Only wings are lacking, thought Folland, only wings, in this blessed soul. He shut his eyes a moment, and Prisca floated in front of him. He opened them to the splendid reality, and made his bow.

'Miss Place, your servant.'

'My Lord,' and she curtsied, so that he thought she was jesting, and laughed at it. She felt a little hurt, but reflected how difficult it had been to bring this meeting about, with her father and her brother at the wharf, her mother still abed, snoring off the last night's brandy, and if she woke now not likely to do more than call for more spirits, Mellin in his pantry, three housemaids at the wash, the cook at market and the parlour maid, the only other person in the house, waiting by the bedroom door and not brave enough to move. All this she had arranged with Kettlestang, in a conversation after Church, in a few words walking on the walls above her own garden in the cool of the evening. She would not waste this, when there was a coronet at stake. She smiled, determined at all costs to keep his incognito. He was big enough, and fine enough, to be a Lord, therefore he must be one, and she would be a Lady. At all costs. She held out her hand. He took it, and found himself drawn closer to her.

'Master Folland,' she told him, 'you must not avoid us so. This house is always open to you.'

He almost laughed in her face.

'Miss, your brother is hardly my best friend.'

'My brother will do what his father tells him.'

'And your father?'

'I will see to that. You must come here, meet my mother, eat at our table, see that wine merchants are not as debauched as you might suppose.'

'I had not supposed they were.'

This was gallant of him. She knew everyone in town talked about her mother. And he would understand more than that. It was not the custom in Wrackham to entertain strangers. The Burgesses fed their apprentices, they might have their own kinsmen to eat at their tables, so long as it cost nothing and promised a profit. If Robert came to dinner in the Place house, then it was more than hospitality, it was more than a declaration of intent, a laying court. It would be a courtship accepted. He understood. She felt his hand stiffen in hers, and with her inborn Wrackham good sense made exactly the wrong interpretation. In a moment she was in—against, anyway—his arms, pressed to him, his buttons marking her skin.

Robert moved automatically, without willing it, as a male. His arm went round her slim waist, his dry lips brushed hers, his thighs felt hers beyond the skirt and the hoops under it. He thought in an instant, oh, if it were Prisca, and then asked himself why, with this lush body, this wealth his for the asking, he should hold back. It was all dust and ashes in his hands, and she, above the scent of sweat and horses and tobacco, through the bulk of his body and the strength of his arms, felt it.

They stepped back simultaneously. She was pink with emotion, he was brick red with embarrassment. There was a moment's silence. Then Robert reminded her,

'Master Kettlestang is waiting. I believe he looks forward eagerly to your coming.' He avoided her eyes. She settled herself. This was nothing. He might well be taken aback, but there was time yet, and Kettlestang was her friend, would see that there were other times, other opportunities. Sophia knew that she was beautiful, and had wit and spirit, beyond anyone she knew. He could not resist for long. She was confident. She laid her hand, quietly now, on Robert's arm, and they passed through the hall into the street.

They did not talk as they made their way toward the postern gate, till she suddenly asked him,

'And will you ride in the Run?'

'I think that that is Master Kettlestang's intention.'

'You will have to beat my brother. And my grey.'

'Tiger will run as he can.'

'My brother would not be displeased if he did not win.'

'But he has won twice already. Why should he not want to win this time?'

'This used to be a race for the gentry of the county, not for the Burgesses. George was the first townsman ever to ride in it, and he beat all those brave fox hunters. Then he did it last year also. He does not want to draw any more dislike from the County —after all, they buy our wine. But the townsmen want him to ride. If he rides, there is nothing he can do but ride to win.'

'Nothing?' Robert raised his eyebrows.

'He may seem a scoundrel to you, but he has his own idea of honour.'

'What is honour?'

'Only that you are true to yourself, and go on with what you have begun—publicly begun.'

'Or with what you have privately begun.'

'So that is your idea of honour, also?'

'I can leave no business unfinished.' He felt strange. He could talk to this girl calmly, without lust, about harsh abstractions, almost as if she were a man, a comrade. No, there was no feeling he could find for her, except that of companionship . . . was friendship too strong a word? She meant him well, that was clear, but she meant more than that, and he could have it for the asking. True, he was not in love, there was no feeling as deep as that here, not the way he felt, had felt, about Prisca. Still, couples had lived well enough like that, in companionship.

They came to the Millyard. Sophia admired the stable, was walked around on Kettlestang's arm, to see the barns, with their stores of the first of the season's barley marked for the brewers and the distillery, the wheat piled for the Army in Flanders. Folland walked behind, ready to open doors, motion the steve-dores out of the way. To his surprise, he found himself following them out to the quay, and up into the flute moored alongside loading barley in bags to slip down the coast to London.

'It's such a little ship,' she complained.

'Big ships do not come here. The river is not deep enough.'

'I know. I have always wanted to see a great ship.'

'We have a great ship in the river mouth now,' Kettlestang told her. 'A Swede. Robin is going tomorrow with a message. If you wish to see her, I am sure he will escort you.'

'If it is a fine day, I would be pleased to go.'

Robin was taken aback. He could not say no. Nor could he the next day, when it dawned dry, with the sun hiding first behind a heat haze. He took Tiger, and Sophia came to meet him on her own grey. She wore a riding habit in her own colours, yellow coat frogged and faced with green, a pale green waistcoat, and a petticoat of deep green. They rode over Staddle Down in polite silence. They confined their conversation to matters of the road, warnings now and then of rough places or soft patches. They stopped at the Inn on top of the Down, and drank a glass of sack, and looked down on Bratton and the ships lying there. Then they began the descent. And Robert remembered that he had promised Prisca he would take her to see the sea, and now he was taking someone else. He wondered if it were an omen.

Sophia caused a sensation in Bratton. There seldom came such fine ladies into the port. Much less did they demand to be taken out to Swedish ships. The Swedish Captain was both astonished and pleased. His men cheered Sophia as she came out of the wherry and up the companion nimbly as any boy, and as sure. The Swedes are eating out of her hand, thought Folland, as he handed over the fresh bread he had brought, and the eggs. The Swedish Captain stumbled in English. Sophia addressed him in German, they laughed, they chatted, far beyond Robert's hope of comprehension.

The Captain did not think it proper to offer a lady the raw schnapps that he drank with Folland. He brought out of his own lockers a bottle of white wine. Sophia paused from her omelette, sipped it, held it up to the light. The Swedish Captain said,

'It is a good wine. From the Moselle.'

Sophia laughed. 'From the left bank, I think. High up, near Trier. Oberemmel? I think not. Most like Wiltingen.'

'You're right,' cried the Captain. The three mates crowded into the coach with them laughed with delight. A woman who judged her wine like this! Robert felt himself a little proud of her, tried to stifle the warmth, failed. She held the centre of the stage, and he was a mere attendant.

All Bratton saw them go to and from the ship. Half of Wrackham saw them ride out of town in the morning: the whole borough knew when they returned, saw Robert hand her down from her horse at her own door. He rode on to the Millyard, took in to Kettlestang his letters from Sweden, made his report. Kettlestang said nothing, did not enquire about Sophia. Robert offered no information. There was nothing to say. All the way home they had talked about Sweden, whether the King would ever return from Turkey, whether he would continue his war against Russia, what in the end would become of that unhappy country. This was, he had to admit, better informed conversation than he had with Prisca. With Prisca he was always the senior, teaching her. With Sophia he was an equal.

The difference was too confusing. Robert decided to resolve it the only way he knew. He took Bridgward by the arm as the Book-keeper was locking up, and pressed him along to the Black Bull. Azerley found himself guarding Tiger. He was not best pleased to sit there in quiet while his two seniors got drunk with the Dragoons.

19

There were five days now to the Run. Tiger had had his last fast gallop, and now he would only be led out for a little exercise in the early morning. Robert took his relaxation as he was used to: he called Azerley from his lodging to watch the Yard, and he went with Bridgward to the Black Bull. It was a merry evening, Bridgward eager to see the Dragoons' weapons, to hear their tales of the Wars, which of course they all had to make up, and did so with vigour while he was paying for the gin. Folland watched the scene with a smile: then he slipped quietly out, and went back to relieve Azerley.

In the morning, he was at his place by Kettlestang's door. He followed the Banker, as usual, down to the Yard, listening to his instructions for the day. But when they got to the counting house, there was something unusual. Kettlestang looked round.

'Where is Bridgward? In the necessary house again? I'll swear he lives there.' It was not one of his good mornings.

'He has not come in today,' Azerley volunteered.

'Then he must be sent for. No, Azerley, not you, I do not pay you to walk about the streets in the morning. Josh! Go to Obadiah Bridgward's house and see why he is not here today. He knows very well that this is a very busy day, with the Michaelmas rents coming in and all the half-year renewals for Master Pontigarde to draft and have signed.'

Josh was gone a long time. Kettlestang turned on Robert.

'You can do Bridgward's work as well as your own. Set to with his books, and do his entries till he comes. Wait, now—count up the columns carefully that there is nothing missing. He has a fine opportunity to cheat me.'

'But he has worked for you, and your father before you, for thirty years,' Robert objected.

'He has been waiting for his chance,' snarled Kettlestang. Obviously, the very idea that one of his workers should not be exactly where he was wanted, when he was wanted, had never occurred to him, had unsettled him completely.

Josh came back at last. He looked happy and dazed, and Robert, smelling his breath, knew what he had been at. Kettlestang did not notice : it had not occurred to him that anyone could find brandy to drink at nine o'clock in the morning.

'He bain't at home. His wife be fair frantic. She bain't seen him since he went to work yesterday morning.'

'You mean he has not been home all night?'

'Well, she never seed him, if he did.'

'He has run away, and cheated me. It's plain, that's what he has done.'

'His books are in order. There is no cash outstanding.' Robert was quick to get that in. 'When I saw him last, he had no mind to go anywhere.'

'Where was that? Was it when he left the counting house?'

'No. I left him in the Black Bull. He had some fine company, but I had to come back here to watch the horse.'

Kettlestang turned on Josh.

'Off to the Bull. Go and ask what became of Bridgward last night.'

Josh was longer coming back that time. While he was gone, Kettlestang seized Bridgward's day books from Folland, re-worked what he could see, cross-referred to Folland's books, to Azerley's. It was a complex system, so devised that no one man could cheat unless both the others came in with him, and then they did not know what secret records Kettlestang kept himself. If the whole business were not so complicated, Bridgward was used to complain, and if Kettlestang could bring himself to trust one man at a time, then that one man could do a week's work in half a day. But Kettlestang would not be cheated.

When Josh came back, he was merry and smelled of drink so bad that even Kettlestang had to notice, but believing it to be an unusual lapse, he tried to say nothing about it. Perhaps it was a judgement on him to send a man like this on purpose to an inn in the working day.

'Well, what did they say?'

Josh giggled, swayed a little, and then laughed outright.

'Oh, they wouldn't tell me at first. Fred Rook what does the tap told me what happened, all quiet like. So I asks that sergeant outright, and he laughs in my face, and gives me a pint of yale, and tells me to think nothing more of it. And when I said that was not the matter of it, that it was you that wanted to think more of it, he said as if you wanted to know, you could come down yourself and ask him.'

'Ask him what?'

'If it be true, o' course, for it be only a rumour and there's nobody will say if they know the rights and wrongs of it.'

'The rights and wrongs of what? Give me a straight answer now, you drunken buffoon, or I'll turn you out of doors to die on the parish.'

'Aye, and that'd do yer a lot of good when it comes to wanting to be Portreeve, because there's them that will take me in and make a deal of fuss about it, and not to your advantage.' Josh couldn't think of anyone who actually would take him in, except Carines, and he could not depend on him, but it sounded a good thing to say. Kettlestang swallowed it, saying with an effort,

'Now, come, come, Josh, you know well that there's nobody will turn you out' (making up his mind to do just that on the first excuse). 'Tell me now, what it was all about.'

'Well, now, I'll try to tell ye, but seeing that it's dry work all this talking . . .' Robert, without being bidden, poured Josh a pint of dinner ale. 'Thank ye kindly, Master Kettlestang, I'll be telling ye, aye, that's good, well it was like this, now. It were last night, Master Bridgward was a-drinking with the sodgers, and getting very merry, as he often does these days after Master Folland has gone home to his bed like a respectable man that he is, and I'll speak to that before anybody. Wanting as always to know what it is like in the Army, and saying as so often he does, that there is no life like that of a sodger, and how he wished that he were a bachelor again and could go off as a gay Dragoon, they did put more gin into him than a pig's bladderful. In the end he said he would have no more of a cantankerous wife nor a foolish and grudgeful master, and did ask if he could be a gay Dragoon. And the Sergeant did put a shilling into his hand, and it's a Dragoon he is now, and soon be off to Flanders with the Regiment, that they did tell me. And a fine joke they all think it, and it's me that is agreeing with them.' Josh finished his pint, and looked around optimistically for more, but did not get any.

Kettlestang was for a moment speechless. He caught at the air, and asked in a strangled voice,

'Do you mean Bridgward has gone for a soldier?'

'Aye, that's what they be saying, down at the Black Bull. But when I did ask more, they did tell me that if you wanted to know for sure, you had better come down yourself.'

Kettlestang turned to Robert Folland.

'Do you think it is true?'

'I do not doubt it. Bridgward often talks as if he envies soldiers, especially in drink.'

'In drink? I have never seen him in drink in his life.'

'But Master Kettlestang, you do not drink in the taverns where we poor men go. If you were used to places like the Falcon or the Bull, you would know sure enough.' Robert felt no compunction at all. The man had refused to stand by him when he was in trouble, therefore he did not deserve protection.

'Then, Robert . . .' Kettlestang considered, 'you go down to the inn and find out the truth. Perhaps the soldiers will listen to you.'

'Shall I go first to his house, and see if his wife will send him stout shoes, and a spare shirt or two, since I know that these he will find most welcome as he goes into Flanders, or perhaps Spain or the Indies.'

'What are you thinking of? What am I to do here if Bridgward goes off to the wars? Who shall keep my books, when you are out on the road? With business increasing as it does, and the time it takes to train a lad, and——' He was about to say he did not trust Azerley to keep his hands out of the till, but it struck him that it would hardly be politic if he had to depend on the clerks only. 'No, we must have him back, Bob, go and see when he can be sent back to us.'

'Oh, Master Kettlestang, you do not know how these things are managed. If Master Bridgward has truly taken the oath to the Queen, they will never let him go.'

'Oh, no, it cannot be as bad as that, Robin. Now go you to the inn and ask the Sergeant whether he will not let him go.'

'I do not think that you understand——'

'Am I not the Portreeve? Am I not the Chief Citizen of this town? Go and tell the sergeant that the Portreeve demands that he release this man from the Army!'

With relish, Robert departed to give those exact words to Freeman. He, too, was a long time coming back, because it was a fine day to sit in the inn yard and stretch in the sun. Kettlestang and the three junior clerks were all sitting down at table when he joined them.

'Why, have you not brought Bridgward with you? Where is he?'

'Oh, I had speech of him, and he was most reproachful that I had not gone to bring him his best shoes, as he knew from all I had told him that they would be most necessary. Still, I did lend him three shillings, being all I had on me, which he promised me most faithfully to return to me when he comes back from the wars, as he hopes to do alive.'

'Do you mean——?'

'This is very good beef, very good indeed. I suppose we can share out Bridgward's portion between us.'

'But I told you to bring him back.'

'I do not want to offend you, Portreeve——'

'If you cannot bring Bridgward back, you run grave risk of offending me.'

'I acted merely as a messenger. Your Worship, I fear that the Sergeant said he cared nothing for your Worship's power in

Wrackham, or for the Civil Power at all. He says there is now nothing you can do. Bridgward is a soldier.'

Kettlestang turned a strange purply-grey colour. He was silent a moment, probably, thought Robert, saying a prayer. For patience? Or for vengeance? He said at last, gently,

'Now, now, young Robert, it is a trying time, and you must not judge me harshly. You must not take anything I say to heart.'

'Oh, no, of course not.'

'What I mean is, can we not offer the Sergeant something to forget the whole matter?'

'Perhaps Bridgward does not want it forgotten? Do you know Mistress Bridgward? I have known men go to sea to avoid kinder women than she. The Army is mild compared to a ship.'

'What *he* wants forgotten is not the point. *I* want Bridgward. *I* must have him back. How much will the Sergeant want?'

'I think if you had gone yourself, and at once, it could have been managed for seven guineas. That is the standard rate. Sergeants of detachments look on it as a normal method of increasing their pay. Freeman is an honest man and never quite understands what is meant by a bribe, unless it is offered to him plainly. But it is out of Freeman's hands.'

'How so?'

'Bridgward has gone off to join the Regiment proper, which as you may know is quartered in Cambridge.'

'Gone off?'

'Ridden off, with four other Dragoons to look after his every need and make sure that he comes to no harm. I do not think he was tied so tight as to hurt him—there is an art in that, as I know, having done it myself.'

'Did he say anything as he went?'

'I could not make out the words. It was either "Grug-grug" or "Ark-ark", but I could not tell through the gag.'

'Good God!'

'No, I do not think it was that, or any other expression of gratitude for divine providence.' Robert was proud of his polished sentences. He had not been able to talk like this when he came to Wrackham.

'But what are we to do? I have it. Colonel Cutler is a military man. He had a Regiment once. He will be able to go to . . . ?'

'Harley has the Regiment in question.'

'. . . This Colonel Harley and get him to release Bridgward.'

'Then you will go to Cutler?'

'No, Robert, you will go. I am busy at this time. Pontigarde will be here this afternoon, with conveyances for me to sign.'

'I do not think that Colonel Cutler will go so far for me. I was only a Sergeant in his Regiment, and you are the Portreeve.'

'You think I ought to go?'

'I have a list of all the things Master Pontigarde is to bring, and how they are to be signed. If you will leave them with me, I will deal with him, while you ride to see the Colonel.'

'I suppose I must. Arrange all with Pontigarde : I will approve anything you do. I shall take Tiger.'

'Is it worth damaging the horse so near the Run?'

'Perhaps you are right. You are so often right, Robert. I will borrow the grey from Miss Place. A fine girl that, Robin, and my heart sings for you.'

The Portreeve went out on that note, and Robert laughed. There was a great deal for Pontigarde to do, receipts and mortgages, loans and conveyances. It was late at night when all was finished, that Robert Folland sitting in his cottage with the paper work of the day spread out before him heard a knocking at the outer door. He peered through the window, and was satisfied, but still he demanded,

'Who is it?'

'It is I, Master Kettlestang.'

'It sounds like, but I can take no chances. What colour breeches was I wearing this noon?'

'Brown. Your brown ones, with the satin trimmings.'

'How much did I pay for them?'

'You did not pay for them, but I did, and they cost seventeen shillings as you will see in my books.'

Folland laughed. He opened the door, and stuck a pistol into the Portreeve's face, near knocking out his teeth. The Portreeve jerked back into the street, and then came forward more cautiously. He sat on a stool and leaned his head on Folland's table.

'God preserve me from business with the military.'

'You were not well received?'

'Robin, Robin, I have eaten two dinners today and I have drunk two bottles of port, besides much claret and brandy. I am in no condition to do anything.'

'And Master Bridgward, is he safe at home now?'

'By no means. I have been all this time persuading Colonel Cutler to help me, and nothing will suit him but that he and I ride together to Cambridge to see Colonel Harley, an old campaigning comrade. He hopes we will have a dinner of the same kind tomorrow.'

'And will Master Bridgward be brought home? He may be unwilling to come.'

'And all that money wasted? He will ask me to send him home if I have to strangle the words out of him. I had to promise Cutler that anything he does in this matter will be at my charges.'

'And you will have to pay anything that Harley's people want. Those expenses will not be light. But come, Master Kettlestang, look at these papers, all ready for you to sign.'

'Oh, but my head aches. The whole room is going twirly whirly, Robin. I cannot sign things tonight.'

'Master Pontigarde was insistent, your Worship, that all must be done. Look. I have quill and ink here, and sand . . . start here.'

'Oh, yes, here . . . and the next. . . . Oh, have you not a better light than this dip?'

'Not a thing. Perhaps if I hold it so. . . . I am sorry, I did not mean to burn the brim of your Worship's hat.'

'And another . . . and another . . . I had not realized there were so many . . . here . . . and here . . . Is that the end?'

'It is.'

'I must be off before dawn. I will have to borrow another horse. That grey is a dreadful animal, with a rocking gait—I feel quite sick. I will not be here in the morning.'

'Master Pontigarde will come back for the papers.'

'Oh, you can manage. You know all the business.'

Kettlestang went off through the fine rain. Robert declined to accompany him to his house, saying he had to guard the horse, he could not do it from a distance. He rose some time after dawn, saddled Tiger, satisfied himself that the Portreeve had indeed gone away, and hacked quietly the circuit of the town outside the walls. It was a quiet day. Pontigarde came again, looked at the pile of signed deeds, sorted out the copies that he was to keep.

The Portreeve did not return that night. Robert laughed to

himself. That the man should think he was going to ride to Cambridge and see a Colonel of Dragoons and come home again the same night. Robert Folland was the first man in the counting house, and the senior man there too, with no Bridgward, no Kettlestang, sitting himself at the head of the table. And almost as they finished their dinner, Bridgward walked in.

'Why,' Robert asked him, as nonchalantly as he could, 'how are you back from the wars so soon?'

'Oh, Rob, Rob, how can I ever thank you? Oh what a time I have had. If you had not lent me those four guineas and whispered advice to me, I would now be a Dragoon for sure. How can I repay you?'

'Oh, I am repaid already, for I got the money from your wife. But how come you are back so soon?'

'I gave the money to the surgeon, as you recommended me, and I was cast off from the Service almost at once, as not fit to be a soldier. And I have a paper, so I can never be enlisted again.'

'Let me see.' Robert put out his hand for the certificate. 'Oh, I cannot read this, an apothecary's fist if ever I saw one. Here, Azerley, read it to us.'

Before Bridgward could stop him, Azerley was standing across the room by an open window. He read loud and clear, so that the carters below the yard stopped to listen. 'This is to certify that Obadiah Bridgward, a person purporting to be a clerk though he could not satisfy me of his ability to read or write, is unfit to be enlisted into Harley's Dragoons, or into any other corps in the army that is desirous of filling its ranks with honest men, by reason of his infirmities, videlicet, the pox, the ague, corpulence, the gout, foulness of the wind, impotence and general debility, and more, that he hath——'

And although Bridgward succeeded in snatching the paper, the carters were laughing in glee. Robert kept his face serious. He poured Bridgward ale—his dinner was all eaten.

'Did they bring you home?'

Bridgward said things which were not fit for a deacon of the Baptist conventicle to imagine. He recovered himself, and went on,

'They left me without a penny, and I walked home, most of the way, though I would not be here yet if I had not met a rider with a led horse last night at dusk who gave me a lift for twenty miles. He said his name was Taberon. He was most sympathetic to me. When I told him that Master Kettlestang would be following after me to release me, he was very attentive and said he would also look out for him. But I got into town barely an hour ago, and I have only washed my feet and changed my socks, and I find there is a great deal altered while I have been away. We had not heard in Cambridge that the Queen was dead.'

'The Queen dead?' Folland stood immediately. 'Why say you that? It is not true, is it?'

'But she must be. For is not Joseph Carines standing in the Buttermarket in the French King's Coat, with a sword at his side, calling on all loyal subjects of the King to rally to him?'

'Why, that we had not heard. Who has rallied to him?'

Nobody had rallied to him. Carines stood there in the market place, and looked for the men commissioned to act under him. Eustace Keld was to be Captain of Militia, and Joshua Nosterfield his Lieutenant. Levi Gannel was to be Constable, and Elisha Starbutton Harbourmaster, and they were all to be ready that evening to meet the new King when he landed at the Quay. But none of them came. No one came at all. Nobody listened to him. The people of Wrackham went away, and left him to hold the Market Square for King James. Alone.

For there was only one person who ought to have received news, that the Queen was dead or that the King had landed to oust her, and that was the Portreeve. And since the Portreeve was not in town to act, no one acted. The Constable did not arrest Carines, nor did the loyal subjects shout him down. All that was the Portreeve's task, and if he was not there to do it, no one else would, and in any case, where was he at such a time? The answer to that was easy.

Kettlestang limped across the bridge into Wrackham, tired, dusty, almost in tears. His hangover did not help. Cutler was behind him, walking doggedly, mechanically, He turned after Kettlestang along the Quay, but collapsed almost at once into the Black Bull. The Dragoons rushed to pour water into his mouth and to wash his face with brandy. They were, he observed dimly, booted and spurred and armed, ready to ride out.

Kettlestang zig-zagged along the Quay till he reached the counting house. He staggered in and sat down on the nearest bench. The clerks gathered around him, Robert came slowly downstairs.

'Oh, your Worship, did you have a good journey?'

Kettlestang slowly raised his head. He spoke at length. There were words the clerks had never heard before, and words Folland had only heard from bosuns, and words even Folland had never heard before, joined in combinations that were original, counter, strange. After a little, Robert understood that Captain Taberon and Colonel Harley together were being conjured to perform feats beyond the limits either of anatomy or of metaphysics.

'But, sir,' Robert tried to restrain himself, to be more than usually polite, since at this moment he could not risk a break, 'did not Colonel Harley treat you well?'

'No, sir, he did not treat me well. And for why? For that the treating was wholly on my side. Last night, he insisted I should dine with him and his officers, who must have been thirty in number, in the Lion Inn, in Petty Cury. And they uncommon thirsty, and insisted I should drink bumper for bumper with the best of them. I was overcome for the second night together. In the morning, the landlord presented me with the bill for all. I had to run around Cambridge like a demented ferret to find one of my correspondents who would allow me sufficient cash to take care of my commitments. And then, it cost me twenty-five guineas this morning to the Captain and the Sergeant Major and the Surgeon who promised me faithfully that when Bridgward is to be sworn in the next day or two they will contrive that he is found unfit for service.'

Folland tried to keep a face. Bridgward had gone sadly home to his wife. What Kettlestang would do when he found that he had spent money to release a man already free, Robert could not imagine. But he could make guesses.

'And then, when we were not more than ten miles from home, and not less, either, we were set upon by that villain Captain Taberon.' Robert calculated that by now Full Term was over. 'He took all the money we had left, twelve guineas from me, and seven from the Colonel, who insists that is part of the charges I promised to bear. He drove away our horses, and I have walked all the rest of the way, no one being willing to lend me a horse, all being wanted to go to watch the race tomorrow, and Colonel Cutler no longer sure that he will run.'

'Then you will not be asking his help in putting down the rebellion?' Robert asked in an offhand tone. That last letter to Carines had been specific: there would be no landing till the

Abbey Clock struck six, and he would need an hour's grace to deliver a heartening address to his forces. Kettlestang listened to the news quietly. Then he stood up. The fatigue seemed to drop from him. He passed his hand over his face, spoke to Azerley.

'Run to the Bull. Call upon the Dragoons to aid the Civil Power.'

By the time Azerley had returned, Kettlestang had at least washed his face, and revived himself with brandy and bread and cheese. The clerk stood terrified before his revivified master.

'The Sergeant says it's none of his business. He's in the Army to fight the French, and to catch smugglers, and he's busy enough with them jobs. And he's not coming till he hears from his Colonel.'

'Not from that man! I have had enough of Harley. I shall put this rising down myself, or die. Give me a pistol.'

Folland brought one down from the upper room. He loaded with powder but thought it politic to omit the ball. Kettlestang went into the yard. He stood on a cart and shouted to the labourers, wheeling casks of cheese and sacks of flour for the soldiers in Flanders, who would be betrayed if he did not fight now, even to the last, however outnumbered.

'Men! Englishmen! There is a rebellion in the air. Let us catch it before it spreads. Come with me and save the Protestant Succession!'

He wished to make a more eloquent appeal, remind his hearers of their birthright, but before he was through his second sentence, they were thronging around the Portreeve. They carried boathooks and cartwhips, thick leather belts, nailed sticks and hollywood cudgels, the weapons of street fighting in Wrackham since time immemorial. They pressed behind Kettlestang as he led them through the postern, up his own street and out into the Market Square.

Carines was standing there, waiting for his followers. He heard from afar a confused noise of voices. He drew himself up to his full five and a half foot, and began to read for the fourth time,

'James, the Third and Eighth, by the Grace of God——'

He went no further. He stopped as he saw Kettlestang come into the Square, the little army debouch behind him and spread out in a long line. Carines stood paralysed looking at them, and they at him. Kettlestang took a step forward. Carines, casting down his proclamation, ran.

There was shouting and halloing, and a joyous chase. Good Burgesses stayed close indoors as the mob followed their quarry down Abbey Walk and Green Gut, the Shambles and Blood Row, Duck Street and North Gate. Through the narrow lanes, Carines turned and twisted, dodging and ducking sticks and stones that were flung at his head. The hunt was joined by the workers on the Quay. There were other kinds of fun. A market stall overset here, a shop door beaten in there, an inn cleared out —it was a fine night indeed, and every house thought to be a Catholic one, or disloyally inclined, would have its windows smashed, and lucky if it was not turned upside down just for the thrill of it. All except for Carines' own shop. Outside the front door Robert stood with his sword in his hand, at the back was Josh Caddon with his whip. That shop was not looted. But why, wondered Robert, are there no Pards on the street tonight? What a fight there would be if there were.

20

The town was quiet. The rioting, the looting, were over. The streets were empty. Joseph Carines sat in the stocks. He had been caught and dragged out, kicking, from the sewer in the Shambles. Alleys and Sarsens, men who had never bought a suit in their lives, in dirty smocks and heavy boots, hauled him to stand before Kettlestang in the Market Place. There the Portreeve held a hasty court. He began by asking Carines what he had to say. The tailor, unwisely, began to recite, from memory,

'James, by the Grace of God——'

He got no further, for Baker Alley had pressed a dead cat over his mouth. Kettlestang was satisfied. What is not said cannot be taken account of. The man was not treasonous, he found, but merely mad—not entirely mad, mind you, for that would mean locking him up in the Bridewell, and nobody could remember where the keys were, the place being so rarely used. No, merely a little touched, with the heat of the summer and the long hours he spent sitting cross-legged in his shop. The most appropriate treatment would be to stretch those legs out straight. Therefore, he was carried to the stocks on the north side of the market place. The carters and stevedores and lightermen had sport there, throwing horsedung at him and clods and rotten eggs and anything else they could think of which would spoil his fine clothes, but not harm him. For the suit, surely, was part of his madness; the sooner that was spoiled the sooner he would be well.

The pelting was soon over, for there was not much fun in a sitting target. The mob melted away. Some of the bolder lads thought it might be a good ending to the evening to go down to the Black Bull and get the Dragoons to come out and fight, for they could easily be aroused, but there were no soldiers. They had ridden out. Where? Well, across the bridge, but only Baker Sarsen knew for sure; he would not tell. So the lightermen beat him, and the Sarsens and Blackmers came to his help and the youngsters beat the hell out of each other and their seniors drank the Black Bull out of beer, and agreed it was a good evening, and went home, unsteady but happy. And it was Thursday night, the Run would be the next day, and Portreeve Picking the Sunday. There were two more good nights of drinking; if the horses ran right and the Portreeve did what was asked of him, they would be cheap nights too.

They all went home and the dusk came in. Kettlestang was in the Dragon with the Aldermen, all agreeing it had been a wicked deed Carines had done, and a near thing there had not been a rebellion, and they would wait till they had firm news of who was in control at Whitehall before they took sides. Carines sat alone and filthy in his stocks, and wished he had gone to a latrine before he fled. He was thirsty, he itched all over, and he wished heartily that he had never learnt to read.

Nothing moved on the market square, except a few rats and Christopher Gunver's pig come out to clear away the rubbish of the stalls—there were half a dozen women who came to sell small greens every day. There was no moon, only a cloud to hide the stars. He felt sick and tired and lonely. He wished he could sleep.

Carines heard a step on the cobbles. He did not know whether to be frightened or glad. It might be one of the boys come back to torment him—oh, the brave ones, they had stolen his wig and twisted his sparse hair into ringlets with ship-tar, and poured some of it down his neck between skin and shirt. He tried to persuade himself it was a woman's step. Was it his wife? He was not sure—he thought not, she would scream at the sight of a mouse, and she'd never dare to come out alone in the dark. Or perhaps one of the Misguided Sisters? Mistress Carnigill, why didn't she come and see to him, she'd had enough out of him before now, not to tell his wife, but he'd had less than his money's worth. And it was a woman, one woman, he could tell. He could not twist his head to see, held fast in the collar. Perhaps it was Liz Alley, come from the Falcon. Surely Dowgill would send her. There was no law against it, and he and Gunver, Papists both, must be in sympathy with the Stuarts.

The steps reached him. A hand touched his shoulder, and he grunted : he could hardly speak, he was so hoarse with reading his proclamation, and shouting as the crowd chased him. And a voice spoke to him, kindly,

'Now, now, Master Carines, be at ease now.'

He failed at first to recognize it, a voice he rarely heard. She went on,

'Now, we'll soon have all that off your face. Just hold still, there's a good man.'

He felt her pass the warm wet cloth over his eyes and lips. He felt clean again. Someone cared about that. He began to cry. She urged him,

'Now, lift up your heart. There's not long to go.'

'Miss Arkengarth,' he forced out. 'What will be done? Will they hang me?'

Prisca laughed.

'No, no, they won't do anything. I heard Master Kettlestang tell the Constable to let you out as soon as it gets light, and you can go. But don't go back to your house. Come around to the School House. I have your wife and children safe there. We will get you really clean. Don't worry, your shop is safe.'

He tried to thank her, but could not for tears. She asked him,

'Can you drink with your head like that? Can you swallow?'

He thought he could. She held a jug to his lips, and he tasted brandy and hot water—more brandy than water. It gave him strength, and then he found the jug was changed. He smelt hot soup, with fat on the top of it like stars; he gulped at that, and found his mouth full of shreds of meat. She tore up a fresh loaf and put it into his mouth; he was just able to swallow it. Carines

208

was a dainty eater, but this he felt was finer than any Portreeve's banquet. When the soup and the loaf were all gone, Prisca held the other jug to his lips again.

'Oh, thank you, thank you,' he mumbled.

'Come along, drink it up,' she bade him. There seemed a great deal of punch, but she insisted. He got it down, he kept it down.

'It will make you sleep,' Prisca told him. It did more than that. It knocked him out; in ten minutes he was snoring like a grampus. Prisca waited till his head began to sag. She stood and looked around her at the darkened town. Everyone was in bed; she had seen the Portreeve go home from the Dragon. She looked, thinking this, down towards the Portreeve's house, and the Place House opposite it. And she saw the Portreeve again, come out of his own door and knock, quietly, at Master Place's.

Folland was sitting by his fire in the cottage, trying to make up his mind to go to bed. Next day, at four in the afternoon, he would have to ride in a race, and he had half a day's work to do before then, and he had had enough poring over books by day and by candlelight. His eyes stung. What if there had been a riot, that was common enough; everything seemed quiet enough now. He was in shirt and breeches, stockings rolled down beneath his knees, his shoes lying before the door. He had placed his wig on its stand, and did not bother with a nightcap. He decided to go to bed. He turned back the blankets, and stripped off his shirt, for he liked to wash away the sweat of the day before he lay down. He had learnt that in the army; though it might be thought a trifle ornamental in a civilian he could not break the habit.

He dipped his face into the bowl of cold water, and came out of it spluttering. He picked up a towel, rubbed—and stopped rubbing. There was someone knocking at the door. He listened. No, he was right, it was someone knocking. He could not tell who. Ten to one, it was Charley. But why should Charley be coming to him now? It would be better if he kept out of the town. Robert walked to the door, cautiously lifted the bar. The door was pushed violently against him, there was a rustle of silk, someone was inside the room with him, pushing the door shut again. He looked down on Sophia in some amazement.

'Miss Place . . . I do not know . . . I must . . . this is no place for you.' He reached for his shirt, keeping his back to her.

'Do you think,' she enquired acidly, 'that I have never seen a man with his breast bare before? Turn round and talk to me, Robert Folland, like a man—if you are a man.'

'What do you mean, if I am a man?'

'You did not behave like a man in my house. You were like a doll then. Can you behave like a man out of doors?'

He faced her, began to understand. She was wrought up. She could only give herself the courage to approach him in his own house after dark by attacking him. Only the impetus of reproach and accusation would carry the request she was bound to make. He answered,

'Try then, and see.'

She slipped her cloak on to the floor. She was wearing a loose gown tied at the waist with a ribbon. The modesty piece at her bosom was crumpled. She had dressed in haste to run down the street to him. She was wearing soft slippers, not her usual high pattens, so as to make less noise. What was up?

'It is my brother.'

He hardened heart and voice.

'He is no friend of mine.'

'That is nothing.'

'It is something that he tried to kill me.'

'Would you rather you killed him? Or me?'

'You are confused.'

'You know what George does at nights? Some nights?'

'He plays the highwayman, but mostly by day. Has he gone up in the world?'

'Do not tease me. You know he runs brandy.'

'I have heard.'

'Then listen harder. They are running a cargo tonight. On the beach, under Hodman Blackmer's farm.'

'Ought I to know where that is?'

'You ought. Do you think we don't know who stole our brandy? You know where it is.'

Folland shrugged.

'Let us accept I know where it is. Is it important I should know it is coming ashore again tonight? Do you want me to go and steal it again?'

She ignored that.

'They have gone tonight. There will be a cargo. This time the soldiers have gone there. They will cut them off.'

'The Dragoons are out? How do you know? Are you sure they have not gone to the wrong place again?'

'Mistress Bridgward came with the news. We pay her to listen over the wall, and to climb on it to see. She saw them ride out.'

'Which way?'

'Across the bridge. They are going down to Blackmer's beach.'

'It is intriguing news, Miss Place. But why tell me? Ought I not to be glad my enemy will soon be in irons?'

She glared at him. 'My brother *will* be in gaol soon unless someone warns him.'

'That is sure.'

She dropped all pretence. 'Will you not ride and warn him?'

'Why should I?'

'You know the way across the rills down to the beach, as well as anyone. You could ride there fast, you could talk to the Dragoons, persuade them to go elsewhere. You have influence with them.'

'Not that kind of influence.'

'You could warn him.'

'If your brother saw me riding to him across the sand he would put a ball in my head before he took a second glance.'

'Are you a coward?'

'Frequently. Besides, I haven't a horse.'

'You have the best horse of all for it. Isn't he why you are here now, not out doing us other mischief?'

'I could not ride Tiger. I have to race him tomorrow.'

'If you do not, my brother will be dead in ten days.'

'Why should I care? He declared himself my enemy with no reason.'

'Save him now, and he will be your friend for life.'

'Of that I have no doubt, but I live easier without that kind of friend. Come, miss, name me one reason why I should go out, even if I find a horse. What about that grey you went so well on over the Down?'

'My father would hear if I took any of our horses. He must not hear. He forbade George to run another ship before the winter. He will be furious when he hears—if he hears. George is doing this on his own account.'

'I still wait to hear one reason why I should act.'

'All right, Master Folland.' He was shaken at the fury in her voice. 'I will give you one reason, and a good reason enough. I will give you myself.'

'Yourself?'

'Aye, a better bargain than Liz Alley or the London drabs, and richer. Go and warn my brother and you shall have me when you return.'

'You? Have you?'

She was close to him, he could smell her hair, feel her softness against him.

'Aye, have me and all I bring with me. Would you be a wine merchant? Or buy into Master Kettlestang's bank? Or have a farm and be a gentleman? Then marry me, Robert, have what I bring you. Only for that service, you may have me.'

Robert stood petrified by the directness of the proposal. Out on the tide line, the Dragoons stood as still, watching the shore. They neither moved nor made any sound—they were terrified of Perkins. Out to sea, the *Gouda* was standing in, slowly, under topsails. Half a mile away George Place and Grinton sat their horses, watching. The Pards were behind them with wagons. In the Market Square, Carines slept, dead drunk in the stocks. And Prisca stood in the shadows watching what went on in the Place house, watching, she knew, tragedy emerge.

Robert Folland stood still, with Sophia in his arms. She was weeping. She was pressed against him, nuzzled into his bare chest, and wheedled him,

'Go, please go, and see what you can have.' Her arms twined round him, her nails tore into his back to rouse him, and Robert Folland wished he could be roused, knew that he would be roused if he did not know better, a better, and she not willing to look at him. He braced himself to push Sophia away.

The door was burst in. Sophia had not replaced the bar. The Pards took a run at it with a ladder. They came tumbling into the room. Folland tried to push Sophia away, to reach for his sword on the far wall. She screamed in real fear, entangled him, held him tight. There were only four Pards—John Mellin, Cock, Devitt and Matthew Dee. And behind them, tall and fair and blind, but pistol in hand, stood James Place.

They pulled Sophia away, pushed her towards the bed. Cock and Devitt held Robert by the arms, twisting them behind his back, and he forced himself to be silent. Sophia stopped crying.

She shrank there, staring fascinated at her father. He came into the room.

'How were they found?' he asked.

'Ah, here it is they are,' John Mellin told him. 'There's the man, with no clothes on aside from his breeks. And her in not much more than a man can see through, to shame all that's decent.'

'Aye, only just in time we were,' Devitt corroborated. 'For they were about to begin, coming to the preliminaries as you might say, the tasting and the testing before the dish is served.'

'Before or after is no matter,' said James Place. 'There is scandalous conduct here before the face of the whole town. You have gone too far now, miss. Gavilstone was hanged, before he reached this stage. But now . . .' He moved forward. He reached out the pistol. Mellin guided the weapon, till the cold ring of steel pressed hard against Folland's breast.

'Are you a man of honour, then, Sergeant?' Place asked. 'Or do you wish to be buried at the cross-roads, a murderer and a suicide?'

Sophia screamed. She knows, Folland thought, what her father is capable of. He answered,

'I am not a gentleman. But I have been a soldier. I have my honour.'

James Place started. He has never heard me speak before, Robert thought. Yet, why the surprise?

'I believe you. There is something . . . I believe you. Then do this upon your honour, soldier. On Sunday be in the Abbey Church to hear your banns read.'

Folland stood rigid. The pistol pressed against him—well, he had ridden to the gun-line before. But Sophia was a crumpled leaf of terror and tears on his bed. Prisca, he thought . . . Prisca . . . but he had no choice. He answered,

'On my honour. I will be there.'

Place laughed. He dropped his arm. The pistol pointed to the floor. He said to Mellin,

'Bring the bride with me. He shall have her as she is, if she do not behave herself.'

Mellin held Sophia by one arm, Dee by the other. They carried her out after her father, her feet dragging on the floor. Cock and Devitt forced Robert struggling as far as the door. They faced him round to look into the room.

'And if there's any of ours hurt this night through your treachery, then you'll be at wedding and funeral in the same day.' And they flung him across the room, to slam his face against the opposite wall.

Folland lay a moment on the floor. Then he rolled over, picked himself up, and dipped his face into the cold water again. That was better. But the Dragoons? And the brandy-runners? He was already decided what to do, had decided as soon as Sophia asked him. He pulled on his breeches and riding boots. He found his coat. He looked at sword and pistol. There was no point in risking being caught with them. He let himself into the Millyard, and saddled Tiger.

He tried not to go hard. The horse was well fed, and not over-worked. He wanted to run, to have his head. But Folland rode him slowly, quietly, out along the quay over the bridge. A mile from the bridge, he turned left. Here he knew the roads. They were lanes, wide enough for a wagon, firmed with gravel, but still soft. The hooves thudded but did not make as great a noise as on the bridge. It was pitch black, and it took him time to recover his vision after his tallow dip. Soon his sight was coming back, and with his memory of soft and hard patches and little streams to ford and the sudden turns, he was able to hurry. Somewhere in front, perhaps two miles away, there would be soldiers and Pards, and neither friends of his that night. He cudgelled his brains how to warn Place in safety. He could smell the sea, the rotting weed along the beach; he could hear it. But he could see nothing. There were no lights. And then it came to him; lights.

He came to the road that ran parallel to the sea. Further along was the only good place to watch the beach. That was where he had waited. He must not go as far as that. He pulled Tiger up. There was the ruin of a stack, what was left of last year's hay, some distance from this year's stack. That would do. He pulled out hay, spread it out till he had a loose heap, with plenty of empty spaces. He fumbled with tinder, and his knife and a flint he carried to light his pipe when he could find no candle.

The loose hay flickered, began to burn. Robert tore at the stack, piled more on to the fire, saw it firmly alight, then ran backwards as the whole stack burst into yellow flame. The fire soared into the sky, lighting up the farmyard. There was no sound from inside the brick house. Robert knew there would be none. There was no dog to bark, either.

The captain of the Bergen boat, holding towards the lantern, saw the fire burst up a mile from it, and swore. There was no point in running risks. He shouted his orders, backed topsails, swung rudder and spanker over, came round, shook out the courses.

Perkins, on the shore, saw the fire behind him. He did not wait for the ship to change course. He snarled to Freeman,

'Look after the beach. I'll have this one.'

He called to two troopers, led them off through the gap in the hedge, into the lane towards Hod Blackmer's farm.

'Make for the fire!' he told the Dragoons: 'If you catch him, hold him!'

He rode a little behind them, falling back all the time. Robert, in the farmyard, was trying to mount Tiger, but the horse, frisky and hardly extended by the canter to the beach, bucked away from him. Robert swore, and Tiger, hearing a voice and tones he was used to, quieted. Robert got into the saddle, and heard the Dragoons coming up the lane. He waited till they passed him. He could see them, against the fire, going as close as they could to the stack—as if whoever had set light to it would wait for them there, Robert thought. But if they're in the field, I can get past them on the lane. He rode out of the farmyard, and came face to face with Perkins. There was no time to dodge, or say how-d'ye-do. Folland, a big man on a big horse, bundled Perkins and his cob into the hedge. Perkins shouted, and Folland guessed it would be no use now going past the men by the fire. He could only trust to luck he had not been recognized, and ride the way he was facing. That would be across the rear of the Dragoons; with luck they had gone on to the sands.

On the edge of the Big Wood, George Place and Grinton had seen the first spark out of the corners of their eyes as they strained for the Bergen boat. They turned, and saw the fire soar into the sky. There would be no running that night. They sat there, silent, feeling the rage and disappointment of the Pards behind them. They watched the Dragoons ride out on to the sand.

'If they *are* Dragoons,' George was full of his grudge. 'It'd be worth a try at them.'

'But the ship's making off,' Grinton warned him. ''Twould not be worth it just for the vengeance.'

'You're right. Get the Pards away. Get clear, and fast!'

George Place stayed where he was, listening to Grinton shouting orders. He loosened the pistol in its holster. He was ready to threaten to gain a little time, but nobody seemed to be coming up from the beach towards the Big Wood. He supposed the soldiers had set the stack alight to cook their supper—they were stupid enough to do that. At any rate it had saved him. Someone had betrayed him. His mind ran over the possible names. Not Charley—he was having enough to do in the town, the night before the Wrackham Run, and George had not told him. But there were others. Perhaps he had said too much the night before to Liz Alley. It was time to be off. He pulled his horse round, came down through the wood to the path.

Robert was breathless after his collision. Perkins had come off into a puddle, and was now blaspheming as he wrung the water out of his sodden cloak. And there was another pair of stockings ruined, and the damage to his breeches he could not see till morning. It had not been a long encounter, nor had the light been good, but he was fairly sure he had seen who it was. There was no point in chasing him, Freeman would catch him further along.

Freeman was not on the path to stop Robert. He was riding aimlessly up and down the beach. It was simple. Smuggling took place over beaches. Therefore smugglers were caught on beaches. They were not caught on paths back from the sea.

Robert pulled up a little past the gap in the hedge. The Dragoons had been waiting here, he could smell the horse droppings. He could not go back. He did not want to take to the fields : Tiger was knocked up enough already. He could hear no very great noise. The thought came to him, perhaps there had been no smuggling attempt, it had been all arranged to bring him out and tire him and the horse. Or worse than tire. He shuddered at the thought, regretted that he had come without sword or pistol. Out here in the dark anything could happen. He got down, and rooted in the hedge, where he remembered Hodman Blackmer had been working. He found a good long fencing stake, a handy sword's-length. He waved it round his head, approved the balance. He got up again, and went on at a trot. Somewhere further along he could turn right and cast away inland to the main road.

Robert listened as he went. There were occasional voices in the distance, nothing near at hand. The Pards were melting away into the dark. He quickened the horse's pace, and reached the corner of the Big Wood at the same moment as George Place.

The night was too dark for them to see each other clearly at twenty feet. But recognition even of these vague shapes was instant, and mutual. Both men pulled up their mounts sharp.

George spoke first.

'So you've brought the sodgers on us again, have you?'

'I have drawn them away. Don't stop here. They may be along any moment.'

'Aye, they'll follow you all right. I've seen enough of you. You spoil my trade, and you annoy my sister. And you won't do it again.'

He reached for the pistol. Robert could scarcely see the arm movement, but he knew what would come, he heard the sound of the hammer pulling back. The man was too far to strike, there was no time to ride at him—or turn away. He flung the cudgel at his adversary. It was luck, not aim, that took it full into George's stomach. George, winded, fell backwards. The pistol went off, the horse bolted. George, entangled in his stirrup, was bumped after it, over the ruts and stones of the path. Then his foot came free, and he was left lying on the ground.

Robert peered down at him. There would not be much justice if he had come all this way to have the man die on him. There was no knowing where that ball had gone. But he could see no blood, not about the body anyway, although it was trickling from a scratch above the left eye. And the eyes were closed. Dead men don't bleed, and their eyes open, he told himself. He listened. There were more hooves coming towards him, from the way George had been going. He took an instant decision, and leaped Tiger from three paces of run through, rather than over, the low hedge, and went hell for leather across the field. He had a vague idea of where the town lay, and where the main road would run. If Pards were about, they would be in the fields, not on the road. He saw another hedge in front of him. The horse landed too short on the other side, for a moment the hind feet struggled on the crumbling bank of the ditch. That was enough for Robert. The next hedge, he spent time to run along it till he found a gate. He could only find a low place in the hedge, and jumped that, satisfying himself first that the ditch was only on this side. That was where two men sprang up and tried to catch his bridle. Pards, he thought, from their voices—not even Dragoons could swear like that. There were others he could hear in the night. The fields, drained fifty years ago, now teemed again with the Marshmen. He wrenched the horse this way and that off the straight, to avoid the chance of another pistol ball— he did not think there could be two men in the County who could shoot like George, but there was always a chance, or an accident. And then he heard the hard gravel beneath Tiger's hoofs, and he knew he was on the Wrackham road.

21

Josh Caddon saw it in the morning.

'You had 'un out in the night, didn't ye?'

'How did you know? I thought I cleaned him up well.'

'Not like I do. Look, on this brush. You did have him down the Marsh. See that green clay? That be on Hodman Blackmer's farm, we all knows that. There don't be no good clay like that for ten mile. And you galloped 'un, too.'

'I had to. I'd ha' been killed otherwise.'

'You dam' near killed the yoss. He's a bit knocked up.'

'He'll be fit to run.'

'Ah, will 'e? I'm not sure.'

'I've seen horses like this before. In the Army.'

'This bain't the Army, this be serious. There's no playing sodgers when the Wrackham Run's to come.'

'We can rest him——'

'And more than resting. There's only one man for this. Charley Nobbler, if I can find 'un.'

Robert looked at him, aghast.

'He can't come.' The practicalities of the situation struck him. 'If he comes, no one must know. But how d'ye do that in daylight?'

'Lord, it don't matter, half the gentry of the county have had him in already. They all knows the Nobbler. He don't make more difference than a hatful of wind to most of them. But I knows what to tell 'un.'

'All right, get him. Don't tell Master Kettlestang.'

'I wouldn't do that. He'd have the hide off my back near straightway—but not till after he'd had yours.'

Through the day, Robert leant over the books, talked with Kettlestang about markets, about ventures worth going into, about concerns worth staying well out of. The Monday after Portreeve Picking Day, Robert was to ride to London. Now Kettlestang had the half-year's rents either in or accounted for, there were many things to be thought of, tried, tasted, some swallowed, most spat out. But dinner time marked the end of that. Kettlestang seemed happy, light hearted, as if he had done something clever, and sure, thought Robert, if the things he has in his books are true, not mere fronts for me like the *Norman Pride*, he is justified. The Portreeve went round a second time with the ale jug, and this was unusual. He rallied Robert,

'Come on, man. You've not ate enough to keep a sparrow alive.'

'I've eaten too much. Every mouthful is the more for Tiger to carry. I never eat before a fast ride like this.'

'But keep your strength up!'

Robert felt himself at this moment enough at an advantage to say,

'What d'ye take me for? A boy at his first hunt? I've ridden in more races, in Flanders, and in Warwickshire before that, than you've seen ships come home.'

He had a glimpse of Kettlestang's face, incredulous, struggling to answer sweetly, but before answer came he was walking over to the stables. There were two hours to go before the start; he was going to take one of them in sleep.

Josh Caddon called him after three.

'How're ye going to ride? What colours?'

'I'm riding light. Here, see—shirt, breeches, pumps. No hat. Not even a penny piece in my pocket.'

'You'd better have some colours.'

'I'll do without. Where's he?'

'Up at the start, drinking wi' the gentry.'

'How's the horse?'

'I've saddled him. He seems quiet enough. Charley had a look and said he wasn't too bad. I hopes you hasn't rid the spirit out of him.'

'The spirit out of him or the soul out of me. There was no choice.'

'How much is he paying you, Kettlestang? How much?'

'Nothing.'

'Nothing! D'ye know how much he gets if you win?'

'No.'

'There's every owner putting in twenty-five guineas at the start. The winner gets half that, and a silver bowl of a hundred guineas.'

'Who provides the bowl? Gunver?'

'Don't ye be so grudging.'

'What about the rest of the money?'

'All the owners have a dinner after it, in the Dragon, with the Aldermen, out of that money. Besides what Kettlestang will make by betting.'

'He won't bet. That twenty-five guineas for start money he'll grudge.'

'No, but we're all betting on you, you know it. And you're betting on yourself, aren't you? You've got money on with old Gunver, I knows that.'

'Not much you don't know. Well, we'll have to see what comes of it. What's the opposition like?'

'Nowt so much, for all there's near thirty paid themselves in. And the Nobbler was around last night. There's only one to think of, and that's Georgie Place's 'oss, the grey. That's a good stayer, and you want to watch him.'

Robert laughed quietly. Would George be fit to ride today, after the way he had gone down last night? It was nothing but an accident, but lucky. Josh Caddon pressed him again,

'What's you riding for, then? You tell me that.'

'Oh, for the same reason we rode at the French, because there was them as said we couldn't beat them. And so we did, though there, too, there was nothing in it for us save our pay that we were going to get anyway, and risked not getting any more if we were shot.'

They were at the Northgate. It was ten minutes to go. Hugo Grangier was standing on a barrel, shouting names.

'They be calling up,' Josh explained. 'Not to worry, I saw to it. Us comes up near last; we don't have to worry nor hurry.'

The horses were being got into line. There were riders in all kinds of dress, their ordinary clothes, bright coats, one or two like Robert in shirt and breeches.

'Kettlestang!' called Hugo Grangier. 'Kettlestang! Kettlestang here?'

Robert led the horse forward, across the front of the throng. Josh came with him, held the stirrup for him to mount.

'You see where you're a-going, Bob, lad?' He pointed toward the Down. 'See that smoke? That's the Pards at their fair. Mind how you go when you gets there.'

Robert looked at the crowd. He could see many faces, but all Wrackham men. There seemed very few out-of-Wrackham men, Pards or Alleys or sailors. He looked to the gate. He could see a yellow feather in a green hat. Sophia Place, he thought, come on horseback to see the fun. She's not the only one. I wonder where George is? He watched idly as Hugo Grangier called out,

'Place? Where's Place? Place to come to the start.'

Sophia was coming round the front of the start line, and she was riding the grey. She came to Hugo. He could see them talking, arguing. She turned to look at the line of riders.

'Help me, gentlemen,' she called out. 'My brother cannot ride. He is hurt. I want to ride in his stead. Master Grangier here says I cannot. Will you let me ride against you?'

There was a moment of stunned silence. Sure, thought Robert, there has never been such a thing. A woman to ride in a race like this? Impossible. They'll never agree. But what a thought, to go over Hugo's head and ask the other riders. They'll never say yes. But they're a lot of them in liquor. The silence did not last long. Colonel Cutler spoke first.

'I'd never chase a lady away if I had my choice. You can ride with me, whatever the others say.'

And in a moment, the whole line, gentry and ploughboys, yeomen and hired jockeys, were shouting or mumbling agreement or laughing. Only Robert kept silent. He was furious. The idea that she should come out to humiliate him again. He could have held off George if Tiger were fresh. But the grey was rested. Tiger was still feeling the last night's ride. Sophia would give her brother four stone at least and Robert five. Well, he'd have to take it and ride with her—against her.

Sophia turned her horse, came to the end of the line, next to him. There were only one or two riders to come. She flashed him a smile. He looked straight in front of him, bent to steady his horse. She said to him,

'It's only three Sundays to wait, Robert. And why dressed so plain? No colours? Would you like to borrow something of mine?'

But he had no eyes for her. Through the mob who were still thronging around the horses, giving last-minute advice, measuring up condition for betting, there was a small brown form pushing. Prisca came to his side, caught his stirrup, spoke to him for the first time since the fair.

'Rob,' she told him. 'Ride well.'

He looked down at her, incredulous. He could not believe it. He bent to her, away from Sophia.

'If the horse can do it, I will.'

'You've no colours. Take this. And watch for the boys!'

She handed it to him. Folded to a triangle, corner to corner, so that he could pass it over his shoulder, and knot it, was the scarlet shawl he had bought her at the Rag Fair. He slipped it on. She touched his hand a moment, then ducked away into the crowd.

He looked back, defiantly, to Sophia. She glared at him, furious.

'And what, sir, are you playing at?'

'I never play. I ride in earnest.'

Hugo Grangier was shouting for the line to be cleared.

'I shall give you a riding lesson.'

Good, he thought, if she is angry, she may not ride as well. What is she up to? She has shown me she has a nose for wine, an eye for business, an ear for a language. And now she is going to show me she can ride. Does she want to be as good as a man in everything—or only as good as this man? That is a challenge, I will take it. If she thinks she is as good as a man, she shall be beaten like a man.

'Miss,' he told her, 'I shall wait for you here at the end of the day.'

Grangier was holding up a white napkin. He bawled,

'Be ready, then! Ready! Off!'

The napkin came down, Robert dug in his heels, they were off.

He was on the extreme left of the line. There was pushing and jostling. He found himself alongside Colonel Cutler.

'Do your best, lad, for the old Regiment,' the Colonel gasped.

'I shouldn't have come—I ate too much dinner. So did the horse, by the way he's running.'

The Colonel dropped behind. Good old Charley, thought Robert. They were coming down to a cart drawn across to block the road and deflect the field on to the open common. The feel of the ground changed, and the sound of shoes on gravel vanished as hoofs beat on soft turf. This was a long run to the first hedge. He saw the flash of yellow and green on a grey horse. He caught Sophia's eye, and against his better will he smiled at her. She laughed loud, and shouted something. He could not tell what it was. This field was a problem of tactics. The shortest run across it, straight for the pillar of smoke, took you to the worst part of the thorn hedge. That was where Sophia was going, coming across his front. The easiest place to jump was by the gate—in fact over the gate itself was best, but a longer way across the field. He had chosen the gate, and Josh knew it: Sophia was going away to his right, he pulled to his left. It was worth the run to spare the horse the jump. He was well out to the left of the field, now. Even the most cautious were going for the low patch twenty yards to the right of the gate. He pointed the horse at the gate, quickened his pace, prepared to gather the horse in for the jump—and the gate swung open. He was so surprised that he pulled at the reins, slowed the horse, and then recovered his senses, and rode straight through. As he came through the hedge, he looked down and along it. Standing by the gate were three small figures. He knew them, and waved.

'Ride to Almanza!' the schoolboys shouted. 'Hurray for Malplaquet!! Folland for winner!'

This was not Josh's doing. There was only one person who could have sent them out. He patted the scarf, and set himself for the next gate. There were more boys. He did not doubt, but went straight at it full pelt, and saw it swing open just in time. There were two or three had fallen at the first fence, even at the lowest part, there were more in this hedge. But in the third field, the gate was at the opposite corner. The boys were waving at him, pointing him over to it. He pulled Tiger's head round, and rode diagonally across the field through the ruck. He found himself coming straight across Sophia's front. She was still shouting at him, he could not tell what, but she followed him. He came fast at that gate; the grey was a longish way behind as it opened. He went through, and looked back. The boys had closed it after him, quick, and Sophia had to jump. Oh, the grey could afford it, with only eight stone on him. But Tiger was faced with the long climb up the chalk slope.

He was on the right of the race, now. He looked in front. The sheep were usually dotted around the grass, scattered here and there in the senseless way sheep live, just asking for wolves where there are wolves. But today, they were gathered together. He could see the shepherd, waving as the ruck galloped past him. He was whistling, in the way that shepherds do, to his dogs. He chose his moment carefully. Half the riders were coming with Folland right of the flock, and half to the left. At the critical moment, the whole mass of sheep began to bolt down the hill into the oncoming riders. Into the left-hand group. Folland came away up the hill, and looked back. There was a sea of sheep around a few islands of horse, faint shouts brought to him on the wind. He laughed. There were only a dozen riders left and still he had Sophia close to him. They were in the rear of the race, but he comforted himself that Tiger was a stayer. And if he could stay with Sophia, with that light weight . . . It was obsessive now, he did not want to win, it was enough if he could beat Sophia, he magnified her advantages, felt satisfied only to keep up. As long as he could hang on to her tail . . . he could just do it.

On the top of the Down, Sergeant Freeman sat weary on his weary horse. To spend the night out on the shore, and know that he had to go straight up to the top of this blasted hill, in case the Pards started anything. They were having their own festivities, a fair of their peculiar kind. Late in season as it was, every man of them wore roses, two roses, in his hat. They had a maypole set in a hole that had been cut in the chalk long before anyone could remember, and they had come up to it every Run Day since creation, up out of the Marsh. They had a bonfire, and the Pards were roasting a couple of sheep. Where they came from Freeman was glad he didn't have to ask, since he was a quiet-tempered man and didn't want the guts wrapped round his neck. He watched the riders come up the Down towards him. The Pards were watching them, too. They would be here any moment.

The Pards were waiting. They were resentful. This was their Run, by rights, that the gentry had stolen from them. Year after year they had been watching it like this, sullenly, but only in the last year or two had there been anything they could do about it.

They had not needed to do anything in the last two years, but this time—they could see the green and yellow, and it was well down. So they went out to do what they could.

The first rider up the hill was Colonel Cutler. The Pards came round him, shouting.

'What do you want?' Luke Devitt shouted into his face. 'Who do you think you are, riding through folk's dinner? Go back with you!' The Pards formed in a solid mass across the way. The rest of the riders came up, were slowed down, snatched at, clogged to a standstill as well by Pards as by sheep. Freeman watched it, at ease. There was no profit in going in there, yet.

Robert came up the hill close on Sophia's heels. The grey's tail, he thought, was being useful, wiping the flies off Tiger. He saw the jumbled mass in front. They flung themselves into it. He kept close by her. The Pards closed round them. He had a glimpse of someone handing her up a flask. She did look magnificent, he had to admit, head back, hair streaming down now that her hat had blown away, tilting her head back to drink. Then he had other things to look at beside her, because there were Pards all around, trying to pull him off his horse. He beat and kicked at them, the men grasped for his arms, women and brats pulled at his legs. Someone aimed a blow at him with a board studded with nails. And it was then Sergeant Freeman decided it was time for him to interfere. For preference he might have left Folland to take what he got, like the Colonel, but there was a bit of money on that horse. He waved his troop forward, and they slammed into the crowd, laying about them with the flats of their swords. The mob dissolved. Robert had a vague memory that Josh Mellin had smacked Sophia's horse across the rump with a switch, shouting to her,

'Ride like the Lords of Loone!'

In any case, she had gone. She was off down the hill, and there was nothing to do but follow her, and hope that the others would be held up. He was worried about the horse. The night before was having its effect. He'd go till he dropped, but these jumps would take the spirit out of him, and drop him the earlier.

Colonel Cutler caught up with him and two or three more, cursing the Pards and the sheep but above all their pesky horses that wouldn't run today like they ought to. And on the edge of the village, Robert caught Sophia. She was stopped, furious, held up by a line of carts across the street. There were a little gaggle of people there, small brown men mostly, Alleys and Sarsens, and the burden of their song was simple. They said it to Sophia, and they said it to Cutler. They wanted to be paid for passage through their home. A penny a leg they wanted, and an extra penny for their trouble in moving the wagons. Folland was purposely last in the field. He pressed against the house wall on his left, and came softly up to the barricade. The Alleys saw him; the cart that carried brandy from the river two months before rolled back to let him through. But he was not quick enough. Sophia was after him, almost beside him, and they were both into the first field, running lightly over the barley stubble.

She was riding near enough to him to shout at him. Nearer again, and she could talk, in jerks with the motion of the horse and her own breathlessness and the exertion of riding. He could not think what it was she wanted to say. She had said nothing last night, when the damage had been done—either in her own defence, or in condemnation of himself. But now she wanted to talk to him, running full gallop across a wide space and a low hedge in front to be jumped, with a fall to the ditch on the other side. He looked over his shoulder. There was not another horse in sight. If Tiger was a stayer, so was the grey. As if by agreement, but without word spoken, they both eased up, dropped to a trot.

Sophia had been talking to him for a long time shouting across the gap of wind, the noise of the horses' running, the shouts of Pards and Alleys. She never doubted that he heard all she had said, taken it in through his pores rather than listened to the words. She did not ask him, or herself, whether he heard. She spoke; that was enough in her self-centred world. By God, Robert thought, she'd be a pair for Kettlestang, they have the same air of ordering the world whether it wants to be ordered or not. Is that what comes of a long line of Aldermen?

'. . . is how we will have it,' he heard. 'Would a man like you be content with a useless wife? You must have a wife who can ride like you, who can talk like you, trade and bargain and plan like you. And a wife who can and will dare like you, risk herself like you.'

'There must be a way out,' he called back. She did not hear, or did not choose to understand.

'And you shall choose. Will *we* sell wine or will *we* sell grain? Kettlestang talks of going to London to settle, leaving you to be master here under him. Will that not be something for us to have?'

'He did not speak to me.'

'When you have a Wrackham wife, then he may talk about it. But till you are a Wrackham man he will not fully trust you.'

They were over the hedge running to the great bank, raised long ago by Oliver's prisoners from the Scotch wars, that enclosed the washes of the Loone and kept the floods from the marsh land. They scrambled up the easy slope to the top of the bank. For a moment, Robert looked each way along the river. There were boats there, skiffs and lighters, with people watching, raising a cheer at the sight of the first riders. He had his plan made. He slithered down the other side on to the washes, risking a strained pastern or a twisted hock. Now he was twenty feet below Sophia. She looked down, and laughed. He heard her call, 'Coward!' In the same moment, he was fully aware of Tiger's failing strength. The horse would not be able to leap another hedge, or ditch, and there were three drains that ran through the banks into the washes, draining the marshes, protected themselves by sluices. Three chasms in the bank, and cut across the washes, eight feet across, a drop from the top of the bank the better part of twenty feet into the water, the lesser height from the level of the washes not making them any easier or narrower. The ground here was soft, cut up by molehills, and Robert did not want to follow King William to heaven. While Sophia galloped, he came back to a mere canter. He saw her, far ahead, coming to the first drain, and leap it, a trailing comet of yellow and green; then he was coming to his first drain.

There was no need to leap it. There were men waiting for him, dressed something like Marsh Pards, sailors out of a Swedish ship, standing in two groups about the edge of the drain, motioning him to run between them. He urged the horse faster, and came to the men. His hooves clattered on planks they had laid across for him. There were two more drains to cross, and sailors and schoolboys by each of them, calling to him and shouting encouragement. He was not far behind Sophia at the second drain, and as he ran down to it he saw her coming to the chasm. And then it happened, that he could not have hoped for. Her horse baulked at the leap, came to a shuddering stop with forelegs stiff, skidding in the mud of the bank. Sophia did not lose

227

her seat, or her determination, not even her temper. She sat still a moment, soothing the horse in a soft voice. She coaxed him into a turn, and rode him back a hundred paces. That was where Robert passed her, to be first over the second chasm. But when he reached the third bridge of planks, he saw her out of the corner of his eyes, leaping at the same moment. But even after that she gained on him, and though she took great care and lost time in sliding down the bank on to the last stretch of the washes, she came level with him.

'I'll show you how to ride,' she shouted. He could not have cared what she said; he was tired with a night awake and this long hard second ride, his thighs were stiff as his back. But he looked at her, and beauty struck him like a blow in the face. Her fair hair was streaming in the wind of her riding. The rush of air and the strain left her face flushed, her green eyes were wild. She was still talking to him, as if she had never noticed that he had left her side, as if he had heard, must have heard and understood all that she had been saying.

'And all that we shall have. Because you shall have a wife who can ride as well as you, who can speak as well as you, better than you, who can beat you!' He could hear the stream of words, understood that she was carried away with her own rage and her exertions. Nothing mattered now to her but the noises that were their own sense, their own reasons and cues. 'I will beat you, and first, I will beat that absurd . . . thing . . . from your back!'

He saw, glancing sideways, the way her arm rose and fell, and he felt her leather-bound switch across his back, once, twice, thrice. He wished, for the first time, that he had one in his own hands : he could not swerve away, he would be in the river; he could only urge the horse onward, pushing at his shoulders. The switch caught him again, lower on his back, across his kidneys, as if her aim was slackening or as if he had gained a foot on her. She struck again, and missed, the slashes came, fast, one-two-three across Tiger's back. This treatment the horse had never had before. Robert had never taken any kind of whip to him, out of pride, nor had Kettlestang, out of fear. Pain was new to Tiger. He screamed, and leapt forward, as if it had given him a new kind of strength. He went forward as if he were fresh out of the stable, leaping away, almost unsettling his rider, scattering the Wrackham men who stood there about the last hundred yards of the run. They were cheering, some of them. The out-of-Wrackham men were cheering more. Tiger came striding home, lathered and sweating and mud-spattered, to win, five lengths ahead of the grey, five minutes ahead of the field.

There was a throng about Robert. He yelled to Josh Caddon to hold the horse's head while he got down, and fumbled with the buckles to unsaddle. Azerley was ready with a blanket to throw over the beast's back. Bridgward came with a pewter pot, and Folland took it. It was mulled wine, hot, it made him sweat. He looked for the grey. Sophia was trying to force a way to him, but there were Pards about her, John Mellin catching at the bridle to tug her away, through the gate to where her father was standing, stony faced.

Kettlestang came to him, beaming. In one hand he was holding the silver cup. The other he reached out to pummel Robert's back, shake his hand, pat the horse's neck, shouting,

'I knew we'd do it, I knew we'd win.'

Robert felt impatience. What in hell had he done to win this race, beyond have the horse in his stables? He did not even know what a horse he really had, that would run ten miles in the dark, and win a race like this the next day. Josh Caddon answered,

'Aye, Master, I knew us'd do it, us have worked for this day. Now, now, Tiger, I'll have ye back in your own stall in a winkie, quiet there my beauty. Come along there, now, come——'

'Let him alone,' Kettlestang shouted, in a fury which astonished everybody. 'Let go that horse!' Josh looked at him dimly. Kettlestang repeated,

'Let go of him. That's a valuable horse. I'll have a proper groom for him from now on. Let go of him. Widdybank! Widdybank!! Take the horse from him. Take Tiger back to the Millyard and groom him, properly. See he is comfortable.'

Josh Caddon shrank away into the crowd, backwards, cowering against the men behind him, as if struck in the face. Robert almost opened his mouth to object, remembered his own plans, shut it tight. And then, there was more shouting, and he saw Colonel Cutler coming in, third. He gave a cheer himself. Cutler dismounted, came across, thumped him on the back, laughing.

'That was a run, Folland, that was a run! There's never been one like it. Never one with so little foul play. Not since Randolph Sainterme bribed the shepherds to fire the stubble when the race was run in mist, and we all went astray but him, never such an open race. And the way you two went! If I can't have Tiger, I'll buy the grey. Where's she to now?'

For Sophia had gone. The crowd was drifting away, ignoring the horses straggling back. Debts were being settled, bets collected, sometimes with the aid of blunt instruments of a delicious variety of designs. The activity was moving into the town. Folland felt chilled. His shirt, wet with sweat, clung to his body. He untied the shawl from his shoulders and wrapped it round himself. The exhilaration of the race had died. He faced, now, the reality of life.

22

It was a warm evening. In the town, money was paid, refused, extorted, argued for, fought over, stolen, spent on drink, on women. The Greyhound, the Falcon, even the Black Bull, were full of drinkers. The Two Roses was quiet. Kettlestang sat with the other Aldermen in the parlour of the Dragon. Robert Folland stood for a while in the tap of the Black Bull, where the troopers cheered him, and laid out the shillings they had won from Pards. But Freeman looked at him sideways. Shillmoors and Cutlers, Saintermes and Pendoggets, the squires kept their company in the White Hart. Robert passed them by, and appeared in the Kitchen of the Falcon. There Pontigarde and Carines, Gunver and Matthew Dowgill saw him, in silence. But nobody saw Josh Caddon.

Prisca sat in the kitchen of the School House. She had the pile of mending that never grew any smaller. She had little Martha Widdybank to live in now, but for all she was near on thirteen she could not seam or darn without making it stand out like a pansy in a parsley bed. Prisca's eyes ached. The tallow dip was not enough, and it danced shadows across her work. The time Prisca had wasted going out to see the start of the Run was asking to be made up.

There was a scratching at the back door. She sat straight and listened. There it was again, not a scratching as much as a tapping of a fingernail. It was someone used to the house, because the dog had not barked. But not Charley, he would have come straight in. She called out,

'Who is it?' She clutched her scissors like a dagger. 'Who's there?'

The door opened; she stood up. Robert Folland slipped through. She gaped at him. He gave no greeting, only said, dully,

'I have come to bring back your favour.'

He unbuttoned his coat, and laid it on the table. The shawl was knotted about his chest as it had been that afternoon, though his shirt was clean. He stood very still, one hand groping from force of habit to the hilt of his sword. She walked towards him, silent, and untied the knot. She trembled, being so close to him, and expected him to take her, hold her. He stood very still, forcing himself, trembling too. She spread out the silk on the table. It was wet and muddy, but not torn. It would need only a wash and iron to be as good as new. She said so. He looked at her as if it did not matter. He had worn it, he had brought it back. But she, seeing him there, could not let him go. She said,

'Sit down. I have ham, and some cheese. Let us have a clout, as we used to.'

'It is a long time since we sat together.'

'And you know whose fault that was.'

'Oh, do not upbraid me. You sent me away.'

At that she did bridle.

'Why must you take anything I say as an assault? They say that soldiers are touchy beings, but I did not realize they were as bad as this. I asked you a question. Whose fault do you think it was?'

He shook his head.

'I only suppose it was mine.'

She busied about, set bread to toast, and the cheese to run on it.

'Do you know how much that Organ is costing, that will be the glory of the Church and make us all think of Kettlestang of a Sunday whether he be here or not?'

'In the books, I know he has already paid——'

'Not the cost, soldier that is now a book-keeper, not the cost. What price did your master set on it, d'ye know?'

'I do not understand.'

'Then let me tell you. That day, that last day, the day that . . .' She hung a moment, could not say it was the day her mother died, Robert filled in for her.

'The day of Rag Fair.'

'That was the day. Late that day, and my father in the state he was, Kettlestang came to him. He told him he would pay for the Organ, but on condition.' She poured the cans, small beer for herself, strong ale for him. 'Better than you get in the Falcon,' she reminded him.

He knew that. She brewed it herself. He asked,

'What condition?'

'Very simple. That he cast you out, and forbid you to see me, or me to speak to you.'

'That you have done.'

'True. And he has not spoken to you, either, in the Falcon.'

'That . . . that I had noticed. I do not go to the Falcon to talk.'

'I obeyed him. And the Organ was built.'

'Yet today you came to me, gave me this, in front of Kettlestang, everyone.'

'There is no harm done. The Organ is built.'

'It looks but half built to me.'

'The pipes are in, and the bellows, and all the machinery. 'Tis set up, and 'twill play. There is only the case to be made, and that will be as expensive and as troublesome as two organs uncased. Kettlestang has made so much cry about his organ that he can neither draw back now nor dismantle what has been built.'

He drank. He felt heavy, slow.

'So, now you think it safe to talk to me again. But that is too late.'

'Is it indeed?'

'Is it not?'

'Think better of me than that. You are now in a fine state of trouble.'

'They will call my banns and Sophia Place's on Sunday morning.'

'Then flee the town.'

'Life is not as simple. I will lose a great deal of money if I do, but I still would count it money well lost.'

'Then why not run?'

'Miss, I am a Dragoon. I have a little honour. I swore to Master Place I would be there.'

'Willingly?'

'He pressed his pistol to my breast, and would have killed me had I not sworn.'

'That oath is void.'

'In law, perhaps, but not in my honour. I would give my life to be out of this match——'

'Why?' She had him now, she forced him.

'That I might match with you.' It cost him to say so.

'First, let us see you free. There is one key to this.'

'What is that?'

'How came Master Place to break in on you? Who told him?'

'Why, the Pards, or so I supposed.'

'I watched. I stood there with Master Carines in the stocks. Master Kettlestang came out of his door when Miss Place came out of hers, and tip-toe like a mouse he went after her. Master Carines and I laughed at the thought of a liaison between them in despite of her father, their being so ill matched in age and temper, and 'twas the first time that Master Carines had laughed that day as you may imagine, and I had to wake him to do it. But in ten minutes by the town clock, Kettlestang was back at Place's front door, and then inside, and soon after there was Place and Mellin and the other Pards come out with him, and down they go towards your cottage. Kettlestang stood there in the street laughing, and then back into his own house.'

'Master Kettlestang brought Place down on me?'

'I saw it.' She placed his clout by him, on a tin plate, passed him a knife. He meditated, chewing, then began to add up the column.

'Master Kettlestang brought me into this town. He persuaded me he had made great sums of money for me, and put it to my credit in his books. He made much of me, and would have me believe I was a great man. He told me often that I ought to marry well, and almost persuaded me that Sophia Place would look kindly on me. But I walked out with you. So he separated us, and used his money to do it. And then, he made sure that I would have to marry Sophia.'

'He set a trap for you, Robert.'

'He has not set a trap for me. He has set a trap for someone he has imagined. D'ye know what he calls me? Robin, Bobbie, young Rob, lad, my boy. He has set a trap for a boy. I am a man, Prisca, I am a sergeant. I have fought the French and the Spaniards. Shall I not fight a banker and win this battle too?'

'But how?'

'There is a reason behind all this.'

'How shall we find it?'

'We? Why would you help me, that have let myself be enmeshed like this, and promised myself to another for fear of a mere pocket pistol?'

She did not answer, *because I love you*. She only said,

'Because I trust you. And you have treated us all alike, even poor Charley; you have shown that he too was a real man, not just a vagabond and good-for-nothing. You have got him work on Colonel Cutler's new house.'

'You do not know the half of it. How shall we do this? How can we find out why?'

'We cannot ask him.'

'I have asked his papers, as far as I could get at them. I have read everything he keeps in the Mill. But the private papers which are in his house——'

Now there was a knocking at the front door, a hammering and screeching. Robert pushed himself in front of Prisca.

'You do not know who it is. Let me——' and he had his sword out before he opened the bolt and swung the door wide.

'Oh, Master Folland,' gasped Nance Hartsop, 'I was only hoping you'd be here, or they'd know where to find you. It's a dreadful business. I'm sure that there's no one but you can settle it. I'm so frightened, I must sit down, and me legs is bad, and my heart too, oh, thank you, the strong if you please, there, that's better.' She drained the pot with as much dash as anyone in the Kitchen of the Falcon, but noisier. 'There, I'm a lot better now, but, Master Folland, won't you come and help settle it?'

'Settle what?'

'It's Josh Caddon, that's what it is.'

'Is he lost? I haven't seen him since the end of the race. I've been looking for him, because I promised him five shillings extra for looking after the horse out of my winnings.'

'Then you didn't look at all where he's always to be found, in Tiger's stall.'

'But Master Kettlestang told him he wasn't to go near Tiger's stall. I made sure of that because I asked Malachi Widdybank.'

'Not the new stall, by the Millyard. I mean the old stall, in Kettlestang's yard. He went there straight away, and I'm thinking he's got some drink there, because I could hear him shouting and cursing something fearful, swearing that he'd bring Kettlestang down with sorrow to his grave and drown him and all his in hell fire, or in earthly fire if hell was not convenient to hand. He always was used to go and smoke his pipe in the hay and put me in fear and trembling of my life, because it would be easy for him to burn all the town down, as once they did in London, though that was a baker's boy that was evil inclined as I've heard tell although a Miller's next thing to a baker. And——'

'Now, now, Nance, it won't be as bad as you think. I'd better be down there to see to him.'

Prisca looked a moment into her soul. In for a penny, she thought. I will not draw back from this afternoon. She asked,

'Nance, will you look after the house? I'm going there too.'

'Well, I've got a mountain of things that I ought——'

Prisca did not waste time on persuasion. She poured another pint of strong ale, and left the jug on the table. She put out bread and cheese, and, after some deliberation, a round of ham. Nance nodded, her mouth too full to let her speak. Prisca pulled her cloak around her. They went out into the summer night. Across the Butter Market they went, down the cobbled street towards Kettlestang's house. They did not care for any flash of white at the window opposite.

Outside Kettlestang's house they stopped, and listened, with the crowd already gathered. They could hear something inside, a shouting and a singing and a great noise as if it were ten old men, not one. As to where that old man was, in his own mind, why, that was clear. There were gibes at Fairfax, aspersions on Manchester's virility, insults to Monck. He was inside the yard, beyond the garden wall and the high gate.

'Can you go in through the house?' Prisca asked. The gate was bolted from the inside. Robert had not been able to shift it.

'No. Nance had the key, and she would not let me have it. She said Kettlestang would kill her if she let anyone else have it. She was probably right.'

'Then what?'

'If I can find—here, Freeman. What are you doing? Can you help me?'

'I've just had a pint in the tap of the Falcon. I won thirty shilling on you this afternoon. What d'ye want?'

'Give me a leg up. I'm going over the wall.'

A heave, a grunt, and Robert was sitting astride the wall. There was nothing to be seen, only the raucous voice, now casting abuse on the Scotch in general and on General Leslie in particular. Robert had to cast about to remember who that could be. He called, 'Josh! Josh!!' For his pains he got cursed as a whoreson Scotch cur, and decided it was not worth the effort. He dropped into the yard, waited a moment, expecting Josh to rush at him, but nothing happened. He unbolted the gate and opened it. They all came in—Prisca, Freeman, two other Dragoons that happened to be passing, Baker Alley. Once into Kettlestang's stable yard, they looked about not certain what to do next. Robert walked ahead of them, towards the stall. He called softly,

'Josh? Josh Caddon? Come here, Dad, come here and talk to me, won't ye?' This was the voice he would have used to a frightened horse. He used it for Josh. But Josh was silent. They had no lantern, and Robert cursed himself for a fool that he had not brought one. Then there came a glimmer of light behind him, and for a moment he blessed Freeman that must have thought of it. But when he turned, the light was not in the yard, but in the house itself.

They stood and watched the lantern moving through the house, from room to room. Josh Caddon had got in, somehow. As they watched him, they heard the crash of glass and the splintering of wood as he did what damage his old limbs could accomplish. The shouting started again. Manchester and Leslie, Monck and Essex were forgiven. The hatred now was all for Kettlestang. Robert could not guess where they could enter after him. But suddenly he saved them the trouble, because one of the Dragoons ventured too close to peer through the window, and took a chair full in his face, that carried the glass and window frame before it. As he rolled whimpering on the cobbles, Robert looked at Freeman.

'You go in first. You're supposed to support the civil power.'

'Not me. Nobody's appealed for help.'

'I'm appealing. You go in.'

'But you aren't a magistrate. You work for Kettlestang, though. It's your place to protect his property.'

Their argument might have gone on for an hour. But Prisca stopped them, saying urgently,

'I can smell it. He's set the house on fire.'

And so he had. Robert saw the smoke already billowing out of the inner rooms. He waited no longer, but went in over the sill. He came again into the same room where he had first met Kettlestang. The Turkey carpet on the floor was well ablaze, and the hanging on the wall. He snatched it down, tried to roll the fabric up, and then realized that there were fires in the hall, under the stairs, in the rooms above. He charged up the stairs, looked first into one bedroom and then another, lit by flames that showed dust of years upon the floor. The last room was Kettlestang's sleeping place, and there he found Josh Caddon, lying on the bed sound asleep.

Robert swore. He picked the old man up. He was completely relaxed, unconscious, as easy to handle as a sack of meal, sagging and slipping. He stank of brandy. That was what he had used to start the fires. Robert heaved him to the head of the stairs, and looked at the well of flames. Should he go down it? It was as bad before the guns at Malplaquet, he told himself, but then reflected that he no longer had to ride against a gun-line. He went back to the bedroom, and shouted down. The yard was full of people. This was another window to kick out; at least that attracted attention. Some of the men below understood what Robert was trying to do. They fetched boxes from the stables, and stood on them so that he could lower Josh into their hands. When the old man was safe, Robert himself dropped to the ground. He looked round for Josh, but Baker Alley and Hod Sarsen had whisked him off.

Half the town seemed to be in the stable yard now. The lower half of the town, that was. The Aldermen at their great dinner in the Dragon had not been disturbed—everyone was agreed there was no need to spoil the fun yet. A dozen Pards had brought thatch hooks from the Place house, and were tearing the roof off Kettlestang's home with gusto. Freeman took a kind of charge and shouted,

'We can't let his furniture burn! In, lads, let's get what we can into the garden.'

But to get in, it was necessary to break down all the outside doors, and beat in the rest of the windows. Of course, that was all to the good because the sudden rush of air through these gaps was the best thing to blow the fire out and what was always sought. And in went the crowd and out came the goods, tables and chairs, candlesticks and kettles.

Robert looked frantically around. Half his mind was on Prisca, the other half still tried to save what he could of Kettlestang's goods. He trampled into the Portreeve's salad beds, and here, with some difficulty he established a furniture stack. By now, the parish fire-pump had been brought, and the leather hoses were taken to the well in Kettlestang's garden. A crowd of men laid to the handles, and water began to hiss into the upper rooms. The stairs were the worst problem, and a chain of Dragoons were got to pass buckets into the ground floor to throw into the stair well. Robert handed over his pile of furniture to Bridgward, and went back to the street gate to meet Kettlestang, running hard, and torn between drink and tragedy.

'My papers!' he shouted to Folland. 'My papers in the press in my front room. Let no one touch my papers, no one at all!'

It was as if he had given a signal, or a clear direction what to do. A dozen strong hands took the press and threw it through the window half across the street. It fell on one corner, the doors burst open, the frame collapsed, back and sides came away. The street was covered in an instant with a mass of papers, bundles and single sheets, handwritten scrawls, fine engrossed deeds, printed folios, schedules, mortgages, letters. The air was full of paper. Kettlestang snatched at the sheets as they whirled past in the draughts of the fire, shouting, almost demented. Robert found himself, in spite of his better judgement, doing the same. Bridgward and Azerley were gathering eagerly all these records of which they had been kept ignorant, the missing pieces of the puzzles which they spent their days piecing together.

The air was full of smoke and steam, smuts and sparks and papers. Robert came slowly to himself, slid away from Kettlestang's wails and shouts. Standing back, he could see there was little permanent damage done to the house, and most of that on purpose. The roof was gone, each of the rooms was foul with smoke and soot. The stairs were charred, the treads unsafe. But otherwise, there was nothing that could not be repaired. In fact, he reflected, the worst item the Portreeve would have to pay would be the fee for the Parish Engine, and the money for the pumpers. That would make him bad tempered enough, but the worst damage would be to his confidence. He had been so confident that he had no rival, no one who could know his secrets, and now on a sudden, all his secrets were scattered about the streets. Robert had had enough keeping this man's secrets. He had lost interest. He pushed about through the crowd again, seeking Prisca, and found her.

She was flushed of face and shining of eyes. Her cloak was smeared with soot, and her hands were dirty.

'Where were you?' he asked. 'I was worried to death in case——'

'I was in the house,' she cut him short. 'Where else would I be?'

'In the house? But why?' He cast about for a reason, found one selfishly, 'I was perfectly safe.'

'Oh, you can look after yourself—up to a point. Come back with me.' She began to hurry him away. A piece of paper floated in front of them. She reached into the air, and caught it. She opened her cloak, and stuffed it unconcernedly into her pinafore.

'We never know what may not come in useful,' she laughed.

They were at the School House door. Nance Hartsop came to let them in, worried.

'Off to Kettlestang's!' Robert told her. 'There's cleaning to keep you busy for the rest of the year.'

They came into the kitchen. Robert sank down on to a stool by the table. Prisca looked at the single tallow dip with distaste, and ferreted into the cupboards till she found three more, and six inches of wax candle. These she stood on the table to give a light such as he had never seen before in such a mean room. He did not ask her directly, only raised his eyebrows. It was now that she hung up her cloak.

'I found it a most intriguing evening, Master Folland,' she told him. 'Or is it Master Bowbank?'

He started . . . recovered himself, answered,

'Of all possible names that is the last one I am entitled to bear. He told me to my face I was a bastard and no son of his. But how . . . ?'

She settled herself opposite him.

'I was not idle in the house. I took a poker to every likely piece of furniture till I found the cupboard that was full of papers. And the fire gave enough light to see. Master Kettlestang was most methodical. I merely had to find the right shelf, and the right bundle, and I had everything.' She reached first into her pockets, then into the front of her dress, and covered the table with little bundles of papers, tied neatly and marked with names on the outside. 'See what I have found.'

'You stole all that?'

'I rescued it from the fire.'

'But Kettlestang will know that you have . . . that someone has taken all that, and he will guess.'

'Kettlestang will never be quite sure what he lost tonight. Why else do you think I had Solly and Joe Blackmer throw the whole thing through the window? All his papers are scattered to the winds, and there is enough ash in the house to account for what is missing.'

Robert sat and looked at her.

'Did you do this on purpose? I cannot trust your eyes. Did you *have* this house burnt down?'

'I had hopes it might happen. I did mention it to Josh—he came round here crying after Kettlestang cast him off, and it took a great dish of boiled beef and carrots to make him sensible again.'

He stared at her. If she thought herself capable of settling Kettlestang, then could she settle Sophia Place?

'He is the key to all this,' Prisca told him. 'If we find out what Kettlestang is up to, we can save ourselves. Look at this.'

It was wrapped in a sheet of paper labelled, simply, 'Robert'. Robert himself unfolded it, saw the familiar hand, read,

Sir:

I am in receipt of your enquiry as to the whereabouts of Robert, known as Bowbank, who has passed for my son. I have told him, on the death of his mother, that he is no kin of mine. He has left my household. Where he is now, I neither know nor care, although it is rumoured that he is gone for a Dragoon. I pray that the outcome may be that which I desire. For there is nothing I desire less in addition, than to have any further communication from yourself, or from anyone belonging to my native town.

Robert read it, said,

'He hated me. All his life he hated me. I could not understand why my father should hate me and love my brothers. Only after she was dead did he tell me he was my mother's husband, but not my father.'

240

'There is more,' she told him. 'Who was John Farmer?'

'He was the Colonel of the Regiment when I joined it. Before Cutler bought it from him. Cutler was my first Squadron Officer.'

'He too will have nothing to do with Kettlestang. But there are letters from Cutler. . . .'

They read. Short notes, that said, yes, this lad is in my Squadron, is a bugler, rides well. He will come with us to Spain. He is in Spain, has lived through Almanza, prospers. Now I have the Regiment, I can keep him under my eyes. He is a corporal, a sergeant. And then, at last, he is wounded. 'If I have any influence in the matter, I shall have him mustered out of the service as unfit, though indeed he will be capable of any exertion when once the thrust is healed. And then I shall find occasion to send him to you.'

Robert sat, appalled.

'All that time, that I thought Cutler was not only my Colonel, but my friend, he was watching me, writing of me to this man. It is not a plot against any old soldier that was convenient. He designed this for me, and for me alone.'

'You do not know,' she reminded him, 'that it is meant to do you harm. Where is the malevolence?'

'You know the man,' he reminded her. 'When he goes about a thing so secretly, would there be anything in it but evil?'

'Is it so necessary that you find out why?'

'I must. Before Sunday. Before the banns are called.'

And the kitchen door opened. For the second time in twenty-four hours, Robert Folland was found in a room alone with a young woman, by that young woman's father. Parson Arkengarth stood there, breathing the brandy all over them, holding to the edge of the door, swaying. He made two reaching, groping strides across the room and sat down on a settle facing them. Folland turned to him, accusing.

'Who was Bowbank?'

Arkengarth blinked, gasped, then pulled himself together and answered,

'They were a respectable family of this town. Very respectable. I must be discreet, my boy, you understand, I must be discreet. As a clergyman——'

'Who was Bowbank?' Robert Folland was standing. He thumped his fist hard on the table. *'Who was Bowbank?* Twenty-seven years ago in this town, who was *Bowbank?'*

Arkengarth stared at this man, so intent to spoil his sleep. There was something . . . he remembered.

'Young man, I will not have you in my house. You are forbidden to——'

'The organ is built. Tell me, tell me *now*! Who was Bowbank?'

Arkengarth seemed to shrink into the corner of the settle. He looked in terror at this huge figure. He looked for support to Prisca, but found none. Her gaze was stony as Robert's.

'I had a curate named Bowbank. Just about then.'

'That went to Warwickshire?'

'A living was found for him. It was a very worthwhile preferment indeed. It was two hundred pound a year, he ought to have been grateful for it. It—the advowson belonged to a friend of the Saintermes. He went to Warwickshire. That was that. We never heard of him again.'

'Never?'

'Never. Not a sight of him.'

'But your memory. What was that?'

Arkengarth stared back at him, sobered. He was silent a long minute. Then he whispered,

'That was what I swore. I have no memory of him.'

'You swore? What did you swear?'

'I tell you, that was what I swore. I promised it, I gave my word, it was as good as an oath, it always has been.'

Prisca was scornful.

'Let us hear no more of oaths in this house. Have we not been ruined by an oath?'

'My word is my soul. You cannot ask me to break my word. I would rather die.'

'Not for your daughter's happiness, her future?' Robert hung over, threatening.

'Not for my own salvation.'

Robert stood over him, half tempted to argue on, to thump the table, to curse and shout it out of him. And what good would that do? He sank back on to his stool. And the old man opposite him, suddenly, without a reason, spoke again.

'It was done decently and in order. It was all in the Church Book.'

23

Saturday was clouded, still, quiet. It was the day between the Run and Portreeve Picking. The streets were slowly cleared of the debris of the night's drinking. Men worked on till half-way to dusk, to finish work left undone on the half day before. Robert Folland and Bridgward, Azerley and the other clerks, leaned over their books in the counting house. They knew Kettlestang had slept upstairs, and sat there now, still and quiet. Nance Hartsop came in at midday, served them their dinner, took a tray up the stairs, and a bottle of claret. Bridgward took the Portreeve's place. The others did not talk.

The afternoon drowsed on. When the wind brought them the sound of the Abbey clock striking six, Bridgward closed his ledger. He looked at his companions, nodded towards the stairs.

'D'ye think I ought to tell him we're a-going?'

'Let him be,' said Azerley. 'I got enough here for a sup for us all as we go. Come on, Rob, you won it for us, have a pint on me.'

Robert hesitated, then said,

'All right, just the one, then. Where'll it be? The Falcon?'

'What, with that dead-alive crew? I'm for the Black Bull.'

They left the counting house. Bridgward came out last, looked at them, then turned away without a word and slipped through the postern gate into the town. Azerley laughed.

'I thought that would get rid of the old bastard. We'll have our drink in peace. He won't come into the Black Bull any more.'

Azerley, thought Robert, there's another one I may need. He drank Azerley's pint, and one on Freeman, bought beer for all the Dragoons, sang with them, and then slipped out into the dusk and walked swiftly back to his cottage. Across the yard in the upper floor of the counting house, he knew Kettlestang was sitting. Robert drew the curtain, and began to pack his own possessions into a big leather bag. His sword he belted around his waist. He was wearing his riding suit and his heaviest boots. He slid his horse-pistol into the pocket of his frock, loaded. It would come out easy, smoothly. He humped the bag, and went out into the rain.

It was much later he returned. The gate of the Millyard was locked. Robert first climbed the town wall, and looked for a light.

'No, you're all right,' Solly Blackmer told him. 'He ain't moved. He's still there.'

Kettlestang sat there still, in his upper room. He wondered when his house would be fit to live in. He had done nothing about it today. He had thought of sending to ask Francis Conrig to come and talk, for there would only be inside work to do, stairs to replace and panelling to patch up. And he would know, too, to find a parcel of Pards who would thatch the roof again. But not today. He was still feeling sick from running back to find his home roaring away like a torch and his papers scattered about the streets. He had screamed and shouted at the crowd to save the letters, and they had only laughed at him. But he had run hither and thither snatching at what he could catch, scrabbling in the dust to find if any had been trodden underfoot, and he had had his own hands trodden on. Not by accident, he could swear that. There wasn't a man in the town he could trust. Not the way Place could trust his Pards.

He had found most of them, in the end. When men saw he was serious, they had helped him—there had been five other Aldermen on hands and knees, and he had been torn between fear that things were lost and dread that his friends might read them. But sick and ill and tired as he was, he had not been idle the day. He had been sorting and counting, trying to remember what he had missed. And where things were missing, he could only hope that they had been burnt decently and not thrown into the wrong hands. Even so, the chances of any single paper coming on the wind to the man it concerned was small.

Still, there were things missing. Had they been burnt, or had they blown over the town and into the river? One or other, he was sure of that. In any case, they would be scattered past harming. He had comforted himself with a hot supper that Nance Hartsop had come out to the yard to cook for him. Now he had his bottle of port in front of him, and a dozen more in the cupboard. He did not feel like going to the Dragon on this wet evening. Besides, he had not yet finished his sorting of the letters, and he could not do that on the Sabbath. He poured himself another glass of port, held the dead man up, draining it. He walked across the room, threw it through the window, heard it splash into the river. The Dutchmen in the ship for Flanders were singing there, loud and raucous. He leaned out to listen to them. He held his hand out to see if it were still raining, and felt the breeze—on the back of his neck.

Kettlestang turned, to face a man standing in the doorway. He saw it was Robert, and smiled. It was no harm to keep smiling for another three weeks. It was all certain now. There was no stopping the plan. He invited,

'Sit down, young Robin, sit down, lad. And have a glass of port.'

Robert stood there, silent. He counted ten to keep down his anger. Then he cross-invited,

'Sit down yourself, Master Kettlestang. I have something to ask you.'

He took off his cloak, spread it carelessly over a settle. The hilt of his sword showed through the slit in his frock. Kettlestang, watching him as a man does an adder, came softly across the room, and sat down again in his high-backed chair, his hands still upon the arms.

'Say on, young Robin. I am always glad to listen. Why did you not come this afternoon?' He was busy a moment, opening a new bottle, reaching for a clean glass on the table, pouring the drink, holding it out. Robert ignored his offer, stood silent, waiting.

Then,

'And not me, alone. There are others.'

'What others? Who else would want to speak with me at this time of night?'

Robert said nothing. He turned back towards the door, and beckoned. There was the noise of feet on the stairs, too many feet, thought Kettlestang, to be encouraging. The people entered, coming in order through the narrow door. Kettlestang was not prepared for this. He stared as they came. First Prisca Arkengarth, and her father close behind her carrying a great bound book. And after that, Colonel Cutler in a comfortable old regimental coat with no gorget as if he had been brought from his fireside, and behind him Captain Taberon, who had been to do the bringing. They came into the room, and spread out in a line, facing Kettlestang across the table. Taberon, without asking leave, poked around a little, found more candles and some tall brass sticks for them, and lit the room from corner to corner. He

245

looked with distaste at Kettlestang's bed, and sat on it. He had the air of an usher, not of a principal. And then, last of all, and alone, her entrance carefully planned, Sophia Place entered.

Kettlestang looked at them, counted them, tried to produce an expression of unconcern. He asked, gaily,

'Are we to have a betrothal party? Are you to be a bridesmaid, Miss Arkengarth?'

'We have come to find out,' Robert replied, 'what you are doing.'

'What am I doing? I am sitting by my own fire, and it a more comfortable fire than we saw last night, young Robin.'

'Young Robin, young Robin, lad, boy—what else will you call me?' The words were petulant, but the tone was level, cold. 'That has been your downfall, Portreeve.'

'My downfall? I have not fallen——'

'But you have. You see, Master Kettlestang, I am not young Robin, young Bob, a youth, a lad, a boy. I am a soldier. I have been a sergeant, and I have tasted powder. And I am not to be deluded by any merchant. I am not a passive dupe. Do you not understand, Master Kettlestang, that while you have known your own plan, I have also been making mine? And what your plan is, we have come to find out.'

'This is all beyond my comprehension.'

'Then we will make you understand. You have behaved as if I were malleable wax, shapeless, a blank tablet for you to write on. And that I am not, Portreeve. Let me rehearse what has happened to me.'

'Pray do. I am sure your . . . companions are as anxious as I am to understand what is happening.'

'Let us remember, how I came into this town, seeking employment which you offered me, better employment than ever I thought possible.'

'I paid you well for your skill and your discretion, and are you now throwing all this in my face?'

'It went well enough. I was willing to give you what you paid for. And then you offered me more than my wages. That I took, and I was content. But it did not take me long to find out that you had cheated me, lied to me.'

'Why, how came you to have that strange notion?'

'Did you not think I could talk to other men? To Master Newall? To sea captains? To men who insure bottoms, and gamble on safe returns? No, you never thought of that; you have no thought for what happens outside your own eyesight. You have ordered the doings of this town for so long, Portreeve, that you can no longer conceive that the world will go on outside your knowing. But it does go on, Portreeve. Men talk to each other. Not in business, not in treachery, but in comradeship. And men have talked to me. Men who saw the *Norman Pride* go down.'

Kettlestang did not deny it. He nodded.

'I thought to do you a kindness. I knew you would not take anything you had not earned.'

'But you lied to me, you cheated me. Cheated me backwards. You thought I was a little innocent boy that would never find out, and if I found out I would think nothing of it. And you were wrong. I did begin to think of it. I began to wonder why. What was your plan?'

'I had no——'

'Do not deny it. That there was a plan, I soon knew. I thought it was a plan in general. Against whom it was directed I could not see. I was only afraid that I might be sacrificed in it. An innocent boy might have spoken to you then and there. But I have my own cunning, Portreeve, as intricate as yours. I will not be sacrificed. There was a fire last night, Portreeve. You remembered that a moment ago. What happened to your papers?'

'What, indeed?'

'Some came into my hands. You see? You recognize the writing? You remember what these letters are about?'

Kettlestang shrugged. He pointed to Cutler.

'Ask him. He wrote them. There is nothing there.'

Cutler spoke now.

'There is much there. They are all the letters I wrote you, about Robert Folland. I told you what had happened to him. At the end I sent him to you, as soon as I was able to see that he was mustered out.'

'And is that not a public matter? Why should you have to burgle my house to find that out? Did you not tell him, Colonel Cutler?'

'And was it not yourself who threatened to show him the letters? You persuaded me this was a wicked deceitful thing.' Cutler spoke now to Folland. 'I was ashamed to face you. You were my comrade. We faced the French together. I betrayed you into this man's hands. It was the threat of revelation that kept my voice silent. Now you know. What have you to say to me?'

'I too have been your comrade, remember that. I can forgive you, because at the beginning you did not know what you were doing. But the money—did he not hold that money against you?'

'The money? Oh, that—that was nothing of this matter, it was only in the way of business. Master Kettlestang advanced me money for the remounting of the Regiment through his agents in Holland. I repaid him in this country. Business is a different thing with him, my sergeant. But I could see that he had dragged you into some net of his own, and I was ashamed to warn you.'

'When we found these letters,' Robert went on, 'only then did I know that it was not *any* Dragoon, *any* bully-boy that you wanted for your purpose, but this one alone, Robert Folland, known in his youth as Bowbank. What did you want with me, Portreeve Kettlestang?'

Kettlestang sat silent. Robert waited, went on,

'There was a part of the plan which was clear to me. You wanted to make me think I was a rich man, that I had money in your books, that I was to be your heir. And you wanted other people to think that too.'

'It might well have been true.'

'Not entirely. If true, I will find out tonight and have proof. But you thought I was the Robert Bowbank of your dreams, the boy from the Warwickshire vicarage, who would believe all he was told. I am Robert Folland, you forget that. But there was another plot. There was a man who tried to rob me when I came into the town. There was a man who hoped I would quarrel with him that same night. He tried to kill me in the Rag Fair. And why? What set George Place so dead against me?'

'Why should you ask me?'

'I will tell you why,' and Sophia Place came forward. 'I know who it was told my father, loudly, that you had something coming from London, on Tiger, that was worth a thousand guineas. It was you, Portreeve, who knew every cargo my father wanted run, and told the Excise men about them. It was you who sent Robert to Bratton when there was a cargo to be run. It was you who told us every time Robert had been talking with the soldiers.'

'But when I stole the brandy?'

Kettlestang looked hard at Robert. The Dragoon turned on him.

'Does that surprise you? Had you not thought me capable of it? I made more profit on that than ever I would on a ship, and not in money either.'

'I had not thought it might be you.'

'But you told my father that you were sure that it was him.' Sophia was harsh-voiced. 'You inflamed this quarrel. Did you want them to kill each other?'

And Kettlestang, blenching for the first time before her green eyes, answered very quietly, 'Yes.'

'So the plan is clear,' went on Robert. 'I am to be embroiled in quarrels. But there was something more. Who set out the rumour that I was Lord Wrackham? It was done cleverly. Who did that? Who hinted at it to you, Sophia?'

'It was him. Portreeve Kettlestang, talking quietly into my ear in the street after church, on the walls in the afternoon. He hinted the Earl would return, would come into Kettlestang's house, that it would be that very day when you came.'

'Hinted? Only to you?'

'To me, yes, but also to others. To Hodman Blackmer, and to Liz Alley. There were some of that clan who did not believe it.'

'But many did?'

'And they followed you. Had you not noticed? Would you have won the race otherwise? Would you have had them back you against the Pards if you had not been, in their eyes, a Harne?'

'So, I am built up. To some I am Kettlestang's heir, to others I am a Jacobite Lord. But why? What does this man do next? He has me turned out of house and home. He bought my eviction with an organ.'

'Is this a criminal case?' Kettlestang asked. There was little he could do now to fight back, but he could be biting. 'Or is it a civil action, because if it is civil, then I ought to have counsel for my defence.'

'Plead your own case when you can find it,' said Taberon, from the bed. He was enjoying himself. It was, he thought, a pity he was reading divinity and not law. Prisca ignored him, entered on her cue.

'Master Kettlestang paid for the Organ in condition that

Robert be no longer received in his house. Why, then, was that? Because we were seen too much together? And what harm did that do?'

'What harm? What harm?' Robert repeated. Sophia spoke.

'You threw us together. You saw that I was willing for the match, eager even. You saw to that. You told me lies about him. You played on me. And when that was not enough you told the soldiers that George was gone for another run. You, too, told me that the Dragoons were out, saw that there was no one else I could trust to warn him, so that I went down to beg Robert to go —and to embroil him without doubt in the smuggling.'

'And when she was gone,' Prisca spoke again, 'it was you who went to their house. You told Jemmy Place what was going on, where Sophia was and with whom. I saw you go half-way down the street with them, and hang back when they burst in the door. It was all your doing. This marriage for some reason, you want, and you are willing to lay out your own money and time, and plot and plan for it. Why? Why? Why?'

'Aye, why?' asked Taberon, from the settle. 'I may only be here as a messenger, but I will have my testimony complete.'

'Why?' asked Robert. 'Was it to see Sophia Place wed to a penniless man? Any old soldier would have done for that. But there was trouble taken to bring me into the town. Who am I? It seems, Master Kettlestang, that you knew that better than I did. I was brought up in Warwickshire, with Parson Bowbank for my father. A harsh and stern father I found him, swift to chastise; he treated my brothers always with more kindness. And I never knew why, till the day he was safe to call me a bastard. Never a word did I hear in our house about Wrackham. The place meant nothing to me. But here, the name Bowbank meant something. It meant something to Master Arkengarth——'

'Will you heed the word of that drunken sot?' Kettlestang was angry, waspish. Taberon rose to his feet and rebuked him.

'Have respect for the cloth, sir, if you have none for the man.'

Robert waved Taberon to sit, and went on,

'Master Arkengarth said nothing. He has kept his oath till today, still keeps it. But we went to Parson Quernhow, who knew nothing of all this, and we have brought the great Church Book. Turn, Prisca, to 1684. I was born in May, 1685. Let us see what there is in 1684. Late in the year.'

'Very late in the year,' said Prisca. 'We looked and we found it. A marriage. Of Robert Bowbank, curate to Parson Arkengarth, by Parson Arkengarth. To . . . Margaret Endellion, daughter of Francis Endellion, Steward of Wrackham Hall. The witnesses . . . Francis Endellion, and David Mellin, who signed with a cross.'

'There is nothing here.'

'You remember it?'

'Why should I remember? I was young myself, then, not your age.'

'And almost immediately, Bowbank was found living in a distant part of the country.'

'That is quite possible. He was not a pleasant man. He beat the boys in the School more than was needful. They learned their Latin, though.'

'That is the same man.' Robert shuddered at the memory.

'Are you so sure?'

'Margaret Endellion signed her own name in the register,' Prisca told him. 'The writing is here, in this prayer book.'

'She scored out her own surname,' Robert said bitterly. 'I never knew till this evening what her name was. The only name I knew then was Bowbank, and when I found it was not mine, I took the nearest to hand.'

Taberon stood up again. He said, quite simply, 'I have work to do. It is late, and I have ten miles to ride. Good night, gentles all.'

He went down the stairs. They listened to his boots in the yard, in silence. Kettlestang sipped his port. Robert spoke again.

'There have been three or four times already when George Place and I have been near to blows, and that was due to you. Each time, I was able to pass it over.'

'Pass it over with your fists,' Sophia commented.

'Not always. But I spoke with your brother this evening, outside the Dragon. He promised me something there, in front of enough witnesses to make it serious—that if I married his sister, or even let the banns be read, he would kill me. I know my own strength. If we fight, I will kill him. Was it for this that you plotted and spent all that money, that Margaret Endellion's son should kill George Place? Or, that not knowing me, you wanted Margaret Endellion's son killed by George Place? And whichever happened, it was sure, that the other would be hanged? Margaret Endellion's son? Or . . . whose son? Who am I, Master Kettlestang? Who am I?'

'Aye, who indeed? That was always a question.' Kettlestang was sitting very still. His left hand clung tight to the arm of his chair. He held the glass in his right, all his effort was spent on keeping the surface of the port level and unbroken. As long as he could do that, he told himself, he need not scream. The concentration took up the spare action of his mind, absorbed the emotion. He could pretend that this was only a nightmare, that it had nothing really to do with him.

'A question. But it can be answered. I have tried to answer it.'

'Ask the parson. He was there.'

'And will not tell, whether he knows or not. I look back on all the time I have been here. All this adds up to hatred. You hate someone, Master Kettlestang. You hate someone enough to have men kill each other. You will even spend money to bring it about. And yet, there have been times when I have felt in your voice . . . what shall I say? Regret? Affection? Some emotion, anyway. I would not otherwise have thought that you ever felt emotion.'

'I felt emotion. Why should I not? Am I not as other men?'

'Why? Is the great Portreeve as other men?' This was Sophia. 'Tut, sir, can he who rules the town, and sits in impartial justice, be disturbed by emotions? And what emotions, pray?'

'Affection, almost. Certainly regret. A kind of pride. I thought I perceived them all,' Robert told her. 'I thought I sensed them time and time again.'

'That you did. You were not deceived,' Kettlestang admitted, grudgingly.

'And why? There was something I once heard in a coffee house, where you were known. How once you were cheated of a bride, and had not shown humanity to anyone since. But you showed it to me. You have plotted my death, yet you showed goodwill to me. Why?' Robert towered over the table, the candles threw his shadow faint on every wall of the room. 'Why? Was it Margaret Endellion you wanted, Margaret Endellion you loved?'

'The Endellions,' and this was the first time that Arkengarth had spoken, 'were always a proud, fierce race. Even when they had nothing, even when Francis lived on the Harnes' charity, he would not have his daughter linked with trade.'

'It is true, then? That you wanted to marry Margaret

Endellion? And that when she was pregnant they married her off to the curate? And found him a living where he would keep silent about it? Is that it?'

Kettlestang nodded. He said nothing. He looked at the surface of the port, counted the candle flames in it. He nodded again.

'Then—is that it? For that you would be revenged on the Endellions? For that you would have me killed, in the most exquisite way? Raised almost to the purple of this town, and then killed? Hanged? Is that your revenge on Endellion?'

'Endellion?' Kettlestang murmured the question. Robert stood closer to him, leaned on the table, thrust his face forward.

'Your vengeance? And why? Who am I? Whose son am I? That you should fetch me out of the ends of the earth and clothe me in purple and fine linen and then send me for sacrifice? Was it that you would take vengeance on the Endellions? Or that you would have the Endellions take their vengeance? Is it true, then—are *you* my father? Am I *your* son?'

Kettlestang sat still in his chair. His fingers twisted, he snapped the stem of the glass, and spread port over the table, over his knees. He cried aloud,

'No! NO!!' He sagged back. He mumbled, 'You were the son I ought to have had.'

'Then who?' Robert straddled him, looming huge and threatening. The Portreeve crumpled before him. 'Who was it? Who was my father? Who left my mother alone to be driven away, handed over to the nearest man? Who was it?'

'I was not there. They did it when I was away, they had not dared to marry her out of town had I been there. It was . . . I cannot tell you . . .'

'Tell!'

'It was . . . it was James Place.'

The room was silent. There were four of them staring at the Portreeve. Kettlestang spoke again,

'He would have known you, had he seen you. I knew you the moment you came into my house.' He looked up sudden, at Arkengarth. 'Did you not know them?'

'Aye. As soon as I saw them. Can you not see now, the long Endellion face on a round Place head?'

'But if James Place . . .' Robert stood there, irresolute. 'Then Sophia is my half-sister. And George my brother.' He turned to Sophia. Her face was full of horror. He laughed at her, and her expression melted. He stretched out his hand, and she took it.

'No wonder,' she said, 'we think alike.'

'Yet there was something,' he reminded her, 'between us. A bar and a bond.'

'Something indeed.' She faced Kettlestang. 'Was this your vengeance, then?'

'James Place took her from me when I was in London. He was married then, and yet he seduced her. And left her.'

'This was your vengeance?' The others were too full of anger, so Prisca spoke. 'That the Place family should in one week, one day, suffer incest and fratricide? And a hanging after, to round it off? All that, to come on the proud Vintners of Wrackham? And you, guiltless, to see it all? Was that your vengeance?'

'That was it.' Kettlestang stood. He was shaking, but his voice was steady. 'That is it. I am not done with you, Places and Endellions and Arkengarths, that stole from me my love, my life. I could not do it while she lived, but since she died I have worked and planned for it. I have worked ten years for this——'

'Aye, and the plan has so entered into your soul that you could not see that it could fail. You took me for the boy of ten years ago. And you could not understand that what others did might alter what you had to do. For five years you have ordered this town. Did you think that you now ordered the world?' Robert flung wide his arms, gathered in the two girls, the schoolmaster, the Colonel. 'You are lost, Master Kettlestang. We know you now. Tomorrow is Portreeve Picking Day, is it not? We shall see how you fare when your vengeance is known to all the Aldermen.'

'Go, then. Do what you will. I will have my vengeance yet, on all of you.'

24

In the morning of Portreeve Picking Sunday, the great bell Timothy tolled the hour of Matins. The common people hurried to be first, packing into the church, into the free seats in the nave and the aisles. Only the Guild seats and the two front benches were empty, the one under that golden key of the Harnes, the other under the Arms of Loone. Quernhow stood in his vestry, and watched them come. Not to worship God, he thought, not for that. They have come to watch the show, to see the Aldermen in their furs, and to hear the great new Organ. It was almost at the stroke of eleven. Yet no Aldermen were there. He motioned to Michael Widdybank to toll on. And, against all precedent, the Parson at last walked down the aisle, and looked from the west door into the market square, across the Abbey yard.

Opposite the Abbey door, stood the Dragon. It was built of clunch with corners and window and door frames of freestone. Once it had been the hospice of the Abbey, where pilgrims to Saint Ragnfrith's tomb had slept. Now it was an inn, and some spoke already as if it were in full the George and Dragon, but the Dragon had been the Griffin from the Tudor Arms, in gratitude to the great and good King, that had given the town such a fine hostelry. In front of the Dragon, awnings had been spread over the platform on which the Aldermen would sit to pick the Portreeve, and present him to the Burgesses of Wrackham for their choice to be ratified. And in the square, Quernhow saw a strange sight.

On one side of the market place stood the Aldermen in their furs and velvets, guild by guild, Keld and Nosterfield, Gannel and Starbutton, Vintner and Cooper. They stood grouped around their Portreeve. Opposite them, a less dignified crew, Quernhow saw Maurice Shillmoor, the Justice, and with him Matthew Perkins and a file of Dragoons, dismounted. The people waited, Alleys and Sarsens, wharfingers and weavers, Prisca Arkengarth, George and Sophia Place. They waited, all, under the hazy sky that cast no shadows yet but promised stifling heat later in the day.

What were they waiting for? Quernhow wondered, watched, waited himself. And then, he came.

Robert Folland came into the market square from Watergate Street. He was dressed in his best, in the coat of green he had worn at the Rout, and his silk waistcoat. He had on his head a new wig, full bottomed, and his shoes were silver buckled. At his side he wore still the German blade he had brought with him into the town, his working sword, the tool of his trade. He came striding into the market place like a soldier, and walked between Aldermen and soldiers as if he expected it, as if that were his due, an honour he deserved. He came between them, and Quernhow saw Shillmoor step from his place and stand before Robert Folland.

'Robert Folland?'

'I have gone by that name.'

'I stand here in your arrest.'

'Upon what charge?'

'A capital one. Of arson. I charge you that, on Thursday night last, you did maliciously set alight and burn a rick of hay, that was the property of Hodman Blackmer.'

'I set alight a rick of hay. What of it?'

'Do you not know that it is a grave offence to burn your neighbour's property?'

'You are mistaken, sir. I did not burn my neighbour's property.'

'But 'twas Hodman Blackmer's rick.'

'Why think you that?'

' 'Twas on his farm.'

'Why do you think it was his farm?'

'Why, 'tis the common report——'

'Common reports do not stand up in a court of law, Squire Shillmoor. You need better drafting of charges than that. There is no hanging a man on common report.'

'Is it not Hodman Blackmer's farm? A quibble will not save you.'

'Then there's no justice in England, because I have seen many a quibble hang a man.'

'Do you deny the farm is Hodman Blackmer's?'

'I do.'

'On what grounds?'

'The farm is mine. I bought it.'

Kettlestang stiffened, stepped forward from the group of Aldermen, seemed about to speak, remained silent. Robert looked at him, waited till it was certain that the Portreeve had nothing to say yet, went on,

'Hodman Blackmer could not pay his mortgage. I paid it with the monies remaining to my account in Master Kettlestang's books. I bought the farm from him with other monies belonging to me after trading in London. He will so testify.'

'You say you have bought this farm? When?'

'The deeds were signed on Monday.'

'On Monday?' This was Kettlestang. 'They were signed on Monday?'

'You signed many deeds on Monday. Did you not? How many did you read? Not one. This deed you signed too, and Azerley witnessed it.'

'You slipped this in——'

'You said that day that you depended on me, and that whatever I presented to you, you would approve. Azerley heard it. He will swear to that.'

'Then Azerley will starve in Wrackham from this day on, for there is no more employment he will gain from me.'

'Azerley works for me. He will not starve.'

'Portreeve!' This was Shillmoor. 'Will you dispute the sale?'

All watched Kettlestang. The banker hesitated, then,

'I will acknowledge the sale. What money was involved, Folland has earned. What papers he has prepared, over this whole half-year, have always had my approval. And this too. He holds the farm. But no one in a hundred miles now will buy his grain, that I swear.'

Robert smiled. Shillmoor returned to the attack.

'Ownership is no defence to wanton destruction of property.'

'It was not wanton destruction. I had my reasons.'

'They were?'

'It was last year's rick. It was not the kind of hay anyone would buy. You remember where it stood? By the pond, in *my* yard all mired with clay?'

'Aye.'

'There I wish to build a kiln.'

'A kiln?'

'It is convenient to dig clay there, and burn bricks. Colonel Cutler is building himself a house. Master Charles Arkengarth has made the plans, and will undertake the building. On Black-mer's farm I will make the bricks for that, or for any other man who wants a new house.' He waved his hand around the market place. 'There is scarcely a house in this town that is not moulder-ing into decay. And there is no good brick clay nearer than my farm.'

There was a movement from the group of Aldermen. Noster-field, the Stonemason, asked,

'But how will you burn your bricks? There is no wood between here and the sea.'

'At this moment, Master Newall's brig lies at Bratton. She is unloading coal from Newcastle, that you will not allow to be unloaded here. That is the Portreeve's will.'

There was silence again as Shillmoor watched the group of Aldermen. There were no questions more. The Magistrate said, hesitantly,

'I do not see that you have a case to answer.'

'No more do I,' Robert answered. 'May I proceed to my devotions?'

'There is no reason why you should not. But,' and Shillmoor's voice was hard, 'I am sure that we should thank Master Kettle-stang for bringing this case to my notice.'

Quernhow saw the gathering come apart into its constituent parts. He walked back into his vestry, and waited while the last of his congregation took their places. Robert stood inside the west door as the others passed him, the Aldermen in their order, Waterman and Silk Weavers, Tallow Chandlers and Cord-wainers. Shillmoor went to his seat in the north aisle, the Dragoons sat in a corner under the south-west tower. Last, the Portreeve entered, and walked slowly to his place, marked by the Town Mace. Robert came from his corner by the door as Kettlestang passed, and walked behind him all the way up the nave. The whole town watched him as he passed. The Portreeve turned into his place. And Robert walked on, up towards the chancel steps. And below the steps he halted. He turned to the north, and sat firmly beneath the Loone Arms, still bearing their faded colour, Two Red Roses across the Moon.

Quernhow walked from his vestry to his place, sat above the clerk. As he came, for the first time in a service, the great Organ pealed out, a flower of sound, a fountain of harmony.

Across the town, Bridgward led the rest of the parish band.

They had been dispossessed. They had debated the advantages of the Church of Rome. They had decided against it. They left Gunver to his latinities beneath the Falcon. They played for the tongues of the Misguided Brethren. They might not be able to talk as eloquently as was required, but at least, they could improvise in disharmony.

Quernhow moved, automatically, through the service. The boys stood to sing the Venite, a strange new setting that nobody had ever heard before and that they seemed to know only imperfectly.

Robert sat in his new seat, and listened. The Psalm for the day seemed apt. 'Deliver me, Oh Lord,' he sang softly, 'from the evil man : and preserve me from the wicked man, which imagine mischief in their hearts, and stir up strife all the day long.'

Kettlestang sang it too. He applied it, of course, differently. He waited only to see what should happen at sermon time. There would be no sermon proper. There never was at Portreeve Picking Day. At that point of the service, the congregation would go elsewhere. But at sermon time, the banns of marriage were called. What then would be said? Robert was there, and all the Places. Robert had promised on his honour that the banns would be read. But what then? Would he forbid them on the grounds of consanguinity? Would all be revealed? Kettlestang sat where he was, and wondered. Of only one thing he was still sure. Incest might not come about, but one way or another, fratricide would be attempted that day. Robert was not the only man to carry a sabre : George Place had armed himself for fighting, not for show, with a stout horseman's blade two fingers wide instead of a mere foil. And with him he had his band of Pards.

The collect for the day broke in on Robert's thoughts. 'Grant us grace to forsake all covetous desires, and inordinate love of riches. . . .' But that was not what it was about. This had been a struggle between himself and the Portreeve. It had not been about riches. Riches, for banker and poor soldier alike, had been something incidental. That Robert was going to be rich he had not the slightest doubt. He had taken the measure of the men he would have to compete with, Perkins, Newall, Nosterfield; he knew that he would be able, one day, to buy them all. No, this struggle was about selves and lives and loves. He was ready now for the culmination. He came awake again suddenly.

Kettlestang was also awake, from his dreams of recovery, of

renewed power. Only let him survive the day. Let him be Port-reeve still tomorrow, and he would rise again. There was still hope. The best of his time was to come. He listened.

'I publish the banns of marriage,' and Quernhow found strength in his voice to fill all the church; he had learnt that that was wise in Wrackham, where many strange things had happened, where the linkages of family and guild produced the oddest cases of consanguinity. 'Between Robert Folland, Bachelor of this Parish, and Sophia Place, Spinster of this Parish——' He was not suffered to go further. He was only surprised it was Robert Folland himself who had stood. Complaining parents had forbidden banns before now, furious swains, creditors, even an apothecary once. But that the groom intended should inter-fere was something new even in his experience. 'You have some-thing to say, Master Folland?'

Robert drew himself up, took a deep breath.

'I forbid these banns,' he said.

'What is your standing in this matter?' asked Quernhow, 'and what, in full, is your reason for this action?' He had often found that a delaying request of this kind, a breath of formality, brought objectors to their senses, and got a withdrawal of the objection—in public at least. What could then be arranged, or disarranged, in the vestry or the lawyer's chambers, was neither here nor there.

Kettlestang sat rigid. He had expected it. There were no grounds, that he could think of, if the banns had come to this stage, except that the intended parties were brother and sister. If that all came out in public, now, at Portreeve Picking, then he was ruined. It would kill Jemmy Place, and that was consolation.

'I Robert Folland, alias Endellion, alias Bowbank,' and it was obvious to Kettlestang that Robert was making a proclamation of it, 'do forbid these banns, on the grounds that I am already married.'

'What did you say your name was?' Quernhow genuinely was not sure he had heard aright.

'I am Robert, known as Robert Folland, the son of Margaret Endellion, late of this parish, who married Maurice Bowbank, also once of this parish. And I do forbid these banns as invalid. I am already married to Prisca, daughter of Frederick Arken-garth, Priest, Schoolmaster of this Parish.'

'Have you any documentary proof?'

'It is in the register of this church.'

'That cannot be. I have not married you.'

'Look into the register.' Matthew Widdybank was holding it ready.

'I do not see——'

'Look at today's date.'

'There is indeed a record here. *Who* is this that has signed? Master Arkengarth?'

'I am a priest,' said Arkengarth from his seat at the great organ. 'I have married couples enough. It does not matter that I hold no benefice.'

'But without banns?'

'I hold,' said Robert, 'the Bishop's licence. It was issued in the early hours of this morning. The Lord Bishop lay last night at the house of his Chancellor, and they were both in agreement that here was need for haste and issued the licence without more ado. It is, you will notice, in the Chancellor's own hand, which may be a little difficult to read, but his Lordship's signature is clear enough.' The Chancellor's hand, Taberon had told them at five o'clock that morning, had shaken so much at the sight of the pistol that he had almost been unable to hold a pen, let alone write a fine engrossing script. However, once he and the Bishop had found out that all they were required to do was to write out a licence for a bachelor to marry an unrelated spinster in a hurry, they had cheered up and pressed him to cold chicken and a bottle of port. The licence was genuine enough, Quernhow admitted. But that the marriage had been performed in his church by someone other than himself, and without his knowledge—he asked for Pontigarde's opinion.

'The marriage is irregular,' said the attorney, grudgingly. 'It is none the less valid for that. It is easier to contract a marriage, reverend sir, than to end one. I would that you would impress that upon your parishioners more firmly, since these disputes cause me a great deal of unnecessary work. But pray, what witnesses were there to this match, or is there irregularity in this too?'

Quernhow puzzled over the register.

'There were two witnesses.'

'Both of full age, and not subject to any infirmity of mind?' Pontigarde was conscious of what James Place had told him three days before, of the Vintner's fury over his daughter's obsession, over her lewd behaviour. He sought to find a way to discredit this book entry. Quernhow answered,

'So I believe. The first is Rupert Cutler, sometime Colonel of the Dragoons. A gentleman known to us all, and,' Quernhow looked round the church, found his man, 'present with us here today to answer for his signed name.'

'And the second? There must normally be two.'

'The second is Sophia Place, Spinster of this Parish.'

There was again silence, broken only by a scuffling at the back of the church as the Pards followed George Place out into the market square. Quernhow closed the register, and with a wide gesture tore in two, and then in two again, the paper of the banns. He scattered the fragments over the floor of the crossing. and Arkengarth snapped his fingers. The boy sprang to the pump handle. And the music came.

Sitting among the uncased guts of his organ, the bare unpainted pipes, the exposed keys and levers. Arkengarth began the march of triumph. All his life he had lived true to his word. Now, his word was changed to pure sound. His steadfastness soared in great waves into the roof, to the headless angels holding the oak beams. Arkengarth sat and played his life, as he was not allowed to speak it, to the townsmen of Wrackham, who listened and yet did not know what he told them. His ejection, his humiliation, played soft and plaintive, melded with the soft lights of the great east window, that had once proclaimed clear the Resurrection, and, shattered by Oliver's men, and crammed back anyhow into the leads, now showed only a jumble of colours. His long years of drudgery made a ground bass : above it a complex fugue told of the greater glories of Virgil and Homer, of Livy and Herodotus. The sublime words were transmuted in his fingers into a complexity of mathematical form. Below him, Quernhow moved from his place, doffed his preaching gown and put on again his surplice and hood of black and white silk. He moved into the aisle. Behind him walked Pontigarde, out into the market square. Two by two went the Aldermen, scarlet-gowned and black-furred, and last of all, his mace carried in front of him, with the gold chain about his neck, walked the Portreeve.

And as Kettlestang moved down the aisle, his feet unconsciously danced to Arkengarth's tune, walked in time to the great march that was Arkengarth's triumph. For whatever

262

happened to his body, however bleak life was to be now in the empty School House, sitting alone with none but Nance Hartsop to come in to make him his dinner, with the boys boarded out about the town, with Prisca and all his children gone to live on the edge of the sea, yet Arkengarth still had this—his soul had once, now, this moment, been free.

Robert walked down the aisle. Prisca was not to be seen. He paused a moment at the door, and held out his hand to Sophia. She took it, pressed it, stood back. Then he stepped alone into the market square.

The square was not empty. On the far side, the Aldermen were grouping themselves on the platform, under the awning. People were standing under the platform, and on the sides of the market place. They had left the centre clear, as if for a show. And the show was there. Opposite the church door stood George Place. He had taken off his coat and waistcoat, and given them to John Mellin to hold. His right sleeve was rolled up, his sword unsheathed. He was not alone. At his back, in a half-moon, stood the Pards, Mellin and Devitt, Glass and Dee, Cock and Key, Buick and Keffle. Strong, short men, harsh of face, ragged, with grasshooks and reeding knives in their belts. Robert walked alone from the church to meet them.

He came within three feet of George Place.

'Pray, Master Place, give me leave to pass. In peace.'

'And that you shall not have. Neither leave nor peace.'

'What quarrel have you with me?' Robert asked. He had spoken his name loud in church, had seen James Place start, had watched tears run from the cataracted eyes. The father knew, then. But not the son—his brother. There was still some part of Kettlestang's plan left. He could see the Portreeve, standing on the platform, watching, still hoping. If he had to fight, there was no question, George would kill him if he were left alive. One of them would die. It was a choice, still, for each of them, death by steel or death on the gallows. George was speaking.

'I said I would kill you if you let the banns be read. There is worse happened now. You have enticed my sister, and for all I know have lain with her under this pretext. Now you have deserted her publicly, and made her an accomplice in your filthy plots. And for that—I will kill you. Draw, and fight me like a man, Folland!'

And at that name, a man stepped in front of George Place.

He was a very old Pard, grizzled in the hair and with a stubbly beard. He stood with dignity, and faced Robert. He spoke,

'Bee'st ye Endellion, then? Bee'st ye the Lord of Loone?'

Robert looked back at him, straight, direct. There was no place here for concealment. He answered,

'My mother was Margaret Endellion. But that is—has not been—my name.'

'In the Marsh, 'tis the mother's blood that do count.' Dave Mellin turned to his sons, his cousins, his fellow-Pards. 'Here be th'Endellion! Here be the Lord of Loone! 'Twas to me she said it at the last, "Follow my Love," she said, "till we return again." Endellion do be returned, my lads. The hell wi' Place! We follow the Lord of Loone!'

Silently, lightly, like great cats, as was their custom, the Pards moved. They left George Place and came one by one to stand behind Robert. Dave Mellin had not finished. When the half-moon was complete, backs to the church, he spoke again.

'It do be late in the year, and there is not many that can grow them so late,' and he held out a little basket, like the Marsh women made for posies. 'But we can and we do. Wear 'un for us.'

Robert reached into the basket. He felt as in a dream, as if all that had happened in his life, Warwickshire, Malplaquet, the Wrackham Run, had been an imagined thing, that this alone was real, the part he had been born to play. He took out the two red roses on the single stem, and pinned them to his coat. George Place still faced him, standing his ground alone. Robert Endellion moved his own right hand to his sword—and found his wrist gripped. Luke Key held his hand, John Mellin and Abel Devitt stood before him, their reed knives out.

'There's none,' said John Mellin, 'shall come against Endellion while we lives.'

Robert moved, spoke as in a dream. He knew, now, what to say. He spoke to the men behind him, himself facing across the square, empty but for George Place.

'I can give my people bread. Will ye make bricks with me? Will ye build a new town by the sea?'

He did not wait for an answer. There was no need. Here was his work force, massive, complete, that he had hoped to pick up here and there, man by man, from Alleys and Sarsens, Dutch and Irish. He walked forward. The first pace ought to have taken him almost on to George's toes. But his half-brother was no longer there. He stood aside, the naked sword still in his hand, to watch his Pards, his Pards no longer, follow Robert Endellion across the square.

On the platform, the Aldermen sat in their chairs. Time had been when the Aldermen humbly approached the Abbot as he sat on the dais, and presented for his approval their Portreeve who would collect the Abbot's dues from the river wharves. Now, it was the Aldermen who sat on the dais, and told the people of their choice. And yet, there had been two occasions, once at the beginning of Oliver's war against the King, and again the year the King came back, that the Burgesses had refused to accept the Aldermanic choice. They had shouted against him. And this, Kettlestang knew, could happen again.

Pontigarde the Clerk came forward. He had mustered the Aldermen, name by name, guild by guild. He had taken the vote, had asked for the choices of the Guilds. Now he came to tell the Burgesses. He spoke, loud and clear.

'Burgesses of Wrackham. By the Charter, gift of his most excellent Majesty, Henry, eighth of that name, of England and France by the Grace of God, King, Defender of the Faith, it is ye who may choose a Portreeve to rule us, for five years. I here present to you the advice of your seniors, the Aldermen of this town. It is their counsel that you should choose again that most revered and wise man, Jacob Kettlestang, Alderman of the Millers' Guild.' He turned to his left. Parson Quernhow stood there, last vestige of the Abbey's power. The Portreeve's gold chain hung over his surpliced arm. Pontigarde reached out his hand to take it. Robert Endellion spoke.

'Before you make this man——'

Pontigarde interrupted him.

'Who are you, sir? Are you a Wrackham man or not?'

'I do believe that I am a Wrackham man. For my mother married a Wrackham man, Maurice Bowbank. And if that be not enough, then I have married a Wrackham man's daughter.'

'Then you are a Wrackham man. What is your name?'

'I have had many in my time. I have been Robert Bowbank, and I have been Robert Folland. And now, before you all, I will take again my mother's name, and I am Robert Endellion.'

'An Endellion, and a Wrackham man? It has never been before.'

265

'It shall be now. Am I to speak?'

'Speak, then.'

Robert felt Prisca's arm in his. The Pards were close about them. At the edge of the square, by the head of Bridge Street, Charley Arkengarth and Josh Caddon waited with horses, one saddled, one sidesaddled. They would sleep that night safe, in Hod Blackmer's brick house, in sound of the sea. Robert smiled to himself, then spoke.

'You propose that this man be Portreeve over us in Wrackham. But sure, ought not a man who sits in so high a seat to be above suspicion, to be without sin? What if he be a man of infinite wickedness. What——'

But it was not Kettlestang who stood to interrupt. It was James Place. His bleared eyes looked far into the future, far into the past. His ears told him where to look for Robert Endellion.

'You are wrong, young Endellion. What you have in your mind is not relevant. I know you have been wronged by Master Kettlestang. I know too, that there are few men in this town who have not, some time or other, been wronged by him. Myself not least of all. Not least of all.'

He paused. There is no one else who knows how, Robert thought. That man may be, no, is, I know it, my father, and I feel nothing for him. I need no father, I am myself. I am the Lord of Loone. But he must now have guessed the wrong that has almost been done him. And he says . . . what?

'What this man has done for us is worth more than any harm he has done. Or wished to do. We know him. We live in this town, as must men everywhere, from moment to moment, from year to year, from one harvest to another, from one war to another. When the harvest fails, when politics are not what we expect, a merchant faces a long lean time. Many times he faces ruin. In one town, we all depend on each other. If one man fails, then one by one we all fail.

'And if we fail, what can rescue us? What holds us up? Only this, that there is in the town one man who lives, lasts, holds through all bad harvests, through all changes of politics, who has money spread so wide that he cannot fail. We have all, in turn, come to him to carry us over bad times. We have all, in our time, owed him money. We have all, in our time, repaid. Without him we would all have failed long ago, and this our town, our beloved Wrackham, have sunk in ruin to a village. He has up-

266

held us. It is through him that those of us who have had good times have supplied those who had bad times. If it were not for him we would not have been able to help each other.

'That is his function in the town. And that is why, whatever he does, he will be our Portreeve.'

No one, not Robert, nor James Place, not Arkengarth, said any more. Quernhow came across the platform. Ignoring the Clerk, he hung the chain around the Portreeve's neck, set the Oar in his hand. For five more years.

Robert handed Prisca up into her saddle. She was not used to it, and clung on desperately. She told herself she would have to learn to ride now, in the country. Robert swung easily on to his mount. Not as good a horse as Tiger, he thought, but the best Taberon had been able to find him. The four of them rode across the square. They passed close under the platform, and Robert bowed to the Portreeve.

Robert Endellion, that was Robert Folland, rode out of Wrackham in a September noon. He was dressed as a fine gentleman. He had land by the sea, and the horse was his own. He had guineas in his pocket, and money in plenty, safe in South Sea Stock. His wife rode beside him and he drove no one in front of him. Behind him came the Pards, mounted or on foot, all garlanded with roses.

The Lord of Loone bowed to the Portreeve of Wrackham. And the Portreeve neither cursed him nor blessed him. He bowed to him as to an equal. For both, life would continue.